A TEMPERED WARRIOR

BOOK TWO OF THE MILESIAN ACCORDS

Jon R. Osborne

New Mythology Press
Virginia Beach, VA

Chris Kennedy/New Mythology Press
2052 Bierce Dr.
Virginia Beach, VA 23454
http://chriskennedypublishing.com/

Ordering Information:
Quantity sales. Special discounts are available on quantity purchases by corporations, associations, and others. For details, contact the "Special Sales Department" at the address above.

A Tempered Warrior/Jon R. Osborne
ISBN: 978-1948485234

Dedication and Acknowledgment

I'd like to thank all of my players over the years. Almost four decades of game-mastering honed my story-telling skills, but none of it would have been possible without the numerous people who joined me around the table.

Through my players, I learned the difference between telling a story for myself and telling a story for others. Thanks to my players, with the occasional nudge from our dice, I learned how to adapt when a story went off the rails in a new and unexpected direction. At the gaming table, I learned to listen to characters' voices and understand they would grow and evolve in unexpected ways. Those changes would become as important, if not more so, than any goblin or dragon I could throw at them.

My players indulged me as I dabbled in writing, from campaign write-ups to behind-the-scene chapters for their characters and the campaign world. Years of recaps and blue books culminated in the urge to write stories and books for a wider audience, but I got there because of my players' support and feedback.

My players have also given me years, and in some cases decades, of friendship. They not only made me a better writer, they made me a better person.

So to all of my players, from the first ones in junior high to the ones who still pick up dice with me weekly, I say two things. First of all—thank you. Second—roll for initiative.

Jon R. Osborne

Prologue

Mikha'el

Mikha'el perched on the edge of the huge throne-like chair, staring into enormous mirrors on the wall. The building's previous tenants had left the garish piece of furniture behind, a relic from the tawdry acts performed on the same stage where Mikha'el had installed the chair. The seatback, on the verge of falling off the rest of the chair, was propped against a tarnished brass pole that stretched from the stage floor to the ceiling.

Mikha'el's minions wondered why he had chosen this building. It still reeked of sin and hardship, especially to Mikha'el's acute senses. They shook their heads behind his back when he ordered them to mount the throne on the stage. They thought pride was claiming him; they thought he was aggrandizing himself.

The truth was far different, he mused, watching his reflection as he sat in a pool of light in the otherwise dark den of vice. He took a sip from the glass goblet he clutched. The liquid was plain mineral water; he drank nothing that would give him pleasure. Likewise, his meals consisted of bland fare, enough to sustain his corporeal form but nothing his palette would savor. He took his rest on a simple cot in an office in the back of the building.

This throne was hard and uncomfortable. Mikha'el knew the temptations of a flesh and blood form. He had seen his fellow celestials led astray by the seductive sensations that were part and parcel of wearing a shell of meat and nerves. This unforgiving seat reminded him that worldly stimuli came with a danger. The trappings of lust and envy warned him against succumbing to a banal existence.

He had a mission, and he would not be diverted—not by the machinations of others, and especially not by the failings of his flesh. He had been the warden of the Milesian Accords for centuries. The Accords had forced the *nukrayim*, the alien entities who called themselves gods, into exile from the World of Man. The lesser *nukrayim* who served them were also forced into exile, cutting off the flow of magic into the mundane world. While it meant the end of great miracles, as the exercise of divine power allowed the heathen magic to leak back into the world, it also meant the crumbling of the pagan faiths.

Magic and legends were relegated to fairy tales, while the religions born of Avram swept the world. True, the divine host had to do without the *sefir*, the divine spark which fueled miracles, but behind the scenes, they swayed leaders of men by more conventional means. While a few were driven by benevolent fervor, most were motivated by coin and power.

Now the Milesian Accords faced a challenge, the first serious challenge since their inception. It was bad enough that faith was locked in a battle with science; if magic came back to the world, along with the exiled *nukrayim*, it would throw everything into chaos. Centuries-old rules kept Mikha'el from snuffing out the challenge like a flickering candle flame. He had to employ less direct means to derail those who posed the greatest threat.

One of the mirrors fogged, as though filled with smoke, and an image coalesced in the eight-foot tall panel to the left of Mikha'el's reflection. A man in a yellow raincoat endured a downpour, clutching his hood to his head against the wind.

"The scion of Enlil did as promised," the man reported. "He sent a tempest across Illinois. He claims the tempest found the druid and has slain or grievously injured him."

Mikha'el leaned forward, his smile the first genuine one he had worn in quite some time. "He found the *hartummin*?" The mage-priest, or druid as the exiled called him, was crucial to their plans. "Where? Have you confirmed he is dead?"

The man struggled against another blast of wind-driven rain. "Not yet," he replied. "The druid somehow conjured enough wind to uproot the tempest and disperse it. The storm-beast lashed out with its dying spark."

The smile faded as Mikha'el slowly sank back against the carved wood of the throne. "Find out. Use your mundane contacts; a man cooked by lightning will be hard to miss. He will turn up at a morgue or hospital."

The drenched man peered around. "What of your promise to Enlil's grand-spawn?" he asked.

Mikha'el waved a hand dismissively and said, "He fulfilled his obligation. Once the challenge has passed, he may join the celestial host on a provisional basis."

The large mirrored pane to the right of Mikha'el's reflection swirled with mist before it lit up with the image of a woman in a conservative dress and jacket seated behind a desk. Below her, prices for soybeans and pork bellies scrolled by, while a storm-warning icon blazed in the corner.

"What news do you have?" Mikha'el demanded, his tone implying it had best be *good* news.

The woman folded her hands on the desk. "Our intelligence regarding a third party was correct," she said. "Sources reported the fallen known as Iblis has been seeking the druid of the Exiled Folk."

Mikha'el's free hand clenched into a fist. "Are you certain?"

"He has been reported operating in the central Illinois region," the woman replied. A moving graphic replaced her image; it resembled a cyclone over Illinois, drawn in red and blue. "These are the currents of *sefir* and the magical energy the pagans refer to as *lledrith*. We assume the *lledrith* is the druid, and unless you have an operative in the area calling upon divine forces, the *sefir* is likely Iblis."

"Why is there a hole in the middle?" Mikha'el scowled. "Can't we use it to home in on both of them?"

The woman shrugged. "They are both obfuscated, either by their own design or through a third party," she answered. "Someone of Iblis' experience isn't going to be easily found."

"Work on it," Mikha'el ordered and took another sip of his mineral water. "I will get some eyes in the area at ground level to see if we can turn up anything more conventionally."

Iblis. Mikha'el should have killed the scheming rebel a millennia ago when he had the chance. When Iblis used a different name, he had been Mikha'el's friend, thus the *Elohim* had stayed his hand. It was a human failing on Mikha'el's part; one he vowed not to repeat.

The central mirror filled with fog, replacing Mikha'el's brooding reflection. Falling golden sparks surrounded a vaguely female form. The mirror vibrated with her voice. "Jehoel has been returned to the golden host. The *benyaim* discorporated him."

It meant Jehoel had found the exiled gods' champion, the *benyaim*. Jehoel was not allowed to kill or even seriously harm the *benyaim*, but the *benyaim* had been heading into the Rocky Mountains for some sort of rendezvous. The meeting was important enough for her to trek across the country despite being hunted, which meant it was in Mikha'el's interest to keep it from happening. He had sent Jehoel and a seraphim, along with a Nephilim and a mortal agent

"What happened?" Mikha'el asked. Luckily, Jehoel had not been corporeal for long, so he would take less time to reconstitute himself, but the host may have still learned a little from him.

"The *benyaim* and two *nukrayim* were intercepted by Jehoel and his assistants," the female voice stated. The buzzing mirror brought dust raining down from the ceiling. "One of the *nukrayim* was felled in the struggle. By the time we dispatched a *xerubim* to scout the site, there was no one from either side to be found. We have to assume the *benyaim* made her rendezvous and was removed from the World of Man."

Anger welled up within Mikha'el, and he pulled back his arm to pitch the goblet at the mirror in rage. A stray thought stayed his hand. "Are you certain there were only the three?"

The golden image in the mirror may have nodded; it was hard to tell amid the cascade of golden motes. "We have a clear image gleaned from his memory." A picture of a mortal woman flanked by two of the exiled aliens appeared. "Is this significant?"

"Yes, it is," Mikha'el replied. "The woman has a son, who was with her when she fled her home. He must still be in the mortal world, likely left with the *hartummin*. It is another lead."

"Follow your lead quickly," the voice admonished, bringing down more dust. "Time grows short."

*****

Chapter One

Liam

"Am I dead?"

Liam Knox could see his body lying at the bottom of the knoll. A flash of distant lightning illuminated the scene, backlighting the dolmen at the top of the hill. The entire scene had a dream-like quality.

"Only a little bit," the ancient druid Cathbad replied. He stood next to Liam. "Hopefully the Smith God will have something to jump start you before your spirit untethers from your body. If nothing else, I'm sure the Flower-Maiden will give you mouth to mouth. Pity you're not there to enjoy it."

"I could give him proper CPR," Raven remarked from the other side of Liam, her arms crossed.

"Very funny," Liam grumbled, watching as Gofannon and Pixel ran to his body. How much time had passed? How long before he started suffering brain damage?

"Seriously, I could give you CPR," the witch retorted. "I took the training at the Red Cross for work."

"Well, you're not here corporeally, and if you were, why would you?" Liam glanced toward the dark-haired woman. "After all, your boss gets what he wants now."

"I don't think my mast—my boss as you put it—wants you dead." Raven shook her head. "At least not yet."

"I'm sure he wants to make a deal with you," Cathbad added. The shade of Liam's distant ancestor intently watched the scene on the hill. "It would be hard to do that if you're dead. Luckily, in addition to being a god of smithing, Gofannon in his many incarnations is also a god of brewing."

"How does that help?" Liam scoffed. "They can have a toast to see me off?"

"Being dead must make you dense, lad," Cathbad chided. "Think of the stories and what he brewed."

Realization dawned as Liam turned back to where Gofannon kneeled over his corpse. The hulking smith god held a small flask to the body's lips. "So there really is an 'ale of immortality?'" Liam asked.

"Immortality is a bit of bardic license, but I suspect this will do the trick," Cathbad said. The spectre clapped Liam's ghostly form on the shoulder. "I'll be seeing you soon, Lad."

Liam turned to warn Raven to stay away when he suddenly fell. At least that was how it felt from his perspective as his spirit form was yanked into his physical body. His limbs jerked, and his eyes snapped open. Pixel's luminescent eyes and Gofannon's huge bearded face filled Liam's vision as he gasped for air, then coughed liquid from his windpipe.

"See, I did not drown the druid!" Gofannon's booming voice was louder than thunder. The smith-god had the presence of mind to turn Liam on his side as he sputtered bile and a clover-sweet liquid into the grass. "Not as potent as a golden apple, but strong enough!"

Pixel threw her arms around Liam, heedless of whether he might retch. Her long, purple hair was soaked from the rain. "You were dead!" she cried. Despite the waning storm, he could still smell flowers as she hugged him.

"Only a little bit," Liam said. There seemed to be a slide missing from his photographic memory. His pit stop in the spirit world was foggy, like a dream. "What happened? Last thing I remember was the tempest."

"After you cut the tempest elemental loose from the ground, lightning struck the dolmen." Pixel still clung to him, shivering in the cold rain. "You were electrocuted; your heart stopped."

"Well, I got better." Liam's voice was still raspy. "Let's get out of this rain. We're soaked, and I think the danger has passed."

Pixel nodded and released her hold on him to stand. She took one of his hands in both of hers to help him up. Gofannon caught him under the other arm and bodily hauled him to his feet. As soon as the smith let him go, Liam's legs crumpled under him. Pixel struggled with Liam's collapsing body until Gofannon caught them both mid-fall.

Liam tried to move his legs, then only his feet. Even his toes wouldn't respond. "Guys, there's something wrong. My legs won't work." Liam tried to tamp down the panic rising in his mind. How badly was he messed up?

"Pixel, I will carry the druid to the house," Gofannon said, and scooped Liam up as though he was a child. Liam was too freaked out to be embarrassed. "Gather his things."

Pixel nodded mutely. She quickly collected Liam's staff and sandals and fell in behind the smith-god. Wind whipped around them as Gofannon strode toward the farmhouse. The rain abated as they reached the garage.

"Dad! What happened?" Tim shouted in alarm. Einar had barely managed to keep the boy from running out into the storm. The dwarf stood next to Tim, watching gravely as Gofannon brought him through the garage.

"I had a close call with a lightning bolt," Liam replied before one of the others blurted out something more alarming. Liam flexed his hands experimentally; both worked, but they felt tingly, like they had fallen asleep recently.

"Where should I take you?" Gofannon asked. The smith managed to navigate the door into the kitchen without clocking Liam's skull on the doorframe. "You may only weigh 14 stone, but I am not going to carry you around all night."

"Take him up to his room," Pixel instructed and led the way. Liam barely noticed the soaked t-shirt plastered to her skin and really didn't want to consider what else might not be working. She said, "We need to get him out of those soaked clothes."

"Of pocking course," Einar muttered, drawing a violet glare from Pixel in response.

"He's drenched," the fae retorted, continuing up the stairs. "Unless you want to do it?"

Einar threw his hands up. "Fine, you molest him. I'll check on the house and see if there is any damage."

"The house is fine," Tim said. "The danger is gone. It's not afraid anymore."

"We may have another problem," Liam said over the smith's shoulder. "Raven, Iblis' witch, may know where we are. She was out there in her spirit form."

Einar muttered something Scandinavian sounding under his breath. "Nothing to pocking do about it now. I'll make sure everything is buttoned up in case he sends any of his skraelings calling."

Gofannon continued up the stairs, the wood creaking under him. Liam's bedroom door swung open unbidden. Given what had happened tonight, it registered low on Liam's weird-o-meter, but he made a mental note to talk to his son about Tim's recent comments treating the house as though it was a living thing.

"Where do you want him?" Gofannon rumbled to Pixel. Again, Liam was grateful his skull hadn't been clonked on a doorframe.

"Set him on the edge of the bed." Pixel slipped past the smith-god and patted the comforter of the antique, four-post bed.

"Shouldn't we take him to a hospital?" Tim asked. Of course, the twelve-year-old would be the only voice of reason.

"What is this hospital?" Gofannon asked. "And how far do I have to carry the druid?"

Pixel bit her lip and watched Liam for guidance. She replied, "It's a place with doctors."

"No, no hospital for the moment." Liam didn't want to explain any more than necessary to the uninitiated. He hated hospitals. Gofannon set him on the edge of the bed, then waited to see if Liam could sit up under his own power before letting go. "They would ask a lot of questions, and with the storms, they are probably busy. Let's see how I am in the morning. More to the point, someone check the bottom of my feet and see how cooked they got by the near miss."

"You've got red marks and blisters," Tim replied. "I think those are second degree burns."

Liam rattled off a list of supplies to fetch from the bathroom and kitchen. It gave Tim something to do to keep his mind off his father's nearly being fried. At least no one had brought up the fact that his heart had stopped.

Once Tim rushed off down the stairs, Liam shucked off his cold, clammy t-shirt and tossed it in the general direction of the hamper. Usually he wasn't so careless about his clothes, but partial paralysis gave him a pass.

"I will see if Einar needs help," Gofannon announced. He turned and lumbered out the door; the groaning wood marked his passage.

Pixel picked up a towel and handed it to Liam. Liam realized there were also dry clothes piled on the bed next to him.

"This isn't how I planned to get your pants off," Pixel teased and smiled weakly. She helped him strip the rest of his clothes off, then picked up another towel, and began to dry his legs. Liam wished he could feel it, or at least something would respond.

Tim clomping up the stairs gave Liam enough warning to drape his towel over his lap. Tim poked his head around the door, then entered with a basket holding the supplies Liam had requested. The same basket had held Idunn's apples.

"Is this to make some sort of magical healing unguent?" Tim asked as he set the basket down next to Liam.

"Sadly, no." Liam wished he had some sort of healing magic. "This is to clean me up and help prevent infection."

"Oh." Tim didn't seem impressed.

"Susan is good at this stuff," Liam remarked. He hesitated to bother his friend this late. "A lot better than I am. She may think of something I haven't studied."

"Surely you know enough." Pixel obviously didn't want to share her sudden caretaker role.

"Maybe, but I really don't want infected burns on the bottom of my feet when I'm able to walk again," Liam countered. He held Pixel's gaze until she relented and nodded. Liam turned to Tim and recited Susan's phone number. "Try not to worry her. Tell her I have second degree burns on the bottom of my feet, but don't volunteer anything else."

"Do you want me to lie to her?" Tim asked. Liam swore children must be born barristers.

"No. I don't want her freaking out and driving over here recklessly," Liam replied. "Tell her I'll explain everything when she gets here, but I can't hobble to the phone right now."

Tim nodded and dashed off, noisily descending the stairs.

"He's a good kid." Pixel resumed drying off Liam's legs, slowly working her way up. "I don't suppose this is returning any feeling?"

"I wish." There was no stirring under the towel in his lap. Liam really hoped it wasn't a permanent condition. He picked up a pair of boxers from the pile. "That's good enough. I need to get dressed."

"But I haven't dried off your bum," Pixel protested with a smirk.

"I'll have to take my chances." Liam replied. He held out the boxers. "I still need your help to get dressed so I don't embarrass my friend when she arrives."

"So, she's never seen you naked?" Pixel asked mischievously. After she slid the boxers up far enough for Liam to reach them, she picked up a pair of sweat pants from the bed. "You've never been friends with benefits?"

Liam shook his head as he struggled to shift his weight without help from his lower extremities. "I told you Susan and I have never been an item."

"Well, given how you and Erin have been running hot then cold the last few days, I wondered," Pixel remarked as she went to the oak dresser and pulled out another of Liam's t-shirts. She stripped off the soaked t-shirt she had worn into the rainstorm and returned to pick up the towel she had used to dry Liam's legs. Liam kept his ears pricked for anyone coming up the stairs as he tried not to stare. After Pixel toweled off, she slipped on the fresh shirt, then glanced at Liam's crotch. "Nothing?"

"I'm sure if I hadn't had a gigawatt lightning bolt strike a few yards away, there would have been something," Liam conceded. He could hear Tim pounding up the stairs and was thankful everyone was clothed as Tim pushed the door the rest of the way open.

"Susan said she'll be here in twenty minutes," Tim gasped, out of breath. "She said don't put butter or ice on your burns."

"Great. Now can you find Einar and Gofannon to let them know Susan is coming?" Liam didn't want them jumping to conclusions when they saw headlights. Everyone was on edge after what had happened.

Tim nodded breathlessly and turned back toward the stairway.

"If I didn't know better, I'd say you're trying to wear him out," Pixel observed as she knelt by his feet and pulled the supplies close. "Do you really think Susan will make a difference, or are you worried about being alone with me when you can't get away?"

"Is there any aloe vera in those supplies?" Liam asked. He didn't want to mention that in his current state Pixel would be hard pressed to take advantage of him.

Pixel rummaged through the basket. "What's aloe vera?"

"It's a desert succulent useful for treating burns, but I haven't kept any around since I stopped messing with smithing." Liam remembered getting a handful of burns during his bladesmith phase. "Susan keeps an extensive stock of herbs and useful plants and knows the best way to apply them."

"So, what's all this stuff?" Pixel gestured to the supplies Tim had gathered.

"We can still clean the affected areas before Susan gets here," Liam replied. He listened for the pounding of his son's feet on the stairs, but there was only silence. "It also gave Tim something to do besides freak out."

"I'm a hand-maiden and a familiar." Pixel picked up a cloth and dipped it in a basin of water. "I'm not a chirurgeon."

"Just clean off the bottoms of my feet and try not to break any blisters," Liam instructed. He still remembered the basics. Liam had studied first aid for burns when he had the idea to work with metal. At least the lightning hadn't fried his memories.

Pixel watched for a reaction as she began to gently dab at his foot, holding it over the basin. Liam tensed when she first started but didn't feel anything. Pain would have been preferable; it would have been a sign his condition wasn't permanent.

"So, did they break the conditions of the Accords?" Liam asked as Pixel switched feet. "Surely sending a storm monster after me is against the rules."

"I'm guessing the Avramites will claim they didn't send it after you; you got in its way and could have let it pass by," Pixel replied. "Assuming it wasn't Iblis and his witch."

"I don't think it was them; Raven seemed as surprised as we were." Liam wished Cathbad would return and answer some questions. He felt like he had skipped several chapters in a book. He had no clue why what he'd done had worked against the tempest elemental; it had been instinct. "I think Iblis might be playing his own game, maybe pitting both sides against each other."

"I guess." Pixel shrugged, picked up a dry cloth, and carefully patted away the moisture from his feet. "I still don't like the bitch."

Liam made a noncommittal noise. Raven definitely couldn't be trusted, but she might be a way to get more information. He asked, "Is it me or is it stuffy in here?"

"Do you want me to open a window?' Pixel asked. She folded the cloths she had used, then stood up. "Will the wind spirits come inside?"

"I don't know if they will, but since it's still raining, we can turn on the fan." Liam realized the zephyrs hadn't come through the door with them. Was it against their nature to be indoors, or was it the wards protecting the house? There was a click and the ceiling fan whirred to life.

Pixel pointed at the switch with a puzzled expression. "Did you do that?"

"No. Maybe it was Scooter?" Liam suggested. He suspected the brownie could turn invisible in addition to changing into a cat or casting a very convincing glamour he was a cat.

"Twasn't me, Druid." The voice, nasal and thick with a Scottish accent, came from across the room, by the clothes hamper. All the wet clothes were gone from the floor, and a small man stood there. It was the first time Liam had seen Scooter not looking like a plump housecat. He wore black breeches, an ivory white tunic, and a black, flat woolen cap. His shoes were polished black leather. "Twas your house itself."

"It would explain Tim's comments," Liam said as he leaned back on his elbows. He had to resist the urge to thank the brownie for all the work he had been doing around the house. According to lore, if you thanked a brownie directly, they were compelled to leave. Liam made a mental note to save some bacon from the next meal to put with the cream and beer he had left out the last few nights. "So, is the house alive?"

"Aye, twould be one way o' looking at it." The brownie gestured overhead. "Tis a lot o' magic infused in the bones o' the house and twas woke up."

Thudding on the stairs heralded Tim's return. Liam's attention was drawn to the door as the boy entered, panting from running up the stairs again. When Liam glanced back toward the hamper, Scooter was gone.

"Okay, Dad, what else do you need me to do?" Tim gasped as he caught his breath.

"I think it's time for you to go back to bed," Liam's stated.

"I'm not tired," Tim protested. "You might need my help."

"You've been plenty of help. The rest is the boring stuff." Liam wished he could go to sleep. With the adrenaline gone, he was weary and a little light-headed. "Once Susan takes care of my burns, I'm going to try to sleep. Besides, I might need your help in the morning, so you need to be rested."

Tim took a moment to search for a counterpoint before relenting. "Okay. Wake me up if anything cool happens."

"Sure." Liam waited until his son left, and he heard the door across the hall click shut. "I really hope we don't have any more excitement tonight. I'm exhausted."

Pixel bit back a remark, probably about excitement. The creaking stairs caught her attention and headed off any quips she might be considering.

"What did you do now?" Susan asked from the doorway. Her eyes flicked to where Pixel knelt on the floor before her gaze returned to Liam. "Were you playing in your forge barefoot in the middle of the night?"

"Know the storm that rolled through?" Liam nodded at the windows even though they faced the wrong direction. "It was fueled by a big, nasty, magical monster, and it took a parting shot at me with a lightning bolt."

"I knew the storm felt wrong." Susan set her bag down on the bed. "If you were hit by lightning, why aren't you in the hospital?"

"It was more of a near-miss. I was close enough to catch some current through my feet, hence the burns," he answered. Liam decided to omit the part about his heart stopping.

Susan knelt down next to Pixel, eyeing the purple-haired girl until she moved aside. "I get the feeling there's a lot more to this story," Susan remarked. "Lift your feet so I can see how badly you were burned."

"I can't," Liam admitted. He braced for the admonishment he knew was coming. "My legs won't work. They're numb."

"Gods, Liam, you need to go to the hospital," Susan scolded. She cupped his left foot behind the heel and lifted so she could examine the sole. "You're right, you have second degree burns. I can whip up something to help prevent infection and soothe the pain, but I really think you should go to the ER. You don't know how the jolt could have screwed up your nervous system."

"What can they do about it?" Liam retorted, shaking his head. "There's too much going on to hassle with all the red tape and questions."

"Doesn't anyone here have some sort of magic that can help you?" Susan pulled her bag to her and dug through it. She pulled out a mortar and pestle first, then spread out a cloth and lined up ingredients. "I mean, you have a god crashing in one of your guest rooms."

"Apparently there's only so much magic ale or mead can do." Liam almost slipped and mentioned jump-starting his heart.

"Most of the Folk's medicinal magic merely accelerates natural healing," Pixel remarked. "Ironically, the Avramites have some miraculous healers, but they are extremely rare because back in the early days after the Accords they were burnt or hung as witches."

"Figures." Susan snorted and poured liquid from a small brown bottle into the mortar. She added pinches of herbs and several bright green bits of aloe vera plant. "So, the whole faith healing shtick is for real?"

"No, they're usually charlatans." Pixel moved to sit next to Liam on the bed. "From what I understand, the kind of people who get the healing gift tend not to be attention seekers. Add the limitations on how much magical energy can be drawn into the Dunwold, and it keeps them from being able to do it often."

"But the forces of the Abrahamic religions won." Susan worked the pestle energetically as she spoke. "They're still limited on how much power they can pull into our world?"

"Exactly. The Exiled Folk were more reliant on magic, so the Avramites limited the amount allowed in the mortal world, the Dunwold, to how much the Avramites themselves used. The fact they've been using more energy and drawing more celestial creatures into the mundane world is what let us slip over. It's also why Liam's magic is growing." Pixel patted him on the shoulder. "It's why he pulled off what he did tonight. It's probably why Cathbad could actually manifest as well."

Liam resisted the urge to lie back on the bed. "Sounds like someone made a big tactical mistake when they called up the storm-monster."

"What do you mean by celestial creatures?" Susan asked as she set aside the pestle. She fished a pair of latex gloves out of her bag and donned them. Scooping some of the mixture from the mortar, she began gingerly applying it.

"Mostly various sorts of Nephilim, Seraphim, and Elohim," Pixel replied. "In general, people would call them angels."

"Of course, there are angels running around." Susan looked up. "Are they as powerful as implied in the Bible?"

"The writers of the scriptures the Bible is based on may have taken some artistic license. That being said, the Elohim can be scary powerful, especially those you would call archangels." She patted Liam's leg. "Fixing Liam would be a snap for one of them. They're rarely on the Dunwold anymore. They don't need to be, given what the Avramites have accomplished using temporal power over the centuries."

"Could one of them or a Seraphim have conjured up the elemental in the storm?" Liam added something else to his mental list of things to worry about—pissed off angels.

"Not a Seraphim," Pixel replied. The fae hadn't moved her hand from Liam's leg, but he hadn't noticed until he glanced down. "They are more warrior-types, though individuals could have different gifts or knacks, but nothing on that scale. Elohim? Absolutely."

"What about Iblis, could he be some sort of fallen angel, like Lucifer?" Liam thought back to his theology studies. Unlike some of his classmates, he hadn't recoiled from researching the negative side of Abrahamic religions and the various adversary myths that had become stories of Satan and Shaitan. "While I don't think of Lucifer as having to resort to hiring bikers to rough people up, could Iblis be some sort of fallen celestial who has adopted one of the names of Satan?"

Pixel shrugged. "Maybe. It's hard to tell since he's been acting through agents. Either he doesn't have very much power, or there's some reason he doesn't want to use it directly. It's also possible he's something else entirely and adopted the name to throw people off."

"So, there could be a third faction?" Susan began working on the other foot. "Like a totally different set of pantheons? You guys seem to represent western and northern Europe, which leaves a lot of other divinities to come into play."

"A lot of the pre-Abrahamaic powers have lost interest in the World of Man or have faded away entirely. The old Tigris-Euphrates pantheons had already waned by the time of the Milesian Accords. The Heliopitans and Olympians are still out there, mainly due to their persistent fascination with the Dunwold." Pixel paused, as though going through a mental list. "The various Meso-American pantheons are still flickering, but they are also a lot scarier. Iblis seems too civilized and patient for them. I guess we can't rule out an indigenous trickster god; it seems totally in their wheelhouse to meddle in this using some of the motifs of the cultures who virtually wiped out their people."

"I get the feeling the list could go on for a while, but it sounds like the gods of ancient cultures which have no adherents or are of no significant interest have gone away," Liam observed while Susan loosely bandaged his feet, trying to keep the pressure off the blisters.

He imagined the dressing would smell wonderful in the morning. "All of this speculation won't really help. Iblis has unknown motives but doesn't seem to want to act too directly. We'll have to deal with whatever comes up."

Susan finished applying the bandages. "I'll come back in the morning to check on you and change the dressings. Don't try to put any weight on your feet, it would be ugly."

"You can crash here if you don't want to drive back and forth," Liam suggested; he felt guilty his friend was going to all this trouble on his account. "Aunt Millie's room is open since Erin is off on her training mission."

Susan thought about it, glanced at Pixel, and nodded. "I'll grab my overnight bag out of the car."

"Time to tuck you in," Pixel said after Susan left.

"Well, it has to be easier than the first night you were here when I got wrecked on tequila." Liam used his arms to haul himself the rest of the way onto the bed. He was less successful at grabbing his sweats and adjusting his legs so he wasn't sprawled at an awkward angle.

Pixel helped him with his numb legs. "At least I don't have to worry about you throwing up on me this time."

*****

Chapter Two

Erin

"Where are we?"

Erin looked around. The antenna farm to the north had vanished, and the sky had a monochromatic cast. Though the sun was overhead, the light reminded her of summer nighttime up north in Alaska, when the sun did not set. An ancient fortification loomed ahead, the twenty-foot tall wall composed of rough stone on its lower half, topped by a palisade of timber.

"This is Dunos Scaith," Scathach replied, gesturing toward the fort with a long spear. The striking, redheaded warrior watched as two attendants hurried past bearing Izzy. Scathach wore practical, hardened leather armor on her upper torso and chainmail covering her hips and upper legs over a loose red skirt. Erin suspected the woman had more armor under the skirt.

A blood-soaked bandage covered Izzy's throat, and she was as pale as paper. Those carrying her rapidly disappeared around the curve of the wall. Derek spared Erin a haunted glance as he trailed behind his sister.

"Is she…?" Erin let the question trail off, not wanting to give voice to the words.

"It remains to be seen," Scathach stated solemnly. "Her wound is quite grave, but we have a skilled chirurgeon. Injuries are common when training warriors. You bear the marks of your recent battle." Scathach marched silently toward the fortress.

Erin's left side stung from the stone shrapnel that had pierced her clothes and bit into her flash. She assumed the wounds were superficial; the bleeding had nearly stopped. Still, it wouldn't be fun when someone plucked the chips of stone from her skin. At least she hadn't broken her foot when she'd kicked the angel; if she hadn't been wearing steel-toed boots, she probably wouldn't be able to walk now. He had appeared flesh and blood, but it felt like kicking a statue.

A huge gate came into view. The ironclad timber doors hung ajar, and guards bearing spears and shields milled in the entryway. As Scathach and Erin approached the entrance, the guards bowed their heads to the tall redhead, then regarded Erin with curiosity. The guards were tall and slender, and an even mix between male and female, at least those whose gender Erin could discern. Their armor was a mix of hardened leather and bronze scale tunics. There were no swelling breastplates typical of pop art and movies that revealed women and highlighted their assets; it was all simple, practical, and effective.

Erin cast a glimpse down the mountain slope, toward where Colorado Springs should be. Instead of the state park and the city, the rough slope gave way to a scrub forest that stretched out toward a dim horizon. The distant terrain had the same monochromatic hue as the sky.

"I understand this is Dunos Scaith, but where are we?" Erin asked again. "I don't see the city or any roads."

Scathach led them into the courtyard. "Dunos Scaith lies between the Dunwold, the Glaswold, and the Murkwold. Only those I choose find it. Otherwise I would be flooded with entreaties to train aspiring warriors, especially now."

"You mean because of the challenge to the Milesian Accords?" Erin surveyed the interior of the fortress, surprised by the eclectic nature of the structures within. Buildings plucked from different eras populated the interior of the fort. The area encompassed by the walls was larger than a football stadium, and a squat, stone keep dominated the center of the space. Cruder stone and timber longhouses were along one wall. A medieval smithy belched smoke not far from the gatehouse. A trio of Quonset huts from World War II or the Korean War were opposite the longhouses.

"Yes, there are many spoiling for a fight if the Exiled Folk return to the Dunwold," Scathach admitted. The redheaded woman guided them toward the central keep. "I have neither the time nor inclination to deal with such foolishness."

"Yet you agreed to take seven years to train me?" Erin tried to discern where the attendants had taken Izzy.

"I train heroes and champions, not peacocks and thugs." Scathach sniffed. "Technically you only get 333 weeks."

"That's an odd number." Erin resisted the urge to figure out how much it reduced her 'sentence.' "Where did they take Izzy?"

"The infirmary is behind the keep, adjacent to the practice yard. You need to have your wounds tended to as well. Fighting an infection is not how I intend to begin your training," Scathach answered. She led the way, and Erin saw a stone building similar to an old, small church. As they drew closer, Erin could see great windows in place of stained glass, with the shutters open. The structure lacked a church's steeple, but great wooden doors opened out toward a marked off square in the yard. Scathach guided her inside.

Curtained partitions lined one side of what would be the nave in a church, taking up the whole right side of the chamber. To the left were several tables; the closest had several people crowded around it, including Derek. Tears had left tracks through the dust on Derek's face.

A woman wearing a blood-spattered grey robe glanced up as they approached. "The wound is too grievous. All we can do is ease her passing."

"Put her in The Sleep," Derek implored.

"Derecho, you are being selfish," Scathach chided. "Your sister earned a warrior's death; let her pass with dignity. Keeping her suspended would only delay the inevitable."

"There is the Pilgrim," one of the attendants suggested, shuffling her feet nervously. "I've heard he can heal any wound."

"I have heard this as well, but he has no love for us." Scathach's gaze went from the attendant to Derek. "It only brings false hope."

"Please, before she's gone, and there really is no hope!" Derek pleaded. "I'll seek out this Pilgrim and get his help."

"Very well," Scathach relented. She gestured, and a crone stepped forward. The old woman held her withered hands over Izzy's prone form and muttered an incantation. Unlike everyone else's words, Erin could not make out what the crone said. She wondered if everyone else had been speaking English for her benefit or if there was some sort of magic at work letting her understand.

"It is done," the crone rasped and teetered away, leaning heavily on a gnarled staff not unlike the one Liam had used.

"I'll go with you," Erin stated and caught Derek's eye, who nodded gratefully.

"What of your training?" Scathach demanded. "Your time is limited. You could lose weeks seeking the Pilgrim, assuming you can convince him to return."

"Izzy fought for me and was willing to die for me," Erin retorted. "If I can help save her, I will. Besides, as an outsider I might be able to convince this Pilgrim to help."

Scathach held Erin's gaze, her eyes blazing emerald before turning away. "Very well. I see I cannot dissuade you. At least have your injuries tended to first."

"Infection, right." Erin followed one of the attendants to an empty table and hopped up onto it. Tugging up her shirt on her left side, she winced as the fabric dragged over the wounds. "Let's get this over with."

An attendant set to work with a pair of forceps and plucked out the shards of granite. Erin resisted the urge to complain; a local anesthetic would have been nice. She wasn't sure what was worse, the spikes of pain from extracting stone from her flesh or the burn from whatever antiseptic they used to clean her wounds.

When the attendant finished bandaging Erin, she gave her a nod. Erin pushed off the table, her foot still a bit tender but not enough to make her limp.

Scathach was waiting outside. She no longer wore the armor, nor bore the spear and shield, but she was no less imposing. She watched as Erin approached, then said, "Let us find Nechtan; he can act as your guide in the outlands."

Derek stopped pacing.

"What can you tell us about this Pilgrim?" Erin asked, falling into step with Scathach as she strode back into the fort's courtyard.

"He is a Nephilim." There was an edge of contempt in Scathach's voice.

"What is the spawn of an angel doing here?" Derek asked.

"As I said, he dwells in the outlands roughly ten leagues north along the mountains." Scathach guided them toward one of the Quonset huts. "He treats with some of the denizens of the Glas-wold."

"It's only what, thirty miles or so?" Erin asked as she peered north to where the highest peak was visible over the wall. "It shouldn't take us long to get there and back."

"It may not seem long to us, but once we leave Dunos Scaith, the flow of time will not be the same," Derek said. "At the boundaries between the worlds time can get a bit unpredictable."

"I have slowed Dunos Scaith to a crawl in the river of time to facilitate your training, Erin." Scathach stopped before the hut closest to the gate. "It is not something I can do on a whim."

"I'm still going," Erin stated, shouldering her backpack.

"Do we take a boat or go for a swim in this river of time?" A man dressed in leather stood in the doorway of the Quonset hut. Erin wondered how much of his outfit he had killed and skinned himself. His accent sounded Irish, and the cadence of his voice was singsong, as if he was expecting a bodhran drum and fiddle to start playing behind him. He met Erin's gaze with piercing blue eyes, then turned to Scathach. "I take it since you're standing on my stoop, you've got a task for me, Milady?"

"Nechtan, this is Erin, scion of Cu Chulainn," Scathach said and placed a firm hand on Erin's shoulder.

Nechtan's stubbled face broke into an easy grin, lighting up his eyes. "Our champion? I knew she'd be tough, but I didn't think she'd be lovely as well."

Scathach narrowed her jade eyes slightly. "Really?"

"Not to say a woman can't be both, Milady," Nechtan added hastily. He took Erin's hand, and she was afraid he would kiss it. When he didn't and shook it instead, though, she found herself disappointed. "Of course, I remember Derecho. Where is your sister?"

"She is the reason we need your help," Derek replied evenly. "My sister is gravely wounded, and we need to find the healer called the Pilgrim."

Nechtan appeared surprised and glanced at Scathach, who nodded. "I'm sorry to hear that, Derecho," he said. "Let me grab a few things, and we can be off."

"As charming as ever," Derek muttered to Erin, the faintest hint of humor returning to his voice. "It's a shame he's straight as a board. He'd fancy you much more than me."

"I hadn't given it any thought," Erin protested.

* * * * *

Chapter Three

Iblis

"What happened?"

Iblis waited impatiently for an answer as Raven's eyes fluttered open. He knew the witch had spirit-walked to the heart of the tempest-elemental, but Iblis had been unable to pinpoint her location. There were several surges of magical power, and not all were from the storm Mikha'el had called.

Raven glanced around the dim room, as she slowly rose from where she reclined on a couch. "The creature in the storm killed the druid."

"What?" Even with the *sefir*, the divine spark Iblis had managed to siphon off amidst the latest upheaval, he was nowhere close to having enough to deal with the Exiled Gods or his own brethren. "The fool! What has he done?"

"The druid got better." Raven paused for dramatic effect, which annoyed Iblis. "They resuscitated him, though he might still be pretty messed up. They had to carry him away."

"Where? Where did they carry him off to?" If he could get the druid's location out of this fiasco, that would at least be something. Especially if the druid was incapacitated but alive. The conditions for the challenge would remain until the clock ticked down, and odds were both sides would try to draw more magic into the mortal world.

"I'm sorry, but once he left the spirit realm it was hard to keep track of him." Raven furrowed her brown eyes in concentration. "I think there was something like Stonehenge in the physical world; I saw it light up when the lightning hit it."

Iblis scowled. It was north of where he was, and based on the weather radar he had followed, east of Peoria. It still left a lot of farmland, but it would be hard to hide something the size of Stonehenge. He regarded his witch, who leaned back into the couch. He wondered if she was telling him everything, or if she had developed a fascination with the druid. Had she grown jealous from the addition of new witches to their coterie, diluting her influence on Iblis?

He would have to bring the neophytes up to speed. While Iblis had poured a portion of his power into each one, it would take tutelage to get them as proficient as Raven. Right now, they were little more than toys and reservoirs for his *sefir*.

"Very well, it gives us something to work with." Iblis debated tasking Mad Dog and Mikey with driving up and down country roads searching for stonework circles but dismissed the idea. All it would take was a row of trees to hide the henge from the road. Maybe Don Potts would know something. If he didn't, maybe someone in this Druidic Fellowship of America Potts belonged to would have heard of someone local building their own Stonehenge.

"Raven, why don't you get some rest?" Iblis suggested, still turning over ideas on how to use the new information. "Perhaps you'll remember more after a good night's sleep."

Raven nodded and rose slowly from the couch, obviously exhausted. "Perhaps you are right, Master."

Iblis watched her leave and returned to his thoughts. He could send the bikers to talk to Potts. Could the meatheads actually keep the questions straight, let alone any answers Potts might give? Iblis decided to send Gypsy along with them. It would be a good chance to see how his new witch took instructions, and Potts might be more encouraged by Gypsy batting her eyelashes at him than the bikers menacing him. Mad Dog and Mikey definitely wouldn't complain about taking the young woman on an errand. Spreading out the responsibility among his witches would also help keep Raven's burgeoning ego in check.

Iblis scrutinized the computer monitor on the desk. The screen was replaying a radar loop from the freak storm, where the front sweeping across the state ground to a halt, then began retracing its path, orange and red congealing along the middle of the front as it crawled west. The storm slowed to a halt again, then the entire line crumbled; the remains drifted back east.

Iblis thought about waking Orliath, his other new witch. While her magical acumen wasn't on a par with the others, she was proficient with technology. Maybe she could narrow the search pattern based on the radar data. Iblis decided it could wait until morning. The initiation ceremony had exhausted his witches, and he had given Orliath some extra potent wine to calm her nerves afterwards. Now she was sprawled, snoring, on a futon in one of the back offices.

Iblis watched the loop again. If the struggle had taken place on the spirit plane, the druid could have projected miles from his physical location. It was a start. Between this and the stonework Raven saw, Iblis knew it was merely a matter of time before he found the druid.

*****

Chapter Four

Erin

"We had best stop for the night."

Nechtan halted and peered toward the northern horizon. He pointed upslope toward a cleft in the foothills. "There is a creek over there; the clearing next to it will make a good camp spot."

Erin glanced up at the sky. Despite the weird monochromatic tint, it appeared they still had a couple of hours before it got dark. "We could cover more ground before nightfall," she suggested.

"I am good to press on," Derek protested. "We need not stop so soon."

Nechtan regarded them both. "I do not doubt your stamina. We are near the boundary of Scathach's domain. Once we cross out of it, time no longer flows according to her whim, and our champion loses precious time."

"Time is precious for my sister as well," Derek retorted.

Nechtan shook his head. "Not really. If they enspelled her, put her in the Sleep, she has more time than any of us."

Derek frowned, but said nothing. Erin put her hand on his shoulder. "I want to get this healer back to Izzy as soon as possible, but I know nothing about this flow of time stuff," she said. "Besides, if we press on, we might not find a decent spot to hunker down for the night."

Derek nodded wordlessly.

"I do not know what this 'hunker' is, but what you say is true." Nechtan started in the direction of the cleft. "It is better to take a good camp site than risk wandering around in the dark hunting for a spot."

"So, you're not using some sort of magic to translate," Erin remarked as she fell into step behind Nechtan. She caught herself admiring his athletic posterior and immediately felt guilty. "You speak English pretty well."

"Thank you." Nechtan gave her a brilliant smile over his shoulder, then returned his attention to picking a path. "Learning Dunwold languages helps pass the time, not to mention how useful it will be when the Exile ends. I speak English, Spanish, passable Arabic, and a bit of Hebrew."

"Know thy enemy?" Derek asked from the rear of their column.

"More or less," Nechtan agreed. "Those languages represent the great majority of the various Abrahamic religions the Avramites preach and follow." Nechtan paused to survey the cleft now that they were closer. The creek was visible, spilling out and tumbling downhill. "I don't reckon my native tongue will come in handy, nor would the patois we've developed in the Glaswold be of much help."

"Where did you come from? Were you born on the Dunwold?" Erin asked as she stopped next to Nechtan. A flat, grassy clearing about twenty yards from the creek bank appeared promising.

Nechtan strode toward the clearing; Erin fell into step behind him. "I was born in Ulster, sometime shortly before the end of the first millennia," he replied. "My father was daoine sidhe, one of the folk who managed to hide from the exile or slipped back through. My mother was a weaver's widow. When the Norsemen came raiding, I fought back. I hunted them from the woods with my bow, or my sword if they came hunting for me."

Erin really hoped the handsome guide wasn't a dead man, some sort of ghost. His grip had seemed solid and warm. "What happened? Did they kill you?"

"Things must be getting interesting on the Dunwold if you can ask such a question so plainly." Nechtan shook his head. "No, I am quite alive, despite the Vikings' best efforts. I finally annoyed them enough for them to send an entire band of warriors into the woods after me. They stopped giving me easy targets. I was injured in a skirmish and forced to flee. I put my bloody hand on a stone in a passing circle and fell into the Glaswold. Scathach was impressed enough to take me on and train me. I have served her and Dunos Scaith ever since."

"Why aren't you the champion then?" Erin unshouldered her pack as they reached the clearing. She hadn't wanted to let on how fatigued she was, but she had been going for 24 hours from her perspective. "It sounds like you were pretty bad ass to begin with, and you have been training for literally centuries."

"I bet he has never killed a seraphim," Derek remarked. He lowered his pack and slumped onto a log.

Nechtan's eyes widened in surprise as he turned to Erin. "Truly, you killed a seraphim? That should be explanation enough."

"It was some sort of surfer angel dude with a white sword," Erin said. She was afraid if she sat down, she wouldn't get back up. "Since he evaporated after I stabbed him, I don't know if I really killed him. I hope I did; he was an asshole."

"If nothing else, she destroyed his corporeal form." Derek made an exploding gesture with his fingers.

"It doesn't explain why you, or someone else who has been here forever, wouldn't be a better pick for this challenge." Erin opened her pack and pulled out the bundled up tent, along with a handful of metal spikes.

"This site has been used before, there is a fire pit here," Nechtan observed as he nudged the charred remains of a campfire with his boot. "I'll gather some wood for a fire. You two are exhausted; get what you need from your packs and rest. Erin, I'll answer your question once we set up. I suspect the answer will bring more questions than we have daylight to answer."

By the time Nechtan returned, Erin had set up the tent and staked it down, then unfurled her sleeping bag inside. Nechtan quickly built a small fire and retrieved some water from the creek, which he pronounced safe to drink. Dinner was an assortment of trail rations; Erin and Derek's were MREs, while Nechtan had dried meat and a hard bread he softened with water to make it chewable.

"So, you've already learned time can be tricky in the Glaswold, especially when you get the domains of various powerful folk and boundaries to other worlds involved." Nechtan pulled a flask from his belt and took a swig, then offered it to Erin. "It gets stranger for those of us who aren't what you would call human. We experience time in a different manner, not in the hour-by-hour, day-by-day manner you or others from the Dunwold do."

"You're from the Dunwold." Erin accepted the flask and took a swig. It tasted like whiskey and fire, and it burned her throat on the way down. She was afraid to cough toward the fire for fear of igniting her breath.

"Yes, but my father was not. There are many terms for the folk: Tuatha De Danaan, Aos Sidhe, Daoine Sith, Twyleth Teg, the list goes on. I've heard faery folk or fair folk tossed around as a more encompassing term." Nechtan nodded toward Derek. "Derecho's people have their own terms as well."

"I get it. You're all supernatural, and I'm a dunnie," Erin said as she handed the flask to Derek, watching his reaction out of the corner of her eye. He took a swallow with no ill effect and reached over to hand the flask to Nechtan.

"The point I am trying to get to is, because of who we are, time tends to skip over us." Nechtan accepted the flask, took another drink and tucked it away. "It's why I haven't aged to dust and bones, but it also means we don't learn the same way as you, especially when it comes to physical skills. What is a month of drill and practice for you could be a nap and a leisurely walk to the well for us."

"Whatever. This time stuff is making my head hurt," Erin complained. The exhaustion didn't help, not to mention the liquid fire she had drunk.

"You two get some sleep." Nechtan pointed toward the tent. "I will keep watch; later one of you can take over long enough for me to rest my eyes."

Erin nodded wearily and went to the tent; Derek followed her. "No funny stuff," she warned as she crawled in and found her sleeping bag by feel.

"Truthfully, Champion, I am too tired to flirt," Derek replied, then collapsed next to her.

Erin rolled over on her sleeping bag and was out like a light. When something tapped her boot, startling her awake, Erin was merely tired as opposed to exhausted. Firelight spilled through the tent door where it had been unzipped. Rolling forward from her sleeping bag, Erin stuck her head out.

Nechtan was crouched next to the tent. "I'd let you sleep longer, but we have company, and I don't want to risk drifting off."

Erin nodded and extracted herself from the tent, accepting Nechtan's hand as he helped her stand. He smelled of smoke, leather, and a hint of whiskey. Any distraction evaporated when he stepped aside so she could see the fire, or rather what was on the other side of the campfire.

A huge, black dog regarded them with eyes glowing like dull red embers. The dog didn't growl, snarl, or pace; it simply stared at them. Erin found it more unsettling than if the beast had bared its fangs.

"I would guess it is a moddi dhu, a kind of barghest. If it was a cwn annwn, there would be more, and they would be white not black." Nechtan kept his voice low and steady, as though the neighbor's Doberman was in the yard, and not some supernatural dog-monster who lurked barely outside their camp. "I do not think it is a yeth hound; it has made no noise."

"So, what do we do?" Erin tried to keep the dog in sight without staring it down. "You have a bow; can't you shoot it?"

"I do not want to piss it off, especially if it means us no harm." Nechtan also kept the creature in his peripheral vision. "I think if you keep the fire burning bright, it will keep the beast at bay. It is only a few hours until sunrise."

"Me? What are you going to do?" Erin reached in her pocket to find the *alf-vassi* holding her sword. She slipped her hand in the small bag and found the hilt of the weapon Gofannon had forged for her.

"Remember all the talk about time?" Nechtan waited for her nod before he continued. "Well, you are grounded in the moment; you can't drift off. Though being around you grounds us, it is taxing, and I need to rest before we set out again."

"Fine," Erin replied. When she pulled out the sword, she expected the black dog to react. It sat there and stared. "I hope this works on dog-monsters as well as it does on asshole angels."

"I imagine it would, but do not brandish it at the beast, or you might provoke it." Nechtan glanced more fully at the dog then back at her. Unlike Derek, Nechtan's eyes didn't have an unnatural glow in the fire light. "It does not seem to want to come further into the light, but if you make it mad, it might change its mind."

"All right. I'll yell if anything happens," Erin promised and nodded toward the tent. "You can sleep on my sleeping bag. It's not much, but it's better than the ground."

"Thank you. Wake us when the sun breaks the horizon." Nechtan turned and ducked into the tent. Erin intentionally did not watch him as he crawled in. After Nechtan fumbled a moment with the zipper, he closed the tent, and Erin was alone with the dog.

She walked over to the log near the fire pit. Erin hoped the wood piled near the pit would be enough to last until morning. Sitting down, she set her sword across her legs. She risked a peek at the dog, which hadn't moved. "I don't suppose you have any answers?"

The dog remained silent.

"I didn't think so."

*****

Chapter Five

Lee

"Pastor Haskins?"

Lee startled awake. He had been dreaming about Joel's fiery disintegration after the woman ran the angel through. It took a moment for him to remember he was in a veterinary clinic in Colorado Springs, sprawled on a couch in the lobby. He had found Qashmet bleeding in the woods halfway to the truck. Not knowing what else to do, Lee had picked up the injured canine and brought him here. He hoped Qashmet's unusual parentage didn't preclude the vet from helping him.

A sympathetic vet technician smiled at him. She wasn't the same one he had checked in with the previous night. She said, "The doctor says Qashmet is out of danger, at least enough so you can go home and get some rest."

The last thing Lee remembered before falling asleep was they were doing surgery to deal with the stab wound that had punctured one of Qashmet's lungs. He glanced at his watch. It had been eight hours.

"How is he?" Lee asked. He realized he was parched; his voice was raspy. The staff had taken his distress last night as being upset over his dog being attacked. In truth, he vacillated between shocked by what happened and panicked over the consequences. He had failed; would it mean Mikha'el would withdraw whatever he had done to cure Lee's wife of cancer?

"He's a strong boy." The tech used the tone animal lovers use when talking about dogs. "It might be a day or two before you can take him home though."

Lee heard the clicking of claws on linoleum as Qashmet rounded the corner. The half-angel's eyes met Lee's; they were far too intelligent for a dog's. Lee almost expected Qashmet to speak up right there. A beleaguered veterinary technician followed the dog.

"He got out of his kennel somehow," the new tech lamented and gestured helplessly as Qashmet trotted over to Lee. Stitches were visible on the dog's flank.

"Oh." The young lady who had been speaking to Lee sounded surprised. "He shouldn't be up and about."

"Tell him that," the other vet tech, a young Hispanic man, replied. "One minute I was getting his cone, the next minute the door to his kennel was open, and he was halfway across the room."

"Well, he is a willful dog," Lee remarked and glanced down at Qashmet. "Why don't you set us up with whatever he needs to keep any infection from setting in, and we'll square our accounts and be on our way."

"You know, if you got him fixed, he might be more docile," the young man suggested.

Qashmet turned and growled.

"No, I don't think so," Lee said. He had already paid upfront for Qashmet's medical attention, using the credit card Mikha'el had provided at the beginning of the mission. He hoped the card still worked; surely, by now Mikha'el knew they had failed.

"Alright. Jaime, why don't you get the cone for Pastor Haskins? I'll take care of the rest." The female vet tech turned toward the reception area. "Pastor, if you'll follow me, we'll get you all checked out."

Lee was impressed Qashmet held his tongue while the vet tech explained the medication prescribed to counter possible infection and went through the paperwork needed to discharge him. Another charge to the card cleared; it gave Lee a glimmer of hope. Maybe Mikha'el knew what had happened; they had done their best to stop the *benayim*, the pagan champion, from reaching her goal.

Lee and Qashmet walked out to the truck in silence. Lee followed the dog to the passenger side; the door popped open without Lee's intervention. Qashmet hopped up onto the cab seat. Lee closed the door, walked around to the driver's side, and climbed in.

"How are you feeling?" Lee asked. He set the small bag with the pills on the seat between them and tossed the cone-collar over his shoulder. He knew Qashmet wouldn't brook the cone. Hopefully, he was smart enough not to gnaw at his stitches.

"Better than I have a right to," Qashmet replied. "Thanks, Collar. You did me a solid; I owe you. You could have left me."

"No, I couldn't," Lee stated and started the truck. "As much as I wanted to run and get the heck out of there, I couldn't leave you there to bleed out. If nothing else, we're both servants of the Lord."

"I thought you didn't approve of my mercenary ways?" the dog retorted. Lee barely noticed Qashmet's mouth didn't move when he spoke. Originally, he had found it quite disconcerting.

"It's not for me to approve," Lee replied as he put the truck in gear and pulled out. He headed for a nearby cheap hotel he had spotted. "And you're welcome."

"So, what now?" The dog turned to gaze out the window. "I lost track of what happened once the faerie bitch shanked me."

"The woman we were supposed to stop, Miss Donnelly, ran Joel through." Lee remembered the scene vividly. "He exploded into a bunch of sparks. Does that mean he's dead?"

"Holy sh- I mean crap!" Qashmet sounded surprised. "Seraphim are pretty hard to really kill, but she probably stabbed his ass off the mortal plane. I'll bet he's *pissed.*"

Lee felt a little relief. As much as the angel-turned-surfer-dude had annoyed Lee, he didn't want to see him dead. What did it mean for an angel? Didn't they dwell in heaven already? Lee decided he was too tired to ponder such matters.

"Right now, I guess we catch our breath and see if we get any new instructions." Lee pulled into the parking lot of the hotel. It seemed like it specialized in truckers and school sports teams on a budget. It would suit him fine. If the card was declined, Lee didn't want to find himself on the hook for a big room charge.

Lee's worries regarding the credit card proved unfounded. The hotel clerk didn't bat an eye when he ran it and handed the card back to Lee. Luckily, the room was at the back of the complex, so the clerk wouldn't be able to see Qashmet. He wasn't the only one with a dog, but he didn't want any complications. If anyone noticed the Doberman follow him into the room, there was no indication.

Once settled in, Lee made a brief call to his wife. There was no hint of distress in her voice; she told him she was feeling fine, though Lee was careful not to probe too much. If Mikha'el rescinded their deal, how quickly would the cancer return? Would it revert to the way Christine was when Mikha'el had first approached Lee? It had been Stage 4, in several organs and the lymph nodes. If it started from scratch, would it make a difference? Could the doctors catch it early enough to treat it?

"Hey Collar, can you get me one of the pills?" Qashmet had waited until Lee said good-bye to Christine before he spoke up. "The stupid bottle is kid-proof."

"So, I'm not going to have to trick you into taking the pills?" Lee asked. He pulled the bottle out of the little, white bag and read the instructions. A pamphlet included tips on giving pills to dogs.

"Are you kidding? I listened to what the vet said," Qashmet replied. The dog sat down in front of Lee, watching expectantly. "If you want to hide it in a taco, you can, or just toss it to me."

Lee fought with the safety cap until he managed to twist it open and extricate one of the pills. "It says you need to take two a day until the bottle is finished."

Lee flicked the pill toward Qashmet, who snapped it out of the air and trotted toward the bathroom. Lee half expected to hear Qashmet slurping water from the toilet, but instead there was a rush of water from the sink faucet. A few moments later, the dog returned, water dripping from his muzzle.

Qashmet eyed the dark television set. "Afraid to turn on the TV?"

"Yes. I imagine Mikha'el is furious." Lee replied as he picked up the remote and pointed it at the television. "I can only suppose what the fallout will be."

The screen flickered to life, showing the news report on a local station. National stories were interspersed with local interest pieces, eventually followed by the weather, but there was nothing directed toward Pastor Haskins.

"I guess we'll get our marching orders soon enough," Qashmet remarked. He jumped up on the other bed, which reminded Lee of Joel's absence. The seraphim had made Qashmet sleep on the floor. "Until then, we might as well rest up. I still hurt like Hell, and I can tell you're gassed."

"I suppose you're right," Lee conceded. He propped up some pillows and leaned back. "I'll order a pizza; I'm too tired to go back out."

"Now you're talking." The dog's tongue lolled out as he smiled. "Get plenty of meat and no onions unless you want to sleep with the windows open."

*****

Chapter Six

Erin

"I see our friend is gone."

Nechtan sat down next to Erin on the log and pulled on his tall, leather boots.

"What friend?" Derek yawned from the entrance of the tent, stretching.

"There was a creepy black dog with red eyes staring at us all night," Erin replied. She was relieved the creature was gone, more so now that the others had awakened. "As soon as the sky started to lighten, it slipped off downhill toward the thicker woods."

"Some sort of barghest?" Derek asked as he approached the fire.

"Aye." Nechtan nodded, as he searched in his pack until he found some dried meat. "Probably a moddi dhu. Definitely not a harbinger hound."

"That's a relief." Derek found his own breakfast, an energy bar. "So, how far is it until we reach the Pilgrim?"

"Probably a hard day's walk, assuming we don't run into any trouble." Nechtan stared north, where the eastern face of the mountain range was brightening in the pre-dawn light.

"How likely are we to not run into any trouble?" Erin asked, following his gaze.

"If I was travelling alone, very likely." Nechtan gave her a quick grin. "I've gotten pretty good at avoiding trouble over the years."

"With us along, not very likely," Derek suggested. Erin knew what he wasn't saying. She suspected Derek could travel nearly as silently as Nechtan. She was the one likely to bring trouble, the dunnie tromping around in their faerie world. Maybe she should have listened to Scathach and let Nechtan and Derek go themselves.

Nothing to do about it now, she thought, and retrieved her own breakfast. Besides, she was going to make sure the Pilgrim came back and helped Izzy, even if she had to drag him along the mountains herself. "Well, we might as well strike camp and get going."

* * *

An hour later, Erin realized the sky had turned from gray to bright blue. In the morning light, colors seemed more vivid. The three of them had been angling downhill and north for half an hour, passing through a sparse patch of woods.

"We've left Scathach's domain," Nechtan announced, leading them confidently down a path only he could see. "On the bright side, it's not so dreary. On the downside, most denizens of the Glaswold avoid her territory, usually out of instinct. Gods only know what we'll run into now."

"It still looks kind of desolate," Erin remarked. She peered around as they continued marching. The woods thinned out to low-hilled scrub along the base of the mountains. There were no signs of civilization, though they were hiking straight toward where Denver would be in the Dunwold. "I take it not a lot of people live around here."

"No, they do not," Nechtan said as he made a sweeping gesture. "This used to be thick with the spirits associated with the indigenous peoples. The Avramites couldn't brook the presence of the native spirits. Therefore, when their folk invaded the land, they did everything they could to stamp out the native faith and the magic associated with it.

"Like what happened with the Exiled Folk, once the native practices dwindled from a combination of forced conversion, uprooting tribes, and outright extermination, the magical beings associated with the tribes drifted deeper into the Murkwold. Few still walk the land here, and some who do are rightfully angry."

Nechtan paused a moment to scan the route ahead. "Now, if all we had to worry about were the holdouts from the indigenous spirits and creatures of this land, America's Glaswold if you will, it is unlikely we would stumble across trouble. When the dunnies from our homelands crossed over the ocean, it opened the way for Exiled Folk and creatures to follow them."

"So, are the Glaswold and Murkwold reflections of the Dunwold?" Erin scanned along the mountains. They appeared the same as when she, Izzy, and Derek had driven west on I-70.

"More or less." Nechtan rocked his head side-to-side. "A mountain in one existence will be there in the others. Think of the Wolds as layers draped over the globe, although the Murkwold is a bit squishier."

"So, the Tuatha and the others landed on the east coast and migrated west?" Erin asked. Like with her son's monster-fighting game, if Erin heard the terminology repeated enough, she picked it up.

"Up until you get into the Rockies. We are on the western edge of the lands inhabited by various folk driven under The Veil by the Milesian Accords." Nechtan strode off across a flat expanse of scrub brush. "I do not know if it is because there are major reservations of indigenous peoples, but westward expansion screeched to a halt. Rumor has it the Council of the Folk reached some sort of deal with the Elder Spirits of the various tribes. There are no holts west of the Mississippi, save for Dunos Scaith; we leave them alone, and they leave us alone."

"What's a holt?" Erin asked as she worked to keep up with Nechtan. He wasn't much taller than she was, but he seemed to eat up the trail with each stride. She looked away when she caught herself admiring his leather-clad physique.

"It's a settlement of one of the folk such as Tuatha, Twylyth, or Xanosi," Derek replied. He seemed content to drift along behind Erin and Nechtan. "Any of the faerie folk really, as you would call them."

"What about California?" Erin asked. "Seems to me it would be ideal for magical folk."

"Is that some sort of gay joke?" Derek's tone bordered between mocking and accusatory.

"No!" Erin protested. "I meant that there are all of those New Age types out there. Crystal wavers, Wiccans, psychics, Scientologists; it seems like it would be a natural fit for people with magical origins."

"As a general rule, we don't go to the West Coast," Derek replied. "It's too weird."

"He is right. You've got a lot of Nephilim out there, not to mention some beasties and spirits dragged north by descendants of the Aztecs." Nechtan chuckled. "And there are weird pockets of banality and trickster entities hoping to take advantage of naïve dunnies playing with spirit-boards and crystal balls. It's a mess, both on the Glaswold and the Murkwold."

"Good thing I never really wanted to go to California," Erin muttered.

"Well, I have good news and bad news," Nechtan said as he halted on a hilltop free of scrub and trees. "The good news is the Pilgrim should be next to the small lake past the next rise, maybe an hour or so away."

"I'm afraid to ask the bad news," Erin remarked and looked around warily. "Here it seems to be worse than, 'oh, bad news, you need new tires.'"

"I am not sure what you mean, but we are being stalked." Nechtan slowly pulled the bow from his back and drew an arrow from his quiver. It seemed like he had a meager supply of arrows.

"Do you know by what?" Derek asked, producing a pair of long, thin knives.

Erin pulled her sword out of its extra-dimensional pocket. She wondered if her friend from last night had gotten hungry enough to come out in the daylight. Nechtan didn't seem to think the black dog was a great threat.

"Derek, do you know what a devil-bear is?" Nechtan asked. The hunter nocked his arrow as he watched the tree line.

"No, and I'm not encouraged by the name," Derek replied.

"Are they covered by the metal pact?" Erin asked. "The one protecting faery folk from most metals besides iron?"

"The Fiwer Pact?" Nechtan shook his head. "No, but I don't know what difference it makes."

A huge, red bear burst from the tree line. It resembled a grizzly on steroids, dipped in blood. It silently charged them, crossing open ground up the hillside at alarming speed. Erin planted her sword in the dirt and reached into her jacket. Nechtan unleashed his first arrow, followed immediately by another. Both arrows sunk into the bear's chest but did nothing to slow it down. They did draw the devil-bear's fury, and it closed on Nechtan.

Nechtan loosed a third arrow before casting aside his bow and drawing his own sword. Two feet of steel seemed pitifully inadequate as the beast reared up and roared for the first time.

A boom drowned out the bear, causing both the bear and Nechtan to flinch. Erin adjusted her aim and pulled the trigger again. This time the .357 struck the bear in the side of the head. There was a gout of bloody fur, but the bear shook its huge head and turned toward Erin, ready to lunge.

Two more reports from the gun produced two red wounds that blossomed on the bear's throat under its jaw. It tried to roar through a bullet-savaged windpipe as arterial blood gushed from the other neck wound. Another pair of hurried shots barked from the pistol. The first struck the bear in the chest amid the arrows, with as little effect; the second impacted it below the eye and caused the bear to snap its head aside as it lunged forward.

Erin dodged to the side and snagged her sword from the dirt. The bear smote the earth where she had been standing a fraction of a second earlier, then spun, searching for its quarry. Erin stashed the pistol in her pocket, so she could use both hands to wield her sword. The bear shook its head, wheezing, and spotted her. It lumbered toward her and lashed out with a paw the size of her head, tipped with four-inch claws.

Erin sidestepped and brought the sword down with all her strength, her fury matching the bear's. The blade's arc carried it through the ursine's paw and severed it. Blood frothed from the beast's maw as it tried to roar in rage and pain. It took a clumsy half step in Erin's direction then slumped to the grass. For good measure, Erin brought the sword up and chopped at the bear's neck, below the skull. It felt like she had struck an oak tree when her weapon hit the spine; the blade disappeared below the fur until she wrenched it free.

"Color me impressed," Nechtan remarked. "No wonder you are the champion. I can only wonder how formidable you will be with Scathach's tutelage."

"I was certain we were going to need at least one favor from the Pilgrim before we broached the subject of my sister to him." Derek sheathed his blades, and they vanished from sight.

"I got lucky," Erin panted, coming down from the adrenaline surge. "The caliber was too small to be effective against such a large beast. I really should have used a .44 or a .50 caliber."

"I do not know what this 'caliber' is, but I suspect the hands wielding the weapons made up for any difference." Nechtan gave her an admiring smile.

"If you say so." Erin wiped the blood off her blade on the bear's pelt, then took out a handkerchief and wiped it further. She would need to give the weapon a proper cleaning when they made camp. "Let's find this Pilgrim."

*****

Chapter Seven

Tim

"I can manage myself!"

Tim could hear his father's voice through the thick wooden door. He debated knocking on it, but he was afraid he would walk in on something embarrassing.

"Quit being stubborn and let me help you." Pixel's voice was harder to understand after the oak muffled it. She added something else Tim couldn't make out.

"It's not polite to eavesdrop." Tim jumped, not having heard Susan approach. She stood behind him, arms crossed. She looked like she had just gotten out of bed as well. She gave the door an irritated glance as Pixel said something unintelligible.

"I wasn't trying to listen," Tim protested. "I was afraid they were…you know…"

"Wrong kind of yelling," Susan replied and reached past Tim. She rapped on the stout door. "Liam, I'm coming in! I hope you're decent."

The door didn't budge when Susan turned the knob and pushed. "Did that purple-haired snot really lock the door?" Susan muttered.

There was an audible click from the door, and Tim nodded toward it. "Try again."

This time the door swung open. Tim followed Susan into the room. Pixel was glaring at the closed bathroom door. If she was surprised they were able to get past the locked door from the hall, she didn't show it.

"I woke up, and he was dragging himself across the room." The small woman poked a thumb at the door. "He's too much of a prude to let someone help him in the bathroom. Dummy."

"I can hear you," Liam called back through the bathroom door.

Susan went over to a large shoulder bag sitting next to the foot of the bed. She pulled rolls of gauze and jars out of the bag, then lined them up on the floor. "He's always been a bit uptight. He doesn't do sky clad or skinny-dipping."

"Pity," Pixel remarked. She was about to say something else, but spotted Tim.

The toilet's flush drowned out what may have been curse words uttered behind the bathroom door, followed by the sink running. Finally, the bathroom door swung open. Tim's father held himself up on the doorframe.

"Good morning." Liam said through gritted teeth. Sweat beaded on his forehead, and his knuckles were white where he clung to the woodwork, leaning against the frame. "See, I was fine."

"Bull," Susan retorted. She moved over to him. "You can barely stand, let alone walk. I told you not to try walking."

"I'm not an invalid," Liam protested, but he didn't resist when she threw his free arm over her shoulders.

"Let your feet get infected, and we'll see about that." Susan beckoned to Tim. "Help me get you stubborn father back to the bed."

Tim nodded and positioned himself on the other side, next to the door. As his father lurched forward, Tim threw himself into Liam, keeping him from toppling over. Between the two of them, they managed to help Liam stagger back across the room.

"Thanks," Liam gasped as he plopped down onto the bed. Tears welled up in his eyes as he obviously bit back the pain. "The good news is I'm not paralyzed, and the plumbing works."

"It looks like you're hurting a lot," Tim said as he moved aside.

Susan knelt down and started unwrapping the bandages on Liam's feet.

His father nodded. "You know when your leg falls asleep, and when it wakes up you get the pins-and needles-sensation?" Liam asked. "Turn it up to eleven and set my feet on fire."

"I've got a few prescription pain pills left from when I had my wisdom teeth pulled," Susan suggested as she placed the used dressings in a pile.

Liam shook his head. "Give me a couple of ibuprofen and put something topical on my feet. I'll tough out the rest."

"Your father is a terrible patient." Susan made a sour face as she examined Liam's feet and glowered up at him. "Congratulations, you managed to break blisters on both feet. Exactly what I warned you not to do."

"Isn't there some sort of magic that could help him?" In the games Tim played, there were always some sort of magic spells or potions to heal people.

"We're lucky Gofannon's mead restarted his heart," Pixel remarked.

"What!" Susan exclaimed. She gave Pixel, then Liam, an accusatory glare. "You didn't say anything about dying last night!"

"You died?" Tim was confused. Last night when the thunder boomed, the house had been really upset, but then settled down after a minute. Tim had thought it was because of the storm.

"Let's not be over-dramatic," Liam protested. "Yes, my heart stopped for a moment, but it restarted, and I'm alive."

"I ought to have Gofannon throw you in the back of my car," Susan fumed as she sat back. She turned her attention to Liam's feet. "Tim, can you do me a favor?"

Tim perked up. "Sure! What can I do?"

"Ask Einar to boil a couple gallons of water and bring them to me," Susan replied.

"This isn't so you can yell at Dad some more?" Tim asked as he paused at the door. Susan still seemed angry.

"Oh, I'm going to yell at him some more." She gave Liam another annoyed glance. "But I really do need boiled water to clean everything."

"Okay." Tim dashed off, taking the familiar staircase two steps at a time. His nose told him Einar was in the kitchen working on breakfast.

"Good morning, Boy," Einar said without taking his eyes from the skillet. "If you're down to fetch some breakfast for the druid, it'll be a few minutes."

"Actually, Susan asked for two gallons of boiled water." Tim spied several empty plates, but no food yet. His stomach growled.

"Fine, give me ten minutes," Einar said. "Gofannon should be sniffing around soon, so I can have him carry the hot kettle up to them." Einar snagged a large copper kettle from a hook near the stove. "Do me a favor and fill this with water. I'll have some food for you in a bit as well."

Tim did as instructed then set the kettle within the dwarf's reach. "I'm going to wait in the living room."

Einar nodded and picked up the kettle with one hand while he dumped a bowl of chopped up meat into a pan full of hash browns. "Good idea. A watched pot doesn't boil."

Tim knew that wasn't true but said nothing as he sought out a comfortable chair in the living room. All the curtains were closed, so it was dim despite the morning light outside. Sinking into the antique upholstery, he debated turning on the television.

"Hello, Tim," a voice said from the darkest corner of the room. "I think it's time for us to have a little chat."

Tim jumped. A man stood in the corner, older than his father but not quite grandfatherly in appearance. The man wore a long, dark robe. Tim noticed the stranger had mismatched eyes like his father. Somehow, Tim wasn't surprised when he realized he could see through the man. The house seemed unconcerned about the apparition.

Tim swallowed the lump of fear in the back of his throat. "Who are you?"

"I'm Cathbad," the ghost replied. "Your ancestor on your father's side of the family."

"You're the one who warned me." Tim eyed the spectral druid. "At the intersection, when the truck would have hit us."

"Correct." Cathbad nodded. He silently walked to the couch and sat down. Tim wondered if ghosts really needed to sit, or if Cathbad was doing it to seem less scary. "Luckily, I was able to reach you."

"Would we have died?" Tim asked. The thought made him shudder.

Cathbad shrugged before he replied, "Quite possibly. I could not take the chance. It was because of our shared blood I was able to reach you. Blood is potent when it comes to magic."

"Thank you." Tim didn't know what else to say. He wondered if someone walked into the room, whether they would see Cathbad, or if it would appear Tim was talking to an empty room. "Is that why you're here?"

"You are welcome and not really." Cathbad steepled his fingers in thought for a moment. "What happened last night brought a torrent of magic into the world."

"Do you mean the *Gwuedd*?" Tim had heard others use the term in reference to magic. It was like ley-lines or a power grid for magical energy.

Cathbad smiled. "Very good. The *Gwuedd* has more power in the Dunwold now. The Avramites pulled it through the storm-elemental from the Murkwold. Most of the power, *lledrith* we would say, infuses the *Gwuedd* around this place."

"Cool." Tim mentally tried to pronounce *lledrith*; the initial sound was challenging. He decided to practice the strange aspirated *ll* later. He had only heard the term once before, without much context. "What does it have to do with me?"

"When your father died, you inherited his birthright for the moment," Cathbad stated solemnly.

"He got better, right?" Tim remembered last night, the crash of thunder, the strange buzzing in his head. "Did he lose his magic?"

"If anything, his magic is stronger now," Cathbad replied, much to Tim's relief. "While you did not retain your father's mantle, the spark of magic has been awakened in you."

"Does that mean I can do magic?" Tim blurted louder than he intended. He dampened down his voice and glanced toward the kitchen. "Does this mean I'm a druid?"

Cathbad shook his head and smiled. "There is much more to becoming a druid than mere magic. You have the potential, if you choose to follow the path. If nothing else, you will be a draoi, a user of magic, at least until the Challenge. If your mother loses, I imagine the Avramites will do whatever they can to purge magic from the world again."

"Will you teach me?" Tim asked eagerly.

"It is difficult for me to remain in the Dunwold," Cathbad replied. "It is important your father not be distracted. He has much to do, much to learn, if we are to succeed. He can't do his job if he is worried about you setting the house on fire or conjuring svartgeists."

Tim slumped in his chair, disappointed.

"If things go well, I will try to come back and talk to you further," Cathbad consoled. "Until then, no experiments."

"Will I need a wand?" Tim hoped he wouldn't need to dress in robes and a funny hat.

"No, this isn't a children's tale." Cathbad's outline began to grow indistinct. "Some users of magic find comfort in props, but they are not needed. Remember what I said."

Tim nodded. "I'll remember."

"Who are you talking to, Boy?" Einar asked from the dining room.

Tim looked from the dwarf to the empty spot on the couch. "No one."

*****

Chapter Eight

Erin

"Doesn't look like much."

Erin watched through the binoculars as a white-haired man fished off the bank of a small lake. Behind him was a simple log cabin; it resembled something out of a museum's pioneer exhibit. The tidy garden would have been at home behind Liam's farmhouse, and a crude canoe rested along the bank.

She realized it was the first time she had thought of Liam since leaving the Dunwold. Erin flicked a guilty glance toward Nechtan, who peered at the white-haired man from under his hand.

The old man wore simple clothing, black pants, an off-white shirt, and a simple black hat. He reminded Erin of the Amish she had seen in rural Ohio. The old man was intently watching the surface of the lake, but then he cocked his head as though listening to something. After a moment, he turned and gazed right at Erin.

"He's seen us." Erin lowered the binoculars, and the man became a distant black and white dot by the lake.

"Aye, he has." Nechtan continued to watch. "I believe he is waving at us. May I use your field glasses?"

Erin nodded and handed them over. She noted the guide still smelled of leather and wood smoke, the hint of whiskey from last night gone, replaced by sweat from the morning hike and the fight with the bear. It was still a good smell.

"At least he seems friendly," Derek remarked hopefully.

"I hope the same goes for the lynx lurking near the cabin." Nechtan lowered the binoculars and handed them back. "Most likely some sort of guardian pet."

"So, he has a cat," Derek scoffed as he stood and walked past Nechtan in the direction of the cabin. Erin could have sworn she saw the blonde man's nostrils flare as he strode by, reminding her Derek was probably as interested in Nechtan as she was.

She admonished herself; now wasn't the time to develop a crush on some leather-clad woodsman. Erin fell into step behind Nechtan. First things first, Izzy needed help; Erin could think about the hunter later…she reminded herself more than a few times in the twenty minutes it took to cover the mile to the cabin.

By the time they came within a hundred yards of the crude, wooden house, the old man had stowed his fishing pole and was cleaning his day's catch on a simple workbench near the garden. Erin was glad the wind was at their back; she could only guess what fertilized his vegetables and herbs. She still saw no sign of the cat Nechtan had spotted.

"Well this is interesting," the fisherman remarked. He set aside his knives and wiped his weathered brow with a shirtsleeve. The man's snow-white hair was in a single braid that fell halfway down his back. His beard, also white, was gathered in a simple leather thong. Despite the whiteness of his hair, the Pilgrim moved energetically. There was no frailness in his tall, lean frame. His accent reminded Erin of the Amish; vaguely Germanic and pitched up at the end of a clause. "Not often I get visitors from the Lady of Blood."

"Hello, Elam," Nechtan greeted the Pilgrim cheerily. "I see you remember me."

"I do, Pathfinder. I would be hard pressed to forget a man such as you." Elam dunked his hands in a bucket of water and wiped them on his apron. The hands were calloused from hard work but not gnarled from age. "You did a service for me, and I did one for you. However, I told you I would not play surgeon so the Lady of Blood can have men practice killing each other."

Derek stepped forward. "It's not for one of Scathach's warriors; it is for my sister."

"If your sister plays with swords, she has to expect to get cut," Elam admonished. "Matthew 26:52."

"She was hurt protecting me," Erin snapped, remembering her earlier threats to drag the Pilgrim back to Dunos Scaith if needed. "This wasn't some game or training, and without help she will lose her life."

Elam regarded her coolly with gold-green eyes. "Who are you? Another want-to-be hero from the World of Man?"

"Elam, this is Erin," Nechtan replied. "You may have heard of the champion who will be challenging the Milesian Accords." Nechtan put a hand on Erin's shoulder. "Minions sent by one of the Elohim tried to keep her from reaching Dunos Scaith. That is how Izquierda was injured."

"I thought the pagan priest was supposed to issue the challenge?" Elam asked, looking from Erin to Nechtan. "Is it really that time?"

"Yes, it is." Nechtan nodded. "I am sure you know, once the druid issues the challenge, the champion takes it up."

"Which Elohim?" Elam demanded, peering at Erin intently. "Which one of the archangels is arrayed against you?"

Erin shrugged and replied, "I have no idea. I don't know their names; they keep sending goons after me and my son."

"I reckon it was that bastard Mikha'el," Elam muttered before he turned to Derek. "What is your sister's condition?"

"She was mauled by a hound," Derek replied. "It tried to tear out her throat. She has been placed in the Sleep to keep her condition from deteriorating."

"Well, the Fair Folk would not bring out the big magicks for just anyone." Elam stroked his white beard. "Very well. I will help your sister."

"Thank you." Derek visibly sagged in relief.

Elam turned to Nechtan. "Do not let your mistress think I have changed my mind about her bloody ways," Elam stated. "I do this for someone who would sacrifice themselves to protect others. It is what He would want."

"Understood." Nechtan nodded.

"It is fortunate I had luck fishing this morning." Elam turned back toward the workbench. "Or maybe the fish knew I would have many to feed?"

"Shouldn't we get going immediately?" Erin asked, eager to get back now that the Pilgrim had been convinced.

"She is in the Sleep. Surely you have heard the tale of Sleeping Beauty?" the old man inquired. Picking up a wooden board, he moved the half dozen fish from the bench to the board. "Your friend could wait a century for our arrival; it is still a nap to her. The day is half gone. We shall eat, and first thing in the morning we shall set out."

Erin bit back a protest; she could tell Derek did the same. Nechtan's cautioning look gave them both pause. Erin reluctantly unshouldered her pack. "In that case, is there anything we can do to help?"

"An English with a bit of manners," Elam observed with a smile. Despite the wrinkles increasing with his grin, it made him appear younger. Erin had originally thought he was at least 70, now she deducted a decade from her guess. "If you would take the empty bucket over yonder to the creek, it would help."

Like everything else, the bucket was simple and hand-made. Erin gazed in the direction Elam indicated; fifty yards away a small creek flowed toward the lake. She nodded and said, "Certainly."

"If you spot Daniel, pay him no mind," Elam advised, then he turned his attention to the fire pit in front of his cabin. He began selecting wood from the adjacent pile. "He will come sniffing around soon enough once the fish are cooking; you will have nothing he wants."

Erin eyed her companions. Derek shrugged his shoulders and shook his head. Nechtan held his hands to his face and pantomimed whiskers. Erin remembered the comment about a cat. Nodding, she picked up the bucket and said, "No problem, I'll be right back."

The woods encroached on the far bank of the creek, but the side facing the cabin remained clear. Scattered stumps gave testimony to the cabin's origins. Erin wondered how long the Pilgrim had been living here, but quickly pushed the question aside as she tried to consider the weirdness of how time flowed here.

The creek ran clear and fast. Before kneeling down, she scanned the clearing up slope and peered into the woods as far as the dense foliage would allow. She didn't want any surprises like the devil-bear.

After filling the bucket, Erin took a long drink from her canteen and refilled it with the cool mountain water. She glanced up as she secured the cap on her canteen and met the gaze of a huge lynx. The feline regarded her with unblinking golden eyes. This was no mere bobcat; it was easily as large as a mountain lion. Erin didn't know lynxes could grow that large.

"I hope you're Daniel," Erin whispered, trying to keep her voice calm. She clutched the full bucket with one hand, so she could reach under her jacket for the reassuring grip of her .357 Ruger LCR. She kept the pistol holstered though as there was no logical reason to expect the cat to recognize a firearm as a threat. "I'm going to take this water back to Elam."

The lynx didn't budge as she backed away from the creek. She remembered hearing it was a bad idea to turn your back on great cats. She didn't know if it applied to mutant felines in a fairyland, but better safe than sorry.

At twenty yards, Erin decided the lynx had no interest in following her. If she hadn't been watching it the whole time, she wouldn't have been able to pick the feline out. She cautiously walked back to the cabin, peeking over her shoulder after several paces. The cat was nowhere to be seen.

* * * * *

Chapter Nine

Liam

"You have got to be the worst patient ever."

Liam wanted to disagree with Susan's assessment, but this morning had proven otherwise. He had been so frustrated about feeling helpless, being able to do something, do anything, outweighed any pain or consequences.

"She's right," Pixel agreed. If Susan and Pixel agreed on something, it must be the end-times. "You could have asked for help."

Liam nodded mutely. From his waist to his knees was mildly tingly but from the knees down felt like an acupuncture convention, with hot coals under his feet added in for good measure. At least now, he could wiggle his toes.

"I should take the Druid out to the forge." Gofannon's voice wasn't quite loud enough to rattle the china. "We have lost most of the day already."

"Absolutely not," Susan countered. She had gone to work and come by the house afterward to check on him. Liam had half expected her to show up with a pair of orderlies to hustle him off to the hospital.

"Why not? His arms work fine." Gofannon protested, flexing one of his own heavily-muscled arms. "If he cripples himself, he will need all the arm strength he can build."

"I'm not going to cripple myself," Liam protested. Venting some frustration on a hunk of metal might do him some good.

"At least the house is clean, which is saying something with all the people you have traipsing about," Susan commented. She surveyed the dining room, where they sat around the large wooden table. "It's actually cleaner than when you were here by yourself. No going outdoors, especially to that filthy forge. Not for three days; we'll see how your feet have healed then."

Liam slumped back in his chair. It was pointless to argue with Susan. His legs still couldn't hold his weight; Gofannon had carried him downstairs.

"We are going to lose three days?" Gofannon thundered. The god glowered at Susan, who was unmoved. "He is already woefully behind."

"Tough." Susan matched the huge smith's stare until he relented and scowled at Liam.

"Don't act like this is my fault," Liam admonished Gofannon. "I didn't send the storm monster or try to fry myself with a lightning bolt. We'll have to make the best of these circumstances and see where we can make up for lost ground."

Liam leaned forward and added, "Why don't you spend the next three days working up blanks for me to practice on? And, can you finish up the smelter we started on, so when I'm back on my feet we can hit the ground running?"

"I can help with the smelter," Einar suggested. "As much as I enjoy cooking, my fingers are itching to work with something heavier than a frying pan."

"Fine. Your idea has some merit, Druid," Gofannon admitted. "Once your Valkyrie of a nurse releases you, we will have to work very hard."

"I can spend the time going over the Milesian Accords," Liam said. He turned to Pixel and Einar. "I don't suppose you guys happened to bring a copy with you? I really want to read up on the Challenge and get a good idea of what to put in the new pact if we win."

Pixel reached behind her back and produced a scroll. Liam added learning how to make an elf-pocket to his list of things to do. Pixel set the scroll on the table. She explained, "It's in English, so we won't lose time translating it from Old Gaeilge or Latin."

"This doesn't look so bad." Liam picked up the scroll gingerly; the parchment appeared ancient. He had expected a much more robust document, but the rolled scroll was less than two inches in diameter and didn't seem tightly wound. Untying the black ribbon binding the scroll, he began to unroll the document. It reached the other side of the table and showed no sign of ending. The remaining roll of parchment was still just shy of two inches thick. "How long is this damned thing?"

Pixel shrugged. "It might reach from one end of the room to the other. Might go halfway into the living room. I've never unrolled it all the way."

Not so concise after all, Liam thought, and rolled the document back up. "We've got three days to kill. After dinner we can start going over it and taking notes."

"Cool. What do you want me to do?" Tim asked eagerly.

"Check in the study for a blank notebook; there should be a few on top of the filing cabinet," Liam replied. "Then wash up and set the table for dinner."

Tim nodded and scampered off in the direction of the study.

"I mean it. No going outdoors or to the forge for three days," Susan warned sternly. "If you get an infection, you're going to the hospital."

"Don't worry, I'll make sure he stays inside," Pixel offered, "even if I have to tie him to the bed."

*****

Chapter Ten

Erin

"That is the wrong path."

Erin halted, and peered up the slope. She recognized the rock formation they had passed coming down from Dunos Scaith. Turning back to Nechtan, she pointed at stones and said, "We came down this way, to the left of those three boulders."

"That was coming down the mountain," Nechtan replied. He peered south-west, where Cheyenne Mountain was clearly visible. "Dunos Scaith is held apart from the Glaswold. Merely walking to the same spot on the mountain will not get you there. We are near the edge of Scathach's domain, and once we have stepped into it, we can make camp."

"Let me guess, your mistress has been mucking with the flow of time again," Elam remarked sourly. The Pilgrim had largely remained silent on the hike. They had broken camp at his cabin right after first light and marched at a brisk pace. The white-haired man had kept up without complaint, and now he was breathing no harder than Erin. "It is unnatural."

"She doesn't actually change how time flows," Derek corrected. He had been uncharacteristically quiet, which Erin had chalked up to worrying about Izzy. "She moves Dunos Scaith into different currents of time, like you would move a canoe in a river to take advantage of a faster or slower current."

"It is still unnatural." Elam frowned. "Her canoe, as you call it, is nearly ten leagues across."

"She needs the time to ensure the Champion is ready for the challenge," Nechtan said. The hunter searched until he found a route up the hill which met some hidden criteria. "See the gully with the tree across the top of it? There is our route."

A distant rumble caught Erin's ear. The sky was clear, but the others had obviously heard the noise too. Nechtan did not look to the sky, but downhill along the route they had taken as the thudding noise repeated.

"I have a bad feeling about this," Derek muttered as he followed Nechtan's gaze.

"Quickly, up into the gully!" Nechtan waved the rest of them forward and unlimbered his bow.

"You will only make him mad," Elam admonished as he followed Erin up toward the entrance below the tree, a hundred yards away. "I thought maybe he had wandered west and stayed there."

"Only make who mad?" Erin asked as they scrabbled up the rocky hill.

"That would be Uthor," Elam replied. "He is a giant."

"I thought he was King Arthur's dad or something?" Erin glanced back and saw Nechtan bringing up the rear, an arrow nocked on his bowstring.

"You're thinking of Uther Pendragon," Derek said. "Uthor is a cousin of Balor of the Fomoire." Derek gave Elam a hand up over a steep patch in the wash and added, "You might know them as Fomorians. They have nothing to do with King Arthur."

"Totally lost me." Erin turned her attention back to her footing. The booming noise had dissolved into distinct thumps in the distance.

"A lot of mythologies have giants. They are usually other races of man or folk, and scholars threw in the term giant out of convenience," Derek explained as he helped her over the same steep patch. "In this case, it's not a matter of convenience."

Erin peered back downhill once she was on sure footing. Something moved behind a hill three hundred yards away. With a thudding step, the giant strode into view. It was thick-limbed and three stories tall, and each of its lumbering strides ate up distance and smote the ground. A patchwork of hides and pelts covered the giant's torso. Over its shoulder, it bore a long tree trunk stripped of branches. The tree ended in a cluster of metal spikes; it took Erin a moment to realize the spikes were sword blades wedge into the wood.

The giant stopped and sniffed the air, the nostrils on its wide, flat nose flaring. Everyone froze, holding their breath as the huge head swayed back and forth. With a final whiff, the giant turned in their direction, its eyes narrowing as it spied them.

"Go! Go!" Nechtan shouted. "Make sure you go under the tree!"

The tree was only fifty yards away. Erin risked checking behind them and caught a glimpse of the giant lumbering toward them, its enormous feet pounding the earth as it halved the distance to them. The fomorian bellowed as it closed.

Erin could feel tremors in the ground as Uthor gained on them. She debated pulling her pistol, wondering if it would do any good. Ahead of her, Elam and Derek scrambled under the tree and climbed up the gully. Behind her, Nechtan urged her to hurry. Obviously, he had no illusions about stopping to fight the creature out in the open, but she didn't think the gully would give them much protection. Fear was starting to give way to anger. She was really getting tired of being chased.

Reaching the gap under the tree, Erin checked again. Uthor was only twenty yards away and winding up his club. Erin reached for her gun but Nechtan shoved her ahead under the tree, causing her to stumble forward. Catching herself, she spun around to yell at him.

"I don't need to be saved! I'm not some damsel," she snarled.

"No, but your temper makes you stupid," Nechtan shot back. "Take a look."

The giant was frozen ten yards from them. No, not frozen, moving in slow motion Erin realized. Her annoyance dissipated in the confusion. "What's going on?"

"We picked a current to our advantage," Nechtan said. "Do not dawdle though; we do not want to risk his blundering through exactly the right spot."

"Still don't like time manipulation?" Derek asked Elam as they renewed the climb.

Elam glanced back and shook his head. The giant was in mid-stride, its foot ponderously lowering toward the dirt. "It saved our hide, but it is still unnatural."

The cloudless sky was stark grey as opposed to blue. Everything in the distance had a monochrome tinge, as if a printer was running out of color ink. Erin checked to make sure her pistol was secure in the holster before she stomped up the ravine after the group.

"What happens if he breaks the tree we ran under?" Erin inquired, still fuming, but now mostly at herself. She tried to keep it from her voice.

"Then the path will be ruined," Nechtan replied, and then paused to listen. Out of sight, Uthor was out of earshot as well.

"Then Elam will be stuck here?" Erin was sure the Pilgrim would not be pleased with the notion. The old man seemed unconcerned.

"Getting out is easy; you merely walk far enough away," Nechtan answered and renewed his climb, leading up a path out of the gully. "Getting in is the tricky part."

After thirty minutes, the sky had darkened considerably, and Nechtan brought them to a halt on a flattened hilltop. The hunter started a campfire while Derek gathered more deadfall wood.

"Your shelter is a fancy bit of work," Elam stated, watching Erin assemble her tent. "Did a croft-hob make it for you?"

"No, I bought it at All-Mart." Erin set to work staking the finished tent to the ground. "It will be snug, but three of us can sleep in it while one stands watch."

"You're not going to warn him not to try any funny business?" Derek dumped an armload of branches and took out an old, but ornate, hatchet.

"I don't think I have to worry about Elam." Erin turned to the white-haired man and added, "No offense."

"None taken, and you are quite right, you need not warn me," Elam replied. He turned toward the fire and rummaged in his pack. "Now, let us see what I can do about supper."

He prepared a meal of salted fish with radishes and carrots and chunks of sweet bread, which had been baked in a skillet. While Erin wasn't a big fan of salted fish, she wasn't about to complain. She suspected the Pilgrim wouldn't find the MREs she was carrying any more appetizing.

"Elam, if you don't mind my asking, how did you end up living in the Glaswold?" Erin decided she was a fan of the bread, especially when it was warmed over the fire.

"I was cast out from my people." His hazel eyes reflected the fire light as he answered. "Rather forcefully."

"Because you're a Nephilim?" Erin asked. She hoped she wasn't crossing a line. Derek and Nechtan watched silently. "Or because you can use magic to heal?"

"They did not know of my lineage; at the time, I did not know either." The old man continued to stare into the campfire. "As for my gift, they were willing to consider it a miracle from Him. I truly believe it is a blessing from the Almighty, but being a healer was not enough to make up for the taint upon me once it was discovered."

Only the crackling of flames interrupted the following silence. Elam turned his gaze to Erin. He recited, "Leviticus 18:22, thou shalt not lie with another man as thou would lie with a woman; it is a detestable act. The people of my parish found it detestable enough to set fire to my home and barn. They made it quite clear I would find no shelter in the community.

"I wandered the world a spell, but using my gift drew attention. Apparently, it displeased Him, for He sent his servant, Mikha'el, to the World of Man. Mikha'el revealed himself when I cured a man of consumption and warned me to cease meddling in the Lord's plan. To prove his point, Mikha'el sent an angel to take the man I had cured to his final reward.

"Mikha'el threatened to do the same to everyone I had spared the grave; every man, woman, and child would receive a visit from an angel of death. I had to assume he would make good on his threat. I spent the next score years as a hermit. I thought that if I avoided people, my compassion would not drive me to heal them, and thus I would not doom them.

"Finally, I was in a town trying to trade some crafts for supplies and a little girl was trampled by a horse. She would live, but she would be crippled. I thought it was surely a sign; healing her would not be keeping a soul from His Heavenly Presence, it would merely ease her pain and the woes of her family."

Elam's eyes shifted back to the fire, and he leaned forward, resting his elbows on his knees. "The seraphim arrived within a day. It turned out it was not healing which offended Him, for His Son and the disciples healed the sick and lame. But using my gift somehow aided the heathens, though I do not understand how. Mikha'el decided the surest way to stay my hand was to have me struck down. Though the angel wore the guise of a man, I recognized His servant for what he was and fled. The angel tore through the town in pursuit, and I was about to make peace with the fact that it was the end of my days when an old Scotsman beckoned me to hide in his wagon.

"Little did I know the old codger was a sidhe smuggler. The seraphim stalked past and never glanced at the hob or his wagon. After His servant moved on, I told the sidhe about my plight. He brought me to the Glaswold; I think it was as much to tweak the angel's nose as it was the kindness of his heart. I've lived here since."

"How long ago was that?" Erin asked once she shook herself out of her stunned silence.

"What is the year of our Lord?" Elam sat up.

"It's 2017." Erin assumed the anno domini was unnecessary.

"One hundred and sixty years by your reckoning." Elam smiled, crinkling his eyes. "Not bad for a relic of two centuries."

"Silver foxes are in vogue now," Derek quipped with a smirk.

* * *

The next day they came within sight of Dunos Scaith shortly before noon. As they drew closer, Derek had picked up the pace, silently urging the others to hurry. While Erin shared his urgency, she didn't want to hurry Elam. The old man seemed vital, but they had been hiking for a day and a half.

"Run on ahead," Elam told Derek. "Make sure they have fresh dressings pressed against the wound so she does not lose too much blood when they release her from the Sleep." Derek dashed ahead and disappeared around the curve of the fort wall.

"You will be able to save her, won't you?" Erin asked once Derek was out of earshot.

"Most likely, but I will not make any promises," Elam replied. The healer frowned slightly at the guards staring down from the wall. "I never wanted to come back to this place."

A large crowd was waiting in the courtyard beyond the gate. They all kept a respectful distance, leaving a clear, wide path, and a murmur of whispers went through the throng as Elam stepped inside. It was obvious most of them knew about the Pilgrim. In the middle of the path stood Scathach, along with a woman whose fierce countenance resembled his. A handful of attendants hung behind.

Elam stopped a few paces away and tipped his hat to Scathach. "My lady."

"Elam." The warrior-woman nodded. "I am pleased to see the Champion was able to sway you."

"I am here for her and the friend who put herself in harm's way on your champion's behalf," Elam responded, then patted Erin on the shoulder. "Do not think I have changed my mind about this place."

Another murmur ran through the assembled people. Erin assumed it was in reaction to Elam's defiant tone. Erin had the feeling no one here would dare take that attitude with Scathach.

"As you say. Let us see to your patient." Scathach turned with military precision, causing her retinue to scatter out of her path, and led them to the infirmary.

The building was crowded. Erin considered using her status to push her way in but realized she would be of no use and decided she'd better serve everyone by staying out of the way. She slumped onto a stone bench outside the infirmary and shed her pack.

Nechtan plopped his pack on the ground and leaned his bow against the building. He sat next to Erin and watched a handful of people lingering outside the infirmary doors. Nechtan said, "I hope you realize what you have accomplished. Those two have not spoken in an age."

"I didn't do anything other than ask for his help," Erin responded. She was almost too tired to notice the whiff of leather and sweat coming from Nechtan. She didn't want to know what she smelled like after three days of hiking and no shower; somehow she suspected she did not smell as enticing as the hunter did.

"Being a champion means more than fighting." Nechtan took a drink from his water skin, then splashed some over his head. Erin fought back the urge to peek.

Closing her eyes, Erin managed to nap. If there was one thing the military had taught her, it was how to sleep whenever and wherever possible. Too soon, someone nudged her awake, interrupting a dream about bearskin rugs and leather-clad hunters.

Blinking, she quickly took in her surroundings and realized huddles of people were coming out of the infirmary, many whispering and drifting off to different parts of the fort.

Finally, Elam emerged, the denizens of the fort still giving him a wide berth. Blood stained the rolled up sleeves of his shirt. Catching Erin's eye, he nodded, and Erin sagged in relief.

*****

Chapter Eleven

Lee

"Pastor Haskins!"

Lee sat bolt upright. In the other bed, Qashmet thrashed in the blankets, trying to untangle himself after being startled awake. The television was on, and the anchorman glared through the screen at Lee.

Lee hadn't left the television on, but it didn't surprise him that it had powered on of its own accord. He blinked blearily at the screen. "Yes, what can I do for you?"

"Apparently not as much as we hoped," the anchorman retorted. "You allowed the *benayim* to escape."

Maybe it was the stress of the last twenty-four hours or the fatigue of the last few days that caused Lee to snap, "I got your man there in time, but he failed to stop her! The *benayim* turned him into a pile of ash. You wanted me to get your agents across the world of Adam, and I did. I don't know what else you expected. Qashmet and I each brought down one of her heathen helpers, but the bitch was tougher than your angel!"

The anchorman's eyes glowed like molten gold, and Lee thought he was going to reach through the screen for him. The camera panned left to the blonde anchorwomen; her sedate expression appeared forced as did her smile.

"Perhaps the failure is not entirely yours," the blonde woman admitted, tugging at her skirt to cover her knees. "Return east, to Peoria. We have lost track of the *benayim*, but the *hartummin* remains. Also, there is evidence another party is involved."

Great, Lee thought. They still hadn't found the druid. "We saw the *benayim*, Miss Donnelly. We did not see her son."

The camera swung back to the anchorman. His eyes had reverted to their natural blue. "Are you certain? There was no sign of the child?"

"We watched them coming up the path before we ambushed them," Lee replied. He didn't want to be too optimistic, but he felt like he was salvaging something from the train wreck on Cheyenne Mountain. "We only saw Miss Donnelly and those two blonde fairies my boys reported in Ohio."

"Which means she left her son somewhere in the world of Adam," the anchorman remarked. A map of the United States appeared behind him, zooming in on Illinois. "She must have left him with the pagan druid. If we could find her son, it would give us a great deal of leverage over her."

"That would be my guess, as well," Lee said. "If this druid had alien allies, they would most likely have communicated with the pair supporting Miss Donnelly. It makes sense they would have handed off the kid."

"Perhaps you are not useless after all," the anchor stated, staring sternly into the camera.

The camera panned back to the woman. "You and Qashmet will proceed to Peoria pending further instructions."

"Hey, I did my part!" the dog protested to the television.

"You only get your reward if we win," the anchorwoman countered, tugging her jacket closed over her blouse. "Are we clear?"

"Crystal," Qashmet replied sullenly. "Looks like I'm your bitch until this is over."

"Excellent, you do understand," the blonde said. "We will use what resources we can to try to locate the *benayim's* son. Go to Peoria so you can act once we find him."

"Sure thing," Lee replied. The image flickered, and the screen went dark. The pastor looked at the dog. "Guess we're going back east."

"Do we at least have time for breakfast?" Qashmet asked.

"Absolutely." Lee nodded. "It's what Joel would have wanted."

*****

Chapter Twelve

Erin

"Don't get lost."

It took Nechtan a moment to realize Erin had made a joke. He grinned and said, "Afraid you'll miss me if I don't come back?"

Erin tamped down the flush threatening to turn her cheeks red. "I'm sure Scathach will keep me too busy to miss anyone."

"Remember to watch your temper," Nechtan cautioned.

Erin bit back a retort. Two days earlier had been her first on the practice yard. Predictably, Scathach had opponents taunt and frustrate her. Infuriatingly, she fell for the tactics even though she expected them. She managed to embarrass herself and send one of her sparring opponents to the infirmary.

Nechtan and Derek were taking Elam back to his cabin now that Izzy was on the mend. Erin guessed Derek's excuse for tagging along was so he could personally express his gratitude to Elam. If not for concern about the giant, Nechtan would have been content seeing them to the boundary of Scathach's domain and waiting for Derek to return.

"I'll try," Erin promised, meeting the hunter's piercing, blue gaze. The courtyard suddenly seemed warmer. Today Nechtan smelled less of wood smoke, more of freshly-oiled leather. While the linen tunic he wore was different from the one he wore when they met, the leather pants and vest were the same. Erin wished she were going with him.

"The sun is wasting," Nechtan said and gestured for Derek and Elam to follow. "We had best get under way."

"See something you like, Champion?" Izzy whispered next to Erin. This was only the second day Izzy had been up and about, and already she was able to sneak up on Erin. Elam's magic had saved Izzy's life, but it was questionable whether she'd ever recover her full voice. Elam had quoted something about the Lord giving and the Lord taking when asked.

"Am I that obvious?" Erin asked, embarrassed because she knew the answer. It hadn't been three days back home, she realized. Surely, Liam had waited longer before hooking up with the purple-haired fae who undoubtedly was throwing herself at him.

"We have a long time here ahead of us; I would not judge you for seeking comfort," Izzy said in a low, raspy voice. "Especially not from him."

"Have you ever…?" Erin let the rest of the question hang.

"With Nechtan?" Izzy regarded Erin with sky blue eyes before answering. "I may have lain with him a time or two. However, it was long ago, before Scathach moved her domain here. Do not let it stop you, Erin. You have to remember, many of the folk, myself included, do not have the hang-ups you dunnies have about sex."

"Derek has pointed it out a few times," Erin remarked. She turned and walked back toward the Quonset hut Scathach had assigned to Erin, Izzy, and Derek. "Though I would hardly consider your brother an objective source."

"Fair enough," Izzy conceded as she followed Erin. "Are you reticent because of the Druid?"

Erin looked over her shoulder. "Maybe. I don't know. If I wasn't sleeping with Liam, I was trying to sabotage any notion of a relationship. Now we're stuck here for seven years, and there's this hot guy with a sexy accent who wears tight leather, but I feel guilty for some reason."

"Did you promise the Druid anything?" Izzy asked. "Or imply anything? It sounds like the opposite."

"Pretty accurate," Erin conceded as she opened the door to the hut. Wood partitions and canvas drapes divided the 800 square foot interior. Half of the area was communal space, the rest divided among four private 'rooms.' "While I know it's not reasonable for me to wait for seven years, to Liam it will only be seven weeks. What if I've moved on, and we get back to find out he has been waiting for me?"

"Then you deal with it like adults," Izzy rasped, settling on one of the wooden benches flanking the dining table. In the dim light inside the hut, the bright pink scar stood out on her throat. "As you pointed out, you will have a long time to think about it."

"True," Erin replied as she sat on the opposite side of the table. She drew her sword from the sheath on her belt. Surrounded by armed warriors, Erin felt no need to hide her sword in the *alf-vassi*. Instead, she stowed her pistol in the extra-dimensional pocket. "Who knows what will happen by then?"

"You have at least a hundred days or so before Nechtan is back to tempt you," Izzy remarked. "Maybe more depending on how long my brother dawdles at Elam's cabin."

Erin paused and set out her sword-cleaning supplies; she had forgotten about the time dilation when thinking about how long Nechtan would be gone. "Maybe it's as well. Hopefully, by then,

Idunn's apple won't have my libido in overdrive. Meanwhile, I can focus on my training without the distraction."

* * *

A week later, Erin was glad for the lack of distraction. Uathach, Scathach's oldest daughter, was in charge of Erin's initial training. Erin quickly learned a couple of things. The first was that the seraphim had been wearing kid gloves. After the first sparring session with wooden swords, Erin was black and blue all over.

The second was that she wasn't nearly as good with the sword as her previous fights had led her to believe. The angel had been pulling his punches and the devil-bear was dying when she chopped its spine. Her practice partners, Daidh and Mysie, had been at Dunos Scaith for a century by their reckoning. Both had sidhe blood, like Nechtan, though Mysie insisted on referring to her fairy ancestors by the Scottish term sith. Thanks to their supernatural heritage, both were long-lived in the Glaswold.

Mysie was short, barely over five feet tall, with short dark hair and a round face. She was also friendly enough…until she picked up a weapon, even a practice one. As soon as her hands wrapped around a hilt, she became deadly serious and more than once Erin feared her partner had forgotten they were sparring. Erin thought her longer reach would give her an advantage over the diminutive woman, only to find Mysie getting inside her guard over and over.

Trying to land a blow on Mysie was like trying to catch a soaped-up wildcat. The small sith was constantly in motion. When Erin tried to take the fight to her, Mysie would duck and sidestep Erin's attacks. Then she'd be on Erin or knocking her on her ass. Erin found herself having to fight her own anger and not forget they were sparring.

Daidh was the same height as Erin. His head was bald, but his trimmed goatee was brown, leaning toward ginger. While not hostile, Daidh rarely smiled on or off the practice field. Whereas Mysie was lightning fast and aggressive, Daidh fought with the patience of a chess player. He didn't slip inside Erin's guard; Daidh waited until she left herself open and struck hard enough to get her attention. He rarely went on the offense, which at first, Erin mistook for infuriating chauvinism. She would get mad and end up with a new bruise.

The third thing Erin learned was that Uathach held a grudge against Cu Chulainn, Erin's ancestor. It baffled her that these people could talk about events that occurred centuries in the past as if they happened last year. Luckily, Erin did not ask if Uathach was also her ancestor, as that was the crux of Uathach's rancor.

* * *

"Your ancestor was a tremendous warrior," Izzy explained, her voice still hushed from her injury. "It doesn't mean he was a good man. He was driven as much by his lust as his rage. According to legend, there was a nock in his spear-blade for every woman he seduced; by the time he fell, the blade was serrated.

"Uathach was one of those marks. Cu Chulainn lured her to his bed, and when her fiancée found out, he challenged Cu Chulainn. It was nowhere near a fair fight. When Cu Chulainn killed Cochar, he acted as though he was doing Uathach a favor by taking Cochar's place."

"That's why Uathach has a beef with my progenitor?" Erin didn't know how many generations were between her and her legendary predecessor. Evidently not enough.

Mysie laughed. She and Daidh had joined Izzy and Erin for dinner. "Oh no, Lass, it gets better. Your grand-bobby was a right bastard. Not six months afterwards, there's a dust up with Aife, Scathach's biggest rival back in the day. Aife landed on the shores of the Isle o' Skye, where Scathach had parked her holt.

"Cu Chulainn was good and drunk." Mysie's Scottish accent thickened with her mirth. "He staggered down to the beach and challenged Aife to single combat; seeing as Cu Chulainn was barely able to stand upright, she accepted. They tussled back and forth for half a day, the Hound sobering up as they did."

"The Hound?" Erin inquired.

"The Hound of Culann," Daidh interjected, looking up from his ale. "You should add linguistics and history to your curriculum."

"Hush, I'm telling a story," Mysie chided, elbowing Daidh. Erin was still trying to figure out if the pair were more than sparring partners. "Anyhoo, he sobers up, disarms Aife, and knocks her on her arse. With his sword to her throat, Cu Chulainn offers her two choices. Either he can end her right there, or she can bear him a son. You can guess what she picked; supposedly you're descended from her choice."

It took Erin a moment to process. "So, you're saying my great-times-a-lot grandfather raped my great-etcetera-grandmother at sword point."

"That's the long and short o' it," Mysie replied, picking up her ale mug. She grinned smugly, like there was still a piece of the puzzle Erin hadn't grasped.

"If he wanted a son, why didn't he have one with Uathach?" Erin finally asked.

"There you have why she's so full o' piss and vinegar, Lass." Mysie slapped the table.

Erin was confused. "I get why Uathach might be pissed, though you'd think however many centuries would be enough to let it go, but I don't get why my grand-bobby, as you put it, would have picked Aife over Uathach."

"She was already pregnant by Cochar," Daidh remarked quietly. "Or, at least, the child's parentage could have been called into question. The Hound wanted a son he could unreservedly claim as his own."

"Awesome," Erin muttered. "My sensei is mad because my ancestor spurned her for another woman, who happened to be my other ancestor."

"Look on the bright side," Mysie remarked cheerfully, refilling her mug from the pitcher of ale. "Since you're the Champion, she won't let us kill you, though seven years is a really long time to take a beating."

"How did you two get picked to administer my flogging?" Erin asked, hoping to change the subject from her ancestor's reprehensible deeds. "Did you draw the short straws?"

Daidh and Mysie exchanged glances, further cementing Erin's theory they were more than practice buddies. Mysie replied, "She wanted someone who could challenge you, and who wouldn't take it easy on you because you're the Champion challenging the Accords."

"She also wanted warriors who didn't have chips on their shoulders because they weren't chosen to champion the Exiled Folk," Daidh added. He had set down his ale and was poking at what was left of his potatoes. "We have no qualms about giving you a good whack, but we have no delusions of facing Giwargix."

"Thanks, I think," Erin remarked dryly. "Speaking of linguistics, do you know how this translation magic works? As much as I appreciate there not being a language barrier, I feel like I should learn whatever language is being spoken here." She had learned a few phrases in Pashto and Dari while in Afghanistan. If she was going to be 'deployed' here for seven years, Erin figured it would be in her best interest to learn the local lingo.

"Another reason we were chosen," Daidh stated. "We speak English you can understand."

"Not to say we can't speak Goidelc," Mysie added. She had turned her attention to finishing her meal. "Anyone who has been here long enough learns it. We can teach it to you, as well. It will come in handy if you have to deal with anyone from outside o' the fort."

"I thought Scathach kept the location secret?" Erin remarked. Scathach certainly seemed determined to keep glory-seekers from turning up on her doorstep.

Daidh pointed at his nearly-empty plate. "Where do you think the fixings for this meal, or any of our meals, come from?"

"It's not like we have a passle o' farmers here," Mysie added, hefting her mug. "Not to mention brewers or any o' the other craftsmen save the handful encamped here. There is a trade route, some sort o' secret passage, from further east. It lets caravans arrive at our gates to trade."

"How does Scathach keep wannabes from tagging along with the traders?" Erin asked. It didn't seem like it would be difficult. Find a caravan bound for Dunos Scaith and sign up as a guard or drover.

"She draws most of her rank and file guards from those who follow the caravans," Izzy said softly. "In exchange for service, they get training. The exceptional ones, such as our friends here, are recruited for more advanced instruction."

"How can she afford to trade with these caravans?" Erin was still trying to wrap her head around the logistics of Dunos Scaith. There were no fields or herds, only a few dozen chickens and a handful of dairy cows. The only craftsmen supported the needs of the fort.

"There are many a *choucho* willing to part with silver and gold to say they or their offspring were trained by Scathach," Izzy stated. "That is how Derecho and I ended up in Dunos Scaith the last time, when it was on the other side of the Atlantic."

"Your brother is the one who seduced Uathach's daughter, Saidhe!" Mysie slapped the table again, startling Daidh. "Rumor has it he's off buggering the Pilgrim. Is it true?"

"I try not to keep too close tabs on what or who my brother is doing," Izzy responded.

"Plausible deniability." Daidh nodded sagely.

*****

Chapter Thirteen

Liam

"I can manage myself."

Liam grit his teeth as he staggered down the stairs. His legs didn't buckle under him, but walking was still a chore. Each step felt like slapping a sunburn on the bottom of his feet, but the pain was better than the previous numbness. At least that's what Liam told himself as he forced back the tears. He leaned heavily on the old, wooden bannister.

"You have to be the most bull-headed druid I have ever met," Pixel remarked, exasperated.

"Really? How many druids have you met?" Liam retorted, pausing at the landing to catch his breath. "If I have Gofannon carry me everywhere, I won't recover my strength."

"Fine." Pixel threw up her hands. Liam tried not to notice she was cute when she was flustered. It would only be six and a half weeks until Erin returned. Pixel pointed at him and declared, "Remember, if you face plant at the bottom of the stairs, I told you so."

"Duly noted," Liam grunted as he lurched down the remaining steps. Pushing off the wall, he tottered to the dining room table and gratefully collapsed into a chair.

The banging of wooden doors heralded Tim's return from school. Liam wiped the grimace off his face and straightened up in his chair. He felt guilty not being able to drive his son to his first day of school.

Tim seemed surprised to see Liam downstairs. "Hey Dad. Does this mean you're feeling better?"

"I made it downstairs on my own," Liam answered, trying to sound cheerful. "How was the first day at school?"

"Okay, I guess," Tim replied and dropped his backpack on the floor by the stairs. "I'm the new kid, so I have to figure out how to fit in."

"I'm sure you'll make friends," Pixel remarked cheerfully.

Tim eyed her dubiously. "I hope so. Otherwise, lunch will be boring. Plus, it's hard because I'm so out of touch."

"I thought you'd have an advantage," Liam said. "These kids probably haven't heard of half the stuff you know about."

"You'd be surprised." Was there a touch of bitterness in Tim's voice? "Most of my classmates have internet or smartphones."

"Your mother was explicit regarding those phones," Liam reminded Tim. Erin had been adamant, certain Tim's grades would tank if he had the constant distraction of a smartphone. Liam couldn't say she was wrong; he had seen too many people with their noses in their phones instead of paying attention to the world around them. "Don't you get enough internet at school?"

"Only during lunch; they make us work on studying and homework during study hall," Tim lamented.

"Those brutes. It's like they expect you to learn something," Liam teased. He pointed to the school bag on the floor. "How much homework do you have?"

Tim sighed. "Two chapters and twenty problems. Not much, but it's only the first day."

"Why don't you see if you can get one of those chapters knocked out before dinner?" Liam suggested.

"Okay." Tim collected his backpack and took it upstairs.

Liam waited until after Tim was out of earshot then lowered his voice conspiratorially. "How hard would it be to get this broadband internet at the house?"

Pixel didn't have to think before answering. "You're too far out for cable, but you could get DSL."

"Translate into Luddite for me," Liam said. He thought cable was for cable television.

"It means you can't get the fastest internet, but since you probably don't want Tim playing online games, which require a fast connection, it's just as well," Pixel replied. "This will probably get you a 'Best Dad Ever' for at least 15 minutes."

"It's not like we can't afford it, and as much as I hate to admit it, it could come in useful for networking," Liam observed. He reached for the notebook they had been using to write down anything related to the Milesian Accords. "I'm thinking it could be real useful for making contact with pagan groups before the challenge."

"Which ones?" Pixel asked, intrigued. "You've not mentioned much about the rest of the neo-pagan world; you certainly didn't seem to have much use for the local groups. It made you hard to track down."

"Which reminds me, we should put the internet service in the farm name, not mine since I don't have the same surname as my aunt and uncle," Liam remarked. There were still people searching for him; he was glad he never got around to changing the name to Hard Knox Farm. "As for which group? All of them. At least as many as we can manage. Organizing them will be like herding cats, but I think we could give ourselves an ace up our sleeves if the Avramites don't play straight when we win."

Pixel smiled and scooted closer. Her floral scent tickled his nose. She asked, "So you think we'll win?"

"Planning to lose is self-defeating," Liam replied. Gears turned in Liam's mind; they would have to make sure the conditions of the victory pact allowed them to capitalize on his idea, especially if the Avramites turned out to be sore losers. "Susan will be a big help; unlike me, she is in good standing with most of the local groups and some of the broader ones."

* * *

Dinner was fried chicken, broasted potatoes, and green beans. Despite Einar's protest that he wanted to work with something heavier than cookware, he spent over an hour in the kitchen trying to cook one of Aunt Millie's recipes. The result was almost as good as Aunt Millie's, Liam thought, but he didn't let Einar know it had fallen short of the original. The meal reminded Liam of his family filling the house a decade ago. Looking at the people gathered around the antique table, he realized he had a new family.

"I took the liberty of tinkering with your aunt's pecan cobbler recipe," Einar announced as he served dessert. Liam tried not to appear skeptical; his Aunt Millie's pecan cobbler was heaven in a pan, especially with vanilla ice cream. Einar set down a slice in front of Liam and said, "I added a little bit of bourbon."

Liam took a tentative bite, making sure to collect some of the ice cream with the cobbler. He hated to admit it, but Einar might have improved Aunt Millie's recipe. "Gods, this is delicious."

"You mean there's booze in this?" Tim asked, quickly downing a bite in case one of the grownups wanted to stop him. He didn't realize the alcohol had cooked off. "Wow, no wonder you guys drink so much!"

"Liquor doesn't normally taste like pecan pie," Liam chuckled. "When you first try real booze, it won't be near as tasty and will probably make you sick."

"Then why do you drink it?" Tim spooned up another bite.

"It's an acquired taste; adults develop a liking for it because of all the crap they have to deal with," Liam replied, gathering another spoonful. "Things you don't have to worry about yet."

*****

Chapter Fourteen

Erin

"How could I have been so stupid?"

"Accidents happen," the chirurgeon replied, unflustered by Erin's outburst. Ynidd was an older woman with feathers instead of hair. She dealt with injuries and ailments at the fort. "It wouldn't be the first time this has happened to a trainee here. It happens less often because the folk are less fecund. Otherwise the Glaswold would be overrun."

Erin scowled. "This will put a wrinkle in my training. I already lost three months fetching the Pilgrim." She turned to Ynidd. "I would do it again in a heartbeat, but this, I could kick myself. I should have known better, even if I was on the pill."

"The pill?" The feather-haired woman seemed curious.

"It's called birth control," Erin explained. She patted her abdomen, trying not to think about how it would look in a few months. "It's supposed to prevent what happened to me."

"We have an herbal tea which does the same thing; I could have given you some." The chirurgeon smiled apologetically. "I hadn't heard you had actually lain with Nechtan."

"I haven't," Erin snapped back, a bit more bitterly than she intended. It would be at least a few weeks before Nechtan returned. She still hadn't decided anything regarding the hunter, and this complicated matters. "I haven't been with anyone here. I know whose fault this is. Stupid apples."

"Apples?"

Erin sighed. "We both ate these magic golden apples given to us by a Norse dwarf. They're supposed to keep us from aging for seven years; they made us as randy as teenagers going to the prom. Liam and I couldn't keep our hands off each other." As she remembered their encounters, Erin found herself missing Liam until she remembered she was pregnant.

"Were those Idunn's apples?" Ynidd asked.

"Yes, that's what they were called," Erin replied. "They offered me one since I would be here for seven years, and the purple-haired wench fed one to Liam because she wanted to bang him."

"So, the Druid is the father?" Ynidd chuckled softly. "It is no wonder you are with child; the life-giving magic of the apples would have been far more potent than any tea or pill. Once you add the way your fates are intertwined, it's as if the Norns wove your fate."

"Tell this Norns to stay the hell away from my womb," Erin growled. She worked out the time in her head; she was nine weeks along. She had originally attributed her symptoms to a combination of adjusting to the food and quitting the pill. She only had a month's supply, so there was no point in taking them when Liam was on another world and Nechtan was on a fifteen-week hike. Then the symptoms reminded her of when she was carrying Tim, and she sought out the chirurgeon. She would have to break the news to Scathach and Uathach. She didn't look forward to it.

* * *

"This changes nothing," Scathach pronounced once Erin told her about Ynidd's prognosis. She sounded as though Erin had told her she had twisted her ankle. Scathach folded her hands on the table. Her pale skin, framed by long, copper tresses, stood out against the dark stone wall behind her. In the corner, a bronze and gold orrery ticked. "We have limited time. We will have to make the most of it. You will practice as long as you can stand; as soon as you are back on your feet you will resume your training."

"I'm going to have a baby, not a hang nail," Erin protested, her hands on her hips. "You don't have an OB/GYN ward in the infirmary. Not to mention if something goes wrong, if I die in childbirth, the whole challenge goes up in smoke."

"You are correct," Scathach admitted pensively. Her gaze went past Erin, but Erin had the feeling Scathach really wasn't interested in the far wall. She was staring into the distance, past the walls of the fort.

Erin wondered how much of a hassle it would be to show up at a Colorado Springs hospital with no doctor's reference or records regarding her pregnancy. They couldn't turn her away. If the insurance company raised a stink, she and Liam could dip into their proverbial pots of gold.

Would anyone be waiting to ambush them? Heavily pregnant, she wouldn't be much use in a fight. Maybe she could talk Nechtan, Mysie, and Daidh into tagging along to make sure she made it safely to a hospital? It would even the odds and then some.

Nechtan. This would certainly put a crimp on starting anything with him, especially once she started ballooning. Maybe it would give her time to rethink the whole thing; between the apple and her hormones, she doubted whether she was being objective.

"It would not do to lose the champion to birthing complications," Scathach mused, shaking her head. "So, we will send Izquierda to intercept Derecho and Nechtan. Hopefully, she can catch them before they cross into my domain. With any luck they can implore the Pilgrim to return."

"Wouldn't it be better for me to go to a hospital in the Dunwold?" Erin countered. Nechtan being gone longer and her giving birth in a stone and timber hovel wasn't what she was hoping to hear. "I could be tended to by modern doctors and medicine. It would probably get me back on my feet a lot faster."

"It would cost far more precious time," Scathach replied dismissively, waving away the suggestion with a long-fingered hand. "If you were in the Dunwold for two weeks, it would cost you two years here. That assumes there are no complications from mortal authorities or Avram agents."

Erin scowled as she tried to crunch the numbers in her head. Yes, Elam could easily be here before she was due. Even with a magic healer, she was worried about giving birth in primitive conditions. Sure, women used to do it all the time, but childbirth then was very risky for mother and child compared to modern day.

Uathach stood behind her mother, silent. The two could have been mistaken for sisters; Uathach's hair was auburn, but they shared the same green eyes and fierce nose. Was Uathach mad at the interruption in the agenda? She stuck to a very strict schedule. Or was she amused by Erin's predicament, knowing Erin's training was going to be more miserable?

"I'll go speak to Izzy," Erin said after a long moment of silence and turned toward the door.

"Don't forget to be on the practice field at sun-up," Uathach called after her. Definitely amused.

* * *

"Congratulations!" Mysie exclaimed, her brogue thickening with her excitement. "It has been quite a spell since we've had a wee one underfoot."

"I get the impression you are feeling less than celebratory," Daidh said quietly over his tankard of ale.

"I can't say I'm surprised," Izzy added quietly. She sat with the others at the wooden picnic table which had appeared one day in front of the Quonset hut. In the afternoon and evening, the shadow of the hut shaded the table, making it a convenient gathering spot. "The way you and the Druid were in rut, I thought you were trying to inaugurate every room of the house."

"We weren't that bad," Erin protested, blushing at the memory of trashing the study. She thought they had gotten lucky and no one heard the racket when they knocked everything off the desk. Now, she suspected the others had politely ignored the commotion she and Liam had made.

Mysie leaned forward, grinning. "You were mounting the Druid?"

"Repeatedly," Izzy remarked. "You would have thought they were drunken teens on Beltaine. On the Dunwold, beds have metal springs under them. They squeaked loudly when—"

"There were extenuating circumstances—history and apples," Erin interrupted, still trying to fight down the flush in her cheeks. "Those stupid apples."

"Your child will be doubly blessed," Daidh commented. He traced a knotwork pattern on the table with his finger. "With two fated bloodlines coming together, your child will likely be destined for greatness."

"What are you blathering about?" Mysie asked as she picked up the pitcher and refilled everyone's cups.

"Erin is descended from Cu Chulainn. The Druid, her lover, is descended from Cathbad," Daidh explained and tapped the table as though his finger had left a trace. "A child born of those two lines, woven together in the Loom of Fate, has great potential. Stories could be written about them."

"We already have a son," Erin remarked, wondering if her cheeks could turn a deeper shade of crimson. "And the Druid isn't my…I don't know; it's complicated."

"How was it?" Mysie asked scandalously. She plunked the mugs down as she filled them. "Obviously good enough for another go or three. I heard druids used to call on the Land to bolster their vitality, if you know what I mean." She finished with a wink.

"It was fine," Erin replied, noncommittally. She looked down at the mug in front of her and realized she shouldn't be drinking.

"It was fine at least three or four times," Izzy added. She looked at the lengthening shadows. "I should go if I want to catch my brother and Nechtan before they cross back into our flow of time."

"We have to have a toast first!" Mysie proclaimed as she set the pitcher down. "To congratulate our Champion on her impending wee one!"

Erin regarded the mug. "I shouldn't drink alcohol now that I'm pregnant."

"That's daft," Mysie protested. "My mum drank when she was carrying me. Daidh's mum was drunk, or she wouldn't have carried him." She elbowed the bald man playfully.

"I guess drinking a toast wouldn't hurt." Erin picked up the frothy drink.

"Slainte," Daidh offered, raising his ale. The others echoed, and they all drank. Mugs clattered to the wooden table. Daidh grabbed the pitcher and refilled his and Mysie's empty mugs. "You may not want to drink more, so we'll have to pick up the slack for you."

* * * * *

Chapter Fifteen

Lee

"I already said no."

Somehow, the dog managed to pout. "Come on, priest, we've been stuck in Podunk, Illinois, all day," Qashmet complained. "We're only two blocks from the casino. We can say I'm your service dog. Tell them you get seizures."

Lee rubbed his forehead. They had already played the service animal card when paying for the room. Lee's guilt was mollified when he spotted the lady with the Chihuahua in a handbag; she claimed the tiny dog was an emotional support animal. Qashmet had snarked the only thing the teacup dog could support was a nervous tic.

Lee had learned Cash could speak to him without others hearing. Lee wasn't sure how it worked, and he didn't want to delve too deeply. Lee wished he could reply to the canine's ongoing banter without being overheard; having a one-sided argument with a dog made you seem insane.

At least they were alone in their room. The television was on the news channel, but muted. Lee was tired of hearing the same news cycle every fifteen minutes, and he figured if the powers above could turn the television on, they could restore the volume. "Gambling is a vice I choose not to indulge in," Lee said. "There are two televisions; watch a movie channel on the other one, but not one full of filth."

"Sure, suck all of the fun out of the road trip," the dog complained. At least he was recovering from his wounds and taking his medications without a fuss. "We could make a killing at the poker tables."

Lee had chosen the hotel on the east side of the Illinois River for convenience; the Route 150 bridge was only two miles to the north, and I-474 was three miles to the south. In addition, the rates were reasonable enough for him to opt for the suite without feeling guilty.

"I do not cheat," Lee retorted. "Gambling is bad enough but cheating is a sin."

Qashmet snorted. "Fine, I'm going to check the woods out back."

The dog padded to the door and pawed at the handle. Lee knew he would have to let Qashmet back into the room; the dog didn't have pockets for a key card, even if he could operate one.

Lee briefly heard the latest Hollywood scandal blaring from the television before it went silent again. He turned around; the two morning show hosts regarded him from the screen. Lee said, "I was wondering when we'd hear from you."

The platinum blonde adjusted her position on the high stool she was perched upon, swiveling her knees away from the camera. "Unfortunately, our agents did not recover belongings from the *benayim's* son," the anchorwoman said. "It is possible they may do so at a future date, but at this point we must make do. As school recently started, we hoped there might be a potential avenue there."

Lee nodded. "You suspected Donnelly left her son with the druid fellow. Did she enroll him in a local school?"

The other anchor, a man with brilliant white teeth and artfully greyed hair, picked up a sheathe of papers. "There have been seventeen children named Tim enrolled in schools within a 50-mile radius for the fall semester. This only includes children in the expected age range. None have the surname Donnelly, so he must be enrolled under a false name."

Lee's phone and tablet chirped to announce the arrival of a new e-mail, undoubtedly with the list attached. They were assuming the boy was only enrolled under a false surname. "So, you want me to go to schools searching for this child? This won't seem creepy."

"How you complete your assignment is your problem," the male anchor said. "However, this is not your only task."

A picture appeared on the screen behind the hosts. It showed a handsome man, probably in his late thirties, with jet-black hair and a healthy tan. His smile was every bit as bright as the morning show anchors.' "We believe this individual is attempting to meddle in the challenge of the Milesian Accords. He has his own agenda; consider him dangerous. If you encounter this person, or learn of him, you are to report that information immediately. Do you understand, Pastor Haskins?"

Lee nodded, studying the picture. His devices chirped again with another e-mail. "Who is he?"

"He is a servant of the greatest enemy," the blonde woman stated, glaring from the screen. "Do not trust him; he is the Deceiver made flesh. Consider any words he utters falsehoods."

"Any idea where to find him?" Lee asked. He didn't want to give voice to the implications this was Lucifer. According to Qashmet, the major figures of religion didn't actually walk the Earth, but aspects of them could.

The male show host frowned, shaking his head. "Not yet; we suspect he is operating in the area, attempting to manipulate events to his own cause."

"If the infidels win, won't he be out of luck as well?" Lee asked. If the pagan gods and their underworld minions invaded the World of Man, surely they wouldn't allow an incarnation of Satan to remain in the world.

"We do not know what angle he is playing," the blonde woman admitted. "In his case, it is prudent to assume the worst. Keep your eyes open, Pastor Haskins."

The volume faded as the program returned to yet another Hollywood celebrity's history coming back to bite him. "I think I need to stretch my legs," Lee said, and walked to the door.

Lee descended to the ground floor and used a side exit facing the half-full parking lot. As Lee watched, an elderly man followed his wife's electric mobility scooter across the asphalt. The electric motor labored as much as the grey-haired man as they headed for the casino.

Qashmet made a chuffing noise, his equivalent of a laugh, and sat next to Lee. "Maybe if she shared her dinner with Gramps, she wouldn't have blown out her knees."

Lee gave the dog a sidelong glance. "That's an uncharitable thing to say," Lee admonished. "How do you know she doesn't have a medical condition?"

"Collar, we both know her problems are probably brought on by super-sized servings of junk food," Qashmet countered. "How many people in this country qualify as obese?"

Lee brushed away a fly as he brought the picture up on his tablet. "What do you know about this fellow they've added to our to-do list?"

Qashmet peered at the screen. "I think his name is Iblis."

Iblis certainly sounded less terrifying than Satan or Lucifer. Lee reminded himself the Prince of Lies likely didn't carry around a driver's license with "The Devil" printed on it under a horned photo. "Is he…you-know-who?"

The dog shifted his paws nervously. "No, not Old Scratch, but you know the story about him getting cast out after defying the Big Guy?"

Lee nodded, waving again at the annoying insect buzzing around his face. "Of course."

"He wasn't the only one kicked out of the heavenly realm," Qashmet said. "He was the ring-leader of the rebellion, but all the angels who followed him were exiled, as well. Most Nephilim are descended from those angels. Sure, there are a few produced by angels who walked the world too long wearing meat suits and caved into the urges endemic to incarnation, but most first-generation Nephilim are born from Nick's cohorts."

"Is this Iblis a Nephilim?" Lee asked. The sun beat down on the asphalt. Lee wandered toward the south end of the hotel, leading Qashmet around behind it. Trees concealed the view of the adjacent industrial park, but more importantly, there was shade. To an observer, it would look like the pastor was taking his dog to do his business.

"I think he's one of the original lieutenants," Qashmet replied, pausing to sniff a shrub. "In his glory days, he was probably on par with Mikha'el."

"Not a comforting thought," Lee remarked. "You said in his glory days. What about now?"

Qashmet managed an approximation of a shrug. "I don't know. Some of Iblis' ilk were recruited from the cast off gods from the fall of the Tigris-Euphrates civilizations. The Big Guy insisted on treating everyone equally, but a faction felt like second-class celestials. They were recruited because they had some innate power, and it was better to bring them into the fold rather than have them run loose and stir up trouble. Others refused to join; they chose to serve forgotten gods rather than bow to the Big Guy.

"When the rebels got the boot and landed dirt-side, they were cut off from the divine spark, *sefir*, in Heaven. They could only tap into what was available down here." Qashmet stopped to lick himself, causing Lee to avert his gaze. The dog chuffed and said, "Don't knock it until you try it. Where was I?"

"They could tap into the spark in the World of Man," Lee replied.

Qashmet sat down in the shade. "Right. In the old days, there was a lot more mojo in the world. All the old stories about miracles and magic? They had a source; granted they were usually embellished for entertainment or propaganda value, but they started somewhere. Someone convinced the One-Over-Others it would be a good idea to cut off anything beyond mortal ability. This was at the same time religion was going from being a regional faith to something bigger."

"Thou shalt not suffer a witch to live, Exodus 22:18." Lee intoned. "Also, Deuteronomy 18 has some relevant passages on the subject."

"We can debate Bible translations later," Qashmet said. "When ex-employees of Up-Above get cut off, they can only use whatever *sefir* they can gather on the mortal world. This directly relates to how much magic, in general, is loose on the face of the Earth. Some say they are the same, and some say they are merely entwined. Regardless, they agree the more you have of one, the more there is of the other."

Lee leaned against the wall and waved his hand in front of his face. He suspected the same pesky fly had managed to follow him. "So, was the point of the battle with the heathens to deny the rebels access to this spark?"

The dog shook his head, a very human gesture. "It was a bonus. The whole point of the Accords was to cut off pagan magic and drive the *nukrayim* out of the mortal world. For centuries, the powers-that-be persecuted not only those suspected of heathen magic, but also anyone mortal or Nephilim who tapped into the *sefir*."

Lee scratched his head. Had a mosquito bitten him? "If we won, why can't we use all the *sefir* we want?"

The dog snorted, reminding Lee of his fourth-grade teacher. At least Qashmet didn't have an eraser to throw. "The more *sefir* we use, the more of their magic leaks into the world," Qashmet said. "You know why you don't hear about miracles and why faith healers are considered charlatans? It's because even though we kicked them off the world and managed to close most of the entries, magic allows *nukrayim* to sneak back over. Mikha'el has been the chief enforcer regarding magic for centuries, and he is zealous in his duty."

"How does this help Iblis?" Lee asked. He wished there were somewhere to sit other than the concrete trim surrounding the base of the building. "If he uses this spark, won't Mikha'el come down on him like a ton of bricks?"

"You would think so," Qashmet conceded. "Nothing is simple with him, though. Maybe he has recruited pagans to harvest magic from their side in addition to the increased *sefir* used by our side. From what I know of modern pagan worshipers, they are largely marginalized. Someone like Iblis could exploit this to gain their trust."

"To what end?" Lee asked. "If he gains a bunch of power, what does he hope to do? Once we win the challenge, surely the Lord will send Mikha'el to put Iblis in his place."

Qashmet hunched his shoulders in a canine shrug. "Unless Iblis gathers enough power to stand up to Mikha'el. Whatever he is up to, I would wager Iblis has thought this game out three moves in advance. Remember, all we have to do is report him if we find him; I'm guessing Mikha'el wants to nip this in the bud before facing the challenge."

Lee rubbed a temple. The sun was about to crest the building and deprive them of their shade. "I need to think this through, preferably not on an empty stomach."

The dog perked up. "Now you're talking," he said. "The casino has an awesome buffet. All-you-can-eat prime rib, even for lunch."

"Fine, but we're not gambling," Lee responded. The buffet sounded good; the past day and a half had been filled with drive-thru and gas station food. "Gambling is a vice."

The dog fell into step and looked up at Lee. "How does Bingo work?" Qashmet asked.

* * * * *

Chapter Sixteen

Erin

"I liked it better when you were armed." Mysie spat out practice-field dirt and rolled over. She added, "You're more dangerous with your bare hands."

Erin extended a hand and helped Mysie up. Uathach had instructed them to spar without weapons; Erin was eager to have the advantage for a change. During weeks of training in sword and staff, which mostly consisted of her getting beaten black and blue, Erin had focused on learning those weapons. Now she was getting to put a couple of her black belts to good use.

Erin took Mysie by surprise when she caught Mysie's arm mid-punch and flipped her, landing Mysie in the dirt. As soon as the short woman got up, Erin swept Mysie's legs, knocking her prone again. Erin finished the bout with her fist frozen in a hammer strike an inch from Mysie's nose.

Uathach watched with interest. She had been quick to criticize Erin but slow to praise her. Uathach gestured at Daidh to take Mysie's place opposite Erin. Erin waited, sweating in the padding she was wearing. The armor was quilting over leather, and it felt like she was wearing her grandmother's comforter over her workout clothes.

Daidh took his position facing Erin, and they exchanged bows. Erin had shared the martial arts tradition with her sparring partners, and they had enthusiastically adopted it. Following the bow, Daidh brought his hands up in an approximation of a boxer's stance. Erin went into a traditional tae kwon do starting position, then launched her attack.

She feigned a punch; Daidh's block came up as soon as her fist started moving. Instead of stepping into the punch, though, she sent a snap kick at his belly. His other hand moved to catch her foot, but she turned and caught him in the ribs with a roundhouse. Her momentum carried her forward, and she caught the side of his helmet with her elbow. The blow caused Daidh to stagger back a step. Erin kept turning, launching a spin kick. Despite pulling her strength, when her heel struck the same spot as her elbow had a moment earlier, the blow knocked Daidh to the ground.

"Oh shit!" Erin exclaimed. She had expected Daidh to block or duck her foot. Neither Mysie nor Daidh had seen modern martial arts, and they had no idea what she was capable of. "Are you okay? I didn't mean to hit you so hard."

Daidh held up a hand and slowly got to his feet. He shook his head and adjusted the leather helmet. "I am not hurt; you just rang my bell. What was that?"

"Tae kwon do, mixed with a little kung fu and karate," Erin replied, still feeling guilty—as much for clocking him as for the thrill of triumph she felt for a split second. "I'm really sorry."

Uathach was still observing quietly. Had she finally been impressed? "So, you've been playing us for fools?" she accused.

"What?" Erin was baffled.

"For the last few weeks, you've hidden this training, only to spring it on us to humiliate your practice opponents," Uathach stated coldly. "Has this been a game to you?"

"No!" Erin protested. Of course, the redheaded bitch would find a way to turn this against her. "This is the first time we've done martial arts sparring. Until now, all the training has been with swords and staves."

"Wrong!" Uathach thundered, her pale face flushing red. "It has been fighting! When you fight, you use every weapon at your disposal! Do you think the Avram champion will hold back? Do you think he will fight you on your terms?"

"You know what? You've been on my ass since I got here!" Erin exclaimed, feeling her blood grow warm. She'd had enough of this bitch riding her. "I've had a lot of teachers, and you're the worst. You've hardly taught me anything; we only drill and spar over and over!"

"You want a lesson?" Uathach marched over to the racks of practice weapons and pulled out two wooden swords. She tossed one into the dirt at Erin's feet. "Be glad I don't teach you with steel."

Erin snatched the practice weapon off the ground. She fought to keep the red from her vision, to hold her anger in check. Uathach wanted her to lose her temper so she could embarrass Erin and put her in her place. Uathach wasn't human; she was some sort of demigoddess trained by her mother, Scathach, the paragon of the fighting arts. Uathach had centuries of practice; Erin had only been playing with wooden swords for a few weeks.

Uathach didn't bother to don practice armor before striding onto the practice field. "How like your progenitor," Uathach scolded, assuming the ready position. "So hot-headed and ready to rush in."

"Is that how he ended up in your bed?" Erin taunted. Two could play this game. "He must have had something going for him for you to cheat on your boyfriend."

Uathach's somber facade cracked into a sneer. Her weapon blurred as she forced Erin to give ground, barely parrying the flurry of blows. Erin knew she couldn't fight on Uathach's terms. Uathach was watching for her to kick, and Erin knew she'd get a whack on the knee or shin if she tried. Traditional tae kwon do wasn't good for close in fighting, and neither were the wooden swords. Fortunately, Erin had learned a lot more than the traditional style.

When Erin parried the next swing, instead of stepping back she surged forward, aiming a palm strike at Uathach's solar plexus. The redhead managed to turn aside so Erin's hand merely brushed her, but Erin jabbed her elbow into Uathach's ribs then swept the arm up to catch Uathach's wrists as the instructor brought her sword around to catch Erin's exposed flank.

Erin drove Uathach's hands up. With her weapon hand, Erin punched at the side of her opponent's head. Uathach spun backward and reversed her stroke, aiming for Erin's sword arm. Erin tried to yank her limb clear, but the blow caught her on the arm guard. If not for the armor, her arm would have broken. As it was, Erin's sword tumbled into the dirt.

Erin's other hand grabbed Uathach's weapon and tugged. Uathach refused to release her grip and stood her ground. Erin brought up her knee as she was drawn toward her opponent, but Uathach twisted so the impact was on her hip, not her belly, and quickly stepped back before Erin could hook her heel and trip her.

Still gripping the wooden blade, Erin thrust it forward, and the hilt jabbed Uathach below the sternum, causing her to gasp for breath. Snarling, Uathach released one hand from the grip and punched Erin in the abdomen. Erin managed to catch most of the impact with her free arm, but it still stung.

Erin's eyes narrowed as her vision turned red. She wrenched the end of the wooden weapon up, toward Uathach's face, stepping into the push. As Uathach returned to a two-handed hold, Erin's free hand drove into Uathach's armpit. Erin was rewarded with a yelp of pain as Uathach fought to keep her center of gravity. Two more rapid punches at the same nerve cluster forced Erin's opponent to block with one hand.

Uathach caught the next punch, seizing Erin's wrist. Erin slammed her skull in Uathach's face. Even with the padding of Erin's leather helmet, the blow staggered Uathach.

Uathach flung the wooden sword aside as she lost her grip on both the weapon and Erin's wrist and fell back a step to widen the gap. Erin gave Uathach a feral grin as the champion half-turned, and her foot pistoned across the space between them. The sidekick caught Uathach square in chest, and the impact launched her as though a horse had kicked her.

Erin seized the dropped weapon and charged toward Uathach, who rolled to her feet, into a defensive stance. There was no finesse to the sword's arc, just fury-driven speed. Uathach barely managed to get an arm up; there was a loud crack as both bone and wood snapped. Erin followed with a punch to Uathach's jaw, snapping the redhead's skull back.

"Hold!" The imperious command penetrated the rage-induced fog in Erin's mind. She froze, her fist drawn back for another punch. The gathered crowd parted, revealing Scathach, her expression furious.

"Like Cu Chulainn, she has the frenzy," Uathach hissed through clenched teeth. "How can we put the hopes of the Exiled Folk in her hands?"

"Because it was ordained," Scathach stated, stalking toward the two combatants.

"She's not one of us; she cannot champion us," Uathach said, clutching her broken arm. "She is mortal and of the Dunwold."

"Go have Ynidd tend to your arm," Scathach said. There was no sympathy in her tone. She lowered her voice and said, "Do not think I am fooled. I know you took the practice field to goad the Champion into losing her temper. I had hoped you put the past behind you; obviously, I was mistaken."

Uathach started to protest, but her mother cut her off.

"Go," Scathach commanded. Once Uathach departed, she turned to Erin. "You must get your temper under control. It can give you great strength, but if you let it run rampant, it will get you killed."

Erin nodded, trying to contain her shaking as the adrenaline rush wore off.

"I think we've had enough practice for today," Scathach announced. "I will see you here in the morning."

"You?" Erin asked, still quelling the after-effects of her berserker rage.

"Yes," Scathach replied. "I will oversee the rest of your training myself."

*****

Chapter Seventeen

Erin

"We have a question for you."

Erin looked up from toweling off. She was drenched with sweat after three hours of calisthenics and spear drilling. They had only added spears to the regimen last week. Erin wondered why, since she knew she would be wielding a sword in the challenge, but she didn't want to question Scathach.

"What's your question, Mysie?" Erin asked as she dropped the towel onto the bench.

"Daidh and I were wondering if you would teach us your martial arts." Mysie glanced around conspiratorially. A group of caravan guards had joined them for spear practice, but none of them loitered near Erin. Their fellows quickly warned off a few who had regarded her with interest. "Just not around this lot."

"Why not around them?" Erin assessed the warriors, who were wandering off in search of dinner. For them, the practice had been exercises and drills. They were proficient with spears and seemed like competent soldiers, not neophytes like the freshly-enrolled white belts at the various dojos Erin had attended.

The dozen guards, male and female, were tall and long-limbed; most of them were attractive. A few had eyed Mysie and Daidh, but the pair didn't seem to return the interest. Erin had decided Mysie and Daidh hadn't slept together yet, but a couple of well-timed tankards of ale or an especially intense sparring match would likely push them across the threshold.

Mysie grinned impishly. "You don't show your opponent every dagger you have."

"It's not like she couldn't drink most of them under the table," Daidh remarked, running a cloth over his bald scalp. "She wants to be able to literally kick their asses, too."

After a few mugs of ale, scuffles were not uncommon, especially against the warriors who protected the merchants who supplied Dunos Scaith and the soldiers who traded manning the walls and gates for training. "Which explains her interest. Why do you want to learn martial arts?" Erin asked Daidh, amused.

"Someone has to watch her back," Daidh answered matter-of-factly. "Plus, we've seen what you can do. I consider myself a fair brawler, but you make me look like a child tussling with his mates."

"Sure, I'll teach you guys," Erin said. She hadn't been an instructor before, but she had studied enough to convey the basics. "It seems like the least I can do after all you've done for me."

"What is this conspiracy?" None of them had heard Scathach approach. The tall redhead stood next to a rack of practice spears, turning one of the weapons over in her hands. Erin wondered if Scathach missed being a warrior, rather than some sort of icon of prowess surrounded by students and walls.

Erin quickly dismissed the idea of lying. "Mysie and Daidh asked me to teach them martial arts from the Dunwold."

Everyone held their breath until Scathach answered. "I think that's an excellent idea."

Erin had expected some pushback. "You do?"

"Yes. Many grow stagnant between the reverie of years, the lack of new ideas, and a resistance to change," Scathach explained. She returned the practice spear to the rack. "There is a reason why we are taking so long to train you, Erin. As a mortal, you can learn day-to-day. The folk of the old gods do not age quickly or breed prolifically, nor do we learn rapidly. What may take you a month to learn could take one of the fae folk a year, a decade, or more to master. To be honest, I think my daughter has learned little in the last few centuries; I am likely guilty of the same."

Erin was surprised, especially given what had happened with Uathach. "You're okay with my teaching Mysie and Daidh martial arts?"

"Absolutely." Scathach nodded. "Teaching does two things. It helps you think about your technique so you can explain it to others, and it improves your patience."

Erin wondered what she was getting herself into. She had never instructed anyone before. "I hope I don't let you guys down. I've never tried to teach."

"Do you not have a son?" Scathach asked, with a hint of a smile.

Erin contemplated the relevance of the question before answering. "Well, yes, but in the Dunwold we send our children to schools to learn. Someone else, a professional teacher, is responsible for their education."

Scathach scoffed. "If you are a mother, you have been teaching since the day your child was born. Your experience will serve you well with this pair."

"Are you calling us children?" Mysie protested, then realized who she was addressing and hastily added, "My Lady."

Scathach smiled knowingly. "When you have children of your own someday, you will understand."

Mysie's eyes flicked to Daidh. "Yes, Mum."

"I am sure you are hungry after the day's exertions," Scathach said, turning toward her keep. "I will leave you to dinner. Tomorrow we will talk about working these lessons into your training regimen."

Erin watched the warrior-matron walk away across the practice field. Even the dust and dirt seemed intimidated, afraid to cling to Scathach's boots and cloak. Then Erin's stomach rumbled, reminding her it was time to eat, and not only for herself.

"Color me surprised," Mysie remarked. "I thought for sure you were going to have to argue with her. Scathach isn't exactly known for her openness to change. The most recent upgrades here are those metal longhouses you and Nechtan live in."

Erin looked toward the Quonset huts to one side of the training ground. "Those probably date back to the Korean War," she said. "They are something like sixty years old."

"Those were set up shortly after Dunos Scaith moved here," Daidh said. "I'm not sure how they got here. Either a scavenger nicked them from the Dunwold, or one of the first caravans brought them. As Mysie said, this place isn't big on change. Once word gets out, you might have as many people knocking on your door as her ladyship."

Erin shook her head and walked toward the canteen. "Which is the last thing I need, especially with a baby coming. At least training you guys will help keep me busy once I'm too far along to spar."

"Maybe it's what Scathach had in mind?" Mysie suggested as she and Daidh fell into step with Erin. "How long do mortals gestate, anyways?"

* * * * *

Chapter Eighteen

Tim

"Anyone home?"

Tim set down his pack and waited to see if anyone would answer. The house seemed quiet, like it was sulking. The muffled pinging of metal on metal told him his father, Gofannon, and likely Einar were out back in the forge.

"Oh, hey Sweetie," Pixel called, coming down the stairs. Her long, purple hair was pulled back under a bright pink bandana. The rest of her outfit consisted of a long, white shirt and pink capris; she looked like she was from one of those old-fashioned television shows from Peoria, which aired during the day. "How was school?"

"It was fine," Tim replied. He still wasn't sure what to think about the fae girl. Sometimes she would act as if she was his step-mother and ask about his homework and chores. Other times, she made an effort to get on his good side, letting him get away with stuff his mom wouldn't, like staying up late or watching scary movies. Sometimes he resented her 'mom act,' especially when he felt she was trying to replace his mother. He tried not to let his irritation show, especially since there were times when he wanted her on his side. "I got an A on my history quiz and a B on my science test."

"Only a B?" She didn't sound disappointed, more concerned. "I thought you were doing well?"

"I was, I mean I am," Tim protested. Normally he aced science classes; they were easy for him. He had gotten distracted this week and had missed some of the material covered on the test. "Though I don't know why I'm worrying so much about science. Once magic comes back, won't science go out the window?"

Pixel glanced at the window, then realized he wasn't being literal. It was another reminder she wasn't really from this world. "When magic becomes more widespread, it doesn't mean science stops working. There's magic now, but only a little of it. Think of magic as cheat codes and science as the programming a game runs on.

"When your mother wins the challenge and the new Accords go into effect, gravity will hold our feet to the ground, not magic." Pixel whispered conspiratorially, "But we will be able to use cheat codes to jump far or even fly."

"We'll be able to use magic to fly? Cool!" Tim nearly forgot why he was in such a hurry to get home.

"In theory, though, flying takes a lot of energy," Pixel said. "It's not as simple as hopping on a broom and taking off. Can you imagine how hard it would be to ride a broom? Witches didn't ride them, but a witch would sometimes disguise her staff as a broom."

"Did it get installed?" Tim quickly changed the subject. He remembered why he had rushed home.

Pixel peered at the clock. "Three and a half minutes. I figured you would have asked before the second minute was up." She held up an index card, grinning mischievously. "I take it you want this?"

"Yes, please." Tim tried not to sound too enthusiastic. The card would have the information he needed to sign on to the wifi for the new internet connection, which had been installed that afternoon, along with the satellite television service.

"Remember the deal with your father," Pixel reminded him, sounding motherly.

"I know, keep my grades up," Tim replied. "Don't do anything to give away where I am. Don't take candy from strangers."

"Okay, here you go." Pixel held out the card which had the wireless network name and password.

"Thanks." Tim took the card. He had hoped she would give him the paperwork that came with the wireless access point; he figured they hadn't bothered to change the administrative login. He could hunt around for the paperwork later. Right now, he wanted to get his tablet on the internet without having to hang out at the public library.

Tim pulled his tablet out of his backpack and took it into the living room. He scarcely noticed the satellite box under the television; he could investigate the new channels later. As soon as his tablet powered up, he brought up the wifi and found the new network. Tim grinned as he put in the password from the card—h0m3w0rk.

He had expected Pixel to linger and chide him about staying online too long before doing his homework, but she had quickly disappeared. She had probably gone out to the forge to make googly eyes at his father while he hammered away. Tim didn't understand it, but it kept her from pestering him with more questions.

The connection speed wasn't as good as the library's, but he wasn't competing with others for bandwidth. It wasn't fast enough for him to play any of the really cool games, the ones his mother didn't want him to play. But, at least he could hit his favorite websites and download short videos.

An hour later, Einar and Pixel came in through the garage. Einar was punctual about when he started working on dinner, so Tim had put away his tablet, still downloading a long video, and had gotten out his homework. Homework was a good excuse for not helping with dinner. If Tim appeared idle, Einar would find something for him to do. If Tim was doing his homework, no one would give him any chores. Since Tim had to do the assignments anyway, he had learned to time them to his advantage.

At least Einar didn't try to make Tim eat anything weird. Tim used to dread when his mother would cook dinner for a boyfriend and want to 'try something new.' Einar stuck to basics. If this was how all dwarves ate, Tim was a fan of dwarf cuisine. Einar's idea of experimenting was spaghetti and ground sausage, though he was considerate enough to make a portion of sauce without sausage for Susan.

As often as not, Susan had been coming to the house for dinner, then working on the new accords afterwards. Tim liked her because she didn't try to be a stepmom, and she didn't seem to be competing with his mother for his father's attentions. In fact, it seemed as if Susan would rather his parents ended up together.

Tonight turned out to be a night she couldn't make it. Tim's father said something about not wanting to burn her out. Einar shrugged and gave the extra grilled cheese sandwich to Gofannon, who scarfed it down. All the other sandwiches had bacon on them. The side dish was a mix of thinly sliced potatoes and carrots, fried in the bacon grease, with sea salt. Einar had also made a small portion in a separate pan without bacon grease; those leftovers also went to the smith god, as did the extra tomato soup.

After the meal, his father tasked Tim with clearing the table and rinsing everything in the sink. Since he didn't actually have to do dishes, he didn't complain much. He knew other kids his age were saddled with washing and drying dishes.

"Hey buddy, all your homework done?" his father asked after Tim finished.

"Yes. I read a chapter of history in study hall, read my English chapter on the bus, and did my math problems before dinner." Tim had learned to be efficient with his homework. It left him more time for fun stuff, like the video, which had been downloading.

"Did you talk to Jenny?" Not only did his father remember everything he read, he remembered everything he had been told, especially if it was embarrassing.

"Who's Jenny?" Of course, Pixel would be interested.

"She's a girl in his science class," Liam replied. "Her folks, the Dittmeyers, own a farm on the east side of town. Her dad, Bob, grows soybeans on 200 of my acres."

"No, I haven't talked to her yet," Tim muttered. He wondered if he could crawl into a hole and hide.

"Is that why you got a B on your science test?" Pixel teased.

"You got a B?" his father asked. "I thought you were the family whiz at science?"

"I'll do better," Tim promised. He would rather talk about his grades than Jenny. Now he regretted asking his father how to talk to girls and letting her name slip. "I know what to study; I'll still get an A for the course."

"Maybe we should invite the Dittmeyers over for a cookout?" Pixel suggested. Tim couldn't tell if she was being earnest or still teasing him.

"What is this cookout?" Gofannon thundered. The smith god must have intuitively sensed food was involved. For a moment, Tim was grateful for anything that drew attention away from his crush on Jenny. Then he realized Gofannon would enthusiastically endorse anything having to do with food.

"It's like having people over for dinner, but you cook on the grill instead of in the kitchen," Liam explained. "Usually people bring over a dish to share, have a few beers, and play horseshoes or corn-hole."

"Do you have a grill, Druid?" Einar asked. "Tell me it's not one of them propane types. I like to cook over an honest fire."

Tim was mortified. Maybe he could hide his interest in Jenny, but word would get back to school that he lived with a bunch of weirdos. He would be a pariah in the lunchroom and a target in gym class.

"Dad, aren't we supposed to be keeping all of this a secret?" Tim hoped playing the paranoia card would pay off. Superheroes, or, in this case, druids, didn't invite the neighbors over for a barbeque. "What if something weird happens, and the Dittmeyers see it?"

His father stopped, contemplating. Had Tim gotten through? Pixel might pass as his father's girlfriend, but what about Einar and Gofannon?

"A good point," Liam said. "Maybe it's not such a good idea to have them over."

Tim wanted to sag in relief and wondered which god he should thank.

"Don't be silly," Pixel countered. "Worst case, I can glamour them, so they forget anything out of the ordinary."

Tim's heart sank.

* * * * *

Chapter Nineteen

Liam

"Dad! Something is in the house!"

If Tim pounding on the door hadn't woken Liam up, his son's words would have. Liam sat up, dislodging Pixel, who had been sleeping with her head on his shoulder. Though Liam was almost healed from the lightning near-miss, she still slept in his bed. It made for some awkward dreams.

Liam extended his senses; the darkness actually helped, as his sight usually dominated the input to his brain. He could perceive the wards in the walls and timbers of the house as an energy field. Since the wards were intact, nothing should have gotten through. If Gofannon couldn't push his way through, what could? Then Liam found it, the hole the technician had drilled to run the feed for the satellite dish through the wall from outside.

Liam jumped into the spirit plane. The spot where the hardware breached the wall was incandescent in the Murkwold. The energy of the house and all the *lledrith* contained within shone through one tiny hole. First things first. He recited the verse of protection and channeled the energy to ward the new addition to the house. Sweeping through the house, he spotted the intruder in the living room. It was hound-shaped and prowling toward the stairs.

By the time Liam snapped back into his body, Pixel had woken up. Liam wasn't sure if she knew what was amiss, but he didn't want to take the time to explain. The stairs led to the hall outside his door, where Tim was standing.

As Liam's feet hit the floor, the door clicked and swung open. Tim stumbled into the room.

"Scooter, wake the others, we have an intruder." Liam didn't know if the brownie was within earshot or not. "Tim, get in here."

Liam stood, the pain in his feet making him wince. It drove away any cobwebs of sleep. He instinctively held out an open hand; his staff leaped from the corner into it. Pixel blinked, her eyes becoming incandescent in the dark.

Tim scrambled into the room and cleared the path between Liam and the door. Liam wondered if Tim had learned to stay out of the line of fire from those games he played. A moment later, a canine form silently padded into view, its golden eyes peering through the doorway.

The creature's gaze locked on Liam. Liam brandished his staff, ready for the hound's pounce, probably for his throat. Then the hound did the last thing Liam expected; it fled.

At least it tried to flee. In the hall, a huge hand seized one of its hind legs. The hound was dashed against the ceiling, then slammed to the floor. Before it could get its remaining paws under itself, the hound was again flung up against the ceiling and again smashed to the floor.

The hound turned and snarled at Gofannon, making a sound for the first time. The noise was cutoff when the god slammed the beast against one wall, then the other. "Any time you want to banish this *ci*, feel free," the smith-god rumbled.

Liam focused magical energy into his staff and jabbed it into the hound. Instead of striking flesh and bone, it popped the hound like a balloon. The canine yelped once, then its outline collapsed, leaving Gofannon empty handed.

"Odin's Eye!" Einar swore from the door to his room. "What is going on?"

"I was sloppy," Liam admitted, staring at the spot the dog had occupied. "I forgot to take into account that any modification through the walls might compromise our wards."

Liam placed his hand against the doorframe, feeling the oak wood. He reached out with his mind, making sure there were no other breaches in the house's wards. The house still seethed at the violation, but the wards were intact.

"You mean running the antenna line broke the wards?" Tim asked. "That must be why the house has been sulking."

"I wish it would have said something," Liam said, double checking the wards again, especially where any hardware passed through the exterior of the building. "All the other utilities were covered."

"Are we found out?" Einar asked.

Liam shook his head. "I don't think so. It was trying to run away; it probably needed to get out of the house to report to its master."

"What was it?" Tim asked. He was still on the floor where he had scrambled out of the way.

"There are all sorts of spectral hounds and ghost dogs," Pixel replied as she clicked on the lamp. "It could have been a moddi dhu, a gwllgi, or a witch-hound."

"Iblis," Liam muttered, "or more likely his witch, Raven." Raven obviously had some magic at her disposal, and likely had an idea about where to search for Liam. Could she have conjured up one of these hounds, possibly from the Murkwold, and sent it hunting for him?

Liam looked around the hall where there should have been a corpse. There was an indentation in the plaster where Gofannon had smote the beast against the wall, but no blood, fur, or other evidence of its existence.

"What do we do now?" Tim asked, poking his head into the hall.

"Go back to bed," Liam replied. "The wards are fixed, the ghost-dog is banished, and you have school in the morning."

Tim frowned and sulked back to his room. He would be grouchy in the morning, Liam thought, because it would take a while for him to fall asleep. Liam wasn't ready to sleep; his nerves were lit up, and his blood was pumping. At least Liam didn't have an algebra test in the morning.

Liam grabbed a pair of sweats and a t-shirt and pulled them on, ignoring the pain in his feet. He had an idea.

"Aren't you coming back to bed?" Pixel asked, watching him.

"We need an alarm system," Liam said, and headed for the stairs. "Something that won't be obvious and will be hard to defeat."

"Some sort of warning spell?" Pixel followed him into the hall. "Adding another layer to the wards? I can help you."

Liam glanced over his shoulder. She hadn't bothered to put on pants; she was wearing one of his old Pagan Pride t-shirts as a night-dress, and her purple hair was tousled. If only things were simpler.

"I had the same thought," Liam replied and descended the stairs. "I was worried the extra spells might make the house or property visible, or maybe create too big a blank area. Then it occurred to me we already have assets we can put to use that won't stick out. Do you want to give me a hand with some arts and crafts?"

"Sure." Pixel nodded eagerly and caught up to him.

Liam led her to the garage, flipping on the light and opening the main door. Immediately a cool breeze swept past.

"There have been more zephyrs around the house since the fight with the tempest-elemental," Liam said and poked around the garage. He needed metal and strong cord. "I'm hoping they will understand what I am trying to do. They seem to react to me instinctively."

Pixel climbed onto the stool she had perched on three weeks ago, when she and Einar had first arrived at Liam's home and told him about his heritage and the challenge. Had it only been three weeks? Liam felt like it had been a lifetime.

"They constantly flock around the house," Pixel agreed. She watched Liam as he gathered random pieces of pipe, some flat metal stock, and three wooden squares from some long-forgotten project. "They can't come in the house, so how can they act as lookouts if they can't warn you?"

Liam smiled. She had followed his line of thought so far. The wind spirits constantly whirred around the farmhouse, and when Liam was out in the forge, they flocked around and through the outbuilding, as well. Liam rummaged through the rack of hardware bins until he found what he needed and added a handful of screw eyes to the growing pile on the workbench.

"Exactly!" Liam retrieved his drill from the pegboard and slapped the battery into the handle like a gunslinger loading a magazine into a semi-automatic. "We're going to make wind chimes. Heavy-duty ones, because I suspect the zephyrs won't be able to resist playing with them, but if something feels wrong they should be able to use them to make a racket."

"Okay, that's pretty clever," Pixel admitted.

"You don't have to sound so surprised," Liam retorted mockingly, retrieving his hacksaw and some clamps from the other end of the bench.

"No, I didn't mean…you are new to all of this, and your idea is something the druids of old would have thought up," Pixel said. She hopped off the stool, the t-shirt riding dangerously up. Liam tried not to notice how much of the tattoo running up her thigh showed. Pixel pointed toward the refrigerator. "Do you want a beer?"

"A beer sounds good." Liam picked up a pair of safety goggles. Gofannon gave him guff over wearing the goggles, but he wasn't about to lose an eye to a flying sliver of metal. When his Uncle Charles had first taught him to use tools in this very garage, he had drilled safety. "I'm surprised Einar and Gofannon left anything to drink."

"I think they noticed you cutting back," Pixel replied from the fridge, the door open. Liam intentionally didn't watch; he knew she was leaning into the refrigerator. "They thought it would be rude to drink you out of house and home."

"I appreciate it," Liam said and pulled on a pair of gloves. "As much as I like beer, I can't keep up with those two, and I don't want Tim's impression of me to be that I am always drinking or drunk."

Pixel set a cold Harter's Stout on the bench and put a hand on Liam's shoulder. "He doesn't think that, and neither do I."

Despite the constant breeze, the aroma of flowers wafted. Six weeks, Liam thought, six weeks until Erin was back. Liam picked up the beer and took a long drink. "Thank you."

"Of course." Pixel climbed back onto the stool. "What do you need me to do?"

"I'm going to cut and drill the pipe and those strips of metal." Liam set the screw eyes in front of her. "You can tie them to the screw eyes. Then I'll sink the screw eyes into the wood squares, and viola, wind chimes."

The purple-haired girl looked through her lashes mischievously. "Anything else you need screwed?"

Liam tried to ignore the sudden warmth in the garage. Six more weeks. He lowered the goggles over his eyes. "Not right now."

One hour and another beer later, they had three sets of wind chimes. There were smaller pipes interspersed with the larger ones. They theorized that if the zephyrs could make a little noise with the chimes whenever they wanted, they could be convinced to save the loud clamor for when there was an intruder.

"We'll wait until daylight to hang these around the house," Liam said. He wasn't about to get up on a ladder in the dark. "Once we hang them, we'll make a jaunt into the Murkwold so I can have a chat with the zephyrs and try to explain the idea behind the chimes. Right now, I'm ready for bed."

"About time," Pixel teased.

Liam rolled his eyes. Six more weeks.

*****

Chapter Twenty

Erin

"I feel like a bloated yak!"

"What's a yak?" Mysie inquired. She paused to wait for Erin, who had stopped to stretch before her outburst.

Erin rolled her shoulders, her back sore. It seemed like it was always sore nowadays. She replied, "A yak is a big, hairy animal from the Dunwold. It's kind of like a big cow."

Both women started walking again. "What did we say about being down on ourselves?" Mysie admonished.

"Half of this 'we' is still fit and petite. So, it's easy for her," Erin said.

"And the other half is carrying a baby, so no fat talk," Mysie countered.

They passed through the gate of the fort. Outside, a caravan of brightly-colored wagons was parked in a half circle; temporary merchant stalls were set up under colorful canopies. Denizens of Dunos Scaith were scattered throughout the transient market.

Erin looked over the assortment of vendors. The market resembled a flea market crossed with a ren faire. She needed some clothes to accommodate her growing belly and widening hips, preferably skirts she could let out as her pregnancy advanced. She was starting her second trimester, so she still had a while before she needed to worry about baby clothes. Erin said, "I didn't think to bring any gold or silver with me. Somehow I doubt they take plastic."

"I don't know what you mean by plastic." Mysie spotted Daidh and caught his attention with a wave. Mysie added, "Your coin wouldn't be any good here anyway."

"Why? because I'm from the Dunwold?" Erin asked.

"No, because you're Erin o' Chullainn, the Champion," Mysie replied. She waved her hand across the wagons. "Not one of these traders would ask a brass farthing of you, or a plastic farthing if you prefer."

Erin was flummoxed. She had spent her adult life scraping to get by; her wants were always a secondary consideration. The big gold payment hadn't really sunk in; it was abstract numbers on paper a world away. "So, I can walk up to one of these vendors and say, 'I want this,' and they'll give it to me?"

Mysie nodded. "That's pretty much the long and short of it."

Daidh walked up to them. "Have you told Erin that Scathach threatened to banish any merchant who doesn't give her anything she wants?"

Mysie glared daggers at Daidh, causing him to step back. She grumbled, "I liked my version better."

"I can't ask them to hand stuff over for free," Erin protested.

"It's not really free," Daidh said. "Remember, most of these fellows have one or more guards, often family members, who were trained here. Plus, they make plenty of coin, so you won't be making paupers of any of them."

Erin nodded. The vendors would be getting services in trade for anything Erin requisitioned. "All right, let's shop before I split the seams of my pants."

Luckily, her clothing needs were easy to fulfill, especially since she favored what the sellers considered 'bland' colors and styles. She was surprised to see a smattering of Dunwold goods mixed in with the merchandise. She made sure to talk to those merchants, more about her future needs. She was going to be here six more years. She didn't want new blue jeans now, but she would after the baby was born. That went double for any feminine hygiene products from the Dunwold.

As Erin finished explaining her wish list to a merchant with contacts in the Dunwold black market, Daidh sidled up to her conspiratorially. He whispered, "Erin, can you help me with something?"

Erin discretely scanned around. Mysie was sampling the wares of a pig-headed fellow who dealt in alcoholic beverages. Erin asked, "How can I help?"

Daidh glanced toward the booze merchant's booth. "I was thinking of getting a gift for Mysie, because, well, you know."

Finally, Erin thought. Any attraction the pair had shared before had only intensified since Mysie and Daidh had started learning martial arts. There were times Erin had thought sparring sessions between the two doubled as foreplay, and a grapple would end in a passionate lip-lock. So far, they had both held back, which was infuriating for Erin. So much for Izzy and Derek's proclamation fae folk didn't have the same hang-ups about sex as mundanes. If Erin was stuck being chaste, she could at least live vicariously through them, but they hadn't crossed the threshold.

"Of course, I'll help you," Erin said. She thought about the goods offered in the bazaar, trying to decide what would be the most thoughtful. If Liam or Nechtan were here, what would they give her?

She shoved aside the thought. "What were you thinking about getting for her?"

"I saw a really nice dagger I thought she might like," Daidh replied.

"You want to give her a knife?" Any romantic notions Erin was entertaining dissipated.

Daidh nodded earnestly. "She fancies blades."

"Do you want to sleep with her or get stabbed?" Erin asked. On any world she went to, men were dolts. It was as if those jewelry store commercials were true.

Daidh flushed redder than his beard. "I want to give her something to show…"

"I know, but I think you need something a little more thoughtful than a knife," Erin said. As with her, something frilly or superficial wouldn't impress Mysie. "Come with me."

Erin led Daidh past a couple of stalls, quickly scanning the offered wares. Most of the goods were of a more practical nature; Dunos Scaith didn't lend itself to luxury or frivolity. Erin was about to concede the dagger was the best bet when she spotted something better at the copper-monger's wagon. She glanced back and saw Mysie heading their way with a sack containing at least two bottles. Erin whispered to Daidh, "Look on the blue cloth, pick one of those."

Erin intercepted Mysie. Frowning at the bag, Erin asked, "More booze I can't drink?"

"I'm sure you can have a wee sip." Mysie replied. "It's maple mead."

Erin wasn't sure whether she should be intrigued or disgusted. "What's maple mead? I've never heard of it."

"Here, he has samples." Mysie took Erin by the elbow and steered her back toward the alcohol merchant. "What's Daidh doing?"

"I think he's checking out beard beads," Erin replied. "I told him about this dwarf I know who wears them."

The merchant resembled one of the three little pigs who went to market and got a job, Erin thought. He was wearing a bright blue doublet which matched the canopy over his stall.

"Oh, the Champion," the vendor remarked with a Scottish brogue, unsuccessfully hiding his pained expression. He probably expected Erin to clean him out.

"All I want is to try a sip of the maple mead my friend bought," Erin said, hoping to allay his fears. "In my condition, I can't drink more than a bit. I only want to see what it tastes like."

The porcine merchant brightened visibly. "Of course, I would be happy to give you a sample." He set a wooden vessel roughly the size of a shot glass full of dark brown liquid on the makeshift counter.

Erin took the shot and downed it. It was sweet, far too sweet for her liking, like slurping maple syrup. Based on the burn, she put it at 40- to 50-proof. "This will get you gassed, but it's too cloying for my taste. I bet Daidh would like it, though."

"You know what?" Mysie said to the merchant. "I'll take another two bottles if you have something for me to carry it in."

"Give me a moment, and I'll find something, Lass." The pig-man ducked into his wagon, audibly rummaging.

"So, you really think Daidh will like this?" Mysie asked.

If they were on the Dunwold, Erin would have bought them a bottle of tequila. "If he likes booze and maple syrup, absolutely. Don't get him so plastered he passes out."

The merchant returned with another burlap bag. "Here you go."

Erin resisted the urge to say 'that'll do.' As Mysie got the new bottles stowed, Daidh joined them. Standing behind Mysie, he gave Erin a wink.

"Here, you need to give this a try," Mysie said. "It is mead made with maple syrup instead of honey."

"It's not mead then," Daidh stated.

Erin affixed Daidh with a glare. "Just try it," she ordered.

Daidh shrugged. "Okay, fine." He accepted the sample shot from the merchant and gulped it down. "A bit sweet, but if you cut it with about half whiskey, you would have something."

"Let's talk whiskey," Mysie said to the vendor.

Erin moved back through the arc of wagons. She had spotted a few items she was interested in and wanted to talk to those merchants. Only a couple seemed reluctant to deal with her; one seemed outright enthusiastic. The latter, a middle-aged woman attired in brilliant scarves over a plain white dress, kept trying to get Erin to accept extra clothes, all colorful. Erin relented and accepted half of what the woman offered.

"I will cover the Champion's purchases with coin," a familiar voice said from behind Erin. Erin turned to see Uathach standing there; they had not spoken since the dust-up on the practice field weeks ago.

"Thank you," Erin said simply. She didn't know what else to say.

"Do not think of this as some sort of apology," Uathach stated. "I do not want Dunos Scaith to be indebted because of you." Uathach paid the woman and moved on to the next merchant.

"What was she on about?" Mysie asked after Uathach left.

"Reminding me she has a millennia-old grudge," Erin replied.

"Actually, I think it's about a millennia and a half," Daidh said, drawing scowls from both women. "Just saying."

*****

Chapter Twenty-One

Erin

"You two don't have to be so smug about it."

Mysie and Daidh looked over at Erin's remark. "We're not being smug," Mysie protested. Daidh was silent, a goofy grin on his face. It reminded Erin of a certain druid.

It had been a week since Daidh gave Mysie the torc he bought. It was cute and awkward, the way they stumbled over words trying to get through to their feelings. Erin felt like she was watching a cheesy television show; the results were as predictable. A week later, they still had the new relationship shine, all smiles and cute gestures of affection.

"This better not interfere with our training," Erin said as she picked over her breakfast. "It's bad enough I have to lay off the sparring until after the baby is born." Erin worked on weapon drills to hone her technique and build her upper body strength. Kempo kata and yoga helped maintain her core and teaching the blushing couple shorin kempo helped Erin refresh her own knowledge.

"It should only be a few more weeks until Nechtan is back," Mysie said. "Maybe you'll have something to be smug about."

Erin sighed. She was in her second trimester, and she was feeling better. For several weeks, she had no interest in being with anyone. Even if she felt up to it, she thought it unlikely Nechtan, or anyone else, would be interested in her. While she was glad for her friends, she was also a little bit envious.

Erin stared down at her growing belly. By the time Nechtan and the others got back, it would be prominent; she would be near her third trimester. "I don't think so. After breakfast, let's work on Forms San and Go, and then we'll do blocking drills."

It was nearly time for lunch when Erin had Mysie and Daidh take the practice field to spar unarmed. Erin was worried they had lost their competitiveness until Mysie got a gloved hand past Daidh's guard and tagged him on the jaw. Daidh's playfulness vanished, and he returned to the serious demeanor Erin was familiar with on the training yard. Mysie's next lunge at his guard ended with her sprawled in the dirt as Daidh sidestepped and tripped her.

Mysie smiled and hopped to her feet. "Good, I was afraid you were going soft on me."

Daidh shook his head. "You didn't have to worry about me going soft on you last night, and you won't now."

As the pair launched into another exchange, Erin realized Scathach was standing beside her. Behind the regal redhead were half a dozen guards. Erin thought it unusual; the last person in the fort who needed a guard was Scathach.

Scathach watched the bout for a minute before speaking. "I understand they are a couple now."

"Yeah," Erin acknowledged. "It took long enough."

"It is a shame," Scathach said. "One of them will have to leave."

"What? Why?" Erin asked.

"We are here to train warriors, not play matchmaker," Scathach replied. "Their emotions will compromise their usefulness to you."

Erin scowled. "Bullshit. If you kick one out, the other will likely leave, as well."

"We will see." Scathach fixed Erin with an emerald stare. "Do you think they would abandon you so readily?" Scathach stepped to the edge of the training yard. "Hold."

Mysie and Daidh broke away from each other and gave the customary bow before turning toward Scathach. Mysie was grinning, flushed from the exertion, but Daidh appeared concerned.

"Since the two of you have become romantically involved, one of you will have to depart," Scathach stated. "The other will remain behind and continue to assist the champion."

Mysie's grin vanished. "Bollocks!"

Scathach looked from Mysie to Daidh.

"I suppose this is the part where I'm supposed to volunteer to be the one who gets the boot," Daidh said. "What if neither of us leaves?"

Scathach made a circular gesture with one hand. A ring of low, green flame manifested on the practice field. The glowing perimeter was thirty feet across. The six guards split into two ranks, three to a side, and stepped into the ring on opposite sides. "The first one driven from the ring leaves," Scathach said.

Erin muttered a curse and marched into the middle of the ring, standing beside Mysie and Daidh.

"Champion, leave the circle," Scathach ordered.

Erin pointed at the guards. "Have them make me leave."

The guards turned to Scathach for direction. Scathach said, "I'm not going to risk harming your baby."

"Good, because we know what happens when I get pissed," Erin retorted and glowered at the closest guard. The man took a step back.

"I could dismiss them both," Scathach suggested.

Erin regarded the next closest guard and gave him a feral grin. "Then which of these bozos gets to be my practice dummy? Because I'll have a lot of aggression to take out on someone." The guard swallowed and began sweating.

Scathach narrowed her eyes. Erin could tell the Lady of Dunos Scaith was getting annoyed at someone telling her 'no.' And she didn't think Scathach would back down.

"I have a counter-proposal," Erin suggested. "My two opponents and I can take a seat. The remaining guards fight my people unarmed. If they can get all four guards out of the circle, they both stay. Otherwise the first one forced out leaves like you said."

"No weapons?" Scathach's green eyes were slits.

Erin shrugged. "Unless you don't think your guards are well trained?"

The corner of Scathach's mouth curved up. "Very well, Champion. Let us see how well you've trained 'your people.'" Scathach made a dismissive gesture, and the two guards closest to Erin gratefully exited the circle. The remaining guards planted their spears in the dirt outside the flaming green ring, then removed their sword belts and tossed them aside.

"You guys have got this," Erin said and moved to stand beside Scathach.

Daidh and Mysie stood back to back and bowed to their opponents. The guards were dumbfounded and looked to Scathach for direction.

"Begin!" Scathach ordered.

Mysie launched at one of her opponents like a rabid wildcat, bearing him to the ground. The other member of the pair, a tall woman with shocking green hair, grabbed Mysie from above and behind. Mysie snaked an arm behind the woman's knee and stood. Instead of having the presence of mind to hang on, green-hair let go to try to catch herself as she hit the ground.

Daidh was patiently holding off the other pair as they tried to get on opposite sides of him. When one tried to close, Daidh caught the aggressor off guard with a snap kick and spun away before the other guard could capitalize on the distraction. He was so focused on Daidh, he missed Mysie charging him. She hit the man low, with all her weight, and her target stumbled backward and lost his balance, falling into the green flames.

Mysie's original opponents had both regained their feet and rushed Mysie together. Mysie ducked to the left and swept the legs out from under the green-haired woman. She hit the ground face first, her momentum almost taking her to the perimeter. Her partner tried to course correct, only to catch a staggering punch to the ribs. The woman stood, sputtering dirt, as Daidh tripped his second opponent into the green-haired woman. The impact pushed her back, and her foot slipped across the flaming circle, kicking up dust and a gout of flame. She shook her leg for a moment before she realized the fire had burnt her.

Daidh's opponent, a lanky blond, rebounded from the collision and regained his footing as Daidh stepped forward with a palm strike. Daidh's opponent managed to twist aside and snag the sleeve of Daidh's tunic. The blonde man pulled with all his weight, dragging

Daidh toward the edge of the circle. Daidh's opponent must have realized if he pulled Daidh out of the circle with him, his side won.

Daidh began to teeter forward; his feet planted a foot from the flames as Blondie continued to lean back. Erin held her breath. Then Mysie caught the collar of Daidh's tunic with both hands, arresting his fall. With his free hand, Daidh pulled the tunic up, ducking his head and spinning out of the garment. Mysie released her hold, sending the tunic and the guard hanging onto it out of the circle.

Mysie threw herself flat as the last opponent rushed her from behind. The man tripped over her, knocking the wind out of Mysie, but losing his balance in the exchange. He landed, peering down his nose at the green fire. As he got to his hands and knees, Daidh planted a foot on his ass and shoved him forward.

Erin looked over at Scathach, trying not to show how relieved she was. "Satisfied?"

Scathach nodded. "Yes. It would appear your tutelage suffices against unprepared novices. If I have cause to question your partners' discipline again, they will not face such novices." Scathach made a shooing gesture at the guards, who collected their spears. The green circle of fire sputtered and disappeared.

No one spoke until Scathach had disappeared. Mysie broke the silence. She said, "What do you think that was all about? Plenty of people get it on here."

Erin was still staring toward where Scathach had disappeared around the corner of the central keep. "Like everything around here, I think it was a test. The challenge wasn't to see how well you had learned martial arts. It was a teamwork exercise, with a side of seeing if I had passed on my failing in not integrating weapons training into my fighting from the start."

"Do you think she wants us to stop…?" Daidh let the question trail off.

"Pox on that!" Mysie retorted. "It took long enough to get you in my bedroll."

"I think as long as we stay serious on the practice field, you guys can go at it like rabbits," Erin said. Someone might as well be enjoying themselves she thought, memories of a fire-lit night by a dolmen surfacing unbidden. "Remember, Mysie, you don't want to end up like me."

"Aye, I'm drinking my tea, awful as it is," Mysie replied, then smiled at Daidh. "Donnybrooks, awful tea, look at the things I'll do for you."

"You like donnybrooks," Daidh countered.

*****

Chapter Twenty-Two

Liam

"Shit!"

Liam stomped the brakes. In rural Illinois, deer on the road weren't unusual. Giant stags ridden by antlered warriors were another story. Fog oozed from the adjacent fields, turning his car's headlights into white pillars. The stag rider returned his car's glare fearlessly.

"Oh no," Pixel whimpered next to Liam. "I didn't think he could come here."

Liam put the car in park and turned on the hazards. Traffic was rare on the country road, but he didn't want someone hurt from plowing into his car while he was in a pissing match with some supernatural entity. He looked down the road behind his car; a gust of wind cleared the fog from it.

Liam glanced at Pixel. Her purple eyes were huge as she gazed through the windshield. Liam asked, "What am I dealing with?"

Pixel found her voice, though it was still subdued. "Ardduwn. I was promised to him before I accepted this mission. Please don't let him take me."

Liam suspected her pleading tone was to elicit his white-knight response, but she seemed genuinely afraid. He had never asked anything about her life before she became involved in the quest to challenge the Milesian Accords. "He's not taking anyone."

Liam stepped out of the car. He considered the shotgun in the back seat. A survival-nut buddy had sold him several rounds of tungsten-carbide buckshot without asking any questions. Liam had said he needed something without the metals covered by the Fiwer Pact, and Mark had cranked the rounds out a week later, both 12-gauge rounds and .357 loads for Erin's handgun.

Instead, Liam pulled his staff from the back seat. It seemed unimpressive compared to the eight-foot long spear the rider was bearing. If it came to blows, Liam knew he was out of his league. He stepped to the side of the road, so his staff was in contact with the ground instead of the asphalt. Liam was reluctant to draw on the *Gwuedd.* He was several miles from home, on his way back from a meet and greet with Peoria pagans. If he drew power here, someone might detect it, and to be honest, he didn't know what he would do with said power. "Can I help you?"

The huntsman's eyes glowed green, and he gestured at Liam with the spear. Green flames ignited along the metal head of the weapon. Liam had to give the antlered man points for showmanship. The rider said, "You have my bride. Give her to me."

A pair of white hounds with red ears appeared from the fog, snarling. There were too many dog creatures in Celtic myth, Liam thought. White dogs with red ears indicated cwn annwn, the hounds of the Welsh Lord of the Dead. This guy was probably a grandson or a nephew of Arawn. A relative of Herne or Cernunnos was also possible, given the Wild Hunt imagery.

Liam met the huntsman's green, glowing gaze. "No."

"She is mine." A note of petulance crept into the protest. The huntsman brandished his spear again, flames still licking along the business end. "Are you claiming her for yourself?"

"I claim nothing," Liam countered, clutching his staff. "She is free to do as she chooses."

Ardduwn lowered his spear and aimed the tip at Liam. "I challenge you for her!"

"Nope." Liam glanced toward the car, hoping Pixel remembered where the shotgun was if he needed it. "She is not a prize to be won."

"I could take her from you." The green eyes blazed, and the hounds snarled.

"I could knock those fucking silly antlers off your head and turn your ride into roadkill," Liam countered. "I could make it so you and your progenitors never set foot in the Dunwold, or so no more souls ever enter the kingdom of Arawn.

"Since you managed to slip here without drawing attention from the Avramites, I know you're a piss ant," Liam continued. "Come at me, and I'll make those antlers grow into your skull instead of out of it." A blast of wind descended upon Liam with the last statement, driving back the fog. Ardduwn wasn't the only one who could be theatrical. Liam hoped the zephyrs wouldn't draw any magical attention.

"She was promised to me." The huntsman's protest sounded more like a whine. The hounds stopped growling and shifted their red eyes to the antlered man.

"Then you need to figure out how to court the old-fashioned way," Liam said. "Try asking a lady to dinner and a movie, instead of invoking some supernatural pact."

"I will—" the huntsman started.

"Do nothing," Liam interrupted. "Pixel, or Pykllyl, is free from any prior obligations. She serves as my familiar as long as she chooses, and only as she chooses. All previous offers are null and void. Now get the fuck out of my way before the Avramites come raining down on us all."

"You have to honor the previous promises," Arrduwn protested. "It was agreed she would be mine."

"Where are you?" Liam asked.

The antlered huntsman peered around, confused. "The New World?"

"You are on the Dunwold," Liam answered. "I have say over all magical matters here for the Folk. Now, do you relinquish your claim over my familiar, or do I turn you into Bambi?" Wind whirled around Liam, punctuating his statement.

Green flames flared in the huntsman's eyes, then tamped down to a dim glow. The fire on the spear flickered out. "Fine. She is yours."

"No, she is hers," Liam retorted. "She decides her destiny. You, however, better get the fuck out of my sight."

The huntsman and his hounds faded into the fog.

"That was impressive," Raven's spirit-form said from the mist.

Liam resisted the urge to jump. He knew staying out here, exposed, was a risk, though he had been careful about drawing on mystic energy. He realized the witch and her master had probably zeroed in on Ardduwn. "What do you want?"

The witch's translucent image glided out of the fog. Liam realized either he was getting better at seeing into the Murkwold or Raven was getting better at spirit-walking. Maybe both.

"The boss wants to talk," Raven's spirit-form replied. "He still thinks you can strike a deal."

"You mean he wants to hedge his bet because he thinks we have a shot at winning," Liam countered. He checked up and down the road; the fog was beginning to clear, and it was only a matter of time before someone drove by.

Liam was surprised Pixel wasn't already baring her teeth at the witch. Maybe she was still shell-shocked by her ex-fiancé's appearance.

Raven shrugged. "Something like that." At least she was keeping her clothes on.

Liam tossed his staff into the backseat. "Give me a phone number. Maybe I'll talk to him, but any funny business, and he ends up on a rock in the River Styx." Liam didn't know if he could make good on the threat, but Iblis might not know either.

Raven recited a number, then asked, "Aren't you going to write it down?"

"Nope." Liam climbed into the driver seat and put the car in gear. "I might call, but if I see anyone creeping around my place, or anyone hassling my people, I definitely won't be in a mood to parley. Am I clear?"

"Crystal clear, Druid."

Liam pulled away, and the witch winked out of sight. Liam wondered if she was trailing them from the spirit world but didn't want to split his attention from driving.

"I'll bet it's a trap," Pixel finally said.

Liam nodded. "Probably, but I'm more concerned about your ex. He managed to cross into the Dunwold, and he tracked us down even though we were moving."

"He tracked me down," Pixel said. "Between his being a *selgiwr*, a huntsman, and my being promised to him, once he got to the Dunwold, it would have been easy for him, at least away from your home."

"Who comes up with these terms?" Liam asked, taking a left away from home. No point in making it too easy for potential pursuers. "It sounds like someone spliced Irish and Welsh."

Pixel shrugged. "I think the Lexicon Council pulled it from one of the proto-Celtic languages and updated it over the years."

"So why didn't you tell me about him?" Liam took a right down a gravel track; it barely qualified as a road. The car left a dust plume in the taillights. "Is he why you've been so eager to have sex with me? To nullify your contract or whatever it was?"

"No!" Pixel protested. "I mean, it would have been a bonus, to not worry about him anymore."

Liam checked the rearview mirror for signs of pursuit, expecting the bikers with the van to show up. "I knew there was something suspicious about a young girl throwing herself at an old dog like me."

"You're not old; the bits of gray make you look dignified," Pixel remarked. "Plus, I'm not as young as you think."

"I'm hoping you're at least 21," Liam said.

"Try closer to 150," Pixel countered. "I was born shortly after the American Civil War."

"Idunn's apples and Tir na nOg, it's impossible to figure out how old you people are," Liam said, swinging onto the county road leading toward home. "Back to the matter at hand. Is Ardduwn likely to turn back up?"

Pixel gazed out into the dark cornfields. "There's a chance he won't come back. He's descended from Arawn, so maybe he picked up some of his ancestor's sense of honor. On the other hand, he seemed pissed. We could have sex, just to be sure."

Liam rolled his eyes as he pulled into the driveway.

*****

Chapter Twenty-Three

Erin

"They're back!"

Mysie was out of breath, having run from the front gate, where she'd gone to see what the commotion was about.

Erin looked up from her dinner. She really wanted to ask about Nechtan, but instead asked, "Is the Pilgrim with them?"

Mysie nodded, picking up her ale tankard and taking a drink. "Aye, they're all there. They're coming up the causeway, so it will be a short spell before they make it here."

Erin debated getting up to greet them at the gate, butterflies quelling her appetite. It seemed the least she could do; they had gone to all this trouble on her account. On the other hand, she was in her third trimester, and she was bushed from a day of yoga, forms practice, and sword drills. A voice in the back of her mind reminded Erin she wasn't the athletic woman Nechtan had seen a few days ago, from his perspective. She felt like she was smuggling a watermelon in her skirt.

Mysie regarded Erin over her mug. The short woman said, "He's going to see you sooner or later, unless you plan to hide the next couple of months until your wee one is born."

Daidh appeared puzzled but kept quiet.

Erin sighed. "I know, but I don't want to see his reaction in front of everyone else, because they'll see my reaction, and everyone will be gossiping about it for the next week."

"You think they'll stop after a week?" Daidh asked, getting a dire look from Mysie. "What? There's not a lot to do here besides train and gossip."

Erin looked at her two friends. "Does everyone in the fort know I have a crush on Nechtan?" She felt like she was back in high school, although it was rare anyone else came around their 'lunch table.' They were their own clique, though Erin didn't think it was one of the cool ones.

"Pretty much," Daidh responded immediately, earning an elbow from Mysie. "It's true; people tend to forget I'm around, so I overhear quite a bit."

Erin pushed herself up from the table. "If I start now, I should be able to waddle to the gate by the time they get here."

"Don't say such things," Mysie scolded. Two weeks ago, she had started a brawl when one of the guards called Erin fat. Mysie snap-kicked the man right in the nuts. By the time the dust settled, four guards had gone to the infirmary, and Mysie and Daidh had been put on kitchen duty for a week.

As Erin made her way to the gate, she spotted Uathach. They'd mostly avoided each other since their confrontation weeks ago. Erin steadied her gait and refused to show any signs of fatigue. She wouldn't give the redheaded bitch the satisfaction of seeing her physically compromised. Uathach stood near her mother in a small knot of people near the gate. Scathach, as usual, was inscrutable and calm. Uathach seemed annoyed.

Finally, the travelers marched into view. They all appeared haggard. Erin remembered the look well from her stint in the military, brought on by little sleep and plenty of labor. Nechtan was in the lead; Erin held her breath as his gaze swept her way, only for Scathach to say something and draw his attention away. An animated discussion followed; Erin couldn't make out the details from across the courtyard. It sounded like they had run into the giant again.

Izzy and Derek continued across the courtyard, Elam trailing behind them. The old healer was exhausted and pale. Erin felt guilty for what he had endured on her behalf.

"A little bird whispered you were in the family way," Derek said.

"Very funny, brother," Izzy rasped, her voice still not healed from her injury. Erin had to remind herself it had only been a few days for them.

Derek smirked. "I thought so. The druid's handiwork, I presume?"

"Of course," Erin replied. "I'm never letting him near me again. Two times, and both times he got me pregnant though I was on the pill."

"It was a lot more than two times," Derek remarked and began ticking off on his fingers. "You two weren't exactly quiet."

"It's not surprising," Izzy said. "After the spirit-walk, there was a large outburst of energy; I presume it was the two of you out by the dolmen."

"Are you saying he used magic to knock me up?" Erin began to imagine punching a lopsided grin off a certain druid. Was it why she kept sleeping with him? No, magic would make an easy scapegoat, but the bad decisions were on her.

"The two of you were flush with the power of Idunn's apples," Izzy said. "Liam had tapped into primal magic, and the two of you were in his place of power. I'm sure the fates may have had a hand in ensuring there would be another druid and champion from your lines if the need arose."

"Plus, I'll bet it had been a while for the druid," Derek added. "A lot of pent up magic, as it were. I have to admit, I'm surprised he resisted Pixel."

"I heard about it," Erin said, still trying to parse what Izzy had told them. "He drank himself into a coma."

"The first night, yes," Derek agreed. "The second night, when everyone went to bed, Pixel threw herself at the druid. He spurned her in favor of you."

"All of this is quite fascinating, but could we sit down?" Elam gasped, short of breath.

"I'm so sorry, Elam." In her distraction, Erin had forgotten about the old man. Again, she felt guilty. "Let's go over to my cabin; you can sit down and have a bite to eat."

Turning around to lead Elam to her temporary home, Erin realized Daidh and Mysie had been standing behind her the whole time. They had obviously overheard everything. Mysie was bemused; Daidh appeared embarrassed.

"Let's go to the mess and get food and ale for the new arrivals," Daidh suggested, pulling Mysie by the sleeve. "We'll bring it to your cabin, Erin."

"We might miss something juicy." Mysie's voice faded as they rounded the corner of the central keep, heading for the timber building serving as the mess for most of the occupants of Dunos Scaith.

"Who are your friends?" Derek asked as they walked toward Erin's Quonset. "I think I recognize the ginger."

"That means he turned my brother down," Izzy rasped.

"Daidh, and his girlfriend is Mysie," Erin replied. "Might explain why he turned you down."

"Or he has no taste," Derek said.

"Obviously," Elam added with a tired grin.

"Please, don't encourage him," Izzy countered.

"In answer to the rest of your question, they are my sparring partners, and when it comes to martial arts, my students." Erin gestured to the table and benches. "Welcome to my humble abode."

Elam sank onto one of the benches with a sigh. Erin caught Derek giving the white-haired man a concerned glance. "Do not worry yourself, Derecho," Elam said. "A bit of food and a couple days' rest, and I will be right as rain."

Elam patted the bench next to him and smiled at Erin. "Let's have a look at you, young lady."

Erin sat down, not sure what to expect. Elam took her hand and closed his eyes, muttering under his breath in a Germanic-sounding tongue.

"She's quite healthy," Elam announced.

"I feel pretty good, all things considered," Erin said.

Elam smiled, his eyes twinkling despite his fatigue. "I meant your daughter."

"My daughter?" Erin's free hand went to her mouth; tears welled up in her eyes. "I'm going to have a girl?"

Elam nodded and released Erin's hand. "Yes, you are. I see it pleases you."

Erin hadn't really thought about the gender of the baby until now. She certainly hadn't set her heart on having a daughter, so she couldn't explain why it made her so happy.

Mysie and Daidh returned laden with food and ale. Erin noticed Daidh avoided looking at Derek but didn't press him about it. Evidently, Mysie had no such qualms, and after a whispered conversation, she guffawed loudly. Daidh's cheeks matched his beard.

Mysie quelled her laughter and said, "You're so uptight, it's a wonder I got you into my bed."

Daidh rolled his eyes, his embarrassment not abating. He found his ale mug and took a deep drink.

Derek began to say something before Erin cut him off. "Leave him be," Erin said.

"Dinna be embarrassed." Mysie's Scottish accent thickened. "I tell you what…" She leaned close and whispered in Daidh's ear. Whatever she said mollified him and elicited a smile. Erin suspected it would be another noisy night in the Quonset.

Erin looked around. "Where's Nechtan?"

"Probably telling Scathach about the giant," Derek replied, digging into the food. "The *condenado* beast chased us again. We may have to deal with it."

"Uthor only does what he is made to do," Elam countered between bites.

"I do not think this is Isaiah 65," Derek said.

"As much as it pains me, I must agree with my brother," Izzy said after a drink of ale. "If the giant continues to be a menace, we may have to drive him off or put him down."

Elam shook his head, disappointed. "If it comes to that, so be it. Perhaps the grugach can be of help."

"Grugach?" Erin asked. How long did it take to report a giant had chased them? Erin wondered if Nechtan saw her condition and was staying away. She realized the notion bordered on the ridiculous as he lived in the Quonset hut next to hers. Staying away would be impossible. She was being paranoid, she told herself.

"Grugach were to the Neanderthals as the fair folk are to humans," Derek said. He picked up his mug and swirled the contents. "Most of the Bigfoot sightings are grugach who slipped over to the Dunwold. They never find any bodies because in the rare instance a grugach dies on the Dunwold, its physical form reverts to the Glaswold."

Erin's attention returned to the conversation. "So, dead yeti suddenly appear in this world?"

"Yeti are something else," Izzy interjected. "As my brother said, it is a rare occurrence."

"The grugach, as you call them, are gentle creatures," Elam said between mouthfuls of food. "Every so often, a small family of them ranges north of my camp."

Nechtan strode into view. Like the others, he looked haggard. Erin noted his stubble was a bit thicker, threatening to turn into an actual beard. She liked the stubble better. "What did I miss?" he asked as he took the empty spot across from Erin.

"We were discussing the grugach and how they might help with Uthor," Elam replied, dabbing at the stew clinging to his bowl with a hunk of bread.

Nechtan nodded, accepting a plate of food and a tankard of ale. He took a deep draw of ale before he said, "I was telling the Lady the same thing." He turned to Erin. "The grugach can speak to giants, and the giants don't try to squish or eat them. They might be able to get Uthor to leave the ridge north of here. Otherwise, you might get a lesson in giant killing."

Erin tipped her head quizzically. "Me? We have two dozen guys standing around with long spears and bows."

Nechtan shook his head and chuckled. "They would be wheat before the scythe. They might back you up with their bows, but slaying a giant is hero's work. Of course, it will have to wait until your current infirmity has passed."

"Infirmity?" Erin raised an eyebrow and set down her mug.

Nechtan seemed to sense his peril; his accent thickened with nervousness. "I mean you wouldn't want to risk your unborn child by brawling with the likes of Uthor."

Nice save, Erin thought, and picked up her ale, swirling it. "No, I won't risk my daughter duking it out with something three times my size."

"Twenty-seven," Derek corrected. "Assuming Uthor is three times your height, he would be roughly twenty-seven times your mass, three times three times three. Though, right now, he might only be twenty-five times—ow!" Izzy elbowed him as Mysie kicked him under the table.

His joke about her weight didn't bother her. She was managing her weight much better than when she carried Tim. Plenty of exercise and a total lack of junk food helped. What made her wistful was the math comment; it was the same kind of thing Tim would have said. It had been seven months since she had seen him. For Tim, it had been roughly a week, maybe two. She tried to figure out the time spent outside the weird time-flow of Dunos Scaith. Did he miss Erin yet?

Mysie glared across the table at Derek. "If you make her cry, I'll drag you by your pretty hair to the practice field."

"I'm a hermit, and I know better," Elam said.

Erin fought back tears. "It's just, I miss my son, and I'm hormonal. Though, if you want to kick his ass, I won't stop you."

"Little girl, you think you can handle me?" Derek asked Mysie, arching his eyebrow. "Bring along your boyfriend, and we can make it a threesome."

Erin managed to laugh. "It's too late for dueling, so where were we before Derek called me fat?"

"I was talking about the giant," Nechtan said. "Also, Uathach suggested I move into the keep to free up space for the Champion's growing retinue."

Erin's tears evaporated. "She did?" Of course, the red-headed witch would.

Nechtan nodded, oblivious that he was blundering into another emotional minefield. "She said there was a chamber available, and it would free up my hut for Elam and the twins."

"Really?" Erin didn't bother to keep the ice from her tone. At the top of her list of things to do after her daughter was born, Erin put 'break Uathach's arm again.' "So, are you moving in?"

Nechtan picked up his mug and shook his head. He replied, "No, I have all of my stuff here, and I like the neighbors."

A couple of hours later, they had shuffled living arrangements. Elam and Derek would stay with Nechtan. Izzy, Mysie, and Daidh, would stay with Erin. Since Mysie and Daidh would share a room, it would leave a room for Erin's daughter. Erin didn't ask about Derek and Elam's sleeping arrangements.

"You're having a girl?" Nechtan sat on the bench they had pulled over by the fire pit, the flames throwing much of his face into shadow.

It reminded Erin of a campfire months ago. "Yes. It came as a surprise to me."

"The Druid is the father." It wasn't a question; Nechtan stated it. Obviously, Izzy or Derek had told him.

The baby kicked as if in response to the question. "Yes, Liam, the Druid, is the father," Erin said. "I might as well mention he is also the father of my son, back on the Dunwold."

Nechtan gazed into the flames. "An auspicious pairing, if I ever heard one. Is he your husband?"

"What? No!" Erin was grateful Liam wasn't around to hear how vehemently she protested. "We're just, well it's complicated. Co-parents with benefits is the best term I've heard."

Nechtan looked up from the fire. "I understood complicated."

"Before I left the Dunwold, I told Liam I didn't want to commit to a relationship," Erin said. "I've spent all my life being me; I don't want to define myself as someone's girlfriend or someone's wife. I've fought hard to be my own person."

"You were afraid you would be reduced to being the Druid's wife?" Nechtan asked. "You realize, without you winning the challenge, his title is worthless."

"He doesn't care about the title," Erin blurted out. "If it was up to him, we would live in his farmhouse with our kids, and no one would bother us."

"But it's up to you," Nechtan said. "What do you want?"

Erin shrugged, gazing into the flames. "I don't know. We met thirteen years ago, and our son was born from that night. We lost track of each other until right before I came here. We reconnected, and he was overjoyed to find out he had a son…"

"But…" Nechtan said, urging her on.

Erin shrugged. "I don't know. We were drawn to each other, and you can see the result. I don't want to settle because he happened to be the one who knocked me up."

The fire crackled as Nechtan asked, "Do you think he loves you?"

There was a long moment of silence, only broken by pops from the fire pit. "I think he believes he loves me. I think he's seduced by the whole notion of having what he thinks he's been missing, a family. However, there's a fairy girl probably throwing herself at him as we speak, his familiar, whatever that is. I expect the veneer of what he thinks he wants, a nuclear family, will be swept aside by an eager, cute, young pixie."

"Why do you think that?" Nechtan asked.

Erin sighed. "Human nature, especially when it comes to men. No offense."

"None taken."

"In my experience, men have preconceived notions of what they want," Erin said. "Young, fit, cute, those are all things men want. Responsibility, commitment, those are things men don't want."

"So, the Druid has had congress with his familiar?" Nechtan asked.

"No, unless it happened after I left. It's a matter of time, though," Erin replied. "Especially since I pushed him away."

Nechtan drained his mug and set it aside. "It sounds like you're the one who's afraid of commitment."

Erin frowned; she wasn't sure if she was more annoyed Nechtan would make such a presumption or more irritated he was right. She waved the smoke and memories away; she wasn't in the mood right now.

"It has been a long day," Nechtan said, standing with the creak of leather. "I'll see you on the morrow, Erin."

"Nechtan?" she called after him. The huntsman paused at his hut. "Thank you."

"You're welcome," Nechtan replied. "Good night."

Erin sat alone by the fire. What did she want? The baby kicked, reminding her she wasn't alone.

*****

Chapter Twenty-Four

Erin

"Saint George isn't so scary now."

The chirurgeon's assistant, Slaine, looked down at Erin in confusion. "I beg your pardon?"

"Saint George," Erin repeated. "After giving birth without modern drugs, championing the Milesian Accords should be a piece of cake."

Slaine nodded. "As you say, Champion." The woman disappeared around the curtains set up around Erin's bed.

The baby nestled against Erin, sleeping after feeding. Erin felt like she could sleep for a week or two. According to the midwife, a crone with shockingly blue hair, the birth had been one of the easiest she had presided over. The crone wasn't the one who had been in labor for nine hours, Erin mentally grumbled. She hadn't filled Erin with confidence when Erin had asked how long it had been since she had attended a mother, and the crone asked if Erin meant in years.

At least Elam had been there. The Pilgrim had remained at her side the whole time, occasionally butting heads with the crone, who seemed to resent Elam's presence. Erin wasn't sure she cared for his proclamation that she was as healthy as a mule, but she appreciated his reassurance that she and the baby were healthy. She suspected the wave of warmth, which washed over her before he departed, was an exercise of his healing talent.

A commotion kept Erin from drifting off. She had been expecting it as soon as the crone declared her fit, but she had asked Slaine to wait until she had fed the baby her first meal and settled her down.

Mysie was the first around the curtain, grinning widely. Izzy and Derek followed, then Daidh, who appeared distinctly uncomfortable. The fifth person was not who she expected. Scathach was majestic as always. Erin expected the warrior-matron to ask how soon Erin would be on her feet and able to resume her training.

Erin got the impression babies were a novelty among the various Exiled Folk. The tradeoff for their extended lifespans was a low fertility rate, especially in the Glaswold. Izzy had tried to explain it in more detail until Erin decided it wasn't worth the headache of trying to wrap her mind around it. She hoped a fort full of enthralled aunts and uncles wasn't going to spoil her daughter.

Mysie cooed at the sleeping infant. "She's so wee. What will you name her?"

Erin looked to Scathach. "Given where she was born, I thought Skye would be an apt name."

Scathach nodded, with a hint of a smile. In legend, Dunos Scaith was located on the Isle of Skye, near Scotland. "A fitting name indeed."

* * *

Scathach wasn't big on the idea of maternity leave. Erin was certain Elam's ministrations contributed to her speedy recovery, and at the end of a week, she found herself juggling nursing a baby and resuming her training. Whoever wasn't on the practice field with her was on baby duty. While the chirurgeon and her assistant helped, as much due to their fascination with the infant as anything else, Erin always made sure one of 'her people' was also keeping an eye on Skye. She remembered hearing stories about fairies stealing mortal children, and she wasn't about to find out if the tales had some factual basis.

Nechtan and Elam departed the same day Erin resumed her training. Derek had offered to accompany them, but Elam had gently chided Derek, saying he was needed more at Dunos Scaith, especially since the four-day round trip would take 200 subjective days to those within the fort.

Erin and Nechtan hadn't really talked since the night by the fire pit. They weren't shunning each other, but they avoided serious discussion and never seemed to end up alone together. Now he would be gone for over six months, assuming he didn't go on a walkabout.

Maybe it was just as well, Erin thought. Nechtan had been right, she was afraid of commitment. Was her attraction to the hunter a way to distance herself from Liam? Or did a relationship with a built-in expiration date hold an attraction? Erin peered down at the baby contently nursing. Right now, Erin had enough to worry about.

Integrating Izzy and Derek into their training cadre hadn't been as seamless as Erin had hoped, mainly because Derek and Mysie kept clashing. Izzy and Derek were more experienced than Mysie and Daidh. Izzy didn't lord it over the other pair, and Daidh didn't let Derek ruffle his feathers. But, Derek knew how to push Mysie's buttons, and she rose to the occasion, which only encouraged him.

The twins had trained at Dunos Scaith in the past, so they gave Erin more insight into Scathach's techniques and lessons. They had been slightly disappointed the bulk of the weapons training focused on spears and long swords, as opposed to the paired short swords they favored. Both twins fought with a fluid, graceful style, with Izzy more prone to economical moves and Derek more likely to try flashier tricks.

* * *

"Mysie, that's enough," Erin called, burping the baby over her shoulder. Erin had split the group into pairs for unarmed practice for the first time. Derek had been smirking all morning between snide remarks, so Erin squared him against Mysie. "Don't make me put the baby down."

Mysie froze, her gloved fist pulled back to deliver another punch. The short woman had caught Derek off balance when she got inside his guard and swept his feet out from under him. While the takedown had been textbook, as Erin had taught Mysie, the follow-up had been a feral pounce to pin Derek to the dirt, followed by a pair of rapid punches to his face.

Erin couldn't see Derek's face past the sparring helmet, but she could imagine his arched eyebrow when he said, "I seem to have gotten a rise out of you. Keep straddling me, and you might get the same from me."

Something wet land on Erin's tunic, accompanied by a satisfied belch from Skye. "Mysie, no!" Erin barked. "Up!"

Mysie's face twisted in a snarl as she forcefully pushed off Derek's chest to stand. Infuriating as usual, he showed no discomfort, but at least he held his tongue as he climbed to his feet. Mysie was still scowling when she exchanged the post-bout bow with Derek.

Erin grabbed a rag and dabbed at the wet spot on her tunic. "Who takes the baby, and who gets back in the practice square?"

Mysie sighed, the scowl breaking. "I'll take Skye."

Derek smirked. "Ooh, do I get to grapple with her boyfriend now?"

Erin smiled and twisted her head side-to-side until her neck cracked. "No. It's time to see how out of practice I am." She handed the baby to Mysie, who made kissy noises at the infant, all traces of her previous anger erased.

Erin donned her sparring armor. "Before you ask, no, it's not too soon. I need to get back on the horse."

Derek arched an eyebrow. "Are we talking about sparring, or something else? I may not have manly stubble, but I could certainly get you back in the saddle."

Erin pulled the last lace on her padded glove tight. She turned and regarded Derek with a smile as she strode toward the middle of the sparring field. She vowed to make Derek pay for the jibe without losing her cool.

Derek tilted his head. "What are you leering at?"

Erin pounded her gloved fists together, still smiling. "Picturing you in khakis, a button-up shirt, and horn-rimmed glasses."

Derek's smirk faded. "Shit."

* * *

Erin was sore from the afternoon's workout, but not as sore as Derek. Though out of shape and out of practice, she still left him with a couple of bruises. Now her group gathered around the large table one of the carpenters had made, sharing their evening meal and some humor at Derek's expense. Erin was nursing Skye while trying to eat with one hand and laughing at Mysie's joke. Erin looked up when everyone else at the dinner table fell silent. There was a loud pop from the fire pit. "She's behind me, isn't she?" Erin asked. They knew whom she meant.

Daidh nodded.

"Hello, Champion," Scathach said. Someone else might have said something along the lines of 'I hope I'm not intruding,' but Scathach wouldn't consider herself intruding anywhere in Dunos Scaith.

Erin turned, her infant still clinging to her breast. A woven sling, a gift from Slaine, helped keep Skye in place. "What can I do for you, Scathach?"

"It has been a month since the birth of your daughter," the mistress of Dunos Scaith said. "I was wondering how your recovery was going, especially since your training cadre has doubled."

Erin searched for the trap. Everything with Scathach was a test, an exercise, or some sort of challenge. "Well enough. If nothing else, the training is great for shedding baby weight."

Scathach nodded, although Erin suspected the matron of war had never worried about shedding pregnancy weight. "When will you be able to face two of your sparring partners at once?"

Erin was so dumbfounded she didn't notice Skye had stopped suckling and had spit up into her open tunic. She had gotten to the point where she could confidently hold her ground against any one of them, including Izzy or Derek. "I'm going to go out on a limb and assume you mean armed?"

Scathach rolled her emerald eyes. "Of course, unless you think the Avram champion will engage you in fisticuffs?"

Erin bit her tongue. "Of course not, however, it is a bit of a leap to go from one opponent to two. I thought the Milesians only had one champion?"

Scathach sniffed and appeared disappointed. "One champion, who beat a dragon, and has had centuries to practice."

Erin shrugged. "A year? It's a lot harder to defend against multiple opponents, not to mention take them out, than to face one highly-skilled opponent."

Scathach nodded. "A year and a day it is. If you can beat two opponents of my choosing, I will convey you to the Dunwold to communicate with your son. Of course, I will offer appropriate boons to your opponents if they can defeat you."

Erin sighed. "Great."

*****

Chapter Twenty-Five

Liam

"Explain it to me again."

Liam wasn't sure if he hadn't heard right, or if he had trouble believing what he had been told.

Einar scowled under his beard. "Druid, after all you've seen, why do you still pocking doubt what we tell you?"

Liam, Einar, Pixel, Gofannon, and Susan sat around the old oak table, discussing the next move. Liam was acutely aware of the days ticking off the calendar. It had been two weeks since Erin had left. This afternoon, after working in the smithy, Gofannon had announced it was time to get the meteoric iron they would be using for Erin's sword.

"We're going to get a meteor in Russia," Pixel said, not betraying exasperation despite repeating herself. "You'll wold-walk us there from the Glaswold."

Liam glanced at his half-empty beer. "Isn't there a meteor closer?"

Gofannon snorted. "Druid, quit whining. This is the only meteor with the right metal, and we know the location it fell is close-enough to a wold-ford so we can recover it in time without attracting attention."

Pixel put her hand on Liam's arm. Liam didn't need to see Susan to know the gesture would draw a frown from her. Pixel said, "Liam, it's not so different from spirit-walking, and you've gotten really good at that."

That was true. Liam could easily step out of his body, and he could observe the Murkwold without leaving his body. "We're talking about teleportation. The physics are mind-boggling." It hadn't helped that Tim had rattled off a whole bunch of scientific reasons why teleportation shouldn't work before being sent to the living room to study for a test.

Einar wiped beer foam from his moustache. "It's not pocking science."

"Afraid you'll cross the threshold of plausible deniability?" Susan asked. "Spirit journeys and visions could all be dismissed as some sort of hysteric hallucinations. You physically step into another world, there's no denying it's all real."

What Susan said resonated with Liam. Was he still harboring subconscious doubts, worried about crossing a point of no return? "Fine," he relented. "What are these wold-fords and how do they apply to what we're doing?"

"A wold-ford is a crossing point between the worlds, usually the Dunwold and the Glaswold," Pixel replied. She still hadn't removed her hand. "Normally, when you cross over, you appear at the same relative point. However, with enough *lledrith*, you can cross from anywhere on the Glaswold to a wold-ford in the Dunwold."

Liam furrowed his eyebrows. It seemed too easy. "Why didn't we wold-walk Erin and the twins to Dunos Scaith?"

Einar set down his drained bottle. He had taken a liking to Harter Anvil Stout; Liam was certain he had become the brewery's best customer. Einar took a moment to compose his reply. "Because Scathach doesn't allow any open wold-fords near Dunos Scaith. Only she can open the hidden one there. She plays cagey with the merchants who supply her stronghold, so she doesn't end up with a bunch of hero-wannabes knocking at her door. The closest crossing I know of is a good three- or four-day hike away."

Gofannon tossed a stone onto the table. "Here, take the rock. It is from the wold-ford."

Liam picked up the rectangular stone. The faint, eroded lump may have been a bull at one time. "What is this?"

"It's a keystone," Pixel replied. "It will lead you to the ford."

"Would it be out of line to ask how?" Liam turned the stone over in his hand.

Pixel clasped the stone in Liam's palm. "Once we are in the Glaswold, focus on the keystone to cross back to the Dunwold. It should pull us through the wold-ford attuned to the keystone."

Liam picked up his beer with his free hand and took a long drink. "So, we try this in the morning?"

"We should go now," Gofannon replied.

"It's nine o'clock," Liam protested.

"Ja, and there it is six in the morning," Einar countered. "Best to have daylight if we're traipsing around foreign hills."

Liam looked at Susan. "I'll watch Tim," she offered.

"Let me grab a jacket." Liam hoped they weren't going to the Arctic, or he'd be ill-equipped. "Do we need to bring any tools, shovels, or the like?"

"Bring your staff," Pixel suggested. "You can grab it on our way to the dolmen."

"Can I watch?" Tim asked from the doorway to the living room.

"Fine, but once we're gone, get ready for bed," Liam said. "Then go to bed; don't give Susan any trouble."

"Okay," Tim agreed reluctantly.

This seemed insane, Liam thought. The storm monster seemed reasonable compared to jaunting across the world. He collected his staff as they passed through the garage. He debated switching into his ritual garb and decided against it. If this failed, he could put on his garb tomorrow when they tried again.

The fire burning in the fire pit told him the others had planned to go tonight. They had faith he could do this, or at least enough confidence to set everything up.

The aroma of flowers preceded Pixel's voice. "Focus on us stepping through into a green world, like you're stepping through the door into your bedroom," she said. "This part is easy, the rest of us can cross on our own if need be."

Liam nodded, walking toward the opening in the dolmen. Every time his staff touched the ground, he drew a little energy from the *Gwuedd.* As he passed between the menhir, he released the energy and pictured the Glaswold. The slope beneath his feet told him he was walking down the other side of the hill. He opened his eyes, ready to be disappointed.

Instead of corn and soybean fields, he saw a great hedge. Beyond the hedge, he could see scattered treetops. Liam turned around, looking past his fellow travelers. A large, blocky stone protrusion jutting up from the ground replaced the house. In the moonlight, the stone formation appeared roughly the same size as his farmhouse.

The wind kicked up and swirled around Liam, ruffling his clothes and hair. He could sense the zephyrs swooping around him. He hoped they didn't get too enthusiastic; these wind spirits seemed more energetic than the ones on the Dunwold.

Something slammed Liam from behind and interrupted his musing. Stumbling forward, he caught himself with his staff. The healing burns on his feet twinged with the careless steps. They didn't bother Liam much if he was cautious about how he walked and kept his time on his feet to a minimum. He suspected this trip would put them to the test.

"Druid, why did you stop?" Gofannon boomed.

Liam glanced back; the others were dimly visible in the glow cast by a riot of stars and the waxing moon. At least Tim didn't try to follow them through the dolmen. Liam stepped aside to give everyone else space to step away from it. He peered west; there were no signs of the lights of Peoria, or any other town. His gaze went skyward. While he had a good view of the sky at home, out in the countryside, it paled compared to the vista overhead.

"Are there any towns or cities on the Glaswold?" Liam asked.

Einar shook his head. "Not so much. There are holts, which are where the folk gather around more powerful entities, and a smattering of trade settlements where farmers and crafts folk trade their wares and swap tales."

Pixel moved next to Liam, peering up at him, her eyes luminous in the dark. "How do you feel, Liam?"

Liam had been so distracted by being on the Glaswold he hadn't taken stock of himself. He felt like he had been through a moderate workout, enough fatigue to notice but not actually tired. The pain from his feet ebbed. "I feel pretty good, actually. I have a hundred questions, and I wish we had time to explore."

"We do not," Gofannon rumbled. "We should continue; time is short."

Pixel pressed the rectangular keystone in Liam's hand. "This time focus on the keystone, and imagine you are holding a door open for the rest of us. Be sure to draw in plenty of *lledrith* before you open the crossing. It will take a great deal of energy."

Liam nodded, forcing himself to focus. He really wanted to come back here in the daytime and scout around. As soon as he could squeeze it in between learning to make the sword, writing the new accords, taking care of his son, and the half dozen other projects he had going, he planned to return

"This isn't going to put a bulls-eye on us?" Liam asked as he stood in front of the dolmen. "It's got to be noisy, especially with Gofannon along for the ride."

Einar cracked his knuckles. "It may kick up a ruckus where we arrive. Let's see them scamper halfway around the world before we get what we need and are gone."

"Fair enough." Liam planted his staff in the dirt. Immediately, he could feel the magical energy flowing up into him. The *Gwuedd*, the weave of magic, was strong here, by at least an order of magnitude over what he felt on the Dunwold. He imagined the *lledrith* suffusing his body, then channeled it all down his arm into the keystone he held before the dolmen.

Light spilled from between the menhir, morning sunlight on wooded hills. A worn megalithic structure cast a long shadow on the hillside. Einar and Pixel hurried through the dolmen, and then Gofannon grabbed Liam's outstretched hand and pulled him through.

Liam's connection to the *Gwuedd* snapped; he felt like every cell in his body cried out. He lost the strength to stand, and colored stars bloomed in front of his eyes. This time the staff didn't help him stay upright as he collapsed in a heap on the ground.

Pixel rushed to his side. "Are you okay?"

Liam wished the ground would quit rippling like a giant bowl of jello. His stomach flip-flopped and threatened to return dinner. He would have shaken his head, but the action would have cost him control over keeping his last meal down. "I don't feel too good."

Pixel knelt next to him and took the keystone. Liam was surprised he hadn't dropped it when he collapsed. She helped him get into a sitting position and handed him half an orange. "Eat this," she said. "It will help you feel better."

Liam numbly pulled out a slice and ate it. He was aware of Pixel asking Gofannon for something, and then she was holding a small flask. Liam maneuvered his staff to the crook of his arm to take the offered beverage. After another orange slice, he took a swig from the flask. The cloyingly sweet liquid inside was like drinking an energy drink plugged into a light socket.

"What is this stuff?" Liam asked. He was afraid drinking too much would cause his heart to race, even in his depleted state. Another orange slice seemed safer.

"Jumping halfway across the world pulled a lot of energy from your body," Pixel said. "It depleted your blood sugar. The orange slices and the *ynni* mead should set you right in a little bit."

Liam took a measured breath, attempting to control his pulse; he could feel his heart fluttering in his chest. "Don't you think it would have been a good idea to warn me that doing this could put me into diabetic shock?"

"I was afraid it would distract you," Pixel replied apologetically. "I didn't think it would hit you so hard. Obviously, I was prepared, just in case."

Liam wanted to be angry, but there was too much going through his mind. It was daylight, which meant they really were on the other side of the world. His legs felt like a newborn colt's, liable to buckle under him if he stood. His head was still fuzzy. Liam handed the flask back to Pixel and finished the remaining orange slice.

"Well done, Druid!" Gofannon's voice seemed especially loud in the quiet forest. "I was concerned there would be days of trial and error before you succeeded."

Einar squinted at the sky. "Judging by the sun, we're in the right time zone." He spotted the megalithic structure behind him, a squat, boxy monument. "Probably the right spot."

"Don't seem so surprised," Liam grumbled as strength returned to his limbs.

"How can we not be surprised, considering how much you doubt your own abilities?" Gofannon countered. "Cathbad must be proud, well, except for the whining."

Liam resisted the urge to retort, instead focusing on regaining his footing. Between Pixel and his staff, he pushed himself upright. A cool breeze rustled autumn leaves in the surrounding trees. "All right," Liam said. "Let's find this meteor."

Gofannon knelt and placed the palm of his hand against the ground, closing his eyes. "It is south of us, not far. There is little iron in the soil, so it should be easy for the druid to pull it up." The smith god stood and strode downhill.

Liam fell into step beside Gofannon. He struggled to keep up due to his tender feet. "We're not going to dig it up?" Liam asked as Pixel and Einar hurried to catch up.

"No, you will pull it from the ground." Gofannon continued walking. The trees thinned out, and a gravel road was visible ahead.

"More precisely, you'll coax the earth to pop it out," Pixel said. She wasn't winded yet, but she was struggling to keep pace. "Think of it as a ferrous blackhead."

"That's a disgusting analogy," Liam remarked. He hoped there was no traffic on the road; he didn't want to explain their presence to Russian authorities. "Does this tie into the Gaia theory, that the Earth is one interconnected entity?"

"No, think of the three realms," Pixel replied.

As if Liam needed reminding, a gust of wind blew back his hair. "I'm going to ask the land spirits to push it out. Since earth isn't as fluid as air or water, it could take a long time."

"Which is why you need to pep them up with some magic," Einar said. Though he had been jogging to keep up, he wasn't breathing hard. "Gofannon could do it, but it would be noisy, and we'd probably end up with a seraphim or three breathing down our necks."

There wasn't a vehicle in sight as they crossed the road. Then they rounded a copse of trees and Liam spotted a pair of houses and a pole barn about three hundred yards away. There were no signs of people, but smoke rose from the chimneys of both houses.

"This could a problem," Liam whispered, pointing toward the buildings. "Please don't tell me our space rock is under one of those houses."

Gofannon furrowed his great, bushy brows. "No, it is only 50 paces ahead."

Liam jumped at Gofannon's voice, certain it was audible all the way to those homes. "Let's try not to announce our presence to the whole valley."

Gofannon scoffed but lowered his voice. "You worry too much." He led them forward, along the edge of the copse, stopping halfway to the houses. The smith-god pointed at the ground and looked at Liam. "It is here."

It could be worse, Liam thought. It wasn't under any trees or in a water-filled depression. He walked around the spot, studying the ground. He was keenly aware of the others watching him. A snapping twig caught Liam's attention; he spotted three men watching the group.

The men wore heavy jackets, worn work boots, and faded jeans. What really stood out were the rifles they carried. Liam wasn't sure if the guns were older military models or the civilian equivalents. It didn't really matter; they had guns and Liam's group didn't.

One of the men, wearing a bright orange, knit cap, said something Russian sounding. Since Liam had never studied Russian, he could only guess it was something along the lines of "Who are you?"

"I don't suppose you speak English?" Liam asked.

"What are you doing here?" This was another man, with a tightly trimmed beard. His accent was thick but understandable.

Liam watched the guns. None pointed at them yet, but they were held ready to change in a moment. Liam spoke slowly without resorting to the typical American-speaking-to-a-foreigner exaggerated annunciation. "We're geologists. We are going to study some rocks and soil, then we will leave. Is that okay?"

"How much money you have?" the bearded Russian asked. Evidently, his compatriots got the gist of what he was saying and chuckled.

Great, Liam thought, they're going to shake us down. I wonder if they'll shoot us when they realize we don't have any Russian money?

"Boys, wouldn't you rather party?" Pixel stepped forward, immediately becoming the center of attention. Her eyes blazed violet as she batted her eyelashes. "You know, vodka? I bet you could show a girl a good time."

All three Russians nodded and laughed menacingly. "Yes, we show you good time."

Pixel flounced over to them. "This will be so much fun." She waved back toward Liam and said, "You boys find your rock. I'll be back when the party is over."

"We party with you long time," the bearded man said as they led the purple-haired girl toward the houses.

Liam watched them, the three men jockeying for position around Pixel as they walked. "Great, now we have to rescue her."

Gofannon shook his head. "Do not worry about your familiar, druid. Focus on the task at hand."

"There are three of them with guns," Liam protested. "You know what they'll do to her?"

"I'll bet a bottle of whiskey she'll be back before you can get the pocking meteorite out of the ground," Einar countered. "Pixel will have the lot of them eating out of her pocking hand."

Liam watched the receding forms, Pixel's purple hair standing out from the brown and gray landscape. "Are you sure?"

Einar snorted. "I've seen her make a fellow flush his own head in a dirty bar toilet."

Liam turned reluctantly back to the spot on the ground. He decided it would be easier to sit; it would make him feel closer to the earth and take the pressure off his feet. Sitting cross-legged, he rested his staff across his lap, and placed both hands palm down on the turf. He reached for the land spirits as he would the zephyrs. After several minutes, he sensed a presence, then another, and yet another.

It was easy to think of the land and earth in monolithic terms, and something like a mountain might have a large spirit associated with it, but in most places, the ground was an amalgamation of dirt and stones. Instead of a single land spirit here, there were many.

Once he was in tune with the erdlings, the earth spirits, he sought their perception of the meteorite. They felt the presence as a lump of foreign matter. Liam reached for the *Gwuedd*, and felt a void, ten feet down. It matched where the erdlings felt the intrusive chunk of alien metal. He coaxed them to work the meteorite to the surface. He soon got a sense of what a slow and laborious process it would be. The earth was not an element disposed to changing quickly.

Liam remembered to channel some magical energy, *lledrith*, into the work. He didn't want to alert the Avramites to their presence; the last thing they needed was a celestial enforcer set on them. He reached as far across the *Gwuedd* as he could feel; instead of drawing heavily on the weave of magic around him, he would pull a little bit along each strand over a greater area. As magic flowed across the land, Liam drew it into himself then cast it to the land spirits. A depression appeared in the ground before Liam as dirt piled to the sides.

It was like watching a miniature landslide in reverse; dirt and stone continued to flow up the sides of the growing hole. Below the surface, Liam could feel the alien void rising, as the earth was cleared above it and flowed around and under the meteorite. After several minutes, a metallic grey and rust colored lump appeared in the bottom of the pit. It didn't appear impressive, maybe a foot and a half long, about half as thick. Dirt from the piles began to flow back into the hole, continuing to elevate the meteorite. When the last of the soil returned to the depression, the iron-nickel lump was halfway out of the ground.

A distant gunshot snapped Liam's concentration. He clumsily lurched to his feet, remembering his recent paralysis as his limbs reluctantly responded. "Did the shot come from the direction they took Pixel?"

Both Gofannon and Einar gazed in the direction of the buildings. Another report sounded. "Ja, I think so," Einar replied.

They didn't seem to share Liam's alarm. "We have to do something."

"Hey guys, are you done digging up our space rock?" Pixel asked, stepping from the nearby trees.

Liam sagged in relief, leaning heavily on his staff. "Thank the gods, I was afraid something happened to you."

"You are welcome," Gofannon rumbled, turning his attention back to the meteorite.

"You were worried about me? How sweet." Pixel smiled, went to Liam, and hugged him. "You didn't have to worry; I had them eating out of my hand. It sounds like their argument over me got a little heated after I slipped away."

Liam breathed a sigh of relief. Strength was returning to his legs; he wondered how much of his difficulty standing had been due to magical fatigue and how much from his legs falling asleep while he sat on the cold ground. "Hey! This means Einar owes me a bottle of whiskey."

Einar frowned, then shrugged. "Ja, you pulled the pocking thing up before she got back," he conceded, looking down at the meteorite. "I'll make it a good one."

Pixel pulled a bottle of clear liquid from behind her back and held it out toward the dwarf. "Here's a consolation prize," she said. "Genuine Russian vodka. May or may not have been made in a tractor's gas tank."

Einar unscrewed the cap, sniffed the contents, then took a swig. His eyes lit up and he suppressed a cough. "Odin's eye, that's rough! I'll be sure to keep it away from the forge. Thökk!"

"You're welcome." Pixel eyed the gray-brown lump of metal. "Seems like overkill. Do we need the whole thing? It looks heavy."

Liam crunched the numbers in his head based on his estimates of the meteor's volume. It was an impressive amount of metal, and he wouldn't want to lift it. "It has to weigh a couple hundred pounds."

Gofannon squatted down and seized the meteorite with his huge hands. Grunting, he hefted it from the ground. "Better to have too much metal than not enough. We should return to the ford."

"Oh no," Pixel whispered. She was staring in the direction of the buildings.

As Liam watched, a pillar of white mist appeared in the field between them and the houses. The mist coalesced into a white marble statue. Liam realized the statue was moving, and the hairs on the back of his neck stood up. "What is it?"

"A pocking seraphim," Einar uttered. "We need to get out of here."

Liam flinched at the crack of a gunshot. A second shot snapped, followed by the sound of a bullet ricocheting off stone. The seraphim turned toward the houses and began marching across the field toward them. It extended its hand, and fog solidified into a white sword.

Gofannon was already moving in the other direction. Despite his burden, the smith-god's pace was quicker than before. Liam had to jog to catch up and keep pace; Pixel and Einar had to run. Behind them, two more gunshots echoed.

"All they're going to do is piss it off," Einar remarked. Despite running, he wasn't breathing hard yet.

"Let's just hope they keep him busy long enough for us to make the wold-ford," Pixel panted. "Liam, you should run ahead to get ready to cross us over."

Liam considered protesting. At least the strength had returned to his legs, but his feet were already aching.

"She is right," Gofannon grunted. "Go."

Liam picked up his pace. He knew better than to try sprinting; he would be gassed before he got back to the megalithic monument. If he hadn't spent the past two weeks in hard labor in the forge, he wouldn't have had the stamina to make it halfway back. Despite Einar's cooking, he'd lost ten pounds sweating over the anvil.

He cursed as he crossed the road, realizing their path was uphill now. He pumped his legs, running upslope, and his breathing became labored, and the pain intensified. As the trees thickened, Liam took a quick look back. The others were crossing the road. The gunfire had ceased; he hoped it didn't mean the seraphim had turned its attention to them.

Liam was gasping for air by the time he found the megalith and sweating heavily despite the breeze whirling around him. He could hear the others crashing through the undergrowth toward him. Liam tried to collect his thoughts. Crossing to the Glaswold hadn't been as hard as he expected, he merely needed to find the opening. He examined the megalith; the short, squat structure didn't have an obvious opening like Liam's dolmen.

Liam closed his eyes and paced around the area where they had appeared. With his mind, he scryed into the spirit-world. To his left, there was a shimmer in the Murkwold. It didn't resemble a door so much as a cylinder. Maybe it was how a multi-dimensional portal could appear in three-dimensional space without a framework.

Liam planted his staff on the ground and began gathering magical energy. He didn't have time to be subtle; he could hear the others growing close. Gofannon sounded winded, huffing like a locomotive. They crested the hill only twenty yards away.

Something flapped overhead. "Infidels! *Nukrayim!*" The words sounded like steam escaping an angry pipe organ. "Trespassers shall die!" The silhouette of a winged man blocked the sun, his golden eyes blazing with wrath.

A howling wind tore through treetops, slamming into the seraphim. The gale caught his wings and hurled the angel sideways into the forest. Branches, then full trees, snapped as he hurtled through them into a hillside.

Liam turned back to the ford and released his gathered *lledrith* into it, imagining opening a door. The air in front of Liam shimmered like the surface of a pond. Einar ran through the spot and disappeared, followed quickly by Pixel. Gofannon lumbered through, wheezing as he cradled the meteorite.

An angry bellow sounded from the next hill, accompanied by splintering wood. Liam didn't need any further encouragement to step through the wold-ford and let the portal collapse in his wake.

*****

Chapter Twenty-Six

Tim

"They're gone!"

Susan stared astonished at the dolmen. She circled around the stone structure before gawking at Tim. "They're gone," she repeated.

Obviously, Tim thought, only a little less surprised than Susan. Despite everything he had experienced in the past couple of weeks, this had to be the most amazing. He wondered how long it would be before he could cross over to the Glaswold?

"You really don't expect me to go to bed?" Tim asked. "My dad vanished into thin air. It has to be the coolest and creepiest thing I've ever seen."

Susan nodded mutely. Tim wasn't sure if she was agreeing with him, or if she really expected him to try to sleep after witnessing people disappearing in front of his eyes. "Should we wait out here?" she asked.

Tim shrugged, trying to act calmer than he felt. "We don't know when they'll get back. We should probably go inside." The wind had stopped blowing, but it was still chilly.

Susan nodded. "Let's go in," she agreed.

The night was eerily quiet as they walked back toward the house. Tim realized the wind chimes constantly tinkled, but now they were silent. He felt better when he stepped across the threshold into the garage, and the house assured him there was nothing amiss.

"I don't suppose there's any chance of you going to sleep before they come back?" Susan asked, pacing around the living room restlessly. "You know your father will be cross with both of us if he gets home, and you're still up."

Tim picked up his tablet but didn't turn it on. "He won't really be mad at you; he'll know it wasn't your fault," Tim said. "He might act like it in front of me, but only to make me feel guilty."

"He will really be mad at you," Susan countered.

Tim shrugged and said, "He'll forgive me. He wouldn't be able to sleep if I vanished. If they don't get back in a couple of hours, I'll try to go to sleep."

Susan seemed unconvinced.

"We could work on the new accords for a while," Tim suggested. "It would keep our minds off them being gone, and it might be enough like homework to make me sleepy."

"Fine, let's work on them," Susan relented after a few moments of consideration. "If nothing else, it will be more productive than pacing until they come back."

Tim followed Susan into the study. They had updated the room with a computer and printer after convincing Tim's father it would be easier than working by hand. Tim being able to print off his homework had been the final selling point. The large LED monitor was out of place among the antique furnishings in the room.

Tim hoped once the challenge was over, he would be able to play some games on the computer. He could have installed some already, but he had no time to play them between school, working on the new accords, and trying to figure out magic. Of course, if he figured out magic, he might have better things to do than play computer games and fence with internet trolls.

The flat panel display was positioned so both Tim and Susan could see the screen. Tim woke up the computer and brought up the documents they had been working on. Susan opened the spiral notebook where Liam had been writing notes and flipped through it.

Scanning the page, then checking the monitor, she said, "We were working on the rules for magic, specifically who gets to use magic."

Tim leaned back in the wooden chair. It wasn't comfortable compared to the office chair behind the desk, but Liam had impressed on him it was rude to hog the good chair. "I don't understand why there are so many rules if people can break them," Tim said. "Every rule had a bunch of conditions and loopholes in the old treaty. If we win, we could make it simple. The bad guys don't get any magic."

Disappointment clouded Susan's expression. "Your father talked about this. We're not to treat them as the 'bad guys;' a small faction represents the Abrahamic religions. It would be like calling all fae folk jerks because Derek is a jerk."

Tim fidgeted in the chair. He knew Susan and his father were right. It seemed to take the fun out of winning. "Which is why Dad doesn't want to keep magic away from them. He thinks if both sides have magic, it will be fairer."

"Exactly." Susan nodded. "So, instead of fostering centuries of resentment, both sides can work out their disagreements."

"It sounds like when they give everyone a trophy, so the losers don't feel bad," Tim said. He remembered participation awards from his last school. "Seems pretty lame."

Susan sighed and shook her head. "You sound like your father."

"There are a lot more of them than followers of the Old Gods, right?" Tim asked. Maybe if he brought a pillow down to cushion the seat, it wouldn't be so uncomfortable. "Something like a hundred to one? If we make everyone equal, they could still bully the exiled folk and pagans."

Susan rocked back in her seat, still looking at the screen. "Reducing it to two sides is an over-simplification. If we only split magic between the two sides, it leaves out a lot of others. Neither faction is homogenous."

Tim tapped at his tablet, bringing up information regarding world religions. He wiped a bead of sweat from his forehead with the back of his hand. One downside to the computer being in the study was that the small room got warm and stuffy quickly. "Avramites, I mean Abrahamic religions account for more than half the world's population," Tim said, scrolling down the screen. "Non-religious is the next biggest group. Can they be irreligious and still use magic?"

"Maybe?" Susan brushed back a sweaty lock of hair, oblivious to the ceiling fan whirring to life overhead, and the transom creaking open. "But if we divide up magic based on population, we're back to pagans being the nerdy girl in a locker room full of cheerleaders."

"We're not counting the exiled folk in this equation," Tim said.

Susan frowned and flipped through the notebook. "We don't know how many there are. I don't think they know how many there are, especially given the different types of fair folk, *aos sidhe*, and so forth. How do we divvy up things when we don't know how many are on the winning side?"

"Would it be fair to say our faction got as big a slice of the pie as the Avramites?" Tim brought up a spreadsheet he had been working on. A large pie chart dominated half the sheet. He figured the graphic would make it easier to explain to everyone.

Susan paused to think of an objection before conceding, "Sounds fair enough, assuming you're giving everyone some pie."

"Everyone who wants some," Tim said as he copied data from his tablet to the spreadsheet, the chart updating as he did so. "People who don't want anything to do with magic shouldn't count against the total."

Susan watched the chart. "You realize we still don't know how to measure magic."

"We don't need to know," Tim countered, glancing from the small screen to the large monitor. "We only need to know the proportion of the available pool. Whether the pool is 100 iotas of magic or 10,000 iotas of magic, if the Avramite faction gets 34% and the Exiled faction gets 34%, they are still equal."

"Iotas?" Susan flipped to the front of Liam's notebook.

"It's a Greek letter used to denote an imaginary number," Tim replied. "It seemed like a good placeholder if nothing else."

"You really are a smart kid," Susan said, glancing back at the screen. "Now, we need to figure out how to keep any one individual from holding too much power on the Dunwold."

* * *

Two hours later, Tim hoped they had a workable solution. Though his father wasn't back yet, he was tired, and Susan had complained of a headache. Tim finally relented and announced he was going to bed. Working on the new accords was harder than any homework assignment. At least with homework, questions had correct answers.

Tim's father had warned him, as he got older, he would encounter more questions, both in school and in life, where there wasn't a cut and dry answer. Tim hoped that was still a way off; he preferred having a concrete solution over a compromise he had to justify.

At least Tim and Susan had agreed it was important for Liam to remain the strongest magic-user on the Dunwold. Neither of them thought the trouble would end with the challenge. Someone would have to keep supernatural beings returning to the Dunwold in check, especially those hoping for payback after centuries of exile. Likewise, people flush with the power of newfound magic could be a source of trouble.

Outside, Tim could hear the faint tinkle of the wind chimes scattered around the house. It was half an hour after his father and the others disappeared before the wind spirits had begun circling the building again. Tim wondered if they would kick up a ruckus when his father returned.

* * * * *

Chapter Twenty-Seven

Iblis

"Guess what a little bird told me?"

Iblis rolled his eyes. He hated when Raven played guessing games, making it obvious she knew something he didn't. He suspected his annoyance encouraged her. "Why don't you tell me?"

Raven pouted at his unwillingness to play along and leaned against his desk. She was dressed more conservatively than usual, mostly in black. When she wanted something, she showed more cleavage, but now she had buttoned her black silk blouse to her throat. "According to Potts, Liam showed up at the Pagan Meet-Up a few days ago."

Iblis scowled. His minions should know to bring that kind of information straight to him. Iblis leaned back in his office chair, and carefully keeping his tone calm, asked, "When did he tell you this?"

"He told Orliath, and she told me," Raven replied. She grinned wickedly. "Evidently Donald is sweet on our new witch."

Iblis snorted. Of course he fancied the young witch. Pretty and intelligent, Orliath still emanated a sense of innocence a life-weary man like Potts would find intoxicating. Potts might be less enamored with the young woman if he knew the acts Orliath performed for Iblis. If the stuffy bookworm were more useful, Iblis might have given Orliath the task of stringing the man along. Still, this latest tidbit could prove interesting. By all accounts, Knox eschewed engaging the neo-pagan community; it was one of the factors making it hard to track him down.

"What else did he tell Orliath?" Iblis asked, steepling his fingers. Knox and Mikha'el were pulling more power into the mortal world. What Mikha'el was doing concerned Iblis; the smart play would be to limit mystic energy coming into the mortal world as much as possible. Mikha'el had not stopped after the stunt with the tempest demon, but Iblis could not divine the purpose.

Every time they drew power into the world, it left more energy for Iblis to gather through rites with his witches. Some of the power he shared with the women who served him, the rest he hoarded away. If they continued at this rate, Iblis would need additional vessels to contain the power. His witches were more than empowered lackeys; they served as his batteries. He had to grant them a portion of power, but they didn't realize how much more they stored on his behalf.

After Raven developed her rebellious streak, Iblis had become more conservative in granting his essence, the portion that fueled the witches' magical talents. If he gave his familiar, or the other two witches, too much power, they might think they didn't need Iblis anymore.

Raven checked her glossy black fingernails before answering. "Liam has suddenly become interested in networking, not only with the local community, but with other neo-pagan communities as well."

Why the change, Iblis wondered. To establish a power-base if the *benayim* managed to defeat Giwargix? To pave the way for an influx of the various supernatural folk in exile? Surely, he realized none of his peers among the pagans possessed power like he did; they would be inconsequential from a mystic perspective. "Was he with anyone else?" Iblis asked.

Raven snorted. "The little purple-haired bitch and some witch from a Peoria coven."

"What witch?" Up until now, Knox had been spotted only with his familiar, the champion, and a pair Iblis assumed to be the fae working with the champion. The champion and her allies had dropped off the map. This was the first local connection. "A girlfriend, perhaps?"

Raven shrugged and tugged on her sleeves at her wrists. "Maybe. A buxom brunette, a few years younger; it was obvious they knew each other well. I've never seen him with anyone besides his little familiar." Raven didn't bother to hide her disdain.

Iblis pointed at a map of central Illinois tacked to a chipped and pitted corkboard on the office wall. The map was dotted with colored pins and marked with red circles, all tied to locations regarding Knox. "Considering this is all we have, and he hasn't called me after the dust-up in the cornfield you witnessed, I think it is worth investigating. Have Orliath talk to Potts; he seems eager to impress her. Find out what he knows about Knox's witch friend."

Raven stood and smoothed her long black skirt. "Fine."

Iblis barely watched as Raven left the room, her boot heels clicking on the tile. What was Knox up to? Could this witch be used as leverage? Did Mikha'el's minions know about her? Iblis doubted the last part; Mikha'el could barely bring himself to deal with Nephilim, let alone truck with infidels and heathens. One of his shortcomings was having an impractically narrow worldview.

Iblis would have to find out when the next of these meet-ups occurred. He glanced at the calendar. If they were monthly, there would be one three weeks before the challenge. Who should he have approach Knox? It was obvious Raven wanted to be on point; Iblis hadn't missed how she had taken to referring to the druid by his first name, as though they were familiar.

Raven's presence would automatically set Knox on the defensive and tip Iblis' hand, which left Gypsy or Orliath. Gypsy was much more outgoing and eager to please, not to mention manipulative. However, she might be more likely to arouse suspicion, or in the case of the druid's familiar, jealousy. Orliath was shy, but she was a much better student than Gypsy. Those were traits more likely to make her endearing to the druid and less likely to arouse his faerie familiar's suspicions.

If Raven could get the name of Knox's witch friend, Iblis could set his basement trolls to digging up information on the internet. Hopefully she wasn't as social media adverse as Knox. Perhaps Iblis could persuade the witch to influence Knox. Iblis could always use another witch; he had gathered so much mystical energy, it would behoove him to spread it around more.

There were more brutish ways to use Raven to convince Knox to come to the negotiating table. They would be a last resort; if the druid was outright antagonistic, it would be harder to convince him. The carrot was much more useful, though if it came down to the wire, Iblis had no qualms about employing the stick.

*****

Chapter Twenty-Eight

Erin

"Five months."

Izzy stirred from her reverie in response to Erin's muttering. "What did you say?" Izzy asked. "I was lost in thought."

Erin shifted Skye, who couldn't seem to make up her mind if she wanted to nap or nurse. Erin couldn't blame the baby; it was cold and wet outside. Rain pattered against the metal roof of the Quonset. "It has been five months since Nechtan left to take Elam home."

Izzy nodded, her eyes reflecting the flickering flame from the lantern. Oil lamps and candles took the place of electric lights in Dunos Scaith. When Erin had suggested wind turbines, solar panels, and electric lights, Scathach had been uninterested. The two burning lamps seemed feeble and dim on a day like today.

"He could be back anytime, depending on how much the rain slows him," Izzy said. She had explained how the seasons in the Glaswold reflected in the Dunwold. The weather was more complicated, especially with Scathach's tampering with the flow of time around her holt.

What had started as late summer was slowly progressing toward autumn. At least they would be gone before winter arrived. Erin didn't want to consider being stuck in the Rocky Mountains for an extended winter.

"Unless he is hurrying, he probably won't be back for a couple of weeks." Erin carefully sat up straight, so she could reach her mug of lukewarm coffee without disturbing the baby. At least there were *some* imports from the Dunwold. "Assuming he doesn't decide to go on a walkabout."

Izzy smiled. "I think he has sufficient motivation to return quickly."

"Really?" Erin took a sip of her coffee. It wasn't particularly good, but it was warm and had caffeine. "When he left, we were barely saying two words to each other. I didn't exactly give him cause to rush back."

"You *dynion.*" Izzy chuckled. "Now I think I understand why so many of your television shows revolve around your inability to deal with how you feel about one another. It is quite amusing."

"I'm glad you think it's funny," Erin said, bristling, causing the baby to stir. Erin had to remind herself she wasn't irritated at Izzy; she was annoyed with herself. "I guess I have to figure out what I want."

"Don't take too long," Izzy said. "We've already been here for nearly two years, at least according to the calendar, here, in Dunos Scaith. At this rate, by the time the two of you finish dancing around, it will be time to return to the Dunwold."

Erin sighed, setting her coffee down. "What if I decide to let things proceed with Nechtan? In five years, we go back to the Dunwold. Either I leave him behind, or he comes along, and my life gets more complicated. Plus, the jury is still out on how I feel about Liam."

"Why is it so difficult?" Izzy scoffed. "If you don't want to get romantically entangled, you can still be...what's the term? You can be friends with benefits."

"Do you mean with Nechtan, or Liam?" Erin asked. Outside, there was a metallic ringing, audible over the rain drumming on the roof. "What's that?"

"The alarm," Izzy replied, standing and crossing to the door. Erin heard Izzy mutter, "Thank the gods."

They both went out onto the porch built onto the front of the Quonset hut. The recent wood addition was enough to shelter them from the rain. Guards began running toward the armory in response to the alarm. Mysie, Daidh, and Derek emerged from the hut next door and dashed through the rain to join Izzy and Erin.

"What do you think is going on?" Erin had trouble believing someone would be stupid enough to attack Dunos Scaith, especially given Scathach's reputation. "Who would be stupid enough to attack here?"

A guard skidded to a halt in the wet grass and mud, catching himself on the large table. "Champion! Scathach instructed me to tell you a giant has breached the perimeter of the domain."

"Uthor, dammit," Erin cursed. "How much do you want to bet he is chasing Nechtan?"

The guard seemed confused and shrugged, his wet, cat-like whiskers drooping.

Erin pointed at the rain-soaked man. "Get me two stout spears and meet me at the gate! Go!"

The guard scurried off, slipping in his haste before he gained his footing and dashed through the puddles across the central yard.

Erin turned to Mysie. "Here, take Skye. You and Daidh stay with her." The baby squawked at the commotion and began to cry. Erin quelled the instinctive tug at her heartstrings and went into the hut. Grabbing her sheathed sword, she slid the baldric over her head and attached the sheath to her belt.

She scanned around the dim room, searching for anything else that might be useful against the lumbering beast. The rain ruled out using flaming oil, which was a shame. Erin would rather chase off Uthor than kill him. Behind her, Erin could hear Mysie comforting the infant as the others followed her inside.

"What do they have in the armory?" Erin asked, deciding nothing here would be useful.

"Spears, swords, bows, arrows, shields, helmets, mail shirts," Daidh replied, ticking off the list on his fingers. "A couple of ballistae and ammunition, but those would require getting the giant in range of the wall or somehow rolling them out to him."

"I'll grab a couple of bows and some arrows," Izzy said, ducking out into the rain.

Erin gestured for Derek to follow and led him out toward the gate. The wet ground made it difficult to go faster than a trot. In front of the central keep, Scathach was standing in the rain, giving orders to groups of guards.

"Champion, I have ordered these men to accompany you." Despite her wet, copper tresses plastered to her head and shoulders, Scathach somehow managed to remain regal. A group of six men and women, armed with spears and bows, stood to the side awaiting Erin's instructions. "What's the rope for?" Erin asked the closest of her troops. Each of them had a coil of rope on their belt.

"We thought it might be useful to bring the giant down," the man replied. His cloud-grey eyes betrayed his doubt about the plan.

"Not likely, it would be like a pack of Chihuahua's trying to bring down a German Shepherd." Erin could see the analogy confused all of them. "Uthor would toss us around like dolls. Hang onto the rope though, we might think of a use on the way."

"Good luck," Scathach said.

"I don't suppose you want to come along?" Erin asked, only half jesting. "I'll bet you're pretty good in a fight."

Scathach shook her head. "If only I could, it would be a worthy fight. I must remain in Dunos Scaith."

"I will go, Mother." Uathach stepped out of the keep into the weather. She had a gleaming, barbed spear. At least the chirurgeon had made sure her nose healed straight, Erin thought.

"I do not think it wise," Scathach stated. "Given your friction with the Champion, it might be best if you remain here."

"We can use the extra spear," Erin remarked, hoping she wasn't going to get a spear-blade in the back. "We don't have a lot of time for the whole mother-daughter debate thing, so unless you want to order her not to join us, we should move out."

"Very well," Scathach conceded. "The giant entered the domain from the north, near the entrance to the large ravine. Go."

Erin gestured to the guards and trudged toward the gate. The whiskered guard waited at the fort's entrance, holding two spears. They certainly weren't as impressive as Uathach's weapon, but they would do the job. As she approached, the guard held both spears out toward Erin.

Erin took one of the weapons, carrying it against her shoulder once she was sure there was enough clear space behind her. It wouldn't do to accidently jab one of her own troops. "Thanks. What's your name?"

"Riogan," he replied once he got over his surprise.

"You're carrying the other spear, Riogan," Erin said. When she spotted his trepidation, she realized he must be a newer guard. "Don't worry, I need you to carry it for me; it's awkward trying to carry two at once. I'm sure they haven't covered giant-slaying 101 in your training yet."

Riogan shook his head and laughed nervously as he fell into step with the rest of the group. One of the other guards muttered, "I don't think they covered giant-slaying for any of us."

The group trudged out of the gates, curving north around the fort before finding a navigable slope downhill. The weather had made footing treacherous; rivulets of water cascaded down the mountain alongside them as the troops picked their way down the slope. Erin wanted to urge everyone to hurry, but she knew they were more likely to be delayed by falls and injuries than gain any time.

Erin and Uathach led the formation, both women using the butts of their spears to control their descent. Erin recognized the path from her journey to retrieve Elam. She hoped Nechtan would use the same route this time. It made sense unless he chose the much harder option of crossing the mountain ridge farther to the north and paralleling the ridgeline.

Once the ground levelled, they were able to pick up the pace. Erin tried not to wonder how long Nechtan could outrun the giant's huge strides. It would normally take six hours to reach the edge of the domain. It had been thirty minutes since the alarm sounded. Erin tried to guess where the two parties were likely to meet; it reminded her of Tim's math homework.

"Do you want us to scout ahead?" Izzy asked. "My brother and I have had experience in the mountains, and he's part goat."

Erin nodded. "Don't get too far ahead."

The twins moved forward, splitting in different directions with Derek veering upslope while Izzy drifted downhill. Erin wished they had radios; the rain cut down on visibility and muffled noise.

They had been hiking for ninety minutes when a rumbling bellow shook the ground. The precipitation slowed to a drizzle, and they risked picking up the pace even more. There was a piercing whistle from high up, toward the ridge. A dark shape loomed in the mist. As everyone readied their spears, a smaller form emerged from the precipitation.

"Nechtan!" Erin called out. She resisted the urge to run toward him; it would cause disarray in the formation as the others tried to figure out whether to follow her or stay put.

The huntsman ran toward them, increasing his pace now that allies were within sight. Behind him, the giant limped into view. Several arrows jutted from his right knee. Uthor roared and slammed the tree he bore as a weapon on the ground. The impromptu club posed a problem. It was long enough for the giant to strike them without being in reach of their spears.

"I should have known you'd come," Nechtan wheezed. He glanced over his shoulder. "The brute's been chasing me for two hours. I thought I lost him when I crossed, but something possessed him to crawl into the entry."

The giant slowed his approach, now that he faced a number of opponents who weren't fleeing. Erin considered it a good sign; perhaps they could deter the monster instead of fighting him.

"How far are we from the downhill perimeter of the domain?" Erin asked, not taking her eyes off Uthor. The giant had come to a halt and glared at them with beady eyes.

"I'd reckon two miles," Nechtan replied, his breathing still labored. "If you're thinking of leading him out, you'd need to find a way back in. It'd have to be a path he couldn't follow."

Uathach scoffed. "We should kill the brute and be done with him. Or are you afraid, Champion?"

"Damn straight I'm afraid. Only an idiot wouldn't be afraid of something like Uthor." Erin resisted the urge to glare at Uathach. "Everyone with spears, spread out. If he decides to rush us, I don't want people tripping over each other to try to get out of the way."

The soldiers moved apart, and the giant swept his gaze over the group. He is probably trying to figure out what we are up to, Erin thought. Uthor squinted, his eyes flicking from person to person.

"So now what, we bore him to death?" Uathach complained.

"If you're so eager to get your head bashed in, be my guest," Erin retorted. The giant snorted at her raised voice. She lowered her voice and hoped Uthor didn't understand English. "I don't suppose there are any convenient cliffs we could trick him over?"

Nechtan hadn't moved away from Erin when the others spread out. "Not this low on the slopes," he replied. "There's a ravine up by the caves, but we'd have to lead him back the other way for a mile."

"Enough of this." Uathach stepped forward, brandished her spear, and yelled at the giant in the Gaelic-based patois the Exiled

Folk used. Erin could make out the gist; it was an order for the dumb brute to leave.

Uthor glowered at Uathach, rainwater running down his sloped brow. Erin didn't know if the giant had understood the imperious redhead's command, but his rage returned. The towering hulk lumbered forward and bellowed, arching its club overhead, like a humongous game of whack-a-mole. Wood splintered, and mud splattered from the impact where Uathach had stood; she lunged forward, jabbing Uthor in his ponderous belly as she slipped past and behind him.

The Fomorian howled in anger, spinning to follow his attacker. The tree trunk followed in a spray of rain and debris, moving faster than Erin would have thought possible for something so huge, but Uathach danced out of its path. Two guards stepped forward and stabbed at the giant's exposed back. Uthor bellowed again as blood trickled from the wounds.

The giant reached back with one hand, keeping the club in the other. The guards scrambled away, one losing his spear as the behemoth snagged it and snapped the haft. Uathach aborted another lunge when Uthor batted at her with the club. It reminded Erin of a bullfight she had seen. Picadors had surrounded the enraged animal. They jabbed and poked the beast, both incensing it and weakening it. It was a cruel way to kill something.

Another guard sprung forward, driving his spear into Uthor's flank. When the giant twisted, the weapon was torn from the warrior's grasp. He tried to backpedal but slipped in the mud, regaining his footing just in time for the backhanded swing with the club to catch him square in the chest. With a sickening crunch, the impact launched the hapless man through the air like a ragdoll.

Uathach struck again, her spear tip sinking into the giant's flabby gut as she dashed through his reach. The giant's outstretched hand snagged her cloak, but she twisted out of the garment. As soon as the club was in motion, Erin made her move. Choking up on the spear, she rammed it into the back of the giant's foot, above his heel. The foot-long blade sank all the way, the point barely emerging through the other side. Wrenching the weapon, she severed the Achilles tendon.

Uathach's scream shook the ground as his leg buckled. Erin abandoned the spear and dashed out of the flailing giant's reach. The tree-club bounced down the slope, bowling the legs out from under an unlucky guard. Uthor slammed into the dirt, dislodging rocks and mud.

The giant slapped the ground, roaring in fury. He swatted at a guard who tried to jab him, only to get stabbed from the other side. Howling in pain, he rolled to his knees, fumbling in the mud in a failed effort to stand. Blood from his wounds joined the rainwater cascading down the slope.

Erin took the second spear from Riogan and circled until she was in front of Uthor. The giant glared at her, its breathing like a laboring steam engine. She hefted the spear; her ancestor was legendary for his prowess with the weapon, a weapon she had been practicing with daily for a year and a half.

"If this was a children's tale, this would be the part where I spare you, and we become friends," Erin said, adjusting her stance to allow for the rain-slickened ground. "We'd nurse you back to health, and you'd show up in the third act to help me out.

"It's a pity things don't really work like they do in the stories. The best I can do is try to give you a quicker death than bleeding out on a hillside in the rain." Erin took two steps forward, putting all her weight into the throw. The spear soared true, the weapon burying itself in the giant's eye to the haft.

Thunder accompanied the giant's howl. One hand clawed for the weapon, the other slipped in the mud. Uthor fell forward and the butt of the spear struck the ground, the weapon sinking in further until the wooden haft snapped.

The giant rolled onto his back, still feebly pawing at his wounded eye. After a long minute, his arm sagged to the ground, and Uthor let out one last, long groan. Overhead thunder rumbled.

*****

Chapter Twenty-Nine

Liam

"Pocking too close for comfort."

Liam nodded, agreeing with Einar as he took in their surroundings. The shape of the hills was the same, but everything seemed more vibrant. The sun blazed overhead, and a smattering of white clouds dotted the sky. "Any chance it can follow us?"

"Not likely," Pixel replied. She put a hand on Liam's shoulder. "How do you feel?"

"He is not the one carrying a huge lump of metal," Gofannon rumbled, dumping the meteorite in the dirt.

Liam took a moment before answering. "Winded, but I don't know how much was from opening a doorway between worlds and how much was from outrunning a homicidal angel." He checked around again. There were no signs of civilization; where he should have been able to glimpse the road was a thin spot in the trees. "Any reason we can't take a breather here?"

"Not too pocking long," Einar replied, eyeing the woods suspiciously. "We're still in a foreign land."

"Right." Liam sat down on a fallen tree. A refreshing breeze whirled around him. Despite the autumn temperatures, running up the hill had left him sweating. Liam wondered if the Slavic gods and their associated supernatural creatures walked this part of the Glaswold. He didn't know as much about the mythology of this region as he would like, especially given the circumstances.

"Here, drink this and finish the orange." Pixel handed him a bottle of water. "As soon as you feel ready, take us home."

Liam opened the water and took a long drink. "Don't I need a keystone?"

"You are the keystone," Pixel replied. "You're attuned to your dolmen. Luckily, it's hard to find from the Glaswold because of the obfuscation around your home. We had to use a wold-ford several miles north of Peoria. We slipped over from the corresponding spot on the Glaswold to keep from making enough noise to draw attention."

"Won't jaunting us back put a bulls-eye on my house?" Liam asked between bites of orange. He didn't want a visit from a seraphim or worse. "It didn't take long for that angel to hunt us down."

"They were pocking quick on the trigger," Einar conceded, stroking his beard. "Not only did you ring a huge pocking bell, you also sat around beating on a drum for a while."

Gofannon squatted over the meteorite, brushing off chinks of dirt. "When we return to the druid's home, we should not wait around outside. Einar, be ready to help the druid; I will have my hands full carrying the meteorite."

It seemed like a good plan, Liam thought. Hopefully, since he knew what to expect, he wouldn't end up in a heap and have to be carried. Something caught Liam's attention while he finished devouring the orange. "I didn't see a house before," he said.

"There shouldn't be any pocking houses." Einar turned to follow Liam's gaze. "Shit. Thor smite me for a fool. Druid, we need to leave."

Liam didn't see what was so alarming about the house. He could make out the crest of a wood-shingled roof and a smoking stone chimney. "It doesn't seem like much. Maybe if we don't mess with them—"

The house moved. They heard the crunching of the undergrowth and the cracking of branches snapped aside as the chimney bobbed and drifted toward the downhill path. The wind fell still as the zephyrs fled.

"Druid, what the dwarf said." Gofannon hefted the metallic lump and stood. "We need to go."

Liam stood and planted his staff on the ground. Downslope, the cottage lurched into view. It resembled a small ramshackle single-room house, with a wooden porch across the front. Under the building were a pair of massive, skeletal legs, the bones entwined with vines and iron wire. The limbs reminded Liam of a tyrannosaurus skeleton. The cottage turned and began striding uphill toward them.

Liam tried to push aside the distraction, and he reached out for the magical energy flowing through the earth. As before, the weave of magic was much stronger than on the mundane world. Liam began gathering it, only to have the web facing the oncoming hut run dry.

An old woman emerged onto the porch, clutching the bannister to steady herself against the house's lurching gait. Long, black fingernails dug into the wooden railing; Liam realized the columns supporting the rail were bones.

"She's messing with the *Gwuedd*," Liam whispered. "I can't pull together enough power to open the ford."

"You going somewhere?" The crone croaked. Her smile bared iron-grey teeth. "We think not."

Liam knew he couldn't return them to the Dunwold in Russia. The enforcer angel likely would still be prowling, eager for some payback.

Einar took a few steps toward the cottage, puffed up his chest, and said something to the crone, but Liam could only pick up a couple of words or cognates in Russian.

The old woman did not seem impressed. "We know who you are." She pointed a bony finger at Liam. "We know he is *drujid*."

"Then you know how important it is to let him go," Einar countered, switching to English. "The Challenge approaches."

The grin spread further across the hag's face, exposing an unsettlingly large maw. "Important to you, us not so much. We know you intend to leave us stuck in *Bogsvar* while you west-folk return to *Zempol*."

"To be honest, we hadn't discussed you," Liam said, drawing an alarmed expression from Pixel and Einar. "If you don't let us go home, you're stuck in *Bogsvar* for sure."

The old woman ran her tongue over her teeth and glowered at Liam. "We cannot trust *drujid*." She pointed a bony finger at Pixel. "Leave the little girl with us. We return her when we walk the fields of men again."

Liam could feel Pixel huddle against him. He didn't think this was one of the purple-haired girl's attempts to manipulate him; she was genuinely afraid. Liam put his free arm around her protectively. Wind rustled the grass as Liam proclaimed, "No, she's not staying."

"Let me play hostage, Druid," Einar said. "You need your familiar; all I do is putter around the kitchen."

Before Liam could protest, the witch snorted. "We do not want the dwarf. We want something of value."

"I'm not leaving someone behind," Liam said. "We really don't have anything of value."

"Give us the sky-rock," the old woman countered. The cottage impatiently shuffled its feet.

"How about half the sky-rock?" Liam countered. He caught Gofannon's nod out of the corner of his eye. There was far more metal than they needed; they could spare some. "We need some of it, or you stay stuck."

"Half the sky-rock and a bone." The unnatural grin split the hag's face again. "A *drujid* bone."

"You want one of my bones?" Liam asked, despite knowing the answer. "I need them."

The hag wiped a hand across cracked lips. "Not all of them. You give one to us; we bring it back when we walk *Zempol*."

Liam didn't like where this was going, but he didn't see any other choice. He'd tried drawing on the *Gwuedd* during the discussion, but it was like trying to catch water with a colander. Any magical energy he tried to draw dispersed before it reached him. "Fine. My pinky toe."

The old woman snorted. "Toes are too easy. Give us a thumb."

"I need my thumbs to smith a sword." Liam held up the pinky finger on his right hand. "The last bone in this finger."

"We will take the bone, but other hand," the witch countered.

"Liam, are you sure you want to do this?" Pixel whispered.

"No, but I don't see a better idea." Liam nodded to the crone. "Agreed."

The old woman chuckled; it sounded like gravel on a chalk board. "Come closer, *drujid*. We will take our bone."

Liam stepped forward, hoping his legs wouldn't shake. The hut squatted down and tipped forward. The woman descended to the lowest step. Liam expected the hag to brandish a cleaver or knife to chop off the end of his finger. Instead she seized his left hand in an iron grip.

"This hurt, *drujid*," the crone snarled, her breath foul with sour milk and rotting meat. "Remember hurt, if *drujid* betray us we use bone to bring more pain."

Liam felt something move inside his finger. The tugging sensation became a tearing one as the distal phalange bone in his pinky finger slowly tore loose from the cartilage in the joint. Liam couldn't keep from screaming in pain as tendon fibers ripped away from the bone, and then the bone began to push through his fingertip. A red dot appeared on the end of his finger before it split open. Covered in blood, the bone poked out, slowly wriggling out of the flesh.

Tears streamed down Liam's face as the bone slid from the ruptured digit; his nerves felt like they were on fire. With a sickening pop, the bone plopped into the hag's waiting palm. She sniffed it, and for a moment, Liam thought she was going to lick it, or worse eat it.

"Much magic." The old woman released her grip on Liam's wrist, and stuffed the bone in a pocket of her apron. "We keep safe, bring back to *drujid*."

Liam clutched the bleeding finger, both in pain and to stem the flow of blood. He heard the tearing of cloth, and Pixel was back at his side with a makeshift bandage. Part of Liam's mind made a note to include a first aid kit on any future forays into the Glaswold.

"The other part of bargain." The old woman glared at Gofannon. "Give us half of star-rock."

"As soon as you quit choking off the flow of magic," Gofannon boomed. "It is no easy task to split this stone, even for me."

The hag's eyes shifted back to Liam, then she nodded, satisfied Liam was in no shape to mount a hasty escape. "Very well," she said.

Liam felt magic flow through the land beneath his feet. He wished there was a way to channel it to close his wound and deaden the pain. The bandage Pixel had tied around the end of the digit was already soaked in blood.

Gofannon grunted with exertion and there was a loud, metallic snap. The meteorite fell into two halves from the smith-god's grasp. Gofannon hefted one of the halves and eyed the witch. Liam suspected the Welsh god was tempted to test the hag's defenses against a hundred pounds of meteoric iron.

"Give her what we bargained," Liam rasped through clenched teeth.

Gofannon frowned and chucked the half meteor onto the cottage porch. The structure rocked with the impact; the old woman clutched the railing to keep from pitching into the grass. Once the house righted itself, she picked up the grey and rust lump in her bony fingers. She handled it as easily as Gofannon.

"Bargained well and done," the hag said. "We will see you again, *drujid*." The house turned on pacing skeletal feet and marched down the hill.

Liam picked up his staff and walked slowly to the wold-ford. "The good news is I no longer care about my feet hurting."

Pixel put a hand on his arm. "Are you going to be able to open the way home?"

Liam nodded and tried not to grimace. "Someone might need to catch me when we arrive."

*****

Chapter Thirty

Erin

"There's nothing glorious about killing giants!"

The guard froze under Erin's glowering gaze. "My apologies, Champion. I meant to commend your prowess."

"She knows you did, Riogan," Nechtan interjected. "It has been a rough day."

The guard nodded and scurried away from Erin's glare. Erin spun and affixed Nechtan with an angry stare.

"I know you don't need me talking for you," Nechtan said and began to walk toward the Quonset huts. He and Erin had come to the mess hall to pick up dinner for the group and were carrying their food back when the young guard off-handedly complimented Erin. "You bit the poor lad's head off; I didn't want you to make him cry."

Even though a month had passed since killing Uthor, it was still a sore subject for Erin. "I feel bad enough about what happened to Uthor, not to mention the guard who died." Erin hadn't known the man who died fighting Uthor. Most of the guards weren't part of her daily life; they were figures on the wall or in line for chow. She followed Nechtan; it was hard to argue with his back. "I don't see why people act like I'm some sort of hero for putting the dumb brute down."

Nechtan looked over his shoulder. "Bards and story-tellers consider giants to be epic foes, worthy of song and tale. Plus, it probably makes the lad feel better knowing his friend died fighting a worthy foe, as opposed to a simple brute."

"Anyone could have done the same," Erin protested. She had avoided the subject for the past month, mostly out of guilt and embarrassment. "All the troops here train constantly, especially with the spear. I'm not some sort of supernatural being like Uathach, or the twins, or…"

"Or me?" Nechtan finished. Rounding the corner of the keep, the Quonset huts came into view ahead. The rest of their ad hoc clan waited at the table by the fire pit, Mysie amusing Skye. "You are, at least in the same way as Skye's father."

Erin snorted, covering up her surprise that Nechtan had mentioned Liam. "Liam is a druid, some sort of wizard. I'm just a soldier with a temper."

"There is more than one kind of magic," Nechtan said. "Not all of it is calling storms or turning the sea to stone. The feats your ancestor performed were beyond the ken of mortal men, even before the bards got hold of the tales. You're not Champion merely because Cu Chulainn is your ancestor; you're Champion because you also inherited his uncanny talent as a warrior. You need to keep learning how to harness it."

Before Erin could make a counter-point, Skye saw her and squealed happily. "Mama!"

"Hello, little girl!" Erin's annoyance dissipated. She set the heavy tray of food on the table, leaving the others to find their meals, while she took a cup of mashed turnips and potatoes soaked in gravy and sat next to the baby. "Are you hungry?"

The child clapped her hands and watched the cup as Erin set it down. "Ith! Ith!" the baby called.

Erin hoped the mélange of languages Skye was exposed to wouldn't be a problem later. Though Scathach had used a charm to let Erin understand those around her in Dunos Scaith, Erin worked on learning the common patois, Goidelc, a simplified dialect of Old Irish heavily peppered with loan words from other languages. A speaker could intentionally exclude their speech from the charm, though most didn't know or didn't bother. The converse was true as well; the magic rendered Erin's English understandable to people around her, unless she concentrated on her words only coming out in English.

As a result, Erin had to focus on speaking English to Skye, so the infant would learn English words. Fortunately, the others in the group usually spoke English to the baby, but occasionally other languages would slip through, predominantly Goidelc. Hence "Eat!" became "Ith!" At least she had four and a half years to sort out her daughter's language before they returned to the Dunwold.

Erin spent most of dinner dodging Skye's attempts to grab the spoon and cup, finally able to eat once she had surrendered the empty cup to the child.

"Don't drink too much ale," Mysie chided Daidh. "It will be a long night on watch; if you fall asleep you'll be on the moon watch another week."

Daidh smiled over his cup. "You'll have to keep me up."

Derek chuckled, and Mysie pointed an accusing finger at him. "You're a bad influence on my *leannain.* Besides, my keeping him up that way would get us both on moon watch for another week."

A single chime sounded high up on the keep, signaling it was half an hour until the next bell. "Well, we should finish up, it's almost ten bells," Daidh said, polishing off his drink. The fort kept time using bells mounted in the keep's single tower. They chimed every two hours, sounding once for every two hours after midnight, and ringing a single note half an hour before the next bell. The main purpose was to notify guard shifts and sound the start of meals from the mess.

Mysie used a hunk of bread to sop up the last of her stew. "Have fun sleeping, you lot. We'll try not to be too loud when we get off."

Derek smirked and raised an eyebrow.

"Off our shift, you Spanish sheep buggerer," Mysie sputtered.

"I'm Gaelic, not Spanish," Derek countered, still grinning.

Daidh took Mysie's hand. "Come on, we need to get kitted up. You could spend the next bell sparring with him."

Mysie hurriedly collected empty plates, bowls, and cups onto one of the trays, shaking her head. "We'll drop this off at the mess on our way to the armory." While they had their own armor and weapons, they drew a spear and ammunition from the armory, as did the other guards. At the end of their shift, they would return it.

After the pair left, Derek stood and picked up his cup. "If you'll excuse me, I'm going to pay a visit to the keep."

Izzy shook her head. "Really, brother? Didn't you learn your lesson last time you dallied with Saidhe?"

"Last time is water under the bridge," Derek replied, still grinning. "Besides, we are merely swapping tales over a few cups of mead. Nothing for you to worry about, Sister."

"Don't do anything you'll regret for the next four years," Izzy said.

Derek sauntered away. "Regret isn't in my vocabulary," he called back.

Izzy quaffed the remaining ale in her cup. "Even though it is early, I am going to call it a night. The shadowcats watching over Dunos Scaith from the Murkwold have reported suspicious activity at the edges of their purview. Scathach is increasing the patrols around the perimeter of the domain."

Erin looked up from giving Skye a drink. "Shadowcat? Why does that sound familiar?"

"The Druid saved one during our journey through the Murkwold," Izzy replied, placing her empty cup on the other tray. "It is one of the sentinels of this place and now owes him a boon."

"One of the shadowcats is indebted to your druid?" Nechtan remarked and refilled his mug from the pitcher of ale. He had been quiet since the meal began. "They do not place themselves in debt easily."

"He's not my druid." Erin managed to distract Skye and add the cup the child had been happily banging on the table to the tray. The baby's deep blue eyes reminded Erin of Liam's left eye. Erin quelled a twinge of guilt. "I should put the baby to bed."

Nechtan sloshed the pitcher he had poured from. "There's a bit left here, and we still have a full one in the other," he said. "I guess everyone else is being a lightweight tonight."

Erin scooped up Skye. "Let me put the baby down, and I'll see if I can help make sure none of it goes to waste." She resisted the urge to peek and see if Nechtan was watching her. Erin knew he did when he didn't think she would see. It wasn't the lascivious leer she remembered from customers at the bar. There was admiration in his gaze, though she occasionally caught a glint of hunger in his piercing blue eyes, which would make butterflies flutter in her chest.

Imagining it now brought back the butterflies, but Erin pushed the feeling aside to focus on getting the baby settled in for the night. Skye yawned and rubbed her eyes with the back of her fists.

"I will listen for the baby," Izzy whispered from the door to her room, her eyes reflecting the dim light like a cat's.

Erin collected the baby's clothes from the day and deposited them in the hamper. In the morning, they would be on the side table, cleaned and folded. A small army of brownies formed an unseen contingent in Dunos Scaith, attending to the housekeeping of the fortress. Erin had never seen one and had been warned not to call out to the diminutive fairies.

Erin slid the door to the baby's room shut. "I thought you had to get rested for your patrol?"

"I do," Izzy replied. "But I can be a light sleeper, and Skye usually sleeps through the night."

Erin raised an eyebrow skeptically. She had the feeling she was being set up. A few butterflies took wing. "Did you send Derek off as well?"

Izzy smiled and replied, "My brother did not need much prodding."

"Did Nechtan put you up to this?" Erin wasn't sure what she wanted the answer to be.

Izzy shook her head. "For such a skilled hunter, Nechtan has done a poor job of pursuing you. Perhaps he fears offending you; your people are known to be hung up on matters involving sex."

Erin remembered Izzy admitting to having been with Nechtan and resisted the urge to ask about it. "In a few years, we are going home," Erin said. "He probably won't want to come with us, and I still don't know—"

"In four years you will face Gwigarix in battle," Izzy interrupted. "Don't let those years be lonely because you don't know what will happen next. Enjoy what happens now."

Erin glanced toward the front door, its window illuminated by firelight. A shadow passed in front of the window; she hoped Nechtan hadn't given up on her returning.

"You've been attracted to Nechtan from the moment you met him," Izzy prodded. "Are your feelings for Liam holding you back?"

"I told Liam we weren't a couple," Erin replied quickly. So why was she holding back? It had been two years since she dashed Liam's romantic notions. By now, he had surely moved on, likely with Pixel. Two weeks, Erin reminded herself. In the mundane world, only a couple of weeks had passed. She'd had this argument with herself countless times since arriving in the Glaswold.

Izzy shook her head. "Were you trying to convince him or yourself?"

Erin walked to the door and stopped, her hand on the handle. Devil bears, seraphim, and giants hadn't frightened her, but her knees trembled at the thought of walking out the door. The butterflies swarmed again as she pulled on the handle and stepped into the cool, night air. Nechtan was at the end of one of the benches, watching the fire, silhouetted by its glow.

Nechtan half turned, his profile visible in the firelight. "I was beginning to think you had gone to bed as well."

Erin sat on the other bench, across the table from Nechtan, and pulled the full ale pitcher toward her. "I seem to remember promising to help you keep this from going to waste." She found her cup and filled it, then held the pitcher out toward the hunter. "Do you need topping off?"

He smiled and reached for the pitcher. His teeth weren't toothpaste-commercial-white like the twins', but he had an honest and healthy smile. "How can I say no?" His hand brushed Erin's as he took the pitcher, his fingers lingering on hers for a moment.

They drank the first round in silence, both watching the flames as the fire began to dwindle.

After sipping from her second mug of ale, Erin found her voice. "Can I ask you something?"

"Absolutely," Nechtan replied and took a long gulp, as though in preparation.

"I know you slept with Izzy before I came here." Erin tried to hide the steadying breath. "Why haven't you since she's been back?"

Nechtan stood and walked to Erin's side of the table, sitting next to her on the wooden bench, his back to the table. He finished his drink and set the cup down. "A poor hunter takes the first shot that presents itself." He refilled his ale, his leather vest creaking as he reached across the table. "A skilled hunter waits for the perfect shot."

"I'm not some deer to be bagged," Erin retorted archly. "I'm not some trophy to mount on your wall or bedpost."

The hunter ran his free hand across his stubbled chin. "I didn't mean…I am not a bard or skald; I don't have a way with words," he said. "Could I have bedded Izquierda? Probably, but I knew it would ruin any chance I had with you, and I knew I wanted a chance with you."

Erin peered down into her half-empty mug. While there wasn't much to see, her other senses heightened. She could smell the mix of leather and the day's sweat on him, plus the smoke wafting from the fire. The heat from her own fire stirred up, driving away the butterflies. Through the chilly autumn air, she could feel the heat of his presence next to her.

"Why have you waited so long?" Erin asked. She knew the ale was fueling the fire; maybe it was the push she needed. "Is it the baby?"

"You did have your hands full," Nechtan answered. He affixed Erin with his piercing blue eyes. "More importantly, you had to admit you were ready."

Erin took a drink, willing the alcohol to batter down her overwrought inhibitions. With all she had been through, and all she was facing, she deserved a little happiness. "You waited a year and a half? Given the chance, I probably would have jumped you long ago."

Nechtan chuckled, still keeping his eyes on her. "A good hunter is patient. I know you are no one's trophy; I merely meant to say I am patient."

Erin finished her ale then took Nechtan's mug and set both cups on the table. She leaned forward and kissed him. The first kiss was tentative; the ones that followed grew in passion and duration. Her fingers entwined in his hair above the back of his neck; his hand started at her waist and slid up her tunic.

"Wait," Erin panted, breaking for air. Nechtan appeared disappointed, probably afraid she had gotten cold feet. She leaned close and whispered, "We shouldn't be giving the guards on the wall a show."

Nechtan stood and offered Erin his hand. He said, "By some coincidence, I have my hut to myself."

Erin allowed him to pull her up from the bench and followed him toward his Quonset, enjoying the view as he walked in front of her. The door had barely closed before they were kissing again.

"There is one thing I have to ask," she breathed in his ear, as their embraced steps took them toward what she presumed was his bedroom.

"What is that?" Nechtan responded, his hand sliding up her back under her tunic.

"How the heck do you get those leather pants off?" Her fingers slid down to punctuate her question, tugging on a lace.

Nechtan kissed her on the neck as he led her through an open doorway, then slid the door closed behind them. "Let me show you how it works."

* * * * *

Chapter Thirty-One

Lee

"I'm sick of bookstores."

Lee glanced down at Qashmet. "I can't leave you in the truck," Lee said as they walked across the gravel parking lot. "Some vegan liberal would break the windows and call the cops, even if I left it running with the air on." Summer hadn't given up yet, and while the heat wasn't stifling, it was enough to elevate the temperature inside a parked vehicle.

Qashmet made the chuffing noise, the equivalent of a canine laugh. "This is the third bookstore we've checked out today. Let's check out the crappy bar across the street, maybe they have some food."

Bishop's Bar and Grill didn't look appealing. The worn brick building had a handful of beat up cars and trucks in the parking lot, and it seemed like a vagrant was sleeping, or more likely passed out, next to the front steps. "We'll get dinner after this, but not in some dive. Remember what happened when you ate those greasy street tacos."

"Oh!" A woman had rounded the corner from the bookstore's entrance and nearly collided with Pastor Haskins. She took a step back, startled by the near collision, as fliers fluttered to the gravel. "I'm sorry; I almost walked right into you and your dog."

"No harm done, Miss." Lee gave her a disarming smile. "I was arguing with my dog over our dinner plans."

She laughed and squatted down, giving Qashmet a clear view of her abundant cleavage as she picked up the scattered papers. "I think you should listen to what he says about the street tacos," she said, using the voice people often did when addressing dogs as though they were children in fur suits. "All that grease isn't good for doggies."

Lee averted his gaze. While the brunette was attractive, in a hippie-chic sort of way, Lee wasn't interested in prurient distractions. "Maybe he'll listen to you," Lee remarked, once the woman stood back up. "Lord knows he won't listen to me."

The woman laughed, waved to Qashmet, and continued toward the parking lot.

Qashmet watched her retreat. "I can't wait until I'm on two legs."

Lee sighed, opening the door to the bookstore, grateful he was the only one who could hear the dog. Unfortunately, Lee didn't have the same luxury when replying, so he couldn't scold Qashmet as he padded past Lee into the store.

"Hey, they have muffins." Qashmet trotted toward the small café, which was little more than a handful of tables, a glass counter, and a couple of commercial coffee machines.

Lee stepped briskly after the dog. "Don't run off!"

Qashmet stopped and stared back at Lee, giving him puppy-dog eyes.

"I told you we'd get dinner next." Lee was grateful that people thought dog owners who spoke to their pets as though the animal understood were only considered slightly eccentric.

"Sir, you can't have a dog in here." The balding, portly man marched out from the back of the store, adjusting his tie. "It's against company policy to allow pets in the store."

Lee studied the approaching man, getting both his and the company's name from the nametag affixed to his button-up shirt. "Am I to take it Word Nerds doesn't adhere to ADA guidelines?" Lee made a point to obviously peer at the nametag. "Am I correct, Clark?"

"Wait, what?" The manager's eyes bugged slightly behind his glasses. "Health code and company rules—"

"Should I contact the county first?" Lee interrupted. "Maybe the media first; you have a newspaper and television news here in Peoria, right? Or would you prefer I contact your corporate office and tell them you refused to admit a customer's service animal?"

Clark sputtered in his haste to protest. "Service animal?"

Lee took on an apologetic tone. "I forgot, he's not wearing his vest right now. He had surgery recently, and the vest chafes his stitches." Qashmet obligingly turned so the scar and stitches were visible through the fuzz of regrown fur. "So, do I need to call your corporate office, Mister…?"

"Hayes," Clark responded automatically. "There's no need to go to any trouble. I'm sorry, I didn't realize your dog was a service animal."

Lee smiled and twitched his eye for effect. "He warns me of impending seizures, usually brought on by stress." For good measure, Lee did it again.

The theatrics were not lost on the manager, who lowered his voice. "Kenna, please give this gentleman whatever he wants from the café. My apologies, sir." Clark adjusted his tie after receiving a confirming nod from Kenna and scurried back toward the rear of the store.

Lee stepped to the counter where a pierced and tattooed coed appeared to be enjoying her boss being taken down a notch.

"What can I get for you, sir?" The girl smiled, probably more from amusement than for customer service.

Lee tried not to wonder what would happen if she ever decided to take the large metal rings out of her earlobes. "A plain black coffee for me, please, and a muffin for my service dog."

The girl nodded. "Coming right up."

Lee scanned around the store. A pair of college students ignored each other across a table in favor of their phones. Half a dozen customers browsed the aisles comprised of mismatched tall bookshelves. Dusty signs suspended from the ceiling denoted book categories.

"Here you go." The pierced girl set the coffee and a blueberry muffin on the counter. "Let me know if you need anything else."

Lee tucked a couple of dollar bills into the tip jar. He guessed a small business like this couldn't afford to pay their employees well. It was a miracle they endured their boss instead of walking out the door. Lee picked up the tokens of the manager's apology. "Thank you."

Qashmet licked his chops as he followed Lee to the table farthest from the door. "Come on, Collar. They'll have to put down a wet floor sign if you leave me drooling much longer."

Lee resisted the urge to laugh and opened the wrapper around the muffin before setting it on the floor. As the dog greedily devoured his prize, Lee took a sip of coffee. Slightly oily and bitter, he was glad it was free. He set the coffee down and retrieved his tablet from his shoulder bag. The tablet's cover bore evidence of Qashmet's handling, tooth marks pocking the faux leather.

Might as well take advantage of the free wifi while I drink my free coffee, Lee thought. Their attempts at locating the druid through the champion's son hadn't yielded any leads. In a way, Lee found it assuring that school administrators were reluctant to share information with a random person claiming to be the mother's pastor. He had been able to eliminate half the potential schools through replies which boiled down to, "we don't have a student by that name." Unfortunately, the other half did due diligence and replied, "we cannot provide any information without parental consent" which left several schools as potential leads.

Lee was loath to visit the remaining schools in person. He had a picture of the boy but lurking outside watching students depart might draw attention. He went back to digging through websites, poring over listings for student councils, drama clubs, and athletic teams. It was time consuming, but it might pay off without risking suspicion.

"Hey, Collar." The dog had finished the muffin in short order and had been waiting under the table. "Check out the flyer on the bulletin board."

Lee looked up from his tablet and spotted the bulletin board mounted on the wall. Setting down his tablet, he went to the board, which was covered in an array of notices. They ran the gamut of everything from babysitters to study groups. Next to a request for players for a game was a notice announcing a pagan meet-up. The last leaflet caught Lee's eye. The woman in the parking lot had dropped the same flyers.

Lee retrieved his tablet, aware one of the youths at the other table had been eyeing the unattended device. Lee brought up the camera and focused on the notice, snapping a clear picture. With the photo on the screen, he took the tablet to the counter. "Excuse me, Miss. I don't suppose you know anything about this flyer?"

The girl stopped cleaning and peered at the image. She obviously recognized it, her eyes going to the bulletin board. "Sure, it's some sort of new age religion meet and greet our old assistant manager is putting together."

"Your old assistant manager? Didn't this notice go up today?" Lee asked. "Was the lady who posted these the druid_knox@illinet.com listed at the bottom?"

The barista shook her head. "That's Liam Knox; he was our assistant manager until a few weeks ago," Kenna answered. She glanced back toward the rear of the store. "He was a much better boss than Clark. Rumor has it he came into some money and went off the grid. It was his friend, maybe girlfriend, who put up the flyer."

Lee sensed this was a huge breakthrough. He could pin down this druid for Mikha'el and not have to worry about Christine's health. They could grow old together. "By chance, do you know how I could find Mr. Knox or his friend?"

The girl behind the counter shrugged. "Sorry. Your best bet is the meet-up the flyer is advertising. Liam hasn't been around since he picked up his last check."

Lee plied her with a smile. "How about his friend? Any idea where I could find her?"

"Sorry." Kenna shrugged again. "She used to come in here when Liam was working, but I have no idea how to find her. Like Clark told those folks a few weeks ago, no one knows where Liam lives."

"Sounds like Mr. Knox is pretty popular," Lee commented, hoping a stray detail might surface to give him a clue. "I take it the other people seeking Liam went away empty-handed?"

The young woman nodded. "Yeah. The lady had Clark eating out of the palm of her hand, but there wasn't anything Clark could tell her or the creepy guy with her."

"Creepy guy?" Lee asked. Could this be a lead on the competition, Iblis?

Kenna lowered her voice conspiratorially. "He gave me goose bumps. He looked like some sort of Hollywood agent, with teeth too white and hair too black. I'm glad he and the goth chick with him didn't see me."

"I don't suppose they left a card?" Lee asked.

"I don't think so," Kenna replied. "Clark acted like he didn't remember them being here."

Another clue they were the party Mikha'el was interested in. Would it be enough to appease the Elohim? If nothing else, it might distract him, so he wasn't haranguing Lee every day. "Thank you, Miss. You've been very helpful." Lee punctuated his statement by tucking a twenty-dollar bill in the tip jar. He might need to return for more information. He collected his coffee; as mediocre as it was, it seemed a shame to let it go to waste. "Come along, Qashmet."

Once they were in the parking lot, Qashmet spoke up. "What are you thinking? We go to this shindig and see if we can pin down this druid, maybe follow him to his hideout?"

Lee nodded as he pulled out his key fob and chirped his truck. "Plus, we give Mikha'el everything we know about these others who are poking around. Hopefully it will be enough to get him off our backs and fulfill our respective agreements with him."

* * * * *

Chapter Thirty-Two

Erin

"I've been looking forward to this."

Erin noted that this time Uathach opted to wear armor. Uathach had tucked her long auburn tresses under her helmet, something Erin made note of for future fights. Her own hair was in a long braid down her back. Her sparring partners had never taken advantage of it, but a true opponent might.

"I'm sure you have," Erin replied and walked toward the center of the practice field. "Good thing you have help; I'm not pregnant this time."

Uathach's partner was one of the guards, Fionna. Uathach had been training with the woman for six months, obviously eager for some payback and to bring Erin down a notch. Like Uathach, Fionna had her snow-white hair up under her helmet, out of reach. Fionna was taller than Erin or Uathach, and long-limbed, giving her an advantage in reach. If Erin had to guess, she would put the guard's age in the mid- to upper-twenties, at least from a physical standpoint. The young woman could be centuries old.

Uathach had a shield and a practice spear, and her partner held a glaive. Both weapons had wooden heads instead of metal. Erin had her favorite practice sword, one that had held up for several months without splintering. Erin's opponents moved to stand opposite her.

The crowd gathered around the practice arena; ropes pegged in the ground marked it. A second rope, six feet further out, marked the perimeter for the spectators. Almost everyone in the fort had turned out to watch the match. The murmuring crowd went silent when Scathach stepped forward.

"Here are the rules," Scathach announced, her voice carrying clearly across the courtyard. A breeze ruffled her green cloak and copper tresses. "If you leave the arena, as marked on the ground, you are eliminated from the bout. If you are struck on the helm, you are eliminated. If you are struck solidly on the torso, you are eliminated. I am the sole arbiter of what constitutes 'solid.' If you are rendered unable to continue, you are eliminated."

Erin gave her opponents a curt martial arts bow, which Fiona began to return until she realized Uathach ignored the gesture. Erin briefly wondered what Fiona had been offered as a prize but pushed the thought aside. Bringing her weapon up, Erin waited for the signal.

"Begin!" Scathach called. The crowd erupted into cheers.

As expected, Erin's opponents split and circled toward her on opposite sides. Erin didn't wait for them to complete the flanking maneuver; she launched herself at Fiona. If Erin could quickly eliminate her, it would turn this bout into a one-on-one duel with Uathach.

Erin knew she only had two seconds before Uathach caught up to her. Fiona choked up on the glaive, sacrificing reach for responsiveness as she parried Erin's first blow. Erin let her sword bounce off the glaive, reversing the arch of her swing to try to hit from the opposite side. Fiona turned with her weapon, catching the second strike.

Erin twisted aside as her instincts warned her the two seconds had run out. Uathach's spear lanced through empty air, missing by a hand's breadth. Erin brought her sword down to drive the spear to the dirt, then had to bring it up to counter the glaive swinging overhead.

Erin and Uathach spun around each other, Erin watching for an opening while Uathach tried to open the space between them enough to use her spear. Movement out of the corner of her eye warned Erin, and she ducked. The wooden glaive whooshed over Erin's head and nearly caught Uathach in the face, forcing Uathach to stumble back behind her shield.

Erin side-kicked the shield, knocking Uathach off her feet, while parrying Fiona's swipe with the glaive's haft. Erin pressed the less-experienced warrior, landing a body punch while their weapons were locked. The armor absorbed most of the blow, which didn't qualify as an eliminating hit, but it forced Fiona back enough to free Erin's weapon.

Uathach jabbed with the spear, forcing Erin to use the heavily-armored vambrace she wore on her off-hand. While Erin didn't use a buckler or shield, the armor piece was designed to let her deflect lighter weapons. She scarcely felt the spearhead glance off it. Erin brought her sword around, aiming for Uathach's unprotected back. Sensing her peril, Uathach twisted away, leaving Erin swinging through empty space.

Erin followed through the sword's trajectory and angled it up, catching the glaive high in its arch. Erin drove her elbow into Fiona's chest and followed through, slamming her shoulder into the taller woman. As Fiona toppled, Erin spun back toward Uathach, who had regained her bearing and held her shield ready.

Erin had to parry a rapid flurry of jabs as she tried to get inside the spear's reach. Once she stepped in, Uathach shoved Erin with the shield, causing her to lose her footing. Erin snagged the haft of the spear to catch herself and arrested her fall for a split second until Uathach let go of the spear.

As soon as she hit the dirt, Erin rolled aside and tossed away the weapon. The glaive smote the ground where she had fallen. Erin kicked up to her feet and swept aside a thrust from the glaive. Erin had begun the reverse stroke, which would either catch Fiona in the chest or force her back when her head jerked back painfully. Instead of retrieving the spear, Uathach had grabbed hold of Erin's braid.

Erin launched a roundhouse kick, catching Fiona in the ribs and knocking her back. She brought her sword down on Uathach's wrist. Uathach released her grip on the braid and stepped in for another shield slam. Erin spun with the impact, deflecting most of the blow, extending her left arm into a spinning backfist.

The reinforced vambrace caught Uathach on the side of her helmet. Erin saw the woman's eyes lose focus as she crumpled to the dirt.

"That's for pulling my hair, you Bitch!" Erin snarled at the prone form.

Something heavy caught Erin in the side, below her left arm. She blinked in confusion as the glaive fell to the dirt. Erin's eyes followed the haft to where Fiona stood. She had thrown the weapon instead of closing. Erin's eyes narrowed and red began to tinge her vision.

"Enough!" Scathach called out, the tower bell punctuating her command. "Uathach and Erin are both eliminated. Fiona has won the bout!"

Erin's blood pounded in her ears. This was her chance to talk to Tim, and the bitch had…Erin took a steadying breath and tried not to grind her teeth. It was her own fault; she had lost track of Fiona in her anger at Uathach. Erin had not considered the woman might pitch the glaive like a spear; Erin had assumed Fiona was going to get close enough for a swing.

Another deep breath and the red began to fade. She turned to Fiona and bowed. "Well fought, Fiona," Erin said over the rumbling of the crowd.

"Thank you, Champion," Fiona replied. She lowered her voice, so it was barely audible over the crowd. "I'm sorry I kept you from contacting your family."

"Champion," Uathach wheezed, having recovered enough of her senses to sit up. She was clutching the side of her face, which was black and blue. Her helmet was on the ground. "'Champion,' you lost."

"At least my face doesn't look like it was used for a hurling ball," Erin retorted. She may have lost the fight, Erin thought, but at least she didn't lose her temper. Erin was certain Scathach chose Uathach as her opponent because of the animosity between them. Scathach was gauging Erin's self-discipline as much as her prowess.

"Well done, Fiona," Scathach remarked, striding to the combatants. "Per your request, your sister may join us. I will send word with the next messenger."

"Thank you, Milady." Fiona bowed and left the practice arena.

"Champion, you fared better than expected," Scathach stated. She had been watching Erin's practice sessions, where Erin had fared poorly sparring against the twins and little better against Mysie and Daidh.

Erin nodded. "I didn't break anyone's bones this time."

* * * * *

Chapter Thirty-Three

Tim

"I still can't believe you gave her your finger."

Tim glanced up from his homework. He was at one end of the huge dining room table, working on his algebra. His father and Susan were at the other end; Susan was changing the dressings on Liam's hand. Tim was relieved to see there was hardly any blood, unlike when Liam and the others had returned from their journey.

"I didn't have much choice," Liam responded, wincing as Susan pulled the fresh bandage tight.

Tim finished writing the answer to the problem he had solved. Two more questions would finish algebra. After dinner, he would have a chapter in history and a page of Spanish vocabulary, and then he would be free to work on the new Accords.

Tim turned the page to the next algebra problem. "Gofannon was with you, and he's a god," Tim said. "Isn't he stronger than some old witch?"

His father rocked his head side to side, a gesture Tim had learned meant 'maybe.' "Gofannon is an aspect of a minor god. The Baba Yaga are much more than witches, especially in their homeland. The one we faced was keeping me from drawing up enough *lledrith* to open the ford."

Susan gathered all the old dressings into a sack. Tim knew those were destined for the fire pit, though he wasn't exactly sure why. "When you did, it nearly killed you," Susan said. "For being so important to their plans, these people are playing awfully loosely with your health. Speaking of which, your finger would heal a lot faster if you would give it a break."

Liam flexed his hand. "I wish we had time. Once Einar and Gofannon get the meteorite smelted down, we need to get to work on Erin's sword."

Tim knew better than to ask for a sword again. Every time he asked, his father countered with 'let's ask your mother.' "Are you going to give Mom's sword a name? Really cool swords, like Excalibur and Glamdring, have names."

Liam smiled and nodded. "I like your idea, Tim. In many traditions, giving something a name conveys power. We'll have to come up with a suitable name for your mother's sword." Liam turned to Susan and said, "Which reminds me, is your friend Tyrone still going to meet us on Saturday?"

Susan sprayed the table where they had been working and wiped it. She added the paper towels to the sack. "He thinks it's some sort of crazy Wicca stuff, but he said if you have the money, he'll hook you up. I know what you're doing, and I think it's crazy."

"What's crazy?" Tim asked, wishing he had set up something to record all the conversations he missed after he went to bed. The house reminded him it wasn't polite to eavesdrop.

Liam pulled a leather glove over his wounded hand and flexed his fingers again. "Iron is really hard to infuse with magic; *lledrith* washes off it, and meteoric iron doubly so. How do you put magic in a blade which repels magic?"

Tim shrugged; this was much more interesting than algebra. He ran through various games he had played or read about; several dealt with magic weapons. "You mix in a metal which conducts magic like electricity?"

Liam paused, finger paused in mid-air, as his answer was derailed. A confused expression spread across his face. "I had asked about alloys, but what if we folded in some layers of copper or silver?"

"Did your son come up with a better idea than your harebrained and ghoulish scheme?" Susan asked. She carefully pulled off one glove, then the other, and dropped them in the sack.

Liam ran his good hand over his beard. "My idea is still on the table; there's a lot of magic precedent. What Tim said about conducting has me wondering if we can thread in some magic conductive material without compromising the integrity of the blade? I'll have to ask Gofannon."

"Like printing a magic circuit board in it?" Tim asked. He wasn't sure if his father knew what a circuit board was. "What was your idea?"

Liam still seemed distracted, as if he was trying to design the magic circuits in his mind. "My thought was to quench the blade in blood. Specifically, my blood since it's supposed to be full of magic."

The answer surprised Tim. "Are you going to stab yourself with a red-hot sword?"

Liam blinked, his focus returning to the here and now. "No, I'm going to have blood drawn and use it in the quenching process."

"Which I still think is insane," Susan chimed in.

Liam frowned at her. "Gofannon and Einar thought it was a good idea."

"How drunk were they?" Susan asked and picked up the bag. "At least Tyrone won't cost you any body parts, but I still think it's nuts." She disappeared into the kitchen, and a moment later the door to the garage clattered.

"Hey, Dad, after the challenge, will you be able to grow your finger bone back?" Tim asked. "You'll have plenty of magic."

Liam shrugged. "Maybe I need to be reminded I'm only human, and there will always be something out there you can't punch, glamour, or zap your way through." He waggled his gloved fingers. "The more powerful the person, the greater the need for humility."

Tim nodded, not knowing what else to say.

"How does pizza sound?" Liam asked, standing up. "I picked up a couple of those take-and-bake pizzas, one for us and one for Gofannon."

"Pizza sounds good," Tim replied. "Isn't Einar cooking?"

Liam shook his head. "Einar is helping Gofannon with the meteorite, so I figured I'd take up the slack." Liam peered around cautiously and whispered, "Especially after lunch."

Tim had been at school, but when he got home the house still reeked of burnt grilled cheese sandwiches and soup. Tim didn't understand how someone could burn soup; evidently, Pixel had figured it out. The fae had been in hiding since, either somewhere upstairs or outside.

"Pizza sounds good," Tim said, as he began working on solving for *x*. Assuming his father didn't burn the pies because he got distracted, pizza did sound good. Tim didn't bother asking if his dad had considered Susan when getting the pies. Sometimes he might be flakey, but his dad always remembered little things, like Tim not wanting mushrooms and onions on his pizza, and that Susan wouldn't eat meat. "Do you need me to do anything?"

"Not really," Liam replied from the kitchen. "Go ahead and finish your math homework. I'll pile plates and silverware in here; everyone can grab what they need."

* * *

"No offense, Druid, but your cul-i-nary skill is not a match for the dwarf's," Gofannon declared between slices of pizza. "Did I get the word right?"

"Culinary? Yes," Liam replied. "No offense taken after being a bachelor for so long, where I didn't do more than the most basic of cooking. Throw a chunk of meat over the fire? I'm good with it. Multiple course meals with fancy foreign dishes? Not so much."

"Don't knock throwing a good cut over a fire," Einar countered. "Bachelor dwarves get by cooking their dinner over the heat of the forge. They don't have time for pocking 'courses.'"

"You did fine, Liam," Susan said. She had plucked the two slices of mushroom and cheese furthest away from the other half, which was sausage and pepperoni. "You used to make a really good stir-fry dish for those pagan potlucks we used to have at the Unitarian Church."

"You mean my hunter-gatherer stir-fried rice?" Liam asked. He had taken one of each side of the pie. "It was pretty easy; I made a big batch of the vegetarian, and then added the chicken and eggs to half."

"I didn't know you could cook." Pixel had been quiet until now. "Maybe you could make some for the meet-up?"

"I can help if you want," Susan added. "Also, gluten-free is really popular nowadays."

Tim pretended not to pay attention. He knew Susan and Pixel didn't get along, although he wasn't sure why. Susan seemed to be annoyed Pixel liked Liam, though Susan didn't like Liam, other than as a friend. Kind of like how Tim liked Jenny Dittmeyer, but he didn't know if she liked him as more than a friend, a smart friend who could help her with homework.

"I can't believe I'm networking again," Liam remarked, taking a sip of soda. A side effect of the injury was Tim's father had cut down on how much booze he drank; something to do with the medicine he was taking. "I hope I can get these people to put aside their witch wars for a couple of months."

"Why do they have witch wars?" Tim asked. Did the witches have factions? Maybe they were from different countries.

"When you get enough people together, trolls pop out from under the bridge," Liam replied. "Some people aren't satisfied unless they think they are in charge. It's one of the reasons I avoid the internet."

Tim nodded. Internet trolls; they were something he could understand. He was still figuring out if he could sneak in some sort of retribution against them into the new accords. He hadn't figured out how, since they were quite mundane, other than infesting the internet with judgmental spirits, and from what Tim had seen there were already enough of those on the net.

* * *

Tim set aside the Spanish vocabulary sheet, along with the filled-in homework. The rote exercise had been easy; it was much harder figuring out tenses. His class had only dabbled in more complex verb use, but Tim knew he couldn't coast on his photographic memory.

At least he was done with his homework. Downstairs, Tim's father had been pitching the idea of embedding a magic circuit in the folds of the metal used to make Erin's sword. Gofannon grumbled the other metal would make the blade too brittle and cause it to snap under duress. Einar had pointed out the presence of metal covered by the Fiwer Pact would make the sword useless against a variety of opponents.

While Tim was tempted to research the metallurgical question on the internet, he was more interested in something else. Popping through chatrooms, he found what, or more properly, who he was searching for.

"Hey," he typed to Jenny's user identity.

"Hey, Timmy!" she replied, opening a private chat window. "Did you already do the algebra homework?"

Tim keyed the 'thumbs up' icon. "Sure, it was pretty easy." He immediately regretted the boast; would it further mark him as a nerd?

"I'm having trouble with a couple of questions," Jenny typed back. "Can you help me out?"

"Sure!" Tim replied. He had already taken pictures of his homework, anticipating this turn of events. "Do you want me to send you a snap of my work?"

"Please!" The response came with a smiley-face icon. "It would help me see what I'm missing."

Tim transferred the file to the chat client and sent it. "Here you go. Let me know if you have any questions." Tim knew he was pretending Jenny wasn't copying his answers, under the guise of figuring out for herself how the math worked. Then again, copying homework would only take Jenny so far; eventually they would have a test.

"You're a life-saver!" Jenny replied. "There are still some things I think I'll need help on. Do you think we could get together after school this week? I think Mrs. Silvasi is going to hit us with a test on Friday."

"Sure," Tim responded, bringing up a Google map in another browser tab. He felt his heart pounding in his chest. He was grateful the conversation was over chat; his voice would probably crack. "Do you want to go to Pizza Hut? I can pick up the library's wifi signal from there." It was only a few blocks from the school.

"Sounds great!" The response appeared with another smiley-face on Tim's screen. "I'll see you tomorrow!"

Tim watched the chat window blink out, giddy. Then he realized he would need to ask someone to pick him up from Pizza Hut instead of his riding the school bus. Pixel would be the easiest to convince; she wanted to get in Tim's favor. Only Tim hadn't ever seen her drive and suspected she couldn't. Einar might do it, and he could drive. Did the dwarf have a license?

His father was the easiest answer; he had a license and could drive. The question was whether Liam could pick Tim up without embarrassing him in front of Jenny. Tim sorted through his options; his father seemed the best bet. There would assuredly be an interrogation afterward; the supernatural folks seemed oblivious about asking awkward questions at the worst time.

There was a knock on the doorframe. "Hey Buddy, how's the homework going?" Liam asked from the doorway.

Tim picked up the filled-in Spanish exercises. "All done. What was the verdict on putting something in the sword to conduct magic?"

"We might test the idea, but from what Gofannon is saying, it would create lines where the blade would fracture under stress." Liam opened and closed his gloved hand. "I'm not a metallurgist, so I can't say for sure, and we don't have a lot of time to experiment. It sounded like a good idea to me."

"So, you're really going to dip Mom's sword in your blood?" Tim made a face; it sounded gross, although he still wanted to watch. He placed his homework in his backpack.

"It'll be a mixture of blood and quenching oil," Liam replied. "It's probably going to stink."

Tim set the backpack on his desk, an old wooden antique with a roll-up top. "Can I ask you a favor?"

His father appeared skeptical, probably thinking Tim was about to take another shot at asking for a sword. "You can ask."

"A friend of mine wants to meet after school, probably tomorrow or Thursday, so we can go over algebra," Tim said. "Could you pick me up from Pizza Hut?"

"Sure," Liam replied. "Do you need money for pizza?" He was probably glad the request didn't risk Tim's mother's wrath, and Liam worried Tim wasn't making friends at school. "Would this friend happen to be Jenny Dittmeyer?"

Here comes the embarrassing part, Tim thought, as he nodded. "Yeah."

"Is this a date?" Liam grinned.

"No!" Tim replied more emphatically than he intended. Lowering his voice, he continued, "We're going over algebra for the next test."

His father looked like he was stifling a laugh over Tim's outburst. "Good, you are too young to start dating," Liam said. "However, if you want to have pizza and study I don't see a problem with it." Liam fished a twenty-dollar bill out of his wallet and handed it to Tim. "Let me know which day. If it helps, we can give Jenny a ride home also; I know where the Dittmeyers live."

"Thanks Dad." Tim was relieved his father had no more questions. "Do you want to work on the Accords for an hour or so?"

"Sure." Liam nodded toward the stairs. "Maybe you can explain these charts you and Susan cooked up."

Tim joined his father in the hall. "You mean the magical progression tables? I got the idea from some of the different games out there. Since the Milesian Accords focused on stifling magic, the agreement didn't bother quantifying magic. If there's going to be magic in the world, and rules governing magic, you need some way of gauging it."

Liam followed Tim down the stairs, still a little slower. Whatever had happened in Russia had left him barely able to walk the next day. "How do you measure magic?" Liam asked.

Tim turned back toward his father. "I call it an iota."

* * * * *

Chapter Thirty-Four

Erin

"If it's so terrible, you don't have to drink it."

Erin choked down another mouthful of bitter tea before replying to Nechtan. "I'm not taking any chances. I've had enough surprises." Her previous surprise was bound to wake up any time, wanting breakfast. "It's preferable to the alternatives, which would include abstinence."

"Well then, drink up," Nechtan said with a grin. He paced around the front room of Erin's Quonset, shirtless, peering at the floor.

"What are you doing?" Erin asked, quaffing the dregs of her preventative tea. She filled her mug with coffee from the kettle on the iron stove and added a dollop of honey. As she stirred in the honey, Erin admired Nechtan's muscled back. The hunter was lean and trim. He possessed a physique honed by a lifetime of hiking and training, without the bulkiness of a weightlifter. When he turned to face her, the knotwork antler tattoo adorning Nechtan's chiseled chest drew Erin's eyes, the inked design joining at his sternum in an abstract representation of a stag's head. "Not that I mind the view."

"I'm hunting for my tunic," Nechtan replied. "I thought I shed it out here when things started to get frisky."

Erin took a sip of coffee. It wasn't barista quality, but it would do. It was one of the luxuries smuggled in from the Dunwold. Erin had asked if anyone had tried to get coffee or chocolate from South America on the Glaswold only for them to stare at her as if she were insane. Evidently you didn't go south on the Glaswold.

"If you hadn't brought the whiskey, we might have made it to the bedroom before clothes started coming off." Erin thanked the gods Skye was a heavy sleeper. Once Erin and Nechtan had finally crossed the threshold of becoming intimate, finding time when there weren't roommates or a squalling child underfoot had been challenging. "Look behind the chair in the corner."

Nechtan leaned over the chair, his leather pants creaking. Erin regretted there hadn't been time for a victory lap. "Here it is!" Nechtan called, holding the tunic like a flag.

Erin sighed as the gray tunic obscured the antler knotwork. "Does your tattoo have some sort of significance?"

"You might call it a gift from my father," Nechtan replied and joined Erin at the small table near the stove. Erin knew Nechtan's father was a daoine sidhe, one of the myriad tribes of fairy folk, but little else. "I don't know I would call it so."

"I'm sorry, I didn't know it was a touchy subject," Erin said.

Nechtan gave her a wry grin as he poured a cup of coffee. "You had no way of knowing. I really don't talk about it. I think maybe it's meant to put things in perspective for me, and, like any good child, I stoutly avoid learning from it."

"Mama!" Skye squealed, toddling into the front room. Erin berated herself for not hearing the child up and about.

"Good morning, Baby Girl!" Erin called back. It was hard to believe her daughter was already 18 months old. With a pang of guilt, Erin realized her son was still 12 years old. She was half of the way through her 'deployment.' A calendar in her bedroom tallied a more accurate figure; Erin knew she was getting closer.

"Uncle Necht!" Skye called. As most children her age, she seemed to lack volume control. If Mysie and Daidh weren't up already, they would be now. The pair had been on the second watch, getting home after midnight.

"Good morning, Wee Girl," Nechtan replied with a smile. "How are you?"

Skye tugged her high chair toward the table. "Ith!"

"Let me warm up some oatmeal for you," Erin said, lifting her daughter into the chair.

"Mama fight Scathach today?" the girl asked. Erin remembered how the child could already pick up on oblique comments, and then remembered who her father was. Liam had an eidetic memory, something he had passed on to their son. Skye may have also inherited the trait, though it could be a child's tendency to parrot every inconvenient thing said within earshot.

"I'm going to spar with her today," Erin said. "It's like play. We aren't angry at each other, it's for practice." Erin was dreading today's bout. It would be the first time she had faced the legendary warrior on the practice field. Erin felt like a high school football player suddenly facing an NFL line.

"I can play?" Skye asked, holding her spoon aloft and launching a dollop of oatmeal.

"When you're older, Baby Girl." Erin resolved to track down the oatmeal projectile after breakfast. She didn't want to leave it for Fib, the brownie who tended to the Quonset. Erin had never seen Fib but took the others' words regarding his presence. The mysteriously completed housework was enough to convince Erin to leave a portion of the evening meal on a small stone slab tucked by the potbelly stove. Every seven days she also left a half shot of whiskey or small cup of ale.

Nechtan drank his coffee while Erin fed the toddler. Equal amounts of oatmeal ended up in and on the child. "I need to get ready for patrol," Nechtan said, standing. "I'll be back in a few days; we're checking the perimeter. Someone or something has been snooping around again. It's enough to put Scathach on edge; she values her privacy."

Erin kissed him as he leaned down, his stubble rough against her cheek. "Don't get lost," she said.

"I'll try not to lose my way, *acushla*," Nechtan replied with a smile. "Good luck with Scathach. Be good, Wee Girl."

"Bye bye!" Skye waved as Nechtan departed, spraying particles of oatmeal. "Uncle Necht coming back?" she asked after the door closed.

Erin picked up a cloth to clean off the child's hands before she splattered any more oatmeal. She tried not to dwell on Nechtan's affectionate appellation; they had promised each other they wouldn't become too attached. "He'll be back," Erin said. "He's only going to be gone for a few days." Erin wondered who she was trying to assure more, her daughter or herself.

* * *

"Are you ready, Champion?" Scathach stood across from Erin. Dressed in the padded leather practice armor, Scathach still exuded a regal bearing. Scathach only stood a couple of inches taller, but she seemed much more imposing.

Erin nodded, though she didn't feel ready. While her practice sessions often drew a few onlookers, today there seemed to be a crowd. "As ready as I'm going to be."

Erin and Scathach exchanged bows and sunk into ready positions. In an instant, Scathach had closed the gap between them, her practice sword already slicing toward Erin's head. Erin barely managed to parry the blow and had to give ground to avoid a quick stab. Erin tried to press a counter-attack, only to find each blow intercepted by Scathach's sword.

Scathach's palm strike caught Erin off guard and hit her in the side of her jaw. As Erin reeled back from the impact, Scathach launched a flurry of swings mixed with thrusts. Erin felt three blows on her own armor, and an especially bruising one on her upper arm.

Regaining her footing, Erin stepped into her block and tried to hook her foot behind Scathach's ankle, hoping to shove her opponent off balance and trip her. Scathach spun aside, letting Erin's momentum throw her forward. Erin was rewarded with another bruise, this one on her upper back.

Was Scathach trying to piss her off? Erin was getting frustrated, but she had worked hard the past couple of years trying to reign in her temper. Erin's reverse stroke didn't catch Scathach by surprise, and the swing as she spun back to face the woman ascribed too great an arc, giving Scathach plenty of time to parry.

The block left Scathach's sword off to the side, so Erin snapped a kick, only to have Scathach dance back and swat Erin on the shin armor. Erin lunged forward, following through the kick, but Scathach sidestepped and caught Erin behind the knee. Erin's leg buckled, and she spilled onto the ground. When she rolled to her back, the wooden blade of Scathach's practice weapon tapped Erin on the chin, under her helmet.

Scathach withdrew the sword and reached down to offer Erin a hand up. Erin grudgingly took it and climbed to her feet. In the space of two minutes, she'd received half a dozen bruising blows.

"I believe we've sparred enough for the first day," Scathach said. "It is a good thing we have three and a half years. Think on your mistakes and have your bruises tended to. We will work on technique tomorrow."

Erin nodded mutely, hoping the helmet hid her embarrassment. She had gotten to the point she could handle any one of her sparring partners readily, but Scathach had schooled her as if she was a cocky yellow-belt.

Scathach pulled off her practice helmet, her coppery tresses spilling out. Only a single curl on her forehead looked dampened by sweat. "If it's any consolation, I gave your progenitor nine welts our first bout. We have to figure out how to channel your anger without it running away with you."

Erin nodded again, and Scathach strode from the practice field. Erin walked to the closest bench and sank onto it, sore in several places. She pulled off her own helmet, and her black hair was soaked from her exertion.

"Mama ow?" Skye asked, wide-eyed.

"Yes, Baby Girl. Mama ow."

*****

Chapter Thirty-Five

Liam

"So?"

Tim peered back in the rearview mirror. "So…what?"

"How was algebra?" Liam suppressed the urge to tease. He vaguely remembered being young, full of hormones and awkwardness.

Tim sighed, watching the town fade to farmland. "It was fine. It wasn't a big deal."

"Pixel wanted to come," Liam said. "I talked her out of it."

"Thank you." Tim replied. "She would have made a fuss and probably said something embarrassing."

Liam nodded. He had assured the fae girl this wasn't a date, but two kids studying. Pixel had promised to only peek and offered to glamour Tim's friend if there was any awkwardness. What Liam hadn't told Pixel or Tim was there was already gossip around town about Liam suddenly having a son with no sign of a mother. Liam could imagine what they would add to the mix if they figured out Pixel was living with him.

Liam had also put the idea of having the Dittmeyers over for a cookout on the back burner. There was too great a chance of something hard to explain happening, and he didn't want to scare them off as acreage tenants. He still half-expected the financial house of cards the Exiled Folk had set up to fall down, and the income from leasing out the farmland looked good on paper.

"Do you have much homework?" Liam asked after a few long minutes of silence. He turned onto the country road that eventually ran in front of the house, checking to see if anyone was following them. What he didn't tell Tim was that while he was in Pizza Hut, Liam had parked across the street at the carwash.

"Not really, I already did my algebra," Tim replied. "I have a chapter to read, and an outline for a paper to finish."

Satisfied no one was following them, Liam slowed and pulled into the driveway. Smoke curled from behind the garage, which meant Einar and Gofannon were still smelting down the meteorite. In another day, Liam would start the lengthy process of hammering down and folding the metal, adding in layers of high carbon steel as they went.

"Dad, did you think someone was following us?" Tim asked as he pulled his backpack from the back seat.

Liam decided to be honest. "I've had this nagging feeling of being watched while out and about."

"Is it because someone is trying to use magic to find you?" Tim shouldered the pack, which looked too big for his young frame, and trudged toward the side door of the garage. "Or, do you think those bikers are back?"

"I wish I could say." Liam retrieved two large sacks of Chinese food from the front seat of the car. With Einar helping Gofannon, the dwarf didn't have time to cook. The wind whirled around in greeting as Liam followed his son. Liam cast a glance at the black tendrils of smoke rising from the forge. The smoke dispersed into haze, which was much less likely to draw attention.

"How was your play date?" Pixel asked Tim as she bounced to Liam and relieved him of one of the bags. "I mean study session," she amended, catching Liam's reproachful glance.

He had lectured her not to use the "D" word. Algebra over pizza was fine; in a couple of years maybe Tim could advance to going to the roller rink.

"It was fine," Tim replied. He turned to Liam. "Since I already ate, can I go up to my room and finish my homework?"

Liam nodded. "Sure." He knew Tim was more interested in avoiding further interrogation than studying. He couldn't blame his son.

"DRUID!" Gofannon's bellow echoed from the forge. It sounded annoyed, rather than alarmed.

Liam sighed and headed for the door. "How does he know I'm back? There's no way they heard us pull up over the racket they are making out there."

"He is a god," Tim replied. "Also, the zephyrs act differently when you're not home; they're not as windy."

"I'd better see what they need." Liam turned to Pixel. "Would you mind setting up for dinner?"

"Of course!" Pixel got the glint in her eye, the same one she got whenever Liam asked her to do something that fell under her definition of wife/girlfriend requests. It always set Susan on edge, raising her feminist hackles.

"Thank you." Liam went through the garage and headed for the forge. He avoided making domestic requests of Pixel; he didn't want Pixel getting it in her head that he was going to make her his *blodyn priod*, or fae-wife as close as he could translate it. Fortunately, Liam was used to fending for himself, so he rarely asked for her help.

"DRUID!"

Liam stepped into the forge shed. Both Gofannon and Einar had their backs to him, concentrating on the smelter Einar had cobbled together outside the building. "I'm right here." A cool breeze accompanied his words, pushing away the oppressive heat gathered under the metal roof. "I doubt you were bellowing at me for air conditioning. What's up?"

"The pocking smelter isn't getting hot enough, even with the blower at full speed," Einar complained. "We need it hotter if we're to separate the metal of the meteorite from impurities."

Gofannon glowered at Liam, as if it was his fault. The smith-god had given him grief about taking time to watch Tim on his study session, complaining Liam could bring the kids to the house and not have to spend a couple of hours away. While true, Liam wanted to spare Tim the inevitable mortification of having one of their guests blurt out something inappropriate or unexplainable in front of Jenny. He considered it two hours well invested.

Liam stared at the smelting furnace for a few minutes. "I have an idea," he finally said. "It'll take a couple of hours of work if we have the parts."

"Let's get on with it, then," Gofannon said.

"Dinner is ready." Liam gestured toward the house.

Gofannon threw down a set of tongs in frustration. "Fine. Let's take another break." He pulled off his thick leather gloves. Liam had seen Gofannon grab a frying pan off the stove with his bare hands, but the smith evidently drew the line at molten metal. "Since you mention it, I am actually hungry."

"There's a surprise," Einar muttered and closed the air intake to dampen the coal fire in the furnace. He switched off the blower motor and asked, "What is your idea, Druid?"

Liam led the procession back through the garage toward the house. "If we could put something to act as a funnel over the air intake, I could get the zephyrs to channel wind into the furnace. It might take some practice to regulate the temperature, but it should let us ramp up the heat."

"Druid, you actually have a good idea," Gofannon conceded, a bit of the surliness bleeding from his tone. "You could do the same with the forge; it would speed up the process quite a bit."

"Here you were bitching because he wasn't pocking Earth-blessed," Einar remarked as they entered the house. "This is much more useful."

The dining room table was arrayed with place settings and Chinese food. Two pitchers of tea were at opposite ends of the table. Pixel beamed with pride, as though she had cooked the repast herself.

Gofannon strode to the heavy-duty chair at one end of the table. Liam had found it at a swap meet; he and Einar had spent a couple of hours bolstering it and adding padding. Gofannon had readily claimed it as his own, appreciating the extra room the enlarged seat gave him.

"What kind of food is this?" Gofannon asked, surveying the spread in anticipation. With less enthusiasm, he added, "It looks rather exotic."

"It's Chinese," Liam replied, pulling up his own chair. "It originated from a land far to the east. I'm not sure how authentic Beijing Garden is; maybe inspired would be a better word."

"It is awfully colorful," Einar grumbled, eyeballing the dishes. "I suspect Susan would approve. Is the witch joining us?"

Liam shook his head and scooped some fried rice onto his plate. "She's going out to dinner with Tyrone. It's kind of a first date."

"The guy who draws your blood?" Pixel asked. She and Susan had reached a détente. Pixel no longer considered Susan a rival for Liam's affections, and Susan no longer expressed her disapproval of Pixel's interest in Liam. Privately, Susan told Liam she hoped he and Erin would get together. "He seems nice, in an urban sort of way."

Liam raised an eyebrow. "Is that a crack about his race?"

"Gods, no!" Pixel appeared mortified. "I meant he seemed like he was more of a big city kind of guy, someone who would live somewhere like New York or Chicago."

Liam decided to take her at face value. He had never discussed race with any of the Exiled Folk; he had no idea whether it registered with them. It seemed like they lumped all 'dunnies' together. "He is from Chicago. Tyrone is studying at Bradley; I think in physical therapy."

"I thought you dunnies gave up drawing blood as medicine," Einar remarked. The dwarf was tentatively poking at the contents of various cartons.

Liam picked up a pair of chopsticks and pointed. "This one has chicken; in fact, it's where I got the inspiration for my cashew chicken fried rice. This one has beef, albeit at a low proportion versus the veggies."

"What are these orange lumps?" Einar asked, pointing at a carton of General Tso's chicken.

"It's another chicken dish, with a spicy sauce," Liam replied. "If you like a little heat, you might enjoy it. The Beijing Garden makes their General Tso's spicier than other Chinese restaurants."

"Fine, I'll try some of this pocking General Chicken," Einar said, shoveling some of the entrée onto his plate. "This rice looks like a tv dinner threw up in it."

"That's vegetable fried rice," Liam said. "There's a carton of plain rice if it's too exotic for your dwarven sensibilities."

Einar's eyebrows furrowed. "Don't forget, Druid, who had to be carried up the stairs the first night we were here. I can stomach anything you can, and then some."

"It was more of a drag than a carry," Pixel remarked. She turned to Liam, "You tried to climb the stairs, but ran out of steam on the landing."

"You are all so fussy about your food." Gofannon had dumped multiple cartons onto the serving platter set in front of him. He shoveled a forkful of spicy pepper beef into his mouth. "I like it! Not to besmirch your cooking, Einar, but it is a pleasant change from meat and potatoes."

Einar sampled a bite of General Tso's chicken, followed by mouthful. "I'll admit, it is an interesting taste."

"Druid, I want to start early tomorrow," Gofannon said, spraying a few grains of rice. "We'll need to restart the coal fire once you make your modifications."

Liam glanced at the windows; the sun was setting. By the time they finished eating, it would be night. He didn't want to rummage through the junk shed in the dark. "First thing in the morning I'll pull together the parts," he said. "Einar, you want to help me with assembly?"

"Ja," the dwarf replied after chewing a mouthful of chicken. "We'll have to fashion some sort of bracket or brace, but it shouldn't be difficult."

"Can I do anything to help?" Pixel asked. Liam noticed she had been staying away from the spicier dishes.

"Can you make breakfast without starting another fire?" Einar responded and reached for a glass of tea. "It would let the Druid and I get to work right away."

Pixel scowled at Einar. "It was a little fire, and yes, I can make breakfast."

Liam remembered the incident. They had quickly snuffed the grease fire, and there had been no damage. Pixel had been embarrassed, and Einar's finding it hilarious didn't help. "You don't need to get too fancy," Liam suggested. "I'm surprised I haven't gotten fat from Einar's cooking."

"You've lost weight," Pixel said. "It's all the hot, sweaty work you've been doing out in the forge." The look she gave him warmed Liam up more than the General Tso's. "Not to mention what it has done for your muscles." She put a warm hand on his bicep.

Liam reached for his iced tea, hoping to cool down and quench his thirst. Einar rolled his eyes and mumbled something. Gofannon obliviously shoveled food in his mouth, pausing to knock rice from his coal black beard.

* * *

"Do you really think she's going to wait for seven years?" Pixel asked, lying next to Liam in bed. He had given up on chasing her out; she used the pretense that it was easier to keep an eye on him in case he went on a walkabout in the Murkwold while sleeping. As usual, she wore one of his shirts, this one a green and black flannel he hadn't worn in ages.

After dinner, they had worked on his magic practice for a couple of hours. He had been getting quicker at harnessing *lledrith*, magical energy, from the *Gwuedd*. With Pixel's help, he could gather energy twice as fast. He had also learned to commune with the earth spirits dwelling around his house. The erdlings weren't as numerous or as energetic as the zephyrs; they were mostly clustered around the garden and the dolmen. They could sense anyone on the property who wasn't in the house. Like the zephyrs, the house was out-of-bounds for them.

Liam had been half-asleep, fatigued from the day's work with a couple of beers mellowing him out. "What do you mean?"

Pixel's eyes glowed dimly in the darkened room. "Erin. She's spending seven years in Dunos Scaith, surrounded by exotic warriors of different *tuaithe*. Are you really hoping she'll save herself for you, after she told you she didn't love you?"

Liam was afraid Pixel would start unbuttoning her shirt. He was sober, so he thought his resolve would hold, but it would probably lead to drama, and he was too tired for that. She had stopped overtly coming on to him, and many nights he was so weary from working in the forge, he was out like a light as soon as he got into bed.

Pixel was voicing the same arguments he'd had with himself. She snuggled up to him, her purple hair draped across his shoulder. "I want you to be happy," she said sleepily and kissed him on the cheek. Pixel rolled over, her head still nestled on his shoulder, and entwined her fingers with his. "Good night."

Sleep claimed Liam before he could dwell too long on what she had said.

* * * * *

Chapter Thirty-Six

Iblis

"I see you're interested in the Occult?"

The willowy blonde blinked at Iblis in surprise. She sat at one of the tables in what passed for a café in the bookstore. A pair of books was stacked on the table, one titled 'Kindreds and Realms: Druidic Magic,' and the other 'Ancient Celtic Religion.' The young woman had been engrossed in her phone and hadn't noticed Iblis approaching.

"I suppose," she replied, staring down at the table. "Occult is a broad term."

Iblis gave her a brilliant smile. "I happen to be a bit of an expert on the Occult."

The woman glanced up, casting her blue eyes everywhere but toward Iblis. "Okay."

"I happened to notice your books." Uninvited, Iblis slid into the chair across from her. "I'm always seeking new students of the Occult." He noticed a flick of her eyes to someone behind him, accompanied by a pleading expression. "I'm sure I can teach you a lot."

"I don't know," the woman stammered.

"Sorry I'm late." A buxom brunette, maybe thirtyish, addressed the blonde. The new arrival turned her gaze on Iblis, her brown eyes hard like topaz. "Is he bothering you?"

Iblis scooted his chair back from the table. "I'm sorry; I didn't mean to intrude on your rendezvous." He stood gracefully, straightening his suit jacket. "I'll leave you ladies to your coffee. Good day."

As far as anyone watching was concerned, Iblis strode purposefully to the door and departed the bookstore. Actually, he stepped into the first aisle out of sight of the café, willing himself to be unobvious. While his magic wasn't as effective at outright illusions and invisibility as the fae folk, he could cause people to regard him as an anonymous and unremarkable person. They had enough awareness of his presence not to bump into him, but little beyond.

Iblis listened through the Bluetooth earpiece. If Raven had been there, he wouldn't have needed to resort to technology. Iblis could have tuned into the senses of his familiar to eavesdrop on what she saw and heard. However, he had been concerned the druid's friend might recognize Raven, if only by description.

"Was that creep bothering you?" the brunette asked. Iblis peeked over the shelf of books; the woman had seated herself in the chair Iblis had vacated.

"He walked up and started talking to me," Orliath replied, clearly audible over the phone. She had come up with the idea of using phones to let Iblis listen in. His phone was muted, to keep stray noise from giving him away. "I'm glad you noticed. I didn't know how to get rid of him. Thank you."

"You're welcome. I'm Susan."

Iblis was certain of the brunette's identity. His internet trolls had found several pictures on social media. While she wasn't a narcissistic selfie poster, Susan was active online, including on Word Nerds' page, where she had a habit of checking in every Wednesday.

Orliath reached across the table and shook Susan's hand. "I'm Renee. Thanks again for running him off. I think he was about to start talking about Gardnerian Wicca and extoling the virtues of going skyclad."

Susan scoffed. "Jerk. If I had a dollar for every time some pervert used 'skyclad' as an excuse to get a woman naked, I could pay off my student loan."

"Can I get you a cup of coffee, to pay you back?" Orliath glanced over at the counter. "I was about to get one myself. I figure I should wait a while to make sure he isn't lurking around outside."

Iblis watched over the top of a book he was 'browsing,' holding his breath as the witch hesitated. Orliath's expression bordered on pleading, as though she really was afraid to walk out of the bookstore. She was a much better actress than Iblis' had expected. Raven was scheming, Gypsy was manipulative, but Orliath turned out to have a talent for deception. It was something Iblis would have to keep an eye on.

Susan glanced at her watch. "Sure, I have a little time."

Splendid, Iblis thought. If Orliath had failed to gain the witch's sympathy, Plan B was to have Mikey and Mad Dog follow Susan to see where she went. Iblis already had her home address, so they could try to tail her any time to see if she would lead them to the druid, but if Orliath could get her talking, Iblis might glean some intel without risking someone spotting his minions.

"What would you like?" Orliath asked with a timid smile.

"A mocha latte," the pierced girl behind the counter stated, and looked over at the brunette. "Unless you want to try something different for a change?"

Susan shook her head. "The usual will be fine." While Orliath waited for their coffee, Susan took out her phone. "Hey, it's me. I'm running a little late. No, it's no big deal; I should be there in an hour or so."

Orliath set one of the steaming cups in front of Susan and returned to her seat. "You must come here a lot if they know your regular order."

Susan shrugged and picked up the latte. "My best friend worked here until a few weeks ago."

Orliath raised her eyebrows. "I'm guessing he didn't get fired, since you're still shopping here."

Susan shook her head. "His boss was a jerk, and he quit," she said. "He got a better offer. Since this is the best place in town to get new age and pagan books, I still come here. Also, he ordered some books, so I'm picking them up since I was coming by anyway."

"Wouldn't it be easier to have them delivered?" Orliath asked. "I mean, I prefer shopping in person, but if you're going to order books, they can bring them to your doorstep."

"My friend is a bit of a Luddite and lives out in the country." Susan took a sip of her mocha. "It's easier for everyone concerned if we pick the order up in the store." She gestured toward the books on the table. "I see you've been doing some shopping yourself."

Orliath placed a slender hand on the books. "I'm from Bloomington, so we don't have a large selection of bookstores specializing in certain topics. I'd heard this store has a decent new age section and doesn't treat pagan religions like a crystal-waving fad."

"You can thank my friend," Susan said. She tapped the pile of books on the table. "He ordered everything in this section himself. Sadly, it will probably decline now that he has left."

"Is your friend a Wiccan also?" Orliath asked. Very good, Iblis thought, draw the information out rather than asking directly.

"Goddess no!" Susan laughed, then stifled her mirth, appearing slightly embarrassed. "He's a Celtic Tribal Reconstructionist, a solitary druid."

Orliath carefully set her coffee down. "He doesn't have a grove? I thought CTR druids were practicing clergy, as opposed to the Druid Fellowship, where everyone is considered a druid."

"You'd have to ask him," Susan replied, taking another sip of her coffee. Iblis made a mental note about how trusting she had been, accepting the drink handed to her by a stranger. "He used to have a grove, but they drifted apart because of mundane world conflicts. Too many soccer games, random work schedules, and too much stress from worrying about bills took the wind out of their sails. People kept cancelling or not showing up, until they were forced to admit the group wasn't a priority."

"That's a shame," Orliath remarked. She picked up the top book. "I would have liked to find a druidic group who had their act together. I've talked some to a DFA guy here in Peoria; he goes by the craftname Taliesin."

Iblis couldn't see the eye roll from his angle, but he guessed it accompanied the snort.

"Taliesin, or Don Potts," Susan said acidly. "He's probably as bad as the creep who was talking to you. Okay, maybe it's an exaggeration, but not a huge one. He's full of his own importance bestowed by some bureaucracy of guys on the internet. He runs the local DFA grove, the Singing Woods Grove."

"I've heard of the grove," Orliath said. "What's wrong with them?"

"Nothing per se," Susan admitted. She picked up her coffee, rolling the cup between her hands before drinking. "Maybe I'm influenced by Liam's opinion, but the DFA seem more concerned about the organization than the religion."

"Liam is your druid friend?" Orliath asked innocently.

Susan's eyes snapped up from her coffee. Iblis could only see the side of her face, but it was obvious she realized she had let something slip. "Yes," she finally relented. "Liam and Potts don't exactly get along. Since Liam is trying to get back into the community, it presents a challenge."

"Is your friend trying to poach members from Potts' grove?" Orliath asked. Very good, Iblis thought, put the witch on the defensive. "I've seen it happen between two covens competing for members. It's not like there's a large pool of potential members. All the infighting is what led me to research druids and Celtic spirituality. The more I read, the more interested I became in the path."

Susan glanced at her phone. "Are you interested in becoming a druid?"

Orliath shrugged. "I think I want to find a druid, find a grove to join. I like to study and learn, but I'd really like someone else to officiate rituals. I'd prefer someone who wasn't trying to get into my pants or convince me the great rite required sex."

Iblis felt vaguely offended at the last remark. After all, passing on his essence required carnal interaction.

Susan sipped on her latte, probably trying to delay and compose an answer. It was obvious she was cautious about giving away information regarding Knox. "Are you in a coven now?" Susan asked.

"I am, and our priest is very…charismatic," Renee replied, fishing a pen out of her purse. "He is very knowledgeable regarding the occult, but I have some issues with the way he treats us."

"Is your priestess aware of this?" Susan asked.

"She is, but she is also subject to his…whims." Orliath flipped over the receipt for the coffee. After tapping the pen on the palm of her hand, she jotted down something on the receipt. "She can't help herself, so I'm certain she can't help anyone else. I don't want to give up the gods, but I don't want to be his plaything anymore." Orliath held the slip of paper toward Susan.

Iblis couldn't see what she had written on the note; he debated edging closer. He wondered who was being conned. Was Orliath searching for a way to escape his grasp or seeking to exploit the witch's benevolent nature to gain access to Knox?

"This is my phone number. Do you think I could talk to your friend?" Orliath inquired. "It sounds like we share similar views on druidic paganism, and he probably won't try to get me in bed."

Susan stared at the note for a moment before picking up her phone. Glancing at the paper, she tapped something into the phone. "I can pass your number along, and I'll talk to him."

"Thank you." Orliath folded the paper and set it on the books. The women drank their coffee in silence for several minutes.

Susan glanced at her phone. "I should get going. Will you be alright?"

Orliath nodded. "Thanks for keeping me company. I hope to hear from your friend."

Susan put away her phone and stood. "I won't make any promises. He's busy right now, but I'll talk to him. Thanks for the coffee, Renee."

After Susan went to the register, Iblis flicked his fingers toward the table. The slip of paper slipped off the books and fluttered to the floor. Orliath was fidgeting with her phone and didn't notice. The brunette witch picked up a package from the register, exchanged pleasantries with the employee, and left.

There was a click as Orliath hung up her phone. Iblis strolled over to the table and picked up the paper off the floor. He unfolded the paper and glanced at it; Orliath's phone number was on the receipt.

Iblis placed the paper on the books. "You dropped something."

Orliath casually stuck the receipt in the top book. "Do we need anything else here?"

"No, I think we got what we came for," Iblis replied with a brilliant smile. Lowering his voice, he whispered, "You did very well. When we get home, I may have to reward you."

Orliath suppressed a shudder, but Iblis spotted it. The girl must be eager with anticipation. His phone chirped, and he tapped his earpiece.

"Boss, you want us to follow the Moore woman?" Mad Dog asked. "She's about to pull out of the lot."

"No, let's not raise suspicion," Iblis replied under his breath. "We'll be out shortly; wait for us." He turned to Orliath. "Shall we, my dear?"

* * * * *

Chapter Thirty-Seven

Erin

"No!"

Erin sighed. She would rather face Scathach on the practice yard than deal with a two-year-old's tantrum. Skye certainly seemed to have inherited the infamous Cu Chulainn temper. Granted, most two-year-olds could be a terror, but Erin didn't remember Tim's toddler outbursts being this intense.

"Sweetie, your blue dress is dirty. Let's put on your brown one." Erin kept her voice calm and her tone soothing. She had never lost her temper with Tim, and she was determined to keep the streak going with Skye.

"No!" The child balled up her fists and plopped down on the floor. "No!"

Erin squatted down to get closer to eye-level. "Come on, Sweetie. This dress is pretty."

"No!" The crying commenced; angry sobs punctuated by sniffles.

Erin sat on the floor and sighed, folding the brown dress in her lap. She was supposed to be on the practice field 15 minutes ago, but Skye had decided to wear her breakfast. Now she refused to put on a clean dress, furious that Erin had removed her oatmeal soaked blue dress.

"How about your green tunic?" Erin suggested. "It's one of your favorites."

"No!" the child wailed.

A small cough from across the room caught Erin's attention. Fib held up Skye's blue dress, clean and dry. "Perhaps this would settle the wee one," the brownie said.

Erin sagged in relief and had to catch herself before she thanked the brownie, breaking one of their taboos. Instead, she said, "You're a life saver, Fib."

Fib draped the dress on the bench and tipped his hat, a bowler festooned with a small green feather. "Twas nothing."

"Look, Baby, Fib cleaned your blue dress." When Erin glanced back from the child to the garment, Fib was gone.

Skye's bawling faltered, and she blinked tears out of her eyes, appearing confused that her demand had been met. "My blue dress?"

Erin picked it up and nodded. "See, good as new. Let's get you dressed."

* * *

Scathach stood like a statue at the edge of the practice yard, barking orders at the class. In this case, it consisted of Izzy, Derek, Daidh, and Mysie. Occasionally others would join them, but not today. Slaine, the chirurgeon's assistant, and Saidhe, Uathach's daughter, sat on the spectator bench closest to the pen Erin termed, "baby jail."

Luckily, both women were willing to entertain Skye while watching the training bouts. Erin always felt guilty putting Skye in the pen, which had a fifty-fifty chance of evoking a tantrum. If an alternative presented itself, Erin took it, as much for her peace of mind as for the child.

"I see you finally decided to join us," Scathach stated, her face solemn.

"You've been a mother," Erin countered, as she began donning her practice armor. "Surely you remember the challenges a toddler can pose. There are days I think facing a dragon would be easier."

"Perhaps you modern folk have too soft a hand with your children," Scathach remarked. "A bit more discipline can work wonders."

Erin scowled as she pulled on the padded helmet. She had never been a fan of corporal punishment; she couldn't think of more than a handful of times she'd had to spank Tim, maybe three at most. She had to resist the urge to defend her 'light touch;' it would be fruitless to debate someone who had been set in their ways for centuries.

Erin pulled a blunt bronze sword from the rack of practice weapons. It was similar in size, shape and weight to her own, but the bronze weapon's blade was slightly narrower to emulate the mass of her steel weapon. The Fiwer pact meant Izzy and Derek were safe from being cut or stabbed by the bronze blade, but it could still leave bruises or, with enough force, break bones.

Mysie and Daidh were at greater risk, as neither of them had inherited the protection from their fairy parents. They wore heavier armor, a mix of leather and chainmail with steel helms. Despite the extra precautions, Erin had given Daidh a nasty gash and Mysie a concussion shortly after Scathach made Erin switch to the bronze weapons.

Over the past couple of months, Erin had improved her control, pulling a strike enough so it was palpable through the armor without leaving a welt. She had also noticed the others were having trouble keeping up with her. Every now and then, Scathach would spar Erin and remind her she still had much to learn.

Izzy strapped a shield to her arm and picked up a wooden broad-sword, twirling the weapon as she paced out to the middle of the practice ring. Erin rolled her neck and flexed her shoulders, then joined Izzy at the center. The women exchanged bows and waited for the signal from Scathach to begin.

Scathach raised her hand and froze, staring of into the distance. "Wait," she said, slowly lowering her hand. Erin wondered if this was some new trick, designed to catch her with her guard down.

Scathach's brows knitted in concentration. "One of the patrols has engaged a beast along the southern slope. Some sort of boar; it is not natural."

"Nechtan?" Erin asked, concerned by the seriousness in Scathach's countenance. Worry warred with the absurdity of having to save her lover from an angry pig.

Scathach shook her head. "His patrol is on the opposite side, to the north. Get real weapons; those warriors need help, or, more like-ly, need to be avenged."

"Daidh and Izzy, come with me." Erin jammed her bronze sword back into the rack. "Saidhe, can you watch Skye for a few hours?"

"Of course, Champion," Saidhe replied.

"What about us?" Mysie protested. "You're not leaving us behind to babysit."

"I don't mind skipping out on fighting a pissed off magical boar," Derek remarked.

"You two load up on arrows, as many broad blade points as you can get in a quiver," Erin said, pulling her sheathed sword from the elf-pocket and fastening it to her belt. "Check with Scathach before you leave, see if the fight has moved significantly and catch up to us."

"Mama?" Skye could sense the tension in the air.

"Sweetie, Mommy has to go play with a big pig." Erin soothed the child. "Maybe I'll bring you back some bacon."

"Don't go," the girl insisted.

"I have to go, Sweetie." Erin felt a pang of guilt. "I'll be back in a little while. Be good for Saidhe."

Erin turned and marched toward the armory, trying to ignore the tug on her heartstrings as Skye cried. Ahead, she could see the quartermaster's assistant leaning long spears with broad steel blades against the timber building.

"I didn't know part of my job was going to be monster fighting," Erin said and grabbed a spear. "I feel like I'm in one of those games my son plays. Find a new monster, fight it, find a tougher monster, rinse and repeat."

"It is good practice," Izzy said, falling into step and carrying her own spear. "The creatures are probably drawn to Dunos Scaith. Between the magic Scathach uses to hold the fort in time and all the heroic tales within its walls waiting to be told, it's like catnip for great beasts. To be honest, I'm surprised we don't see it more often."

"This would be easier with horses." Daidh was bringing up the rear. "Why don't we have horses? There are stables."

"Something to do with a disagreement with Epona is the popular theory," Izzy replied. "The real reason is boring, and it boils down to logistics. It's already hard enough to provision Dunos Scaith because of the difference in the flow of time. Providing enough fodder for horses for seven years was too problematic."

"So, since we get a caravan about every other month, it would have to enter the pathway every day from the outside world," Daidh said. "There must be some sort of supply depot, so caravans can reload and head back here."

"Correct." Izzy gave Daidh an approving glance. "I imagine the various merchants also have stockpiles of wares."

"Logistics are a merciless foe for any fighting force." Erin remembered from her time deployed how supply issues would crop up, especially if a flight or convoy was delayed. "It also seems like it would be difficult to hide such a large operation."

"Another reason for the increased patrols?" Daidh suggested.

Izzy paused to survey the route ahead, where the slope began to descend. "Perhaps. Remember, anyone wanting to take advantage of the situation would only have a few weeks to react, as opposed to our years."

They began picking their way downhill as quickly as the terrain would allow. "Why do we have regular day and night?" Erin asked. The question came to mind every so often, but she always forgot to bring it up. "I mean, our season is stuck based on the actual season in the outside world. It will progress from late summer into autumn during our stay. On the other hand, the day-night cycle seems normal when a night should last something like three weeks."

"That is Scathach's doing." Izzy used her spear like a walking stick to navigate a steep slope. "One of the reasons she never leaves is because she maintains a stranglehold on the flow of time in Dunos Scaith. To keep her domain out of the normal flow, she must be present."

"Then how did she come to us on the Dunwold after the fight?" Erin asked. "She was not only out of Dunos Scaith, but also not on the Glaswold."

Izzy stopped again to get her bearings. "It wasn't physically her; she projected a phantom. It's like spirit-walking but projecting yourself onto the Glaswold or Dunwold. It takes a great deal of magical power and skill, especially to send a phantom through a wold-ford."

"The others are coming," Daidh said and pointed uphill.

Derek and Mysie were jogging to catch up, pointing to the southeast. Erin could see something tiny fluttering in the air in front of the pair. It took a few minutes for their paths to merge, and as she got close, Erin could discern the small paper bird they were following.

The origami bird led their band along a stream until they came to a short cliff. Twenty feet below was a pool at the base of the stream's waterfall. A handful of warriors from Dunos Scaith were huddled against the cliff in shallow water. Another was on the ground near the pool, the spray of blood and entrails leaving no doubt about his fate.

Pacing the edge of the water was a huge boar, its hide and bristles glimmering with a bronze sheen. Erin thought it would have been majestic if not for the blood splattered on its face and the intestines dangling from its tusk. The beast glared at the people huddled in the pool as it stomped back and forth.

"The devil-bear was scarier," Erin remarked. Still, the creature had killed one person and chased the rest into the pool. She had sparred most of the soldiers, so she knew they were no slouches. "I hate magical monsters. I'm going to guess we can't shoot it full of arrows and call it bacon?"

Derek unlimbered his bow and nocked an arrow. "It would seem too easy. Still, nothing ventured, nothing gained."

Mysie pulled an arrow from her quiver and drew a bead on the boar. "Ready when you are, *fiaradh*."

"How can you call me that when you haven't lain with me?" Derek smirked, still holding his arrow steady on the boar. "Now!"

Both arrows struck true, one behind the foreleg, the other a bit higher behind the shoulder. Both arrows bounced off the boar's bronze hide. The beast flinched as the projectiles struck and cast its gaze about, searching for the source. It squinted at the soldiers huddled in the pool and began pacing the water's edge again.

"Weren't those steel arrowheads?" Erin asked, watching over the edge of the bluff.

"Yes, and the pig is well within range for our bows," Derek replied. "I didn't think we would be able to fell him, but the arrows should have pierced his hide."

"Awesome." Erin wished she had a long gun. Wild boars required heavy caliber weapons to bring down quickly. She didn't think her .357 would do much more than annoy it. Erin gauged the distance to the far side of the small pool to be about 60 yards; she could hit the creature. She set down her spear and drew the revolver.

"Why isn't it going after the patrol?" Daidh asked.

"Maybe he sinks like a stone?" Mysie suggested. "He knows where they are but having a tough hide won't keep him from drowning."

Erin laid flat and braced her elbows on the ground to steady her aim. She waited until the boar reached the end of his path and paused to glare at the soldiers. Erin squeezed off two rapid shots; she noticed years of working out all day paid off. She found it much easier to manage the recoil than she remembered.

The first bullet struck the bronze boar right between the eyes, and the second hit two inches higher on his skull and slightly to the left. Both rounds mushroomed against the animal's hide and fell away. The pig staggered and shook its head, spraying a mist of blood and viscera from its earlier victim. After a few moments, it seemed to regain its bearings and squealed in rage.

Erin replaced the spent rounds, pocketing the brass in a belt pouch. "So, it can feel blunt trauma, but our weapons won't pierce its hide. I'd rather not gamble on taking it out by way of concussion before it rips me open with those tusks."

The boar snuffled at the shoreline and resumed its pacing. "Please tell me someone has rope," Erin said.

"I have some," Daidh replied. "Is 60 feet long enough?"

"Why are you carrying rope out here?" Mysie asked.

Derek smirked. "Ooh, kinky."

"It's work rope," Daidh protested, then lowered his voice. "Not the other rope for when—"

"Just get out the rope," Erin interrupted. "I don't need to know more about your bedroom play."

"What are you thinking?" Izzy asked. "Use the rope to bring our people up and hope the boar doesn't figure it out?"

"Pretty much," Erin replied. "It hasn't noticed us; I think pigs are near-sighted. If we can pull our patrol to safety without getting gored by that amazing, metallic pig, I'll count it as a win."

"It's only a 30-foot drop, so it should work," Daidh said and tied a loop in the end of the rope.

"Someone needs to stand ready in case Pork Chops figures out what we're doing," Erin said, watching the pig stalk the perimeter of the pool.

"It should be you," Izzy responded. "If anyone can fend off *Um-ha-Guairi*, it is the Champion."

Derek chuckled. "Did you name the pig to make it worthy off a tale around the campfire? Bronze-Bristles is most apt."

Erin shook her head in exasperation. "Is the rope ready?"

"I put some knots in it to make it easier to grasp," Daidh said.

Erin stood and planted her spear point in the earth. "Lower the rope and start fishing them up. Let's see how long it takes Bronze-Bristles to notice."

The pig continued to stalk and sniff at the edge of the water while they hoisted four of the soldiers to the top of the cliff. Erin gauged the distance the pig would have to traverse once it figured out what was going on. It was at least 200 yards in either direction before the slope became climbable. When the second to last soldier began her ascent, the boar became agitated, snorting and pawing at the dirt.

Erin laid at the edge of the cliff, watching as the rope snaked down to the last refugee. The animal was squealing and splashing in the shallows of the pool, as though trying to work itself up to going into the deeper water. As the warrior put his foot in the loop of rope, someone behind Erin sneezed. It wasn't a muffled, polite sneeze, but vocal and explosive.

Bronze-Bristles froze, its beady eyes scanning the bluff. With a furious grunt, it bolted to the right, its hooves tearing up rocks and sod.

Erin stood and seized her spear. "Shit, the pig is coming!" She hopped over the rope to position herself in the path of the oncoming threat. A glint of bronze caught her eye, and the boar erupted from the brush a hundred yards away. Behind her, the team on the rope redoubled their efforts and called to Pherick, the last person up, to climb as he reached the lip of the cliff.

Erin brandished her spear and screamed at the closing boar, red creeping into the edge of her vision as adrenaline took hold. She strode forward half a dozen paces, angling closer to the edge of the bluff, and planted the butt of her spear in the dirt. The beast zeroed in on Erin and charged across the remaining space.

Time slowed for Erin as she dipped the head of the spear into the boar's path at the last second. Clods of earth and stone churned up under the boar's feet as it dug in for traction. The pig's angry snort turned into a squeal of shock as the steel spear tip hit the roof of its mouth. Bronze-Bristles twisted its head, keeping the spear from going down its throat. The unbreakable hide kept the weapon from cutting its way out through the boar's cheek; momentum drove the steel blade between the pig's skull and its bronze skin.

The shaft of the spear bowed when the tip wedged in the animal, and, with a loud crack, the shaft shattered in a spray of splinters. Erin scarcely noticed the piercing pain lancing from her side and thigh as she threw herself off the bluff. A corner of her mind remembered a swimming hole near the Ohio River where she and her friends would swing out over the water. She hoped the pool here was as deep as she plummeted down.

Above Erin, Bronze-Bristles tried to arrest its forward trajectory, only to have the edge of the cliff crumble under its hooves. Erin caught a split-second glimpse of the huge bronze pig as it tumbled over the bluff, bellowing in fury. Then the cold mountain water washed over her. Luckily, the water was deep enough to buffer her descent, so she didn't break anything when she hit the bottom. She gathered her legs underneath her and kicked off the rocky floor of the pool toward the surface. Erin gasped for air as soon as she emerged from the water.

Her armor pulled her back under, the water still over her head, and Erin stroked toward where she had seen the shore. Another push up and she was in shallow enough water to stand. As Erin trudged out of the pool, Bronze-Bristles thrashed behind her. When Erin was knee-deep in the pool, she pulled her revolver.

The pool frothed as the boar struggled beneath the water, the bubbles tinged pink. When the beast surged up, and its head broke the surface, Erin opened fire. The first shot splashed in the water, the remaining five struck Bronze-Bristles in the head, grouped around its right ear. The flattened bullets plunked into the water, and the boar listed left and sank back down.

"Hydrostatic shock for the win," Erin sneered as she shoved the gun back in the holster and unsheathed her sword. She knew better than to wade in after the pig this soon; she had seen enough monster movies.

Bronze-Bristles lurched up again, blood oozing from its right ear, and its head skewing left. As it tried to gain its footing, it was apparent it had a broken foreleg. Water sprayed from its muzzle and snout as it bellowed. Erin took a few brisk steps toward the floundering boar and raised her sword. Gripping it with both hands, she channeled her anger into the swing. The blade arced down and struck the beast behind its skull, its vertebrae crunching from the impact.

Erin's hands and arms stung from the jarring blow, and she danced backward in the waist deep water. The boar staggered toward the shore and flopped over in knee-deep water. It struggled for a minute, trying to keep its snout out of the water, but then sighed as its body sagged. A minute later the bubbles stopped emerging from the animal's nostrils and mouth.

Erin lumbered out of the pool, weighed down by her sodden armor, and sat on the shore. As the adrenaline slowly drained away, she became aware of her various aches and pains. Wearily, she pulled off the practice helmet and set it aside. She glanced at the boar while she unraveled her dripping hair, which she had tucked up under the helmet.

"Are you all right?" Izzy asked as the others trotted down to the pool. Several of the guards held their spears ready, hoping they wouldn't need them.

Mysie beamed and pointed up toward the cliff edge. "That was amazing and daft! How did you know the pool was deep enough?"

Erin shrugged, causing her armor to tug on a splinter still impaled in her side. "I didn't. I guessed if the pool was too deep for the boar to chase people through, it would be deep enough."

Daidh knelt next to Erin. "You have a couple of pieces of your spear stuck in you. Do you want me to try to pull them out?"

Erin nodded. While Daidh was no chirurgeon, he was at least as knowledgeable as she was about first aid. "There's one in my thigh as well."

The guards stood around Bronze-Bristles, staying at least a spear length away in case the beast sprung back to life. "What do we do now?" one of them asked.

"Use the spears and rope to rig some way to carry the pig," Erin replied. She pulled off her gloves and tossed them next to her helmet. "Someone run back to Dunos Scaith, get some more hands to lug this pig back and see if anyone knows how to skin and butcher a pig with unbreakable hide."

One of the guards, a young woman with long brown hair and cervid ears turned toward Erin. "I will go. I can run what the dunnies call a marathon in a little over a bell."

On the Dunwold, the woman would be flirting with the world record. Erin was embarrassed that she couldn't recall the young woman. "What's your name?"

The woman's deer-like ears twitched as she tried to stifle a shy smile. "Damhnait."

Erin realized she had spent a long time here when her brain translated what sounded like 'Devnet' to the Gaelic mass of letters. "Damhnait, can you run to the fort, pass along my message, and lead some additional help back? I'm guessing our bronze friend is 400 to 600 pounds."

"Sure!" Damhnait stood up straight. "I'll be back shortly." She dashed off toward the end of the bluff.

Daidh had opened his first aid kit, which mostly consisted of bandages, suture thread, needles, a sharp scalpel-like knife, and heavy-duty tweezers. "This will likely sting. Please don't hit me."

"I'm not going to hit—Ow! Sonuvabitch!" Erin gritted her teeth and unbuckled the straps of her armor on the side opposite where Daidh was working. The next spike of pain wasn't enough to make her blurt out expletives, and the third qualified more as an irritation. When he extracted the splinter from her thigh, it was only enough to make Erin wince.

Daidh returned the forceps to his pouch. "I've extracted the ones I can see through the armor."

"Sounds like an excuse to get your clothes off, Champion." Derek smirked and arched his eyebrow.

Daidh blushed, and Erin scowled at Derek. Some things never change, she thought, as she unbuckled the other side of her armor and pulled it over her head. The water-logged mass of leather and chain thudded to the ground. Her wet tunic had ridden up with the armor, and Erin tugged it down enough for modesty's sake without obstructing Daidh's view of her flank.

After removing two smaller splinters and cleaning her wounds with alcohol, Daidh declared he had done all he could do in the field. The punctures were tiny, and he had small adhesive bandages from the Dunwold, which would be more effective than trying to wrap gauze around Erin's torso.

"Aren't you going to ask her to take her jeans off?" Derek teased. "There might be more wood."

Erin, Mysie, and Izzy glowered at Derek; Daidh blushed and packed up his kit.

*****

Chapter Thirty-Eight

Erin

"So, technically, this is magic bacon?"

The cook shrugged at Erin's question. "I heard the hide was tough; the meat was meat."

Erin regarded the pile of bacon the cook had loaded onto her tray to take back to her group. She had already eaten a chunk of the pork from Bronze-Bristles, as her 'hero's portion' at the feast which followed their return to Dunos Scaith with the boar. It tasted like pork.

Luckily, one of the craft-hobs had a pair of shears enchanted to cut anything. While Erin didn't know if it was an exaggeration, the shears had cut through the boar's hide, which was now tanning at the far end of the fort. The cook scooped some scrambled eggs and fried potatoes onto her tray as well. He finished by loading her up with a bowl of oatmeal and a cup of milk for Skye.

Erin carried the laden tray across the compound, reminded of her waitressing job. For her, it had been three years since her last night at Dante's Pub. For her old boss, Ray, it would have been a little over a month. The morning air in Dunos Scaith was chilly, though it would be a while before they saw frost. Time had barely crawled into autumn.

The bacon smelled delicious. It had been smoked with maple syrup, giving it a sweet flavor. Erin had been afraid the boar's flesh would be unusable, but as the cook had said, it was merely meat. A lot of meat; the pig had yielded over 300 pounds. Even with all the mouths to feed, it would provide some variety to their provisions for several days.

Erin reached the door to her Quonset hut at the same time as Mysie. The short Scotswoman had a gallon jug of orange juice, smuggled off the Dunwold and brought in by the last caravan. That was one of the perks of being the 'Champion,' you and yours got the best of everything. While Erin hadn't heard anyone grumble about it, besides possibly Uathach, she had to wonder if any of the guards or staff resented it. The Quonset huts were a testament that things were occasionally brought over from the mundane world, but special effort had gone into garnering as much as possible to cater to Erin.

Dunos Scaith was halfway through the planned 7-year plunge into a slower timestream. While the inhabitants didn't seem to be concerned about the skewed passage of time, it was a logistical pain-in-the-neck. If it hadn't been for the resident skilly-hobs, Erin would have been at a loss for what to do for clothes for Skye. Now the same folk were eagerly enchanting needles and coming up with ideas about what to do with Bronze-Bristle's hide.

Mysie grabbed the door for Erin. "You have your hands full," Mysie remarked in her cheerful brogue.

Erin carefully stepped over the threshold. It would suck to drop everyone's breakfast. "Thanks." The cool morning would have made having breakfast out on the big table chilly; everyone would much rather crowd into the warm front room of Erin's Quonset. Izzy had brewed coffee on the iron stove, and the aroma permeated the room.

"Momma!" Skye cheered as Erin set down the tray. "Ith anois!"

"Yes, Sweetie, you get to eat now," Erin said, picking up the oatmeal and milk. The child was already clutching her favorite wooden spoon. As long as she was in a good mood, Skye would feed herself. Fortunately, this was one of those mornings.

A chilly breeze accompanied Nechtan and Derek as they arrived. Nechtan quickly crossed to Erin and kissed her on the back of her neck. "Good morning, *acushla*," he murmured in her ear, eliciting thoughts not conducive to going out in the cold and practicing.

"Keep it up, and she'll drag you into her room instead of dragging us onto the practice field," Derek remarked with a smirk. "By all means, please continue."

Erin's mood was too good for her to be cross. "If only we could play hooky." With Skye digging into her oatmeal, Erin was able to sit down and see to her own breakfast. Nechtan slid onto the bench next to her as plates were passed around and food was portioned out.

"Brogan thinks they can craft some armor for you from *Umha-Guairi's* hide," Izzy said as she poured herself a cup of coffee. "Whatever enchantment makes the hide immune to penetration didn't end with the beast's life. Luckily, the craftsfolk can put more powerful charms on their needles and knives."

Derek arched an eyebrow. "Isn't Brogan a bit short for you?" Erin had met Brogan, who didn't stand as tall as her chin. He appeared to be middle-aged, with carrot-orange hair, which was slowly receding from his forehead. His eyes reminded Erin of some of the more lecherous patrons at her old job.

"Not where it matters, Brother," Izzy replied with a mischievous grin. "And he has nimble fingers."

Erin glanced uncomfortably toward Skye, who was working on her oatmeal. Erin wasn't sure if Izzy was only messing with her brother, and she didn't really want to know. Izzy's taste seemed very eclectic and had no regard to gender. At one point, she had made a drunken suggestion regarding a three-way with Nechtan, showing as much interest in Erin as the hunter. Nechtan had feigned obliviousness, and the next morning Izzy had a splitting hangover and claimed to have no memory of the conversation.

"Do I need to get with Brogan about this armor?" Erin asked, hoping to deflect the subject of his qualifications regarding more amorous pursuits. "I assume he and the others will need measurements."

"Be sure you take someone with you," Izzy remarked between bites. "Brogan is very skilled, but also a bit of a lech. If there are witnesses, he'll be well behaved."

"Why does Scathach keep him around?" Erin demanded.

"He's very talented, both in leatherwork and magic," Izzy replied. "When he was born a thousand years ago, his advances would have been considered 'flirting.' If he were on the Dunwold now, he would be drummed out of wherever he plied his trade. Here, as long as he doesn't cross the line from suggestion to action, Scathach will put up with him."

Erin frowned. "You slept with him?"

Izzy shrugged. "His advances were assertive, but he is a skilled lover. I found his self-confidence warranted, but I realize others may not appreciate his aggressiveness."

"A five-foot tall pervert puts his hands where they don't belong, and I'll put him through a wall," Erin said.

Izzy sighed. "He may suggest more intimate fittings over mead, but he understands the meaning of 'no.'"

"Fine." Erin stabbed some potatoes on her plate. "Izzy, you come with me. I want to hear more about this armor; it sounds useful for my fight with Giwargix. But if Brogan tries anything, he'll be picking plaster out of his teeth."

"Until now, your defensive strategy has been pretty bare," Daidh remarked. "I know your…" Daidh glanced at Nechtan before continuing, "The Druid is forging you a special sword, but no mention has been made of ensuring you survive your fight with St. George."

Erin picked up a crisp slice of bacon and took a bite. It was leaner than she expected, but still tasty. "We've been hard at work on the conditioning and training but haven't discussed gear. Neither Einar nor Gofannon mentioned armor; they were all about making me a magic sword."

"Erin's defense will be killing him first," Mysie interjected and handed Erin a cup of orange juice. "You've seen how fast she is, especially when she has one of her *saobhi.* The fight with the boar was the quickest I've ever seen anyone move; she was a blur in her warp-frenzy."

"She may be fast, but Giwargix killed a dragon," Daidh said, shaking pepper onto his eggs and potatoes. He reached for the sea salt grinder. "Rumor has it Giwargix ate the dragon's heart after the battle."

Erin wrinkled her nose in disgust. She had become accustomed to the more primitive food here, but the idea of eating a lizard's heart was almost enough to put her off her bacon. "Why would he do that?" Erin asked. She took a sip of juice to wash away the imaginary distaste in her mouth.

"To gain the creature's strength," Izzy suggested. "It was one of the last, if not the last, dragon on the Dunwold. It would have been a very potent source of magic."

Erin set down her juice cup and checked on Skye. The toddler had managed to eat more of the oatmeal than she was wearing. "I thought the Avramites didn't approve of magic?" Erin asked.

"Only when it doesn't suit their needs," Derek replied. "Much like any other kind of knowledge, the higher powers prefer the people they rule remain ignorant and manipulable. Anything which causes them to question the edicts of authorities must be declared evil and banished."

"If he ate the dragon's heart, he got stronger?" Erin pushed aside her bacon and worked on her potatoes. "Can he breathe fire now?"

No one at the table had an answer. For a few minutes, they ate in silence punctuated by Skye blowing bubbles in her milk.

Nechtan broke the hush. "Is there any reason you can't just shoot him? Your gun put down the devil-bear, and you shattered the side of Bronze-Bristle's skull, even if the bullets would not punch through his hide."

Erin had finally worked her way back to the bacon and had to finish chewing before she could answer. Nechtan had paid attention back when she explained firearms. She rarely used the pistol and never wasted ammo on practice. "Somehow, I don't think it will be so easy. Liam was working on getting me tungsten-carbide rounds, but I don't think I can walk out onto the battlefield, pull my gun, and blow several holes in him."

"*Aithir?*" Skye asked, using the Goidelc word for father. The child clutched her milk cup and watched her mother expectantly.

Erin glanced at Nechtan to gauge his reaction; he seemed intent on his scrambled eggs and potatoes.

"Yes, Sweetie," Erin replied. "I was talking about your father." She dreaded the time when the girl would get older and start asking more complicated questions. Erin turned toward the others. "We could put some of the leather from Bronze-Bristles behind my vambrace. My sword couldn't cut into the boar, so the hide might help if, somehow, George's sword cuts through the steel armor."

"It's a shame they can't make you a forearm guard with some of the meteor they are using for your sword," Derek remarked. "The meteor iron would likely diffuse magic, and the bronze-hide backing would keep your arm from getting sliced off."

Nechtan frowned. Erin knew he didn't like it when they talked about putting her in harm's way, but he didn't voice his instinctive, protective male impulses. "Such a blow would still shatter her arm."

Erin checked to see how much attention Skye was paying to the conversation. She didn't like discussing violent matters in front of the child; Skye was catching on quicker than Tim had at the same age. The toddler seemed intent on investigating how her emptied cup would fit in the oatmeal bowl.

"It doesn't matter," Erin said. "We don't have a way to let them know, and the arm-buckler isn't my main defense. I have it for when my blade is out of position, and I really need to block something."

"Someone could cross to the Dunwold and tell them," Derek suggested. He ticked numbers off on his fingers. "Whoever did it would have to cool their heels for about three weeks until the rest of you finished here and crossed back. I'm sure I could find a way to amuse myself."

Izzy scowled. "How generous of you to volunteer."

Derek smirked. "I am a very giving fellow," he countered. "Ask Saidhe."

"When's the last time you opened a wold-ford, Brother?" Izzy held her gaze on her twin. Erin knew Izzy was more proficient at magic than Derek, but she wasn't sure to what degree.

"You could open the ford for me," Derek replied.

Izzy leaned back from the table and crossed her arms. "I could, but why should I go to the trouble to send you back to modern convenience and comfort?"

"Won't they need you to bring Erin back over?" Derek retorted, crossing his arms to match his sister. "They really don't need me for anything."

"The phone." Erin sat up, recollecting her plan from years ago. "Remember, the original idea was for me to cross back after a couple of weeks and call home. We cached a weatherproof container with a phone, a spare charged battery, and one of those hand-cranked containers. Izzy could cross over, make the call, and come back."

"Since we know where the wold-ford is, I don't see why your suggestion wouldn't work," Izzy said. "Sorry, Brother, but hot showers and cable television will have to wait a little longer."

Mysie stifled a snicker in response to Derek's crest-fallen expression. "I understand the appeal of a hot shower, but the other stuff is lost on me. We have a roof, hot food, and ale; how much better can it be?"

Derek shook his head. "You have no idea."

"Before you go, let me write a message for Tim," Erin said, her mind already whirling. She hadn't expected this opportunity. "I'll keep it short. Don't tell anyone about…" Erin flicked her eyes toward Skye, who was stacking her bowl on top of her cup. "I want to break the news myself, in person."

Izzy shrugged. "As you wish. Let me know when you have your message ready. I'll pack a bag in case I'm outdoors longer than a few hours."

* * *

Training interrupted Erin's attempt to pen a concise letter with the right sentiment. She had debated asking Izzy to check out the antenna farm they had spotted during their search atop Cheyenne Mountain to see if there were any mailboxes at the buildings servicing those towers.

Her distraction nearly got her bell rung when Izzy's practice sword came within an inch of her helmet before she ducked back and blocked it. The near hit provoked a scolding from Scathach; Erin mutely nodded. She wished she could be the one to go back to the mundane world, if only to talk to her son for a few minutes. From her perspective, it had been three years since she spoke to him. Luckily, her helmet hid the handful of tears running down her cheek.

"Izzy, I have an extra favor to ask of you." Erin had waited until Scathach left before broaching the subject. "I want to write a letter to send to Tim. Part of my go-bag included envelopes and stamps, just in case. I'm thinking, if there are service buildings for those transmitter towers on top of the mountain, they probably have mailboxes. If you stick a letter in the box, the postal worker should pick it up."

Izzy nodded. "Certainly. Those antennae were less than a quarter of a mile from where we crossed over. It should only take me a few minutes, maybe an hour at the most, to scout them out and return to the ford."

Erin sighed in relief. She didn't have any reason to believe Izzy would deny her, but she couldn't help but think it was too easy. "I'll write a letter for Tim tonight," Erin said.

"No letter for the Druid?" Izzy asked, her tone neutral.

Erin glanced about, scanning for Nechtan. While he hadn't practiced with them, he knew when they usually finished and joined them afterwards for dinner. "No, I don't think so," Erin replied, feeling guilty as she uttered the words. "I'm not sure what I would say to him, and I don't want to get his hopes up."

"You understand his familiar wants to be his fae-wife," Izzy remarked. "If you don't want to write off a future relationship with the Druid, a few words could go a long way. When we departed, you really didn't give him a reason to turn down Pixel's advances."

The mention of the purple-haired fairy's name brought old annoyances to the surface. Erin still occasionally had dreams about the fae girl and Liam. She didn't want to marry Liam, so why did it bother her so much?

"Maybe I'll jot him a note as well," Erin relented. "It would only be polite, but I still want to wait to tell him and Tim about Skye in person." A petty part of her wanted to be there to see Liam's jaw drop when he got the news.

"Understandable," Izzy agreed as they reached the Quonset hut. Nechtan was there, kneeling and stoking the fire pit against the autumn chill.

"What do you think, *acushla*?" Nechtan smiled at Erin. "Is it too cold to eat outside?"

"As long as the wind doesn't pick up, we should be fine," Erin replied. She went over to Nechtan and draped her arms over his shoulders. She leaned forward and kissed a stubbled cheek. "We might as well enjoy the fresh air while we can. The nights are getting bitter."

"Good thing you have a way to stay warm," Derek quipped, setting a cask of ale on the table. He leered at Nechtan and Erin. "You know, more bodies make more heat."

Erin narrowed her eyes. "It isn't that cold."

Derek popped the lid off the cask and grinned. "So you're saying there's a temperature cold enough for you to consider—"

"No!" Erin interrupted. Nechtan chuckled.

Erin managed to finish the notes during dinner, between banter and making sure more food got in Skye than on her. Tim's had been easy to write since she was sending a letter rather than having Izzy recite a message over the phone. By the time she put pen to paper, Erin had composed the whole missive in her head. The short note to Liam was harder; Erin fed the first three iterations to the fire. The fourth draft struck the right balance between warmness and genuine appreciation she had for the time he was spending with their son, without getting sappy or alluding to more affectionate intentions. She folded it and sealed it in the envelope with Tim's letter before she started a fifth draft.

Izzy emerged from the Quonset, clad in layers of clothing, and hefted a backpack. "Are you finished?" she asked as she approached the table.

Erin nodded and held out the envelope. "Sorry it took so long. I wanted to make sure I got the letter to Tim right, seeing as I won't see him for another three years."

Izzy seemed doubtful but said nothing. She took the letter and tucked it into her coat. Erin assumed Izzy was tucking it into one of her *alf-vassi.* The twins each had three of the elf-pockets, which somehow stayed attached to them without being anchored to their garments. They had tried to explain it to Erin but wrapping her brain around it gave her a headache.

"Be careful, Sister," Derek cautioned. His expression was serious; it reminded Erin of when they arrived at Dunos Scaith with Izzy at death's door. "While I doubt they would still be prowling the area after more than three weeks, the Avramites are nothing if not tenacious."

Izzy smiled. A thick wool scarf hid the faint scars on her throat. "Do not worry. This will be four to six hours for me," Izzy said. "I'm more concerned about the trouble you'll get into for the several days I'm away."

Derek gave a dismissive wave with his long fingers. "I'm the picture of caution and prudence."

"Prudence?" Skye parroted. Erin considered herself lucky; Skye took glee in repeating words Derek said which provoked a reaction.

Izzy snorted. "Try to keep him out of trouble, Champion." Izzy strode toward the gates, fading into the dark shadow of the keep.

"Bye bye." Skye waved in the direction of the keep.

"Where is Izquierda off to?" Nechtan asked, returning from the latrines. If Dunos Scaith had a greatest failing, it was the lack of indoor plumbing, especially toilets.

"She's running an errand for me," Erin replied. She suddenly felt guilty about the note to Liam. "She's getting a message to my son, letting him know I'm still alive and well."

Nechtan sat on the bench and scooted close to Erin. "Are you going to tell him about his sister?"

Erin shook her head. "It's not the kind of thing I want to announce through a note. I'd rather break the news in person."

"By then, the news will be what, five years old?" Nechtan nodded toward Skye.

Skye held up two fingers. "I am two years old."

"That's right, Sweetie." Erin smiled at the child. "You are two years old."

"Is she finding a wold-runner to take the message back?" Nechtan asked, pouring himself a mug of ale.

Erin assumed he was referring to one of the smugglers who ran between the Dunwold and the Glaswold for the merchants. She hadn't considered them as an option. "No, she's going to take the original wold-ford we arrived through, go back to Cheyenne Mountain on the Dunwold, and stick the letter in a mailbox."

Nechtan took a draw from his flagon. "I'm surprised Scathach approved."

Erin shrugged. Would Nechtan run off to tell Scathach? Should someone chase after Izzy and stop her before she crossed over to the Dunwold? She decided to stay silent on the matter.

"It feels like it's going to be a cold night," Erin whispered in Nechtan's ear. "How about after I put Skye to bed, we find a way to stay warm?"

* * * * *

Chapter Thirty-Nine

Erin

"Where is Izquierda?"

Erin felt like her Mom had caught her smoking pot. Scathach's question sounded casual, but so did asking why you were burning incense and had the window open in February.

"She's running an errand for me," Erin replied and continued to don her practice armor. "She should be back in a few days."

"Is she taking the merchant's path?" Scathach asked. "The road will not be open for several days, from our perspective."

Erin remembered how her mother would continue to ask questions when she already knew the answers, just to see if she could drag the truth out of Erin. "No, she crossed the wold-ford on top of Cheyenne Mountain. We left some equipment behind she can use to contact my son, and she is mailing a letter. It won't be more than a few hours for her, so she should be back in a few days."

Scathach's green eyes hardened into agates. "No, she won't."

Erin stopped halfway through lacing her last glove. "I doubt those Avramites are still lurking around. It's been more than two weeks for them, and the seraphim I stabbed into dust."

"She will not be able to open the wold-ford to return," Scathach stated. "The fact that she was able to open it at all was an oversight on my part, one I intend to remedy."

Erin stood up. "You're not going to let her come back?"

Scathach seemed to grow a foot taller as she glowered at Erin. "Absolutely not, her transition to the Dunwold may have given us away," Scathach said, fuming. "Opening the ford from the Dunwold side is more likely to draw attention. If you had asked me beforehand, I would have told you."

"I'm sick and tired of trying to guess all of your weird rules," Erin countered. "Maybe if you would be a little more up front instead of playing the inscrutable master, I wouldn't have to wonder."

"I wonder how many people here are sick and tired of being stuck for seven years to help you?" Scathach retorted. "Your little stunt may have endangered everyone here. I hope I don't have to submerge Dunos Scaith deeper in the flow of time to keep our enemies from finding us." The imperious redhead spun on her heel, her cloak flaring out behind her as she strode toward the keep.

"Does this mean practice is cancelled?" Daidh ventured.

Erin snatched a practice sword off the rack and gave it an angry twirl. "No." She stalked out onto the practice field. "What did she mean about sinking us deeper in time?"

Derek took his time putting on his protective gear. No one was eager to join Erin in the sparring ring while she was upset. "You know how she has held Dunos Scaith in a faster current of time to give you more time to practice?" Derek asked. "Right now, time passes for us at fifty times the rate of what it does outside. She could accelerate it further, so if someone came to this 'stream,' they wouldn't find us. The flipside is even the current time-flow is taking most of her power. To go deeper, deep enough to escape notice, would be physically taxing on her."

"So, it isn't something she would do in a fit of pique." Erin stalked back and forth, controlling her breathing. "She wouldn't do it simply to prove a point."

Derek frowned, and then answered, "I don't think so. She may have the famous Celtic redhead temper but moving one's domain in the currents of time is not lightly done. This is good, because I don't want our remaining three years to suddenly turn into six or nine."

Erin stopped in her tracks. "What about Izzy? She'll go back to the ford and won't be able to open it."

Derek snorted. "Pobrecita. She will be stuck in the land of hot baths, central heating, and indoor toilets. She will be fine. She can go down to Colorado Springs, check into a motel, and cool her heels in modern comfort for a few weeks."

"That's why you were so eager to take on the job." Erin regarded Derek through the slits in her practice helmet. "You hoped she would get pissed and seal off the route, stranding you in the mundane, but oh-so-comfy, world."

Derek feigned outrage. "I'm shocked you would think such a thing."

"I'm not shocked," Mysie remarked.

"Me either," Daidh added. "I'm the opposite of shocked."

"On the bright side, she should have the Charger ready for our road trip back to Illinois," Derek said, ignoring the jibes.

Mysie dragged her toe through the dirt outside the practice square. "It could be a lot worse," she said. "We'll miss Izzy, but it sounds like she gets a vacation while waiting for the rest of you to catch up."

"I suppose you're right," Erin relented. "Nechtan remarked about asking Scathach before Izzy left. I'm pretty sure I didn't because I knew what her answer would be, even if I didn't know the ramifications."

"Where do we go from here?" Daidh asked. He wasn't near the line to enter the square with Erin. "Have you calmed down enough so you won't hand us our heads?"

"I suppose so," Erin relented. Her pulse had slowed to a steady beat; as long as she could keep from dwelling on the situation, she shouldn't get riled up. It would be challenging, because she found it was far easier to be mad at herself. "I'm going to miss Izzy. She was the best at two-handed sword, as well as at sword and shield." Those were the two most likely fighting styles for Giwargix to use. "Daidh, why don't you grab a two-hander, and Derek why don't you gear up with sword and board?"

"Are you sure it's wise for you to take on two of us while you're agitated?" Derek asked and walked reluctantly toward the weapon racks. "It seems like a good way to get you frustrated enough to warp-frenzy and send someone whose name starts with a D to the chirurgeon."

Daidh mutely nodded in agreement.

Erin shook her head. "I'm only going to drill today. You're right; I'm too likely to fly off the handle, and I don't want to hurt someone. I think it would be a good idea for you and Daidh to practice with those weapons before sparring me. They represent two of our three best guesses at what Giwargix will use, and we don't have any horses for someone to try a lance charge at me."

* * *

"You know, since Izzy won't be back, you could move in with Nechtan," Mysie suggested as she and Erin stowed the practice armor. "Derek could move in with us, you could put Skye in Derek's old room, and you and Nechtan could play house as much as you want."

Erin managed not to freeze like a deer in the headlights, continuing the motions of putting away her gear and making sure the racks were covered. "That's an interesting idea." More like terrifying, Erin thought. She was training to go one-on-one with a legendary dragon slayer, but the notion of moving in with the guy she was sleeping with was more frightening.

Mysie apparently noticed Erin's stiffness. Erin would never be known for having a poker face. "I'm sorry if I crossed a line," the Scots woman said. "You two seem to get on so well."

"Probably because we don't live together," Erin remarked. She gave the practice area a last once-over. "When I get too serious with someone, things go south. It's usually my fault."

Mysie regarded her quizzically. "What do you mean?"

"I pretty much sabotage my relationships if I'm afraid things are getting too serious," Erin replied. "I used to think guys couldn't handle the fact I'm a mother first, but Liam ruined my theory."

"The Druid?" Mysie asked. "He's Skye's father and the father of your son back on the Dunwold."

Erin nodded. "If I had let him, he would have married me. He had a cute little coed sprite throwing herself at him, but he was ready to give me the white picket fence and dog."

Mysie knitted her eyebrows in puzzlement. "Fence and dog? Also, sprites are tiny."

"I don't know the whole catalog of different fair folk," Erin grumbled. "She was petite, a bit shorter than you, and looked like she was all of twenty years old." Erin tamped down her irritation at the thought of Pixel. "The picket fence and dog are a dunnie reference; they represent an idyllic, happy, traditional family."

"Sounds horrible," Mysie remarked as they crossed the courtyard toward the Quonset huts. "He spurned a young lover to offer you a storybook life."

"I know, right?" Erin stopped,and squinted at Mysie. "Very funny. Now you see what I mean, though. Liam's a good guy, and I'm attracted enough to him to spawn two children, but the idea of marrying him scares the hell out of me, more than giants or monster pigs do."

"The guy who loves you, children and all, ruined the idea of your having a serious relationship?" Mysie asked. "No offense, but you dunnies are really messed up."

"It made me examine my previous relationships," Erin replied. "Yeah, some of those guys were jerks, and a few were just out of their depths. Thinking back, I'm pretty sure I chased at least a few away."

Mysie's eyebrows gathered again. If the woman had a flaw, Erin mused, it was her bushy eyebrows. Erin would love to get her in a salon on the Dunwold. "You're afraid if things get too serious with Nechtan, you'll do something to ruin the relationship and push him away."

"Exactly!" Erin exclaimed louder than she had intended. She peered about awkwardly, but no one seemed to notice.

Mysie placed a consoling hand on Erin's arm. "I'm sorry you feel like you need to punish yourself. It's a shame you can't let yourself be happy."

Erin bit back her protest. Mysie was right; Erin was her own worst enemy. "It seems like Nechtan and I are in a good place. We enjoy each other's company without the specter of commitment. I don't want to rock the boat."

"Forget I brought it up," Mysie said.

Nechtan and Slaine, who had been babysitting Skye, were waiting at the table. The fire pit was stoked and burning hot. Another large metal container had been placed on the far side of the table, filled with timber, and set alight as a second heat source.

"Momma!" Skye exclaimed, throwing her arms in the air. The bundled-up toddler was ensconced in her high chair. "Momma play hard today?"

"Hi Sweetie!" Erin called to the girl. Slaine stepped aside to make room for Erin. "Thank you for keeping an eye on her, Slaine."

"It was no trouble," the chirurgeon's assistant replied. "The cooling weather means less mischief for the guards, and in turn, quieter days for us at the infirmary. I'll be by in the morn to see if you need me to sit with her." The woman hurried off toward the stone infirmary, where her own dinner would be waiting.

"Not to poke a hornet's nest, *acushla*, but I heard Scathach wasn't very happy about Izzy's excursion," Nechtan said after Erin finished cooing at her daughter.

Erin snorted. She was determined to keep her ire in check. "You could say so. Izzy is stuck on the Dunwold; Scathach closed the wold-ford."

Nechtan stroked his stubbled chin, delaying so he could choose his words carefully. He was usually smart enough not to pick pointless fights with Erin. "What's done is done. For Izquierda, it will only be a month, or closer to three weeks, before you return to the Dunwold."

Erin nodded, splitting her attention between her conversation with Nechtan and Skye's insistence on telling Erin about a bird she saw, a bright blue bird. "Was it a pretty blue bird?" Erin asked the child before turning to Nechtan. "As long as she didn't run into any trouble when she emerged back on Earth, I mean the Dunwold, she should be able to cool her heels with pizza and HBO until Derek and I get back."

"It was a mean bird," Skye whispered. "I think it was bad."

"Sweetie, it was probably upset it was cold and should have flown south for the winter," Erin replied without thinking. She wished she could go south; why couldn't Scathach have set up shop in a nice tropical locale? "We'll have to make do without Izzy."

"You know, with Izzy stuck on the Dunwold, it opens up things here," Nechtan said. Despite his piercing blue-eyed gaze, Erin suspected he was working hard to keep his tone casual.

"You're right," Erin replied. "I could turn her room into a guest room, in case Slaine or someone else watching Skye needed to stay over."

"I guess that would be a good idea," Nechtan admitted.

* * * * *

Chapter Forty

Liam

"Iblis was in Word Nerds?"

Liam didn't wait for an answer to his question before he started pacing. This was bad, he thought. The so-called Devil was zeroing in on him. He took a breath and reigned in his skittering thoughts. "What makes you think it was Iblis?"

Susan cradled her coffee cup at the kitchen table. "I would bet money on it," she replied and took a sip. "It was too convenient. I'm positive he was waiting for me to show up."

Liam cracked his knuckles. It was more of a fidget than an aggressive gesture. "I suppose it was a matter of time. Enough people know we're friends; there might be a few pictures out on social media."

"Yet every time I try to take a selfie of us, you get all pissy," Pixel remarked.

"Now you see where pictures lead," Liam countered. He turned back to Susan. "When did this happen?"

"Wednesday, when I went to pick up your order," Susan replied. "I don't know how they knew you had an order, or if they had been casing the store for several days."

Liam debated switching from coffee to beer even though it was before dinner. "It's Saturday. Why did you wait until now?"

"I was concerned they might be using me as a stalking horse," Susan replied. It was obvious she was annoyed. "I didn't want to lead them right to you."

Liam took a deep breath. He had to admit Susan had made a smart decision. If she had called him, he would have gone right over. It would have played right into their hands, assuming that was their plan.

"You're sure he didn't have his goons follow you here?" Einar asked, his eyebrows knitting in concern.

Susan nodded. "Yes. I took the north route, the Highway 17 bridge across the river. Anyone following me would have been obvious."

"The question is—what does Iblis hope to accomplish by tracking Liam down?" Pixel asked. "His bitch, I mean witch, has already said he wants to make a deal."

"Maybe I should call him?" Liam suggested. The room broke into pandemonium.

"You can't trust him!"

"He's the great deceiver!"

"He could be the Avramite devil!"

Liam held up his hands. "Calm down, it was just an idea. I'm guessing he is trying to hedge his bets; he doesn't want to be wiped out if we win."

"He could be the paragon of evil for the Avramites!" Pixel protested. "He could be Satan, himself; how can you deal with someone like that?"

"As opposed to Loki and Gwyddion?" Liam retorted. He seriously doubted Iblis was Satan; his operations seemed low rent for Lucifer. "Surely you don't believe their services are altruistic?"

"They may be tricksters, but they're our tricksters," Pixel replied. "They were the ones who managed to convert Glaswold gold into the financial gobbledygook the Dunwold uses in place of honest coin."

Liam heard Einar stifle a chuckle. The dwarf probably had a better understanding of the shenanigans employed by the trickster gods than Pixel. "My point is no one is aboveboard on these dealings. I'm sure Loki and Gwyddion helped you set up the funds for Erin and me because they could skim something off for themselves. I would guess those funds will fuel further mischief."

"Well, duh." Pixel ran a hand through her purple locks. "It was assumed whatever cut they took for themselves would be acceptable in light of providing for the Druid and the Champion."

Liam stared into his empty coffee mug. It was time for a beer. "What would it take to make sure our tricksters cut Iblis out of the loop?"

Pixel glanced at Einar before answering. "Dealing with them is always fraught with traps."

"Ja, Loki prides himself on tripping up clever wizards, or in your case, druids," Einar added.

"Would Loki get tricky enough to keep himself out of the Dunwold?" Liam asked. "If I lose, he is stuck. Don't get me wrong, I don't relish the thought of unleashing Loki on the world, but if I can keep the world from ending, it's a deal I'm willing to make."

"There's something else you should be aware of," Susan said. Her tone was reluctant; she didn't want to bring this up to Liam, but he could tell she felt compelled. "Renee, if that's her name, had a black dot on her palm."

"What does a black dot mean?" Pixel asked.

"When a woman is the victim of domestic abuse, she'll place a black dot on her palm," Susan replied. "It's a signal to a sympathetic party, but it doesn't draw attention from the abuser."

Einar's eyebrows gathered again. "Wouldn't the bastard who's hurting her see the dot?"

"Some hand sanitizer will take it right off," Susan said, rubbing her thumb across her palm. "The real question is whether this is a cry for help or a trap?"

"This is the same person who sent bikers to kidnap Liam," Pixel retorted. She placed a protective hand on Liam's shoulder. "Of course, it's a trap."

The oven dinged, prompting Einar to hop out of his chair and head for the kitchen. "Dinner will be in 15 minutes. Druid, you should call your son, and someone let Gofannon know."

Liam paced several steps, then caught himself. "I know it's a trap, but on the chance it isn't, we can't blow Renee off. It's entirely possible she works for Iblis, and he abuses her."

"What do you want to do?" Susan asked. "I want to help her, but we have no clue how to deal with Iblis."

"I still think it's too dangerous," Pixel protested. "It's probably another attempt to seduce you, like Raven was. Since her boobs didn't do the trick, they're trying the damsel-in-distress game."

Liam had to admit he had a weakness for the whole white knight routine. "Susan, do you have a way to get in touch with Renee?"

Susan nodded. "She gave me her contact information to pass along."

"Pixel, do you think you can get some net-savvy fae to do some digging?" Liam knew there was a contingent of fae folk schooled in modern technology working to further the Exiled Folk's agenda.

"Maybe they can see if there is any truth to her story. It might also give us some clues regarding Iblis."

Pixel pursed her lips in thought. She seemed reluctant to agree, searching for a flaw in Liam's suggestion. "I suppose. Their Google-Fu is better than mine; they may be able to dig up some dirt."

"Let's set up a meeting with her," Liam said, looking out the high windows lining the dining room. "I have a plan to mitigate the risks; we can see if she is legit or a worm on Iblis' hook."

Susan took out her phone and set it on the table. "Here is her contact information."

"I'll need a burner phone," Liam said. While he wasn't tech savvy, he understood the value of a hard-to-trace phone. Pixel produced a phone from her elf-pocket and set it on the table next to Susan's.

Liam punched in the number. "Hello?" The woman who answered sounded tentative, like someone who was expecting bad news from a hospital.

"I'm calling for Renee," Liam said. "My friend Susan gave me this number."

There was a long pause; Liam thought the woman had hung up. "I'm Renee," she finally said. "Who is this?"

In for a pence, in for a pound, Liam thought. "My name is Liam. My friend said you were searching for someone with a background in druidry."

"Yes! I'd heard there was a druid practicing Celtic Tribal Reconstructionism in Central Illinois," the woman on the other end of the phone said. "I'm not really connecting with what's going on in my Wiccan coven."

Liam could empathize; he'd had a Wiccan phase, and while the religion worked great for some people, it didn't mesh with his spiritual path. "I don't have a grove anymore. I'm not sure how much help I could be to you."

"I really want to talk to someone," Renee whispered, barely audible. "If you're a solitary druid, maybe you could give me some advice. My current priest isn't very helpful."

Liam took a deep breath before uttering the next sentence. "I understand he hasn't had your best interests at heart."

Her pause lasted longer, long enough to make Liam wonder if there was someone else who could overhear her part of the conversation. "You could say so," she finally said. "He has more carnal interest in some of us. There is an implication that how far we rise within the coven is related to how well we serve him."

Liam bottled up his rising ire. If this was a trap, unleashing his ire would be exactly what they wanted. If it wasn't a trap, getting angry would serve no useful purpose. "I'm going to be at a meet-up on the 10th," Liam said. It would be ten days from now.

"Any chance we could meet sooner?" Renee asked. "Just the two of us?"

Liam was glad Pixel couldn't hear the conversation. "I can arrange something. My schedule is tight, but I could meet you tomorrow, at the Brickhouse Pub in East Peoria. Would that work for you?"

"Yes, absolutely," Renee replied. "What time?"

"Let's say 7 p.m.," Liam said, mentally consulting the timetables for sunset. This would be easier if it was dark outside. "Sound good?"

"Yes," Renee answered. "I'll see you then."

"See you then." Liam ended the call and checked the phone to be certain. "It's totally a trap."

"I told you so!" Pixel exclaimed.

"How can you be certain?" Susan asked.

"Renee never asked how she would know it was me at the rendezvous," Liam replied. "She never asked what I looked like, or what I would be wearing, or any other questions to identify me."

"Because she already knows what you look like," Susan said.

"Exactly!" Liam clapped his hands together. "She knows what I look like."

"What are you going to do?" Pixel asked.

Liam grinned. "The only thing that makes sense—spring the trap!"

*****

Chapter Forty-One

Lee

"If you keep eating so much, you're going to get fat."

Qashmet ignored Lee's admonishment, wolfing down the rest of the meatballs. The pizza pub was only half a mile from their hotel and served better food than the casino buffet. The casino had not been agreeable to Lee's feeding Qashmet off the buffet, despite Lee paying for a separate plate for the dog. Lee couldn't really blame the casino given the dog's gluttonous nature.

Brickhouse Pub didn't care if Lee fed Qashmet since they didn't have a buffet. Lee was glad his credit card still worked; the dog had an expensive appetite. Lee had learned not to give Qashmet garlic or mushrooms; the hotel room's windows didn't open.

Lee sipped his beer as he scrolled through sites on his tablet. He had a list of all the schools within 20 miles of Peoria. He had gone through three-quarters of them, checking all the listings and pictures he could find. While he knew more than he ever wanted about mid-Illinois middle school athletics, he was no closer to finding Donnelly's son.

This morning, he received another vague threat over the news channel. Finding a clue regarding the druid initially appeased Mikha'el, as did discovering information about another party interested in the druid, but the goodwill hadn't lasted long. The barista at the bookstore had let leak the 'creepy guy' had been back. Interestingly, the young woman with him had a conversation with the druid's friend. The girl had no idea what they discussed, but she noticed them exchanging contact information.

Lee had also sent an e-mail to the address on the flyer, under the pretense of being a Unitarian minister interested in ecumenical work. A couple days later, Lee received a vague response referencing the meet-up on the flyer.

"If we could get our paws on something belonging to the druid or his buxom girlfriend, I could track them down," Qashmet remarked from under the table. It meant he was out of meatballs, and Lee expected him to plead for more soon. At least the dog's wounds had healed; now he could wear the service dog vest, which meant fewer complaints when Lee brought him into restaurants and stores.

Lee glanced down. "Hindsight being what it is, they should have grabbed some of the kid's personal items in addition to his mother's," Lee whispered, aware the dog could easily hear him. Qashmet still checked for signs of the Champion's trail, but he never found anything. It was as though the woman had vanished from the face of the Earth.

"Collar, you should check out the cutie who sat down in the booth behind you."

Lee sighed. No matter how often Lee explained it to Qashmet, the dog didn't understand Lee had eyes only for Christine. Even ravaged by cancer, she was the most beautiful woman in the world. "It's unnatural for you to be lusting after humans," Lee uttered.

The dog snorted. "If I had two legs, I would totally be chatting her up."

Lee shook his head, pulling up his alternate social media profile. This profile was more open to other faiths and focused on networking among different religions. Lee hoped no one ever connected it to his factual profile; it would be hard to explain to his colleagues and parishioners.

"Oh, my fucking God!" the dog exclaimed.

"Language," Lee retorted under his breath.

"I'm serious, Collar, turn the fuck around," Qashmet growled.

Lee glanced over his shoulder, trying to appear as though he was looking for his waitress. Walking along the booths straight toward him was Knox. There was no mistaking it, despite the scarcity of pictures he had dredged up on the internet. Luckily, Knox seemed focused on someone else.

"Hello Renee," Knox said, clearly audible from the next booth. He slid into the seat across from the young woman Qashmet had noticed. "It's nice to meet you."

"Hi," the young woman replied. Lee wished he had a better view; it was hard to observe the booth behind him without being obvious. "I wasn't sure if you would come."

"How are ya'll doing?" The waitress sounded too southern; Lee wondered if the accent was an affectation, or if she was a transplant. "What can I get for ya'll?"

"I put in an order online," Knox replied. "If the young lady would like anything else, charge it to the same card. It's under Knox."

There was a moment of silence, and Lee wished for eyes in the back of his head. "Whatever my date ordered should be fine to start," the woman replied.

"Sure thing," the waitress remarked. She stepped over to Lee's booth. Fortunately, his beer was still half-full. "Anything I can get for you, Darling?"

Lee shook his head. "No, thank you."

"Ask for another order of meatballs," Qashmet suggested from under the table.

Lee hefted his mug. He never drank more than two beers. The waitress nodded and left.

"Thank you for coming," the young woman in the next booth said. "Did Susan tell you I'm interested in druidry?"

"Let's cut to the chase," Knox countered. "I know you work for Iblis."

"Holy crap!" Qashmet stood, poking his snout out from under the table.

"I—I was recruited by him," Renee admitted after a long silence. "He is obsessed with finding you."

"We hit the double jackpot!" Qashmet wagged his tail excitedly.

Lee strained to hear the pair behind him over the low murmur of the other patrons. "Shh."

"Why?" Knox demanded. "Why is he so keen on finding me?"

There was another moment of silence. Lee found himself holding his breath, not wanting to miss the answer.

"I think he's trying to play both sides," she admitted. "From what I gather, the more energy the Avramites use, the more energy you get to use. Somehow, it means he gets more power to draw on."

"So how do you, and the other witches, figure into all of this?" Knox asked.

"I'm not sure," Renee whispered. Lee could barely make out her words. "I know Raven is his familiar, and Gypsy wants to be his familiar. He has sex with us, to give us a fraction of his power."

"Bad guys always have the most fun," Qashmet remarked.

The waitress returned. "Here we go—two iced teas and an order of garlic cheese bread. Is there anything else I can get for ya'll?"

"This should be fine, thanks," Knox replied. "I prepaid for the order, so make sure they give you your tip."

"Thank you, Darling." The waitress checked on Lee again with a smile and saw he had made little progress on his beer.

"Help yourself," Knox remarked.

"Aren't you going to have any?" Renee asked. Lee could hear silverware clatter as someone unraveled their napkin. "It smells good."

"I had a big dinner." There was another silence before Knox started speaking again. "What's the play? Try to seduce me or tug on my sympathies?"

"Are all druids so cynical?"

"How many druids do you know?" Knox countered.

There was another pause, possibly for chewing rather than stalling. "Only you and Taliesin."

Knox chuckled. "Of course, Potts is in this mess. I can only guess what Iblis promised him, though I don't know why Iblis would want him."

"I take it you don't have a high opinion of Taliesin." There was a soft, mirthful laugh, and she added, "He doesn't think much of you, either."

"He's a puffed up…no, I'm not going to get into this," Knox said. "We don't like each other, and now I know he works for Iblis."

"Unlike you, Potts doesn't have real power," Renee said, lowering her voice so Lee could barely make it out. "I've heard you have real magic. Maybe you can help me get away from Iblis. What—"

"Looks like it's time to go," Knox said. "Tell Iblis to leave me alone, or I'll find a way to leave him with as much magic as Potts."

"Wait! How did you—" Renee sounded astonished. Lee felt the woman shuffle out of the booth behind him. "Don't go!"

Lee leaned out of the booth. Knox was heading for the exit; Renee stood by their booth dumbfounded. "Cash, follow him," Lee whispered urgently. While Qashmet scampered after the druid, Lee threw down a couple of twenties, enough to cover the bill plus a healthy tip.

Knox disappeared around the corner into the vestibule, apparently unaware a dog was hot on his heels. Lee heard a loud thump from the doorway and found Qashmet dazed in front of the door, shaking his head.

"He went through the door." The dog shook his head again.

Lee pushed the door open and let Qashmet precede him. The dog veered left, and Lee followed. Lee spotted Knox walking down the walk along the building. Lee was so intent on following the druid, he didn't notice the two bikers emerging from between two trucks to block Knox's path until they were already on the sidewalk.

"You two bozos?" Knox crossed his arms. "Does your boss really think kidnapping is going to persuade me?"

"We owe you for whatever happened at the bookstore," the taller, bald biker snarled.

"No one to bail you out this time," the other said.

"As funny as this would be, I don't have the energy to deal with you guys." The druid shook his head, as though dizzy, and staggered back a step. Before the bikers could step forward, Knox vanished.

The two bikers stared at the empty space, flabbergasted. Lee had enough presence of mind to step between two parked cars, hoping they wouldn't notice him when they recovered their wits.

"What the hell was that?" one of them asked.

"How the hell should I know?"

"Where did the druid go?" The woman emerged from the pub. "I thought you guys were supposed to wait in the van?"

"I thought you were supposed to sweet talk him," the bald biker retorted. "He was in there for less than ten minutes."

Lee stepped behind a van to block their line of sight. Qashmet crept along beside him.

"I don't think he was there," Renee said. "He was a ghost or something. He knew I served the master and thought this was a trap."

"The boss isn't going to be happy," the shorter biker grumbled.

"Let's go," the first ruffian said.

Lee took it as his cue to cross the parking lot toward his truck. He relied on Qashmet to warn him if they took an interest, but Lee and the dog made it to the truck without incident. As Lee opened the passenger door for Qashmet, he saw the van's lights come on. He memorized the license plate.

Lee circled to the driver's side, and by the time he started the truck, the van was pulling away. Lee didn't think about following it. If Joel had been with him, it would have been a different story.

"Collar, the druid ghosted," Qashmet said as they turned onto the street toward the hotel. "When I said he went through the door,

I meant literally. He didn't open it, he walked through it, and I plowed right into the glass."

"How is that possible?" Lee knew the answer was magic, but there had to be a more nuanced explanation.

"If I had to guess, he used some sort of astral projection," Qashmet replied. "It sounded like he knew the whole thing was a setup, from the girl to the goons in the parking lot. Did you notice how he stumbled at the end, right before he disappeared?"

Lee nodded. "I didn't see either of the thugs swing at him."

"I think he was running on fumes," Qashmet suggested. "He's probably within a few blocks, projecting himself. It's why he prepaid and didn't eat. He couldn't touch anything. I wonder if the garlic bread is still there."

"We're not going back." Lee wondered if it would be worth driving around to search for the druid, but quickly dismissed the idea. There were too many parking lots full of cars to hide in.

"Can we at least go through a drive-through and get some tacos?" the dog pleaded.

* * * * *

Chapter Forty-Two

Tim

"Being fair sucks."

"Why?" Susan asked.

She'd caught Tim off guard; he had expected her to chastise him for his pronouncement, not call upon him to explain it. "When the Avram factions won the last Challenge, they weren't fair. They exiled the old gods and all the supernaturals. They cut off magic."

Susan looked from the computer screen to the whiteboards. Notes from brainstorming sessions covered the boards in a combination of Susan's looping script, Liam's precise lettering, and Tim's enthusiastic scrawl. "Yet they left in provisions for the new Challenge and rules to keep them from bumping off challengers," Susan said.

"Who enforces the rules?" Tim asked. "It seems like both sides break the rules, so who do they get in trouble with?"

Susan frowned. "I'm not sure. Someone must enforce them, or they would have done something drastic, like—well something drastic."

"You mean like kill my mom?" Tim knew Susan held back when she realized she was talking to a kid. Susan's shocked expression confirmed it. "They tried to scare her out of being the Champion, when they could have shot her in the parking lot."

It took a moment for Susan to regain her composure. "Well, yes, you're right. Something kept them from taking the easy way. It implies they are afraid of someone or something who will punish them for breaking the rules, or at least hold them to the clauses in the Milesian Accords saying they forfeit."

"They're like devs in an online game," Tim suggested. He knew he would have to explain further; while Susan wasn't a Luddite like his father, the woman knew very little about gaming. "Devs, or developers, are people who design and run online games, like *Realms of Quests*. They make the rules and are usually the ones who enforce those rules. They can designate people to handle minor infractions, and some stuff the players police among themselves, but the really bad apples usually get banned by the devs."

"I think we have enough work cut out for us without trying to figure out who the 'Devs' are," Susan said. "It seems like an apt analogy. Once the Exiled Folk left the Dunwold, it was up to the Avramites to enforce the exile."

Wind chimes around the house began to jingle. Tim and Susan silently listened to see if the heavier chimes would begin clattering. Those remained quiet.

"Dad must be home," Tim said. A moment later, the house confirmed Liam's return had stirred up the zephyrs. "Yup, they're back."

Susan saved their work on the computer. "Let's see what trouble he's gotten into this time."

Tim followed Susan to the dining room. The door between the kitchen and the garage clattered open.

"Druid, you move slower than my grandfather, and he's 900," Einar groused from the garage.

Liam tottered around the corner, Pixel leaning against him. At first, Tim thought the fae was holding Tim's father up, but they seemed to be supporting each other.

"What happened?" Susan asked. "Should I get the first aid kit?"

Liam shook his head and pulled out one of the old, wooden chairs around the table. "We're spent," Liam muttered, pulling the next chair back so Pixel could sit in the first. Liam sank into his seat. "I'm bone tired, like I ran a marathon."

"When did you ever run a marathon?" Susan moved to the opposite side of the table.

"My point exactly," Liam replied. "I only projected for about twenty minutes, and I nearly ran myself and Pixel out of *lledrith*." Pixel wearily nodded, holding onto Liam's hand.

"I told you, you should have carb-loaded," Susan chided Liam. "Using magic seems to burn blood sugar, essentially making you hypoglycemic when you do big spells."

Liam nodded. "You're right. I should have listened. I need to stop keeling over in the grass every time I draw major mojo."

"It worked?" Tim asked.

"Yeah, it sure did," Liam replied. "Iblis' goons were there. I would have loved to see the expressions on their faces when I vanished."

"It was a trap after all?" Susan sounded disappointed.

Einar plunked down a pecan pie, a pile of plates, and a tub of vanilla ice cream. "Ja, it was a pocking trap." Einar asked Tim, "Grab the silverware from the kitchen, would you? This will fix those two right up."

Having pie and ice cream on a school night? Tim wasn't going to pass that up; he hurried to help. He tried not to rattle the utensils as he scooped them up, so he wouldn't miss anything said in the dining room.

"The black dot was a ruse?" Susan asked. Tim wasn't sure what she meant.

"For good or for ill, it seems so," Liam replied. "I spotted those bikers who jumped me hanging around outside Word Nerds. If batting her baby-blues at me didn't work, and I didn't fall for the damsel in distress ploy, they were Plan C."

"You noticed her eyes?" Pixel glanced up from leaning against Liam.

Tim clattered the silverware onto the table, picking out the scoop and burying it in the vanilla ice cream. Normally, when Pixel got cuddly, his father found an excuse to brush her off. Now he didn't seem bothered by it, which worried Tim. His mom would be back in three weeks, and it would dash Tim's hopes of getting his parents back together if the purple-haired girl became Liam's girlfriend.

"Tim, why don't you dish out some pie and ice cream?" Einar suggested. "You had best hurry before Gofannon gets wind of it and eats the whole pocking pie like a tart."

Tim nodded and began doling out slices of pie and scoops of ice cream.

Einar ducked back into the kitchen and returned with mugs full of coffee. "Tim, I didn't think you'd want any coffee, but there's milk in the fridge."

After Liam had a few forkfuls of pie, he appeared less wan. "She admitted she served Iblis," Liam said. "They have great rites with him in exchange for power."

"They?" Susan set down her coffee cup. "How many witches does Iblis have?"

Liam finished a bite of pie and ice cream before answering. "It sounds like three. She mentioned one other than herself and Raven."

Pixel jabbed at her pie. "I suppose she wants to sleep with you, as well."

Einar laughed. "Like the Druid would want Iblis' sloppy—" Einar's gaze fell on Tim. "Erm, you pocking know what I mean."

"I know," Liam said. "Maybe Renee really is in trouble. Maybe charms and promises lured her, and now she's in over her head. I don't think we can take a chance. If we win the Challenge, we can see if she really needs help and deal with Iblis as needed."

"I feel like an idiot," Susan remarked.

"Don't," Liam countered. "Either she took advantage of your good nature, in which case shame on her, or we're stuck in a situation where we can't help. Neither one is your fault."

Everyone finished their pie in silence. By the time they were done, Liam's and Pixel's pallor improved, but they still seemed fatigued.

"I wish I could sleep for a week," Liam said. "I didn't realize spirit-walking on the Dunwold would be so taxing. I'm going to hit the sack. Tim, help Einar clean up, and don't stay up past your bedtime. Susan, are you staying over?"

Susan shook her head. "I have work in the morning. I'll see you for your blood draw if you're still up to it."

Liam sighed and pushed back from the table. "I have to be. I need to make sure we have enough for when we quench the blade." He stood up. "Thanks for keeping Tim company. Tomorrow night, let's go over what we have so far on the new Accords."

As Liam stepped away from the table, Pixel caught his hand and followed. Tim noticed Susan also watching the pair keenly.

"Erin better get back soon," Susan muttered. "Thanks for the pie, Einar. I'll see you tomorrow."

"Ja. I suppose I should take what's left out to the gullet at the forge." Einar picked up the remaining pie, the half-empty ice cream tub, and the largest spoon. "Tim, put the dishes in the sink, would you?"

Tim nodded. "Bye Susan." He collected the detritus from the impromptu dessert and piled it in the sink. Tim noticed Einar had left a sliver of pie and a dollop of ice cream for Scooter. Tim wished the brownie would show himself more often; he reminded Tim of a cross between a house-elf from a children's story and a leprechaun.

Tim padded up the stairs, avoiding the squeaky spots. His father's closed bedroom door was across the hall from Tim's room. Tim knew he should go to his room; instead, he crept closer to the other door. He held his breath and listened.

After several seconds of silence, Tim breathed a sigh of relief. He debated waiting longer, but the house chided him for eavesdropping. Tim was embarrassed and slinked across the hall to his own room.

"You could at least tell me," Tim whispered after he closed his door. "Are they…you know?"

The house reluctantly assured Tim his father was asleep and reminded Tim he should respect others' privacy.

"I know, but it's less than three weeks until Mom comes back," Tim protested. "I've heard enough to know Pixel wants to be my dad's wife."

Fae-wife, the house corrected.

"Whatever. I want my mom and dad to get back together, and it won't happen if Dad and Pixel are, well, you know."

The house didn't reply.

*****

Chapter Forty-Three

Erin

"Are you insane?"

Scathach serenely ignored Erin's accusation. "It would do the child good, and teaching will help you progress your own skill," the redheaded matriarch stated. The bright autumn sun glowed deceptively warm through the narrow windows of the keep's central tower. Sunlight glinted off the large bronze astrolabe in the corner of Scathach's office. "It will let you spend more time with your daughter."

"She's too young," Erin protested. "She's barely more than three years old. She doesn't have the discipline for it."

Scathach picked up the goblet of mead from her desk. "She is not a normal, mundane child. Skye was born from two potent bloodlines, so she has exceptional potential. It is best to teach her to reign in the infamous Cu Chulainn temper early, before exposing her to other children. It would help you manage your own temper. Nothing can be as trying to a mother's patience as a willful daughter; I speak from experience."

"Not exactly a selling point," Erin remarked and picked up her own cup of mead. She hadn't been a fan of honey-wine when she arrived, but there were no coffee shops or cold beer. What little coffee she had was brewed on an iron stove, and the ale was served warm. "Won't it interfere with my training?"

"I wouldn't expect a child to train all day," Scathach replied. "We'll start with a session first thing in the morning and again near the end of the day. Tutors can begin working with her while she isn't training, so her education doesn't lag behind."

"I didn't think Dunos Scaith was prepared for children." Erin downed another gulp of the sweet mead and set her cup down. Scathach's mead wasn't watered down—unlike the mead and ale served in the mess hall—and was rather potent.

"We hadn't planned for the contingency," Scathach admitted. "In hindsight, we should have better prepared, given it was inevitable there would be pairing up over the seven years. The fair folk are not as fecund as mundane people, but it was still possible we would end up with one or more children. Luckily, we have enough folk with the knowledge, temperament, and inclination to educate Skye."

Erin let the fecund remark slide. She was used to the stereotype of mundane folk as covetous, gluttonous, spoiled children who did little besides breed and despoil the planet. Erin wasn't surprised there were volunteers to school her daughter; the lack of children made Skye a novelty. The little girl had a fort full of ersatz aunts and uncles. "Fine, but no weapons training yet. The last thing I need is her braining someone with a practice sword because she thinks it's a game."

"Agreed," Scathach said. "Unarmed combat is your forte, and you've proven yourself a good teacher. Once Skye gains more discipline, you can work on more challenging subject matter."

* * *

More challenging subject matter, Erin grumbled to herself. Skye had enthusiastically run out to the practice field, only to have a total meltdown. Now the child sobbed and kicked at the dirt. The others drilled, staying as far as possible from the tantrum without leaving the training ground.

"Sweetie, try it," Erin coaxed. She had intended to start with a simple stance, only to have Skye stubbornly refuse to cooperate.

"Noooo!" the child wailed.

* * *

Two months later, Erin was able to keep her daughter focused for half an hour to an hour, depending on the child's mood. Erin had learned the warning signs that indicated Skye was about to throw a fit, although she still had trouble deciphering the cause. The most random circumstances could set off the girl, anything from her gloves chaffing to her remembering she didn't have her favorite breakfast.

When Skye showed symptoms of an oncoming outburst, Erin would quickly wind down the lesson. Most of the time, Erin could defuse the emotional time bomb and hand the girl off to her tutors. Occasionally, best efforts failed to prevent a meltdown, in which case Erin would deal with her daughter, rather than have someone else deal with a raging toddler.

* * *

"Another caravan?" Mysie remarked. They had taken a break from training to eat lunch when the commotion near the gate started. "This makes three in as many weeks."

"They would have to cross over within a few hours of the previous one," Daidh remarked between bites of stew-sopped bread. "The supplies from the last caravan filled the storehouses."

Erin listened for sounds of alarm, or anything unusual. There were only the typical calls for strong backs to move supplies and a murmur of anticipation. For the guards staffing the fort, the merchants' arrival was a welcome break in their routines.

Skye was oblivious to the commotion, eagerly tearing apart her bread and slathering it in stew. She had performed 45 minutes of drills couched as games, then had gone to her lessons without a fuss. Erin couldn't help but wonder when the other shoe would drop.

"After lunch, we can check and see if the merchants brought anything interesting," Erin said. The last caravan had lacked trade goods; it had solely consisted of bulk supplies. Erin couldn't think of anything she needed, but there was always the chance something would catch her eye. Erin tipped her head toward the keep. "Derek, you should see if Saidhe knows anything about the increased traffic and why Scathach is stockpiling for a long winter."

"So now my dalliance with Saidhe is convenient?" Derek retorted mockingly. "Before, it was 'remember what happened last time.'"

"You're not going to listen to advice, so you might as well be useful," Erin replied. With Izzy gone, it had fallen on her to take the wind out of Derek's sails on occasion.

Erin finished her stew, piling her wooden bowl and spoon on the platter in the middle of the table. "I wish Nechtan were here instead of on patrol," she said. Nechtan spent more time leading small groups of guards around the perimeter of Scathach's domain than in the fort. "He might have some idea about what's going on."

"I'm sure that's not the only reason you wish he was back," Derek muttered into his mug, grinning. "Truth be told, I might go out the next time he takes a team on the northern route. I wouldn't mind paying Elam a visit."

"You would miss a couple of months of practice," Daidh pointed out, "assuming you only stayed at the Pilgrim's cabin a day or so from your perspective."

"What a shame." Derek finished his drink and added the empty mug to the platter. "I may stay a few days."

Erin shrugged. "We've got something like two years left. If you want to take a few months to visit Elam, I'm not going to begrudge you. We owe Elam a lot."

Derek appeared puzzled, as though he thought Erin was kidding about being okay with him going. "All right, then. The next time a patrol heads north, I'll tag along."

More bowls and cups clattered onto the platter. "Let's see if there's anything of interest in the wagons," Mysie said.

Erin picked up a cloth and wiped the worst of the detritus of Skye's lunch away. "Come on, Skye, let's go see the wagons."

* * *

The caravan turned out to be a disappointment. Like the previous one, it was laden with bulk goods. The wagons were full of crates, bags and barrels of provisions. Much of the food was preserved or dense staples, reminding Erin of military rations.

"It seems like Scathach is stocking up to cut us off for a while," Erin said, walking along the line of a dozen wagons. In addition to provisions for people, there was fodder for the handful of dairy cattle and feed for the chickens. Erin suspected if Dunos Scaith were cut off from supplies for any length of time, the dairy cows would soon turn into beef.

"The patrols haven't found anything," Daidh remarked. "I know Scathach was worried Izzy's crossing to the Dunwold might give away our location, but with the wold-ford destroyed, they would have to cross elsewhere and, somehow, find one of the paths into the domain."

Derek rapped on a wagon wheel with his knuckles. "On the bright side, Scathach has to make sure you arrive back on the Dunwold in time to face Giwargix, so whatever she is planning has an expiration date."

*****

Chapter Forty-Four

Iblis

"They're back."

Iblis opened his eyes at Raven's announcement. He had detected Orliath's approach several minutes ago. Iblis could sense the presence of his vessels if they weren't over the horizon, which was just shy of three miles away.

The question was how Raven knew they had returned. Iblis could feel Orliath about a block away, too far for Raven to distinguish Mad Dog's van from any of the occasional vehicles passing by.

"I know," Iblis said. He already expected to be disappointed. While Orliath had proven a better liar than Iblis would have imagined, every other ploy with the druid had failed. Worse yet, the druid didn't seem at all threatened by Iblis. If he couldn't cajole Knox into cooperating, Iblis at least wanted to intimidate the druid into expending more magic in the mundane world.

Raven shuffled the tarot deck she had been fiddling with for the past half hour. "What do you think went wrong?" The witch flipped a card off the deck in her hand. "Obviously, Orliath didn't go home with the druid."

Iblis stole a glance at the card. The Fool taunted him from the desk. Maybe Raven needed another lesson to remind her of her place. "Orliath endearing herself so quickly to the druid was a long shot. You've proven he's not a total fool for feminine wiles. I'm hoping she was able to establish some sort of rapport, and perhaps play on his white knight instinct enough to provoke him into meeting me. Knox obviously doesn't see me as a potential ally, nor is he cowed enough to make any sort of deal for his own benefit.

"However, if Knox thought he could help poor little Orliath by confronting me, it might be enough to goad him." Iblis stretched in his luxurious office chair. "Once I get him talking, I can take his measure and figure out what really motivates him. Either I convince him I can be an ally, or I scare him enough to pull as much magic as possible to protect himself against me."

Raven flipped another card onto the desk; this one was The Devil. "I think any chance you had of convincing Liam you could be buddies ended long ago, probably around the time your pet goons tried to jump him outside the bookstore."

The front door of the offices clattered open. The Nine of Swords landed on the previous two cards, displaying a woman waking from a nightmare.

Orliath was the first to enter Iblis' office. Unlike Raven, Orliath had dressed demurely for her rendezvous with Knox. Iblis could hear Mad Dog and Mikey shuffling in the hall. Iblis suspected he was going to need to vent some anger later.

"The druid was onto us," Orliath said without preamble. She began pacing the other side of the office, ignoring the remaining, empty chair. "As soon as he sat down, Knox said he knew I worked for you, and our meeting was a setup. He wanted to know what your game was."

"What did you tell him?" Iblis asked, leaning back in his chair. Showing anger now would either clam her up or cause her to give answers she thought he wanted to hear.

The young woman stopped pacing. She glanced in Iblis' direction, but didn't meet his gaze. "I told him I thought you were trying to play both sides."

Iblis smiled. She really was a good liar. A believable, but vague, truth created credibility. He wondered what else she had said but decided not to press the point for the moment. "What happened next?"

"I reached for his hand, but my fingers went through it," Orliath replied. "As soon as it happened, he got up and walked out."

Iblis leaned forward. "What do you mean 'went through it?'"

"Like he was a ghost," Orliath replied. "I tried to catch his arm to get him to stay, but it was as if he wasn't there. Then, when Mad Dog and Mikey stopped him in the parking lot, the druid vanished."

Iblis was so stunned, he nearly missed the remark about the bikers confronting Knox. "I told you two to stay in the van unless there was trouble," Iblis fumed.

"Way to blow her cover, meatheads," Raven added, ignoring the bikers' scowls. She flipped over another card and added The Hanged Man to the pile. "You guys are toast."

"The hippie was already on to her, Boss," Mad Dog protested. "We were trying to corral him for you."

"And get some payback for the beating at the bookstore," Mikey added.

Mad Dog shot his partner a dirty look. "It didn't matter, because he wasn't really there," Mad Dog said. "He was a hologram or a ghost."

Iblis stood, pleased the bikers instinctively backed away. "You two get out of here. Maybe not getting paid will remind you to follow orders."

Iblis' glare silenced any protests, and the bikers slunk out of the office. Iblis' gaze fell on Orliath; the girl stood frozen like a mouse hiding from a hawk. "Don't fret, my dear," Iblis said with a smile. "You played your part. It may take longer but playing the ingénue in over her head may yet elicit his sympathy."

Orliath nodded mutely, her blue eyes betraying nervousness.

"Meet me in the sanctuary in 30 minutes," Iblis ordered the young witch, tipping her chin up with a single finger. Iblis stepped back and shooed the girl. "Go on, get ready."

"Yes, Master," Orliath stammered and fled from the office.

Iblis sat on the corner of his desk and rubbed his chin thoughtfully. "If Knox can project a phantom, his power has grown faster than I anticipated."

"He has his little purple-haired battery," Raven said. She turned over the Two of Cups, holding up the card with a couple holding a pair of chalices between them, before placing it with the others on the desk. "From the sound of it, he couldn't have kept the illusion going for much longer."

"True, which means he probably won't be able to use it for a longer engagement, such as the pagan meet-up on the 10th," Iblis said. "Add in the number of people, and it would be too likely someone would notice or accidentally walk though him."

Raven added The Magician to the growing stack of face-up cards. "It would certainly impress all of the wannabes. They've never seen real magic; he would have them eating out of his hand. Useful if he's trying to gather allies."

Iblis waved his hand dismissively. "He can gather as many Taliesin's and Moon-Blossom's as he wants," Iblis sneered. "I'm more interested in how much magic he is drawing into the mundane world. We may need to recruit."

"Don't you have enough toys?" Raven displayed a card with three frolicking women holding gold goblets—The Three of Cups. "If Liam is pulling this much power, how come we didn't sense it? Remember the scrying bowl blowing up in my face?"

"Most of the energy would flow through the spirit-world," Iblis replied. "He projected his spirit-form into the mundane world and cast a glamour over it, so people could see and hear him. It's an old school, faerie, magic trick, popular with the druids back in the day. Supposedly they would convene councils via phantoms, saving themselves travel time and impressing the peasants."

"Peasants are a product of the feudal system, which didn't arise until much later," Raven remarked. The Hermit was the next card. "Can you project a phantom?"

"Of course, I can," Iblis replied contemptuously. "However, if I enter the spirit-world, I will draw attention to myself. The last thing I need is Mikha'el and his ilk breathing down my neck."

"Because you don't have enough power to take them on." Raven set the remaining cards down. "If there really is more power to be gathered, maybe you shouldn't waste your time with Orliath. I can give you what you need better than a trembling neophyte, both carnally and magically."

"Maybe later. First I want to let off some steam and add some credence to Orliath's story," Iblis said. He would soon need additional vessels to store the mystic energy. If he put too much power in any one of his minions, someone might notice.

"As you wish." Raven rose and left the office, her heels clicking on the tile in the hall.

The cards caught Iblis' eye. He reached down and turned over the top one. An angel looked down upon people rising from their graves—Judgement.

*****

Chapter Forty-Five

Liam

"I said, 'Can I help with anything?'"

Liam had barely heard Einar over the din of metal hammering on metal, the roar of the forge, and the whir of the blower motors, muffled by his shooter's ear muffs. Gofannon gave Liam guff over the hearing protection, which was still insufficient to quell the smith-god's bellowing voice.

Liam paused from striking the dull, red blade long enough to glance at the clock mounted on the house. It showed two in the afternoon, but the small clock in the smithy displayed five o'clock. Gofannon claimed the time difference was due to their focus on their work, but Liam was sure the Welsh god was somehow slowing down time, letting them steal a few extra hours each day.

Liam hated to admit they needed the extra time. Layering the meteor iron with high carbon steel had proved more difficult than they anticipated. Their first attempt fell apart; like a layered pastry, the different metals flaked apart. The second blade was well along when it warped a third of the way from the tip, likely due to a bubble of impurities. Liam took the unfinished blade to a friend's shop, where they used a plasma cutter to lop off the offending section, but the remaining blade was too short for their purposes.

Liam hoped the third time was the charm. They had no time to start over. Liam flipped the blade on the anvil. "Sorry, Einar. What did you say?"

"I wanted to know if you needed a hand with anything?" the dwarf yelled.

Gofannon chuckled. "Tired of playing farm-wife in the kitchen?"

Einar's brows furrowed in annoyance. Liam knew he felt left out; at this juncture, there was little for Einar to do. The dwarf's help had been indispensable during the smelting process, but now that Liam already had Gofannon looming over his shoulder, there was little point in Einar standing around waiting to hand Liam a tool he could easily pick up himself.

"Not really," Liam said and began pounding away again. He had lost track of how many times they had folded and hammered this blade. His arms told him roughly a thousand. Luckily, he was ambidextrous, which annoyed Gofannon, but it meant Liam could spread the work between both arms. The glow was fading from the metal, so Liam stopped hammering and returned the blade to the forge. "Maybe when we get ready to do some quenching, we can use an extra set of hands."

"You could make us some sandwiches," Gofannon suggested, probably waiting to criticize Liam for letting the blade get too hot.

Liam pulled the glowing metal from the furnace. "Or you could hang out with us if you want." The cool October breeze wafting through the smithy gusted in response to Liam's irritation. Gofannon's thoughtless comment annoyed Liam as much as it bothered Einar. Liam swung the red-hot blade over to the anvil and switched hands.

The dwarf nodded and pulled a stool away from the wall. Einar watched while Liam worked his way down one side of the blade, flipped it, and repeated the process. "You've gotten much better," Einar remarked during a lull while Liam and Gofannon inspected the shape of the blade.

Liam smiled. Positive reinforcement wasn't part of Gofannon's repertoire. "Thanks, Einar."

"It's because he's had a good teacher," Gofannon added.

Liam resisted the urge to roll his eyes. What Gofannon lacked in instructional etiquette, he made up for in expertise. The metal faded to dull yellow-orange, so Liam took up the hammer again. He drew *lledrith* from the earth and channeled it down his arm into his hammer swings. Blue-green flashes mixed with the usual orange sparks each time the hammer struck. The long slab of metal increasingly resembled a sword with each swing.

* * *

"I hope you don't mind sandwiches," Einar said. A spread of meats, cheese, and condiments covered the kitchen table, along with kettle chips and macaroni salad. "The great glutton himself gave me the idea."

Liam hoped Tim didn't blurt out disappointment, but the boy seemed content building a sandwich he probably couldn't finish. Liam knew he should chide his son about being wasteful, but the boy was emulating his father. After spending twelve hours, from his perspective, in the forge laboring away, Liam was famished. It was almost enough to distract him from the ache in his truncated pinky.

Liam followed his son into the dining room. "Tim, how was school?"

"It was okay," Tim replied. Liam learned the simplest response could mean a hundred things, and few meant okay. "I aced my algebra quiz."

"Algebra? How did Jenny do?" Pixel chimed in.

Tim stared down at his plate and mumbled, "Fine."

"Sounds like your tutoring paid off," Liam interjected, before Pixel could keep pressing Tim for details. "How are your other classes going?"

Tim took a convenient bite of his sandwich, giving him time to compose his answer. "Gym stinks, but otherwise okay. I'll have all As."

Liam wondered if the school challenged Tim enough. The problem could wait until Erin returned. Besides, it wasn't like there were many options. Liam had skipped a year in school; while it may have kept him from getting bored, Liam wondered if it impaired him socially. Tim obviously felt awkward in school; Liam didn't want to exacerbate the situation.

Pixel's phone rang. The ringtone was some theme song Liam didn't recognize. Pixel seemed puzzled when she glanced at the screen. "Hello? Izzy?"

Everyone at the table sat up, biting back questions.

"You're stuck?" Pixel asked. Liam tried to puzzle out the conversation from Pixel's side. "We've got some creep we think is a fallen, or descended from one, sniffing around, but no signs of the Avramites. Are you sure? More or less. No, he's fine; we just have trouble keeping him in one piece."

Liam wanted to protest, but the pain in his hand stopped him.

"Sure, Tim is right here." Pixel held the phone out. "Izzy wants to talk to you."

Tim took the phone tentatively. "Hello? Okay. Oh. Okay. Yeah." Tim slid the phone across the table to Liam. "Your turn, Dad."

Liam picked up the phone. "Hello Izzy."

"Druid, I'll save you some questions, as I don't think this phone has much charge left. I've filled in Pixel on some of the details. Erin is fine; I came back to the Dunwold as a messenger and got stuck. My plan is to wait here until they come back from Dunos Scaith. I will call back tomorrow once I've settled in and charged this phone."

Liam had questions but decided he should wait until he heard what Pixel knew. If Erin was okay, everything else could wait until morning. "All right, Izzy. Is there anything you need?"

"No. I was prepared for the Dunwold," Izzy replied. "I'll hike to town and find a hotel to set up camp. I'll talk to you tomorrow." The phone beeped once, and the line went silent.

"A seraphim intercepted them at the wold-ford," Pixel said, anticipating Liam's question. "Erin vanquished it, and Scathach showed up to bring them to Dunos Scaith. For some reason, they decided to have Izzy come back."

"Izzy is mailing me a letter from Mom," Tim interjected.

"Right after Izzy crossed to the Dunwold, the ford vanished," Pixel continued. "She spent all day traipsing around in case it drifted, but she couldn't find it."

"A pocking seraphim came after them? The Champion took it out?" Einar sounded impressed. "I wonder how it knew where to find them?"

Pixel shrugged and nibbled on her sandwich. "I imagine we can get a more detailed account tomorrow. Izzy didn't seem too worried about it."

"They've been in Dunos Scaith for four and a half years, right?" Tim asked. He had started on his sandwich with gusto; Liam suspected he would soon run out of steam. "If the seraphim followed them, they would know by now."

Liam crunched the numbers in his head; Tim's math seemed right. "I would think so. Maybe Scathach has to open the ford for people to cross from the Dunwold. It would explain why Izzy is stuck, and why nothing else crossed over after them."

"One of those pocking angels might be able to spot the wold-ford from the Murkwold," Einar remarked. "It won't do them any good if they can't open it, but it might explain why a seraphim was waiting for them."

"The seraphim would not dare cross to the Glaswold," Gofannon rumbled from the kitchen doorway, "especially not on Scathach's doorstep. It would be a fool's errand. They cannot kill the Champion, or they break the Accords and forfeit. Going after Scathach would hasten their return to their own celestial realm."

"You mean the Oirwold?" Tim asked between bites of sandwich. He gave Liam a proud smile. "I read about it in the Accords."

Liam noticed, for the first time, the smith-god had filaments of silver scattered through his beard. Had they always been there? Liam had patches of grey in his beard and at his temples. He had hoped with Idunn's apple, the grey would retreat, but it remained the same.

"Gofannon, do you mind watching Tim while we're at the pagan meet-up?" Liam asked.

The Welsh god pulled out his extra-large chair at the end of the table and settled into it. "Watch him do what?"

Liam should have known to be more specific. "Make sure he doesn't burn the house down or something."

Tim appeared insulted. "I wouldn't do that!"

"Sounds easy enough," Gofannon replied and set to work assembling sandwiches worthy of Dagwood. "We will be quenching the sword, do not forget."

Liam thought of the pouches of blood accumulated in the refrigerator in the garage. He had been worried about his blood retaining its magical potence for so long, but the encounter with the Russian witch gave him hope it would retain its mystic properties. He flexed his left hand.

"I haven't forgotten," Liam replied. "The meeting isn't until 7:30, which gives us plenty of time to work."

"Can't I go with you, Dad?" Tim asked.

Originally, Liam had been fine with the idea, but with Iblis' goons turning up at the Brickhouse, Liam didn't want to take chances. "Maybe the next one," Liam said. "If this all works out, I suspect I will be attending a lot more gatherings in the future."

"You really think this meeting will be worth the trouble?" Einar asked. The dwarf had agreed to go along and provide an extra set of eyes. It sounded like he was hoping to test his mettle on the bikers.

"In the Pagan Pride Project alone, there are 130 chapters," Liam responded. "If I can get half of those on board and get them to network within their own communities, we could have low five digits turnout on Samhain. Worst case scenario, I donate a crap load of money to organizations who could really use it."

"I think it's a really good idea," Pixel stated, placing her hand on Liam's arm. "If nothing else, it sets up the groundwork for you being First Druid."

"These people have no interest in a pagan pope," Liam said, getting his mind back on track. "I really don't want the job of Chief Cat

Herder. This is to strengthen networking, get myself out in the community, and to sponsor our special event for Samhain."

"You might not want the pocking job, but people will have questions." Einar brushed crumbs from his beard. "They'll be searching for answers, and I think you're better off trying to help them than let them flail about, figuring out magic for themselves."

Liam knew the dwarf was right. "I'm still figuring out the right questions to ask."

*****

Chapter Forty-Six

Erin

"Another caravan?"

Everyone in the training field paused in their practice at Nechtan's statement. Erin listened for the telltale noises; she knew the hunter's senses were more acute than her own. After thirty seconds, she heard the distant trod of draft animals pulling wagons toward the gate.

"We already have a year and a half of supplies," Erin remarked. The storehouses were crammed full, and the horse-less stable had been pressed into service to store additional fodder for the cows and chickens.

"Maybe this is a regular caravan?" Mysie sounded hopeful. "We haven't seen one for nigh on two months."

"They have all been bulk deliveries," Daidh added. "Could we at least take a peek?

Erin chewed on her lip. It was still an hour and a half until the traditional lunch break. She hated to waste a clear, crisp morning. It had been chilly until they started exerting themselves, and the sun rose higher. Now the coolness was refreshing.

"Fine," Erin relented. She debated retrieving Skye from the chirurgeon's building, where Slaine was watching her while schooling her on the alphabet and numbers. Erin decided to let her daughter be; no point in pulling her away from her lessons if this was wagons full of fodder and potatoes.

Erin let Nechtan go ahead of her. She would never dream of wearing leather pants, but watching the hunter tempted her into declaring the rest of the day off.

"Falling behind, *acushla*?" Nechtan's grin increased the temptation to play hooky. Erin could imagine the smell of leather, smoke, and a hint of whiskey.

"The drought is over," Mysie declared as she passed through the gate. Merchants were setting up an ad hoc market, hurrying about setting up canopies and display racks.

Erin wished she had made a list, even if it was a mental one. She knew Mysie would chide her as shopping was half the fun. She wondered what the Scots half-fae would make of Dunwold retail.

It would still be an hour before they could properly shop; the merchants were still pulling their wares from their wagons and putting them on display. Erin wandered along the lines of stalls, taking advantage of the fact the guards had shied away from coming out lest they be pressed into service unloading bulk supplies and porting them into the fort.

"Wilbur, how are you?" Erin asked the pig-headed booze vendor.

The merchant peered up from carefully arranging bottles and corked jugs on shelves. Luckily, his hands were quite human; Erin couldn't imagine how difficult it would be to handle his merchandise with porcine hooves. A smile spread under his snout. "Champion! Always a pleasure," he said. Once Wilbur realized he would be paid for wares given to Erin and her friends, he had become quite eager to see them. "I brought some beer from the Dunwold. Rumor has it, it's the Druid's favorite."

Nechtan looked up from the bottle he was examining. "Oh really? You mean the Druid, as in the Druid of the Challenge?"

"The very one!" Wilbur replied. "Give me a moment, and I'll fetch a bottle."

"You don't need to go to any trouble," Erin protested, suddenly uncomfortable. She knew it was irrational; Skye was a constant reminder of Liam to both of them.

Wilbur waved away her objection. "It's no trouble." He clambered into the wagon.

"Does he have anything interesting?" Mysie asked. She and Daidh had paused at an ironmonger's wagon before catching up to Erin and Nechtan.

"He has some of the Druid's favorite beer," Nechtan said with a hint of a grin.

"He got another delivery from the Dunwold?" Daidh asked. He had developed a fondness for whiskey from the Dunwold. Mysie didn't mind; she claimed the liquor made Daidh 'less reserved.'

"I don't see what the big deal is about some beer Liam likes," Erin remarked, mentally cursing herself for using his name rather than his title.

"Maybe I want to see how our tastes compare, *acushla*," Nechtan teased.

Wilbur emerged from the wagon, clutching a dark bottle. "Here we go, Anvil Stout, by a brewer named Harter. I hear the dunnies insist on drinking their beer cold."

"Sounds daft," Mysie commented. "The only reason we have a cold house is because Scathach is a major lady of the folk. Many crafthobs, dwimmermongers, and draoi try to curry her favor."

Wilbur shrugged and retrieved a bottle opener from his apron. "Care to give it a try? It's not cold, as they drink it, but it's cool from the night chill."

"Absolutely," Nechtan replied, winking at Erin. Wilbur popped the cap off the bottle and handed it to the hunter. Nechtan held the bottle up, scrutinizing the label. He said, "Let's see what the Druid fancies."

"Obviously, he favors something strong," Wilbur commented. "Something packing a lot of punch. Most Dunwold beer is weak and watery. Evidently, the Druid favors something more down-to-earth, with enough sweetness to balance the bitter notes."

Nechtan took a long pull of the beer, then took a moment to savor it. "Pretty much sums it up." Erin hoped she wasn't blushing. Nechtan held the bottle out and asked, "Who else wants to give it a try?"

"Absolutely," Daidh replied, taking the bottle. He gave the label a cursory glance. "It's not whiskey, but you don't turn your nose up at a good stout."

"Especially one that tastes like Erin," Mysie cajoled.

Daidh gave Mysie a quizzical glance, but it didn't stop him from drinking. "I don't know what you're on about," he said after he finished. "It packs more of a wallop than you'd expect, especially given it's a bit sweeter than a regular stout."

"Go ahead and take the bottle," Wilbur suggested. "I need to finish setting up unless you would like me to back my wagon up to your cabin."

"We can't hog all of the booze," Erin said. "We'll come back around in a bit."

Mysie took her turn with the beer as they walked away. "All right, it is pretty good. A few bottles of this would loosen the knickers, if you know what I mean."

Erin accepted the bottle when Mysie handed it to her. She took a long drink and remembered the night at the fire pit. Loosen the knickers, indeed. This was the same beer she and Liam had shared the night they conceived Skye.

"Does it bring back memories of home?" Nechtan asked, pulling Erin out of her reverie.

"I've had it before," Erin replied. Two could play the game. "I guess I should take what reminder I can get since it'll be a couple of years before I go back. Until then I'll have to settle for native fare."

"Ouch," Mysie muttered.

Nechtan sighed and held out a hand for the beer. "Fair enough. If you poke a hive for honey, you're bound to get stung."

"I wonder what those boggers are on about?" Daidh remarked.

A dozen men strode purposefully through the wagons. Their pronounced, hawkish noses caught Erin's attention first. Bronze helmets with a falcon motif emphasized the men's bird-like countenances. As Erin stared at them, they appeared less human. Their eyes were too large, and their ears ended in points, like elves from the movies Tim had begged her to rent. At twenty yards, a quartet peeled off toward her group, and the remaining broke into a trot toward the gate. The strangers pulled weapons from under their robes and charged.

Time slowed down as Erin shouted a warning. Her group was woefully unprepared; having come off the practice field, they were wearing training armor and appeared unarmed. Erin reached into her elf-pocket and gripped the hilt of the sword Gofannon had forged for her.

The attackers were ten yards away. Two had gleaming steel swords with curved, sickle-like blades. The other two had staves. After a moment, each staff lost its rigidity and became a hissing serpent. Bronze armor glinted under the warriors' robes.

One of the snake wielders slid to a halt just out of Erin's reach and snapped the snake like a whip. The serpent bared its fangs as its head flashed forward. As Erin slipped to the side, she flicked her sword down; the snake's head continued on its trajectory as the body recoiled back. Erin's grim satisfaction dissipated as another head bloomed from the bleeding stump of the snake's neck. Her opponent flashed a feral grin.

The other snake bearer stopped short as Mysie threw a pair of knives in rapid succession. One blade clanged off his chest armor, the other pinned the snake to its wielder's hand, causing both to hiss in pain.

A sickle-sword whistled past Nechtan; Erin swore it was close enough to shave his stubble. With one hand, Nechtan shoved his assailant further along his trajectory; with the other he reached behind his back and grasped an arrow. The hunter jammed the arrow at his opponent's shoulder, only to have the shaft shatter when it struck his armor.

Daidh was forced to yield ground as he struggled to stay out of his opponent's reach. The tip of his opponent's sword sliced open the padded leather sparring armor and drew blood. Instead of flinching away, Daidh reached into the backswing and caught his assailant's wrist. He tried to wrest the weapon away, but the swordsman was stronger than he looked.

Nechtan back-pedaled from a backhanded swing, retreating to the iron-monger's wagon. The merchant hadn't brought out any swords yet, so Nechtan snatched a spear from the rack. The swordsman slid to a halt and twisted aside; the spear's leaf-bladed head tore through his robes but glanced off the armor underneath. The hawkish man eyed the spear warily.

"I don't suppose you'd care to surrender?" Nechtan offered.

Daidh and his opponent still wrestled for control of the sword. The pair spun, and the stranger slammed Daidh into a wagon, knocking him loose. Thrown off balance, Daidh caught a wheel to keep from falling. The sickle-sword arched down, and the blade caught Daidh on the wrist, cleaving through flesh and bone. Daidh's hand fell away as the blade continued its arc and buried itself in the wagon wheel.

Erin turned, knowing the next sword swing would ensure Daidh's death. Pebbles and dust flew up as she pushed off in his direction. Instinctively she ducked, a viper lashing where her head had been. Erin could see the swordsman wrench the blade from the wood of the wagon wheel, bringing the weapon around. By the time he realized Erin was closing in on him, the attacker had his sword positioned to finish off Daidh, who clutched his bleeding stump.

Erin's sword caught the warrior below his helm, the impact knocking her target sideways and spoiling his strike at Daidh. The helmet and the head within bounced off the side of the wagon. Erin broke her stride, but her momentum carried her into the wagon. She twisted to allow her padded armor to take as much of the bruising impact as possible. As she caromed off the wood, she kept her footing and brought her sword up defensively. The snake-wielder had chased her, hoping to catch her distracted.

Mysie was having trouble closing on her opponent and was probably out of throwing knives anyway. The Scots warily circled the man, a dagger in each hand. Erin had to give her credit for not letting Daidh's plight distract her. Meanwhile, her opponent managed to shake loose the knife from his hand. While he was bleeding, the snake seemed to have recovered and reared up, baring its fangs.

Erin's original opponent snapped his snake-whip again; the fanged weapon was a blur. As her blood pounded in her ears, the serpent uncoiled in slow motion, its mouth agape. Erin swatted aside the viper with the flat of her blade and grabbed the snake behind the head. She did the last thing her opponent expected; she yanked. Caught off balance, he fell forward, toward Erin's waiting sword. Erin thrust with all her might, and the god-forged sword punched through the man's breastplate, left of his sternum. Erin felt the point of the blade strike the armor on the other side as the light went out in his large eyes. The serpent reverted to a wooden staff and shattered.

Nechtan jabbed at the warrior facing him, who hooked the spearhead with the inside curve of his sword and yanked it aside. Before Nechtan could recover the weapon, the man spun the sickle-sword around and sheared through the haft. The leaf-blade fell to the dirt, leaving Nechtan with a five-foot wooden pole. Emboldened, the warrior lunged. Nechtan struck the flat of his opponent's blade, knocking it off course, and spun aside. Whipping the spear haft around as the warrior passed, Nechtan caught his opponent from behind, only to hear the wood crack against the armor. As he stumbled to the dirt, the warrior rolled aside, evading Nechtan's follow-up blow and kipped up to his feet. His next swing chopped another foot off the spear haft.

Mysie snatched a cloak off a display in a merchant's stall and threw it in the path of the lashing snake, tangling up the reptile. Her dagger sank into her opponent's arm, but her follow-up kick left her with a bruised foot as flesh struck armor.

Erin had to make a snap decision. Her lover was in trouble, but her friend was in mortal danger. Dust burst from her steps as she closed on the remaining snake-wielder. Too late, he realized his peril. He flicked his serpent at Erin. She backhanded the fanged head with her vambrace. The heavy bronze and steel armguard shattered the snake's outstretched fangs and crushed its skull like a grape. Erin drove her sword under her target's helmet. Bone crunched as the blade split a vertebra. The snake fell into splinters of wood. Erin yanked her sword free of the corpse.

The last swordsman turned around in time to parry Erin's swing. Steel rang on steel. Erin was surprised he still held his sword, and he seemed startled by the force of her blow. She grabbed his wrist while their swords pressed together. The warrior shifted his stance, preparing to throw her as his fellow had done with Daidh. Erin twisted her sword in one direction and his arm in the other, and she was rewarded with a loud pop as his wrist broke.

"Western harlot," he snarled in a thick accent, still clutching his weapon.

Nechtan picked up the spear blade. "That's enough out of you." Nechtan jammed the spear point down between the man's collarbone and throat.

"I had him," Erin snapped. Her blood still pounded in her ears.

"I know, but we have other pressing matters." Nechtan reached behind his back and pulled his bow from his elf-pocket. "Besides, it's not polite to hog all the bad guys."

Mysie was crouched over Daidh, tying a tourniquet around his severed limb. Erin heard the din of battle rising from the fort. Skye was somewhere in the fort. Erin ran for the gate, Nechtan at her heels.

The first bodies were at the gate, and the trail of carnage led toward the central keep. Two of the attackers were down; the remainder faced double their number in guards, as well as Scathach, herself. Half a dozen melees swirled in a loose front. The guards were getting in each other's way as much as helping. They trained to be warriors, not soldiers. Two guards fell before Erin was halfway to the conflict.

As Erin sprinted toward the fight, Scathach struck down one of the invaders, swinging her claymore one-handed as though it were made of paper, not steel. The matron of Dunos Scaith was bloodied, but none of her wounds appeared grievous. Uathach slumped in the doorway of the keep; her face contorted with pain as she clutched her arm.

Erin scanned for snake-wielders, judging them to be the most dangerous. Two remained, one trying to whip his serpent past Scathach's shield. Erin charged him, hoping to catch him off guard. One of his compatriots barked something in a guttural language. In the split second of distraction, Scathach beheaded the snake.

Before the staff could regenerate, Erin rammed her sword under the snake-wielder's upraised arm, shearing his right lung and heart, and the snake crumbled.

Erin blocked a sickle-sword with her arm-guard. Sparks flew as the blade bit into the steel armor, but the edge never reached her flesh. Erin pulled her sword free of the collapsing corpse. Black blood sprayed from her blade as she swung and forced her attacker to abort his follow-up parry. As strong as the invader was, Erin's rage made her stronger. The warrior gave ground under a rain of heavy blows.

Arrows whistled from Nechtan's bow as he focused on the remaining snake-wielder. One ricocheted off his armor, the second delivered a flesh wound under his target's pauldron, and the third found the opening in his helmet and pierced the warrior's eye.

Scathach set upon another invader. The warrior was skilled, but he faced the embodiment of prowess. Scathach wasn't fooled by his feint, and when she caught his sickle-sword on her shield, she swung her claymore down and split through his collarbone. The blade bit six inches into his breastplate. He gurgled something ending with "whore" before she kicked him away to free her sword.

Several guards managed to dogpile onto one of the remaining invaders, bearing him to the ground despite his supernatural strength. Two spears were jammed into his gut, the points slipping between the bands of armor protecting his abdomen.

The remaining invader continued to fall back from Erin, only for Scathach to flank him. He lunged at Erin, but she swept his sword aside with a one-handed block. Her free fist hammered him in the cheek, between the hawk-like nose guard and the side of his helmet. As he fell toward the ground, Erin's sword caught his blade from behind the curve, yanking it from his grasp. She clocked him again, this time bludgeoning him with her vambrace.

"Who are you?" Erin demanded. "Why did you attack us?"

"You westerners, you fight with the desert god," the fallen warrior slurred. Erin wasn't sure how much was guttural accent and how much was injury. "If you win, you erase us and our kin."

"Who sent you?" Erin demanded.

"The Forgotten." He paused to wipe blood from his mouth. "The old gods are forgotten, and the people bicker and fight in the name of Avram's god. You and your druid are just another step toward wiping us from the world once and for all."

Erin regarded Uathach, who was gasping in pain. "We need to get Elam," Erin said. "Maybe he can help Daidh and Uathach."

The prisoner chuckled. "The Pilgrim? He is dead."

"What do you mean?" Erin demanded, resisting the urge to put a blade to her prisoner's throat.

"We know of the Pilgrim," the swordsman replied. "He will be dead before you can reach him."

Wilbur slid to a halt, eyes wide with fear as he beheld the battlefield. "Champion! Two of these strangers left to the north, riding the ox which pulled their wagon!"

"They know about Elam," Erin said. "We need a horse. Pull one off one of the wagons. I'll be damned if I'll let these sons-of-bitches get Elam."

Wilbur gestured toward the gate. "There are no steeds. Those are all draft animals."

"*Acushla*, I know how to get there in time," Nechtan stated. "We'll need a saddle from the stables. Go put on your new armor. We'll give these bastards what for."

Erin was torn. She realized Skye was still somewhere in the keep, probably huddled in fear. Well, maybe her caretakers were huddled in fear; they probably had to restrain the child from finding out what was going on.

"Your daughter is safe with Slaine in the infirmary," Scathach stated. She turned to Nechtan, her expression grave. "Are you sure you want to do this?"

"Unless you have a better way for us to catch up before they slaughter the Pilgrim," Nechtan replied. "I reckon Derek is still with him, but the *xanoso* won't be able to fend off two of them."

"I'll grab my armor and be right back," Erin said, then turned to Scathach. "Daidh is out front by the wagons; one of these assassins chopped off his hand."

"You are too late," the prisoner spat. "The infidel qadesh will die. We may have failed to kill you, *benyaim* harlot, but he will die."

"I'll check on Skye and grab my armor and gun," Erin announced, turning on her heel and stalking toward the infirmary. Behind her, Erin heard the meaty thwock of a sword chopping through flesh and bone. "No matter what you have in mind, we need to hurry," Erin called over her shoulder.

*****

Chapter Forty-Seven

Liam

"Are you ready for this?"

Liam nodded in response to Pixel's question. "This could be crucial down the road." He put the car in park and killed the engine. The lot of the Unitarian Church was half-full, about 50 cars in all. Liam quickly scanned the parking lot for the bikers' van. It wasn't there; at least not yet.

They climbed out of the car and retrieved their contributions to the pitch in—Liam's hunter-gatherer fried rice and Einar's buffalo chicken dip. Einar got a little carried away; another pan of the spicy dip was chilling in the refrigerator back home.

"Knox, I'm surprised to see you here." Potts was more smug than usual. "You crawled out of your hermit cave twice in one year? Remarkable."

The wind kicked up around Liam, damp and chilly with the recent rain. He briefly wished he had worn his ritual robes as Pixel suggested. "Times change, Don."

Don spotted Pixel. "Well, Missy, I see you found the druid you were hunting for. I hope you're not disappointed."

"Why should I be?" She put a hand affectionately on Liam's arm. "Not only is he the real deal, he's great in bed."

Liam choked back a cough, while Einar failed to stifle a guffaw. Potts glanced away uncomfortably, then turned and walked briskly toward the doors.

Liam resumed his trek across the parking lot, avoiding puddles while balancing stacked Tupperware. "Did you really need to say we were sleeping together?"

"Well, we are," Pixel countered, her tone teasing.

"This again?" Einar grumbled.

"He's going to tell everyone," Liam said. "These people gossip like old men at Pancake House."

"So? Are you ashamed to sleep with me?" Pixel demanded.

"No, that's not it," Liam protested as they reached the doors. "We're not…I don't…"

"Give it up, Druid," Einar interrupted. "If you're done busting his chops, get the door, Pixel. We have our hands full."

Pixel grabbed one of the glass doors and pulled it open, stepping aside to let Liam and Einar pass with their burdens. Several zephyrs slipped through; Liam hoped they didn't cause too much mischief. When Liam finished arranging his food, he saw Susan eyeing him from across the room.

Susan shook her head as she approached. "So, she finally got to you? I thought you were waiting for Erin."

Liam rolled his eyes. "We didn't…she said it to get a rise out of Potts. Besides, what if I did? She's 150 years old, not 19."

Susan started to retort but stiffened.

Liam followed her gaze; Orliath was standing in the entryway. "Remind me again why I left my house?" Liam muttered.

"Because you need to win some people over," Susan replied. "You don't have connections to the broader pagan community, but some of these folks do. The real question is, what is she doing here?"

"Obviously trying to get her hooks into you," Pixel said. Liam hadn't noticed her approach; he wondered how much she had overheard.

Liam glanced at the large clock in the community room. "Everyone stay on mission. There's five minutes until the program starts, and I speak toward the end. Don't pick a fight with her." Liam met Pixel's eyes. "Don't worry about her. Whether she needs help, or is acting as Iblis' pawn, I have no interest in her."

Pixel appeared unimpressed. "You're saying you don't think she's pretty?"

"Don't do this. Not now," Liam countered. "I need to focus on what I need to do. Either Renee is an abused young woman or a Mata Hari. Either way, she is out-of-bounds. Trust me on this, okay?"

"All right," Pixel relented. She took his hand and squeezed it. "What's the plan?"

"If she approaches us, be civil," Liam replied. "I'm going to have Einar check and see if those goons are lurking around. I'm pretty sure he is under their radar, so they will be less likely to notice him."

"Do you want me to tell him?" Pixel asked.

Liam shook his head, then concentrated. The closest zephyrs whirled around him, ruffling his hair. "Einar, check outside for any suspicious thugs," Liam whispered. "Check for a white panel van." Liam added the plate number, then mentally urged the wind spirits toward Einar.

After a few moments of wind teasing his beard, Einar met Liam's gaze and nodded. The dwarf casually ambled out the door.

"Do you have the packets?" Liam asked Pixel.

She reached behind her back and pulled out a handful of manila envelopes, all marked 'Forging A New Year.' "Here they are. Should I pass them out now?"

"Wait until I make my pitch," Liam said. He resisted the urge to imply she should glamour the recipients to be more agreeable to his suggestion. He also didn't forbid it. "Hopefully the incentives I offer will be enough to get them on board and talking about the project. We don't have much time."

"You realize some people out there will scam you for money?" Susan remarked.

Liam shrugged. "If they do, maybe karma will come back and bite them in the ass. As long as enough people join in, I'll happily spend the money. Maybe it will do some good; the Avramites have certainly benefited from deep pockets over the centuries. I'm barely scratching the surface."

"All right, everyone, we are ready to begin," the organizer of the event, a witch by the name of Gavain announced. "Please be seated in the chapel. Our program is brief, so our food won't get too cold."

"Game time," Liam muttered.

* * *

"How many do you think bought in?" Liam asked, loading his plate with a smattering of the various dishes. "Did I stammer?"

"You did fine," Susan assured him. "I wish we could have made this pitch a month ago."

"You did great," Pixel added. "I'll bet they were all impressed."

"Because you were using a glamour to boost my presence?" Liam suggested. He had felt a tingle of magic during his brief speech and noticed people were paying attention to him rather than their phones as they had during most of the 20-minute program. "Don't get me wrong; I'll take all the help I can get. I know I'm not a natural orator."

"That was a very impressive speech." Renee smiled shyly. She was holding one of the packets handed out during Liam's presentation. "This is a very interesting proposal and very expensive."

"Only if a lot of groups follow through," Liam said with a polite smile. "I've come into some money, and given how most pagan groups operate on a shoestring budget, it seemed appropriate to pay it forward."

"Why the whole 'forging a new year' motif?" She seemed genuinely curious. "I understand it would be on Samhain, but it seems rather specific."

"Like you said, it's Samhain," Liam replied. "It's the Celtic New Year. I'm sure you understand the significance of the day."

Renee nodded. "I want to apologize for what happened in the parking lot. I didn't know those guys were going to mess with you." She tentatively reached out and touched Liam's forearm. Liam thought he heard Pixel growl. "I guess you're really here this time," Renee said. "How did you do it? Was it some sort of astral projection?"

"I'm sure Iblis has parlor tricks of his own," Liam stated. "I'm surprised he's not here."

"I think he's afraid of you," Renee said.

Liam blinked in surprise. "Bullshit."

Renee shrugged, poking a bowl of chili with her plastic spork. "Maybe not you directly, but if he walked in and the two of you threw down magically, only one of you is protected by the Challenge rules."

Liam hadn't thought about that and remembered the pissed off angel in Russia. If Iblis really were some sort of fallen angel, he wouldn't be happy to see one of his old colleagues show up. "What's your play?" Liam asked between bites of the buffet on his plate.

"You could take me with you," Renee suggested. "By the time Iblis realizes I'm not coming back, hopefully, it would be time for the Challenge."

"Try again," Pixel sneered. Liam placed a hand on her shoulder.

"Not going to happen," Liam said. He wasn't about to risk Tim by bringing Renee into the house. "If you really have an interest in druidry, get back to me in three weeks, after the Challenge."

"If I go back to him, especially empty-handed, he's going to, well you can guess." Renee implored Susan, "You saw him at the bookstore; he was being polite and putting on a public face."

Liam pulled an envelope from his coat pocket and set it next to Renee's plate. "If you really want to get away from him, this should be enough money to allow you to hide until after the Challenge."

Liam didn't wait for a response. He got up and started working the room. He recognized half the people there, so he enlisted them to meet the other half. Pixel joined him after a few minutes; it seemed Potts had managed to spread word of their 'relationship,' but Liam didn't want to expend the effort to correct everyone.

Finally, the crowd began to trickle out. All the buffalo dip and most of the rice were gone. Susan had gathered up the plastic containers and pitched the dip's aluminum pan. Liam hoped his proposals were as well received as Einar's cooking.

Liam peered around. "Where is Einar?"

"I was taking a pocking piss, if that's all right with you," Einar grumbled from behind Liam and went to the table. "Maybe we should have brought the other pan of dip."

"Renee slipped away," Susan mentioned.

Pixel sniffed. "She probably took your money and went right back to her master."

Liam shrugged and picked up the Tupperware. "It was the best compromise I could think of. If she is in over her head and wants out, she has the means. If it was a ruse to win my sympathy, I'm simply out some money."

Pixel pushed the door open, letting Liam pass into the night air. At least it hadn't started raining again, he mused. The parking lot was nearly empty; no one lingered in the chilly weather. Susan's car was closer, and she had reached it when the glare of headlights blinded Liam. Tires screeched on wet pavement as the van slid to a halt.

"I'm really getting sick of these guys," Liam muttered. The wind whipped up with his agitation.

"Let's see you pull your fancy tricks now!" the bald driver shouted as he clambered out of the van. His partner came around from the other side. "We owe you, hippie!"

Liam stepped back onto the grass; he wished he had his staff to help him pull *lledrith* from the earth. He focused his ire on the closest thug, the wind howled and slammed into the man, staggering him.

Over the roaring gale, Liam heard Einar shout, "Gun!" The dwarf lunged toward the other goon. Liam caught a glimpse of a huge revolver before Einar eclipsed it. Einar seized the biker's arm, trying to keep him from bringing the gun up.

The boom of the gunshot echoed off the building. The gunman seemed as startled as everyone else, but it didn't keep him from pulling the trigger again as he stumbled back from Einar. Something hissed past Liam and cracked off the brick wall behind him. Einar lurched forward and slugged the shooter with a meaty fist, knocking the thug to the pavement.

Einar reached under his vest. When his hand came out, he was clutching a short-hafted battle-axe. The gunman tried to aim the pistol, but the axe batted it away. The revolver skittered across the wet asphalt, and the biker clutched his hand, yelling in pain.

"You're pocking lucky I didn't take your hand off," Einar roared, brandishing his axe. He took a lurching step forward. "You're…pocking…lucky…" His arm sagged, and the haft slipped from his grip. "Let…me…" The dwarf sank to his knees, then fell on his side.

"No!" Liam ran forward, a jetstream preceding him, and buffeted the gunman. Liam knelt next to Einar; blood was pooling on the pavement, mixing with rainwater. "Einar!"

The dwarf's eyes flickered. "Druid…pocking finish…" Einar grimaced in pain and rasped, "Don't let them win." Einar's head sagged to the pavement with a sigh.

Pixel was on her knees next to Liam. She shook the dwarf by the shoulder. "Einar?" she whispered. "Don't…you can't go."

Liam's head snapped around, and his gaze fell on the biker who'd shot Einar. The thug had regained his feet and was searching for his gun. He met Liam's eyes, and the howling wind fell silent.

"Let's get out of here!" The other biker clambered into the driver's seat and slammed the door.

Liam rose to his feet, holding the shooter transfixed in his stare. The pavement under his feet spider-webbed as erdlings shattered it from below. Liam pulled *lledrith* from the earth; overhead, thunder rumbled.

"Come on man!" the driver shouted. The gunman shook his head and blinked, then ran for the van.

Liam's eyes followed the thug, his anger welling up. The wind roared, rocking the van as the driver spun it on the wet pavement. The vehicle sped across the lot, and the tires screeched as it skidded onto the blacktop road. Another torrent of wind hammered the van mid-turn. The vehicle tipped off balance; one of its tires snagged in a pothole that blossomed in its path. The van flopped on its side and slid to a halt, accompanied by shrieking metal and tinkling glass.

Instinctively, Liam reached a hand toward Pixel while he glared at the van. Her small hand slipped into his, and the connection clicked between them. The van's driver's door was at the top of the flipped vehicle. The door moved as an occupant tried to push it open. White-hot fury burned in Liam's chest.

One of the bikers managed to shove the door up. Liam couldn't tell which thug it was, and he didn't care. He unleashed his rage. There was an incandescent light as lightning flashed from the sly, through the van's forward compartment, and struck the pavement beneath. A second bolt arced down, raking the van's exposed undercarriage. The gas tank exploded.

The clouds opened in a deluge. Liam sat down hard on the pavement next to Einar's corpse. Susan was there. Liam hadn't realized she'd left her car. She had rolled Einar onto his back, but Liam knew it was too late.

Despite the pouring rain and numbing fatigue, Liam was aware of another presence in the parking lot. It was a female, armored form, shrouded in a cloak of black feathers. It took a moment for Liam's mind to assemble the pieces. Modern art depicted Valkyrie as angelic, but they were the shield-maidens of Odin and choosers of the slain, not blonde angels in breastplates.

The armored woman gazed down at Einar's corpse and said something in a Nordic tongue. Pixel realized she was there, but Susan remained oblivious, trying to staunch bleeding from a wound in Einar's chest.

The raven-cloaked woman held out a hand. Liam could see Einar's spirit-form sit up from his body and take her hand. He rose to his feet and met Liam's eyes.

"Finish this, Druid," Einar whispered, then both he and the woman disappeared. Einar's body faded from view, leaving a bewildered Susan.

"What happened?" Susan asked.

"He went home," Pixel sobbed.

*****

Chapter Forty-Eight

Erin

"Where's our ride?"

Erin trotted toward Nechtan and Scathach, fastening the last of the buckles on her armor. So much for not wearing leather pants. There was a saddle and a pile of leather straps on the ground; a couple of skilly-hobs were sorting tack.

"We're working on it," Nechtan replied. "How is Skye?"

Erin slowed to a walk and patted down her gear to make sure everything was in place. "Furious. Someone needs to relieve Slaine," Erin said. Casualties were already flowing into the infirmary. "She has her hands full, and the last thing she needs is a raging child underfoot."

"I will see to it personally," Scathach said.

Erin regarded the pile. "Is someone going to conjure up a ghost horse or something?"

"Not quite," Nechtan replied. He unlaced his leather vest and shucked it off. His tunic followed, dumped unceremoniously to the ground.

Erin wondered if summoning magic required some sort of weird sex rite. "What are you doing?"

He patted his bare chest over the stag tattoo. "Using what my father gave me." He leaned against the stone keep to pull off his boots.

His belt and boots joined the pile. He gave Erin a wry smile as he unlaced his pants. "A pity we don't have more time, *acushla*."

He shoved his pants down and kicked them off. Holding his hand over the stag tattoo, he whispered an intonation. Blue-white sparks erupted across his skin. As the sparks grew to motes and began to merge, he gazed at Erin one last time. "I love you."

Erin's voice caught in her throat. She didn't know what to say. The light enveloped Nechtan, and the color grew greener. As the color changed, so did Nechtan's outline. He fell forward, and the green-blue silhouette grew. His limbs lengthened, spikes erupted from his head and branched into antlers. By the time the glow was verdant green, the shape it illuminated was a great stag, as large as a horse.

The light faded, leaving a dark stag. Black fur faded to brown on the underside, the throat, and the inside of his limbs. Erin took a step toward the animal, holding her hand out. "Nechtan?"

The stag regarded her and snorted once, dipping his head.

Scathach hefted the saddle onto the stag's back. "Quickly now!" The skilly-hobs burst into action, looping and fastening the leather straps to hold the saddle in place. Erin could hear them muttering incantations as they worked.

"I assume they are enchanting it to keep me from falling off?" Erin asked.

"Yes," Scathach replied tersely. "Also, the saddle will fall off when he chooses."

Erin thought it would be easy for her to take it off once they arrived so he could change back. She gathered Nechtan's discarded clothing. As much as she might enjoy seeing him naked, he probably didn't want to go into battle or hike back in the buff.

The hobs stepped back and nodded. Erin shoved the boots and belt into one saddlebag and crammed the rolled-up clothes into the other. The stag turned to watch her when she took hold of the saddle. Erin took a deep breath and sprang up, swinging one leg over the saddle as she hauled herself into position.

"Watch over my daughter!" Erin called as she stag turned and pawed the earth. "We'll be back as quickly as we can."

Nechtan leapt toward the gate, nearly throwing Erin from the saddle. She suspected only the hobs' magic had kept her in her seat. Erin leaned forward and clutched the strap going from the saddle, around the stag, between its forelegs and neck. She quickly found loops of leather, intended for handholds, as Nechtan bolted through the gate and cut left. The caravan wagons were a blur.

Nechtan arced around the fortress, leaping gullies and scrabbling across the loose stone along the fort's exterior. North of the walls, he was able to break into a full gallop. In minutes, they passed the place where Uthor was slain. They streaked past the gulley that was a path back into Scathach's domain and its warped time flow. Nechtan angled downslope, keeping above the scraggly grove of trees that occupied the same spot as Colorado Springs in the Dunwold.

Erin quickly became sore from the jolting ride. She was glad her armor protected her from chaffing. An hour in, Nechtan was still going strong. Erin tried to keep track of landmarks—an old campsite, where they fought the devil-bear, a distinctive rock formation. A second hour ticked by, followed by a third. Erin's arms and legs burned from clinging to the stag.

In the distance, she spotted the wisp of smoke in the direction of Elam's cabin. She whispered a prayer to a variety of gods that it was only chimney smoke and not the cabin turned into a funeral pyre.

Fifteen minutes later, she caught her first glimpse of the cabin; the roof was intact and not aflame. Then she spotted something else, a large bovine creature with two figures clinging to its back.

"I have the cooler ride," she muttered. They hadn't reached Elam and Derek yet, but the Forgotten would get there before Erin and Nechtan could catch them. The Forgotten were only 500 yards from the cabin; Erin and Nechtan were a mile out. Elam and Derek had no clue they were in danger.

Erin pulled out her revolver. "I hope this doesn't spook you," she shouted over the stag's pounding hooves. Holding the gun up, she fired a shot, waited several seconds, then fired another. Erin thought the riders ahead of them peered back in response to the gunshots.

She lost sight of the cabin and the opposition as Nechtan descended into the tree line. Erin spent a minute hugging the stag, her face buried against its neck as branches whipped them. Finally, they broke into the meadow around the cabin. The Forgotten were only a hundred yards away, but Derek had emerged. He spotted the approaching warriors and called back into the cabin.

The hawk-helmed warriors vaulted off their mount, drawing weapons as they landed. Derek pulled twin swords in response and took a defensive stance in front of the cabin door. The ox the Forgotten had rode bellowed; its tail arched up and grew into a giant scorpion tail. The beast's head morphed into a cross between a man and lion. Its human-like mouth split open to reveal a maw full of shark teeth. The creature roared as it stalked behind its riders.

Erin was too far for an accurate pistol shot while riding a stag at breakneck speed. She wondered if Nechtan was going to slow down or charge into the enemies. The scorpion-tailed monster roared again and poised its tail to strike. The warriors gave it room to get at Derek, and the creature tensed to pounce.

Daniel exploded from the grass next to the beast. The giant lynx was a ball of hissing fur and raking claws as it landed on the creature's back, then quickly sprang away. The monster roared and gave chase. The Forgotten both closed on Derek, flanking him. They struck Derek twice in as many seconds, both flesh wounds, but it was obvious he couldn't fend them off for long.

Erin felt Nechtan decelerate; his hooves tearing up great chunks of sod. Erin took a deep breath. These assholes attacked her friends, they might have killed Daidh, and who knew how many others. The edge of her vision turned red, and she felt the rage boil through her blood. She sprang from Nechtan, and kept her fury focused on the warriors before her. As she rose from the crouched landing, she aimed the revolver and fired.

The bullet slammed into the warrior's armor hard enough to throw him off balance. Erin marched toward him and drew her sword with her free hand. Her second shot hit the hawk-shaped helmet. He spun to face Erin and sneered from under his helmet.

Erin holstered the pistol. "Come on, asshole! Let's see how you handle a fair fight!"

He spat something Erin assumed translated to 'western whore' and lunged. The sickle-sword whistled past her head as she ducked. He managed to reverse-block her stroke, so Erin roundhouse kicked him in the gut hard; he slammed against the cabin wall with a crash of armor.

Her opponent advanced behind his whirling blade. The sword was a blur, whipping around in a figure-eight path meant to intimidate. The blade slowed with Erin's fury; she caught the curved weapon from behind on its downward arc, then reversed her stroke. Her blade bit into the underside of his helmet, slicing half an inch into his jawbone.

The Forgotten swung low, the tip of the blade sliding across her shin guard but failing to penetrate the armor made from Bronze-Bristle's hide. Erin swept her blade down, catching her opponent's weapon in its back swing. She planted a sidekick square on his breastplate; the warrior slammed into the cabin again, ten feet away.

Even as he bounced off the wall, the Forgotten brought his sword up. On his first step toward Erin, he began to pull his sword back to strike. Erin held her sword in a one-handed cross guard, her free hand dipped to her side. The warrior's second step closed half the distance, and he had his sword ready to begin its forward arc. Erin's hand came up with the revolver. The third step put him nearly within reach. His sword swung forward, and Erin pulled the trigger. The bullet mushroomed against the helmet from the inside, having blown a path through the warrior's eye socket and skull.

Erin took in the other two fights. Derek was barely holding his own against the remaining Forgotten. The man-lion-bull-scorpion had returned; it faced off against Nechtan. They circled in the grass, the beast's stinger raised high, and the stag's antlers held low. Erin knew she had one shot left. She lined up the pistol and fired. The round drew blood from the creature's forehead, and it staggered. Erin holstered the gun and circled Derek's melee. The remaining Forgotten must have sensed his peril; he switched from a furious offense to a cautious defense.

"You know, Champion, I'm in a giving mood today," Derek remarked. "I don't mind sharing with you."

The Forgotten spun and lunged at Erin; the sickle-sword curved toward her neck. She caught it on her blade with a high block and backhanded him with her vambrace for good measure. The warrior snarled when Derek drove one of his short swords into the unarmored back of his knee. Derek brought his other sword around the warrior's neck. One cut later, and the man fell forward into the dirt.

Erin returned to the fight between the stag and the strange creature. The monster seemed to have shrugged off the gunshot, despite blood flowing between its eyes. The stinger bobbed and weaved as though it had a mind of its own. Erin sheathed her sword and reached into her elf-pocket. Her hand grasped the spear haft, and she drew the weapon out.

"I don't suppose you brought any heavy artillery," Derek panted, keeping up a cheerful front despite his bleeding wounds.

Erin hefted the spear. "We just need to get past the stinger."

The stag snorted and feinted toward the beast. The beast lunged forward, clamping its toothy maw on the stag's throat. The venomous tail whipped forward. Erin charged, but as fast as she was, she was too far away. A feline form leapt into the air and caught the arachnid tail, knocking it off target.

Erin whipped the leaf-blade spear around. She severed the tail, prompting the monster to release Nechtan and roar in pain. It spun toward Erin, baring multiple rows of teeth. Nechtan staggered away, blood glistening on his dark fur.

"Choke on this!" Erin sprang forward and rammed the spear down the beast's throat. The creature gurgled in surprise, then clamped its jaws down on the haft. The wood snapped as razor-sharp teeth shredded it. The beast tried to roar, but it was more of a croak as the rest of the spear remained impaled.

The lynx returned to harry the beast from its flank. As it turned toward the cat, Erin pulled her sword. She sprang forward and drove her blade behind the bull-torso's foreleg. When Erin yanked her blade free, blood bubbled from the wound.

The beast tried to roar, but could only emit a high-pitched rasp. It turned and staggered several steps before collapsing on the grass.

"Nechtan!" Erin sought the stag. It lay on its side in the grass, breathing shallowly. She ran to him. "Don't you dare die on me!"

The stag snorted weakly as Erin hugged it around the neck, tears streaming from her face.

Elam kneeled next to her. "It's not time for his final reward." The white-haired man closed his eyes and laid his hands upon the stag. After what felt like several minutes, the Pilgrim sank back onto the grass.

Erin looked up. "Is he…?"

Elam took a deep breath. "He's lost a lot of blood, but with His grace, Nechtan will be right as rain."

The stag struggled to his hooves. Erin threw her arms around his neck. "Turn back so I can kiss you," she said.

The stag stepped back out of her grasp. The straps holding the tack and saddle on Nechtan gave way as he shook himself free. Erin waited expectantly, then remembered his clothes. She extracted the clothing from the saddlebags in the pile. The stag met her eyes, snorted, then bounded off over the field toward the trees.

"Wait, what is he doing?" Erin stood holding the clothes, bewildered. The stag disappeared into the tree line.

"He didn't tell you?" Derek asked reluctantly.

"Tell me what?" Erin demanded.

"There is a price for using his father's gift," Derek replied. "When he becomes a stag, he must remain so for a year and a day."

Erin gazed at the spot where Nechtan had disappeared. "Why did he run off?"

"Because the longer he remains in the stag's form, the less of him remains." Derek put a hand on her shoulder. "It's amazing he retained his mind this long. Now he has to brave the wild for a year and a day to be himself again."

"Why didn't he warn me?" Erin wavered between anger and sorrow. "He should have warned me."

"If he had, what would you have done?" Derek countered. "He was probably worried you would talk him out of it. If you hadn't arrived when you did, Elam and I would be dead. Nechtan did this to save us."

Erin kicked the dead beast, her anger abating into sadness. "He should have told me." After several minutes of staring at the spot in the trees where the stag had disappeared, Erin sighed and said, "We should get back to Dunos Scaith. A bunch of these guys showed up and attacked the fort; there were a lot of casualties and wounded."

"I'll get some things together," Elam said and went into the cabin.

"For what it's worth, I'm sorry," Derek said. "Unlike me, you aren't generous with your affections, so I know how much you care for Nechtan."

Erin nodded, holding back tears through sheer will. "We need to get back. I need to get back to Skye."

* * *

They marched hard until it was too dark to travel safely. Erin pulled her tent out of her pack and erected it while Derek started a fire. Elam set out provisions he had cobbled together from food in his cabin.

"How old is Skye?" The Pilgrim asked, breaking the silence around the campfire.

Erin turned a hunk of bread over in her hand. She knew she should eat more, but the lump in her throat warred with her body's demand to replenish the energy she had burned. "Not quite four, as long as nothing happens to throw us off track."

Elam shook his head. "It has only been a month since she was born, at least out here. The magic Scathach uses is unnatural. It breaks His rules in ways they shouldn't be bent."

Erin wasn't in the mood to debate supernatural metaphysics. "I thought all magic broke the rules."

"Magic has its own rules," Derek said, taking a drink from his water skin. It was fae-made, and like an elf-pocket, it held much more than it appeared to. "A lot of magic involves drawing energy; some of it involves paying a price. For example, Erin's warp-rage taxes her body, but not to a degree from which she can't recover. Every day Scathach holds Dunos Scaith deeper in time, it ages her as it would a mortal."

Paying a price, Erin thought. Was she paying a price for letting herself think she could be happy? Had Nechtan paid the price for her happiness? Was it why she had been afraid of becoming entangled with Liam? Would he somehow suffer in the end?

"Champion, why don't you get some sleep?" Derek suggested. "We can set off again at first light."

Erin nodded, then wearily crawled into the tent. She was so exhausted, she barely had time to register her tears before sleep claimed her.

* * *

After eight hours of hard hiking, they passed through the arroyo that was one of the entrances to Scathach's domain. They crossed the perimeter, and Erin slackened the pace to let Elam catch his breath. Now they were matching the time in Dunos Scaith minute-for-minute. It had been two months to the occupants of the fort since Erin left. Half an hour would not make a difference now.

Derek gazed along the ridge. "Shouldn't we see the top of the keep from here?"

Erin followed his line of sight. From this vantage point, the tower of the keep should be visible. "Did we miss the entrance?" Erin asked. She stared into the distance. She realized the strange monochromatic effect was missing.

"I'm certain of the path, but we could double back to the perimeter and check," Derek suggested. He had used one of his origami birds to lead the way.

Erin chewed on her lip, debating the options. "Let's press on to the fort. Is it possible Scathach made it invisible?"

Derek shrugged. "Glamour was never her strong suit, but I suppose she could have, or she could have had someone else do it, to hide Dunos Scaith."

"If she did, she'll know we're here." Erin started marching again. "She probably sensed our presence as soon as we crossed the perimeter. As long as we don't blunder into an invisible wall, we should be fine."

Derek helped Elam up from a boulder the old man was resting on. "I hope you're right," Derek said as they fell in behind Erin.

* * *

Ninety minutes later, they were staring at the clearing where Dunos Scaith should have been. Erin took out her spear and prodded the ground ahead of her, like a blind person with a cane. She passed it several times through where the walls should have been.

Derek knelt down next to a small pile of stones. "Erin!" he called. "Take a look at this."

Erin trotted over to Derek. The stones were intentionally stacked, and atop them rested a wooden figurine. Erin picked up the carving; it was a stag with a pale blue ribbon wrapped around it.

Erin turned back toward the empty stretch of ground. "Where's my daughter?"

# # # # #

ABOUT THE AUTHOR

At thirteen years old, Jon Osborne discovered a passion for two things—writing and telling stories. Instead of doing what a normal author-to-be would do and write stories, Jon wrote for his school newspaper and told stories through the medium of running role-playing games for his friends.

Journalism helped pay the way through college, and gaming garnered him lifelong friends. After college, journalism didn't pan out as a career, but Jon continued creating worlds and forging stories with his friends.

Fast forward almost 30 years; Jon is still a gamer who every now and then dabbles with writing. A long-time friend and fellow gamer who had found success as an author, Mark Wandrey, convinced Jon to submit a short story for an anthology. Jon's story was accepted, and it gave him the impetus to finish his first novel, "A Reluctant Druid."

Living in Indianapolis, Jon still games, and continues to write. You can find out more about Jon at jonrosborne.com. Fans who sign up for his mailing list will receive "Chapter 0" of "A Reluctant Druid" and be the first to get the news about Jon's newest books and stories.

* * * * *

Connect with Jon R. Osborne Online

Website: http://jonrosborne.com/

Amazon: https://www.amazon.com/Jon-R.-Osborne/e/B073PKR8GS

Facebook: https://www.facebook.com/jonrosborne/

Twitter: @druidoz

* * * * *

The following is an

Excerpt from Book Three of The Milesian Accords:

A Tangled Fate

Jon R. Osborne

Available soon from New Mythology Press

eBook, Paperback, and Audio

Excerpt from "A Tangled Fate:"

The van gave chase, casting aside all pretense of subtlety, but the boxy vehicle was losing ground, unable to match the Charger's horsepower. A flash caused Erin to duck over Skye. In the army, she had been in a couple of firefights; she knew a muzzle flash when she saw one.

"They're shooting at us!" she yelled. She knew shooting out of a moving vehicle was a lot harder than it looked in the movies, but plenty of people died by dumb luck in firefights.

"Shoot back at them, Momma!" Skye encouraged.

"They're too far away," Erin said. Her pistol wouldn't reach the van, not with any accuracy.

Erin started to get pissed off. She hated feeling helpless and out of control, especially in a fight.

"We've got about ten minutes before we hit Jefferson City," Derek announced. "Even if they don't have agents among the police, I think the police will object to our fast and furious road chase."

"Izzy, ease off a bit, let them catch up to us," Erin said.

"I assume you have a plan?" Izzy asked, slowly letting up on the gas. "Or are we making this up as we go?"

"Call it fifty-fifty," Erin replied. "I think they're trying to take out a tire to slow us down. They've been aiming low."

"You realize letting them get closer only increases their odds?" Izzy remarked. Her words were punctuated by the *spang!* of a bullet glancing off a fender. Erin hoped the close call was luck rather than skill.

"I need them to get within my reach," Erin replied. She reached into an olv-vassi and drew the sword Gofannon had forged for her. "Sweetie, can you hold this for me?"

"Of course." Skye carefully took possession of the sword. "Should I get my sword out as well?"

"Sorry sweetie, your blade is too short for what I have planned," Erin replied.

"Your plan includes attacking a two-ton vehicle travelling 80 miles an hour with melee weapons?" Derek asked incredulously. "What am I saying? Of course it does."

Erin lowered her window. The wind howled through the car, whipping up wrappers and other detritus from their last pit stop. For a split second, Erin was reminded of Liam. She pushed the thought aside, reached into an elf-pocket, and drew forth the best spear in her arsenal. It wasn't forged by a god, like her sword, but skilly-hobs had made its edges magically sharp and the shaft stronger than mere wood.

"Seven minutes," Derek intoned.

"You sound like one of those computers from science fiction movies," Izzy remarked. "Announcing the time, and they're almost always wrong."

"Izzy, on my mark, hit the brakes and swerve over to the oncoming lane," Erin ordered.

"What if there's oncoming traffic?" Derek demanded.

"Then I wait for them to pass, *tonto*," Izzy barked.

Erin braced herself and drew a deep breath. The edge of her version turned red as she let the anger of being chased well up, and then she focused her rage. "Now!"

Izzy stomped the brakes and jerked the wheel. A gunshot sounded; the bullet struck empty pavement. Time slowed to a crawl as the van slid into the space abandoned by the Charger. Erin rammed the spear across the space between the vehicles, and the blade shattered the driver-side window. The van slewed away briefly before the driver realized the peril of the adjacent telephone poles. Ducking away from the weapon, he twisted the wheel, and the van collided with the Charger. Metal shrieked from the front fender of the car as the vehicles bounced off each other.

Erin pulled the spear back, and, without asking, Skye slapped the pommel of the sword into Erin's waiting hand. Izzy hit the brakes as the van slewed back in their direction. In the rage, the split second stretched out long enough for Erin to jab the tip of her sword into the rear tire of van. The tread stripped away from the rest of the tire as Erin gritted her teeth and clung to the hilt of the sword to keep it from being ripped from her grasp.

The van wobbled ahead of them. The driver, likely fearing another spear thrust, failed to regain control of the weaving vehicle. Dust kicked up from the gravel shoulder as the van hit a ditch and flipped over into a harvested field, narrowly missing a telephone pole. A cloud of brown dust rose up around the van as it slid to a halt on its side.

"Giant-Bane, Boar-Foe, and Panel-Van-Slayer," Derek remarked. "Your titles continue to grow."

Erin snorted, and stowed the spear, then the sword. She was grateful she hadn't lost either weapon. "Whatever."

"I think it sounds impressive, Momma," Skye said.

#####

The following is an

Excerpt from Book One of Forge and Sword:

Keep of Glass

Steven G. Johnson

Available Now from New Mythology Press

eBook, Paperback, and (soon) Audio Book

Excerpt from "Keep of Glass:"

Trinadan peered at the spot Forge was examining. She thought she saw a bit of movement.

A second later, the wildlife burst into squawking, scrambling motion all around them. A family of rabbits rushed across the trail in a close grouping, making for the distance with great, stammering hops. Birds exploded from every tree and bush in the vicinity, fleeing upward like ashes from a drenched fire. She heard the bleat of red deer and saw a bluish-green lizard leap from tree to tree on fans of skin under its arms.

Forge was off his horse and on the ground in one step, as smoothly as if his horse were still. In another instant, he unslung and strung his bow, nocking an arrow as he knelt behind a blackberry tangle along the trailside. His gray eyes had not left the bend in the trail behind them.

"Forge, what—"

But then she heard it, the thunder of hoofbeats. Several horses, driven hard, had panicked the animals as they crashed toward the spot on the trail where Trinadan's little convoy stood idle. She barely had time to turn her charger around.

And they were upon her. Three horses, swathed in yellow and blue, rounded the bend at speed, weapons held high. They saw her and pointed, the leader in half-plate and a high bucket helm as he spurred into a full-tilt gallop, taking the lead from his two companions. She saw his lance drop to fighting trim, its head growing enormously as it arrowed toward her at the speed of a maddened horse. The head was not the basket-cup of a jousting lance, but real iron, forged and worked to a cruel point.

*****

Get "Keep of Glass" now at:
https://www.amazon.com/dp/B08RMVLWXV.

Find out more about Steven G. Johnson and "Keep of Glass" at:
https://chriskennedypublishing.com

* * * *

The following is an

Excerpt from Book One of The Endless Ocean:

Responsibility of the Crown

G. Scott Huggins

Available Now from New Mythology Press

eBook, Paperback, and (soon) Audio Book

Excerpt from "Responsibility of the Crown:"

The sky was so big.

She had never been so high up on her own. Thousands of feet, it must have been. She felt as if she could fall forever in the endless blue that was the ocean below and the sky above. Already, she had to strain to pick out the bronze and violet specks that were Elazar and Merav.

Senaatha aimed for the fighters, and they bored in, lines of death shooting from their wings. Suddenly, she seemed to stutter in the air, beating her wings irregularly. She dropped, climbed, and dropped again.

She's throwing off their aim, Azriyqam realized. Consortium planes were fast, but they moved in long curves. They had no wings to beat—*how do they turn?* she wondered—and so they weren't capable of the fast changes in direction a dragon could manage.

Or a halfdragon. The planes sliced through the air on either side of Senaatha, and she whipped her neck around, flaming, but her fiery breath fell short of her targets.

They must be going a hundred miles an hour, thought Azriyqam.

Her heart sank. It was obvious, even to her, that the weapons on the aircraft reached much farther than Senaatha's flame could, and they could use them while going at full speed. Senaatha didn't dare—she'd fly right into her own breath. Even worse, the planes would not get tired. Already, they were looping around for another pass. Senaatha labored for altitude, but the aircraft climbed higher still, nearly to her own height.

Height. She strained against the thin air, found a weak thermal, and rode it upward. The planes settled in for their attack run. Again, the deadly lines of gunfire lashed out.

Two tiny figures dove into them. Elazar slashed downward, Merav flying practically at his wingtip. They twisted between the lines of light and danced in front of the oncoming plane. It veered in the air, yawing and rolling to avoid a collision. Slowing.

Senaatha breathed flame as it passed by her at a distance of fifty feet. The airplane emerged from the stream of flame spinning wildly, a comet of fire trailing black smoke, every surface ablaze.

Then the second plane's guns punched heavy bullets through Senaatha's right wing.

Blood flew like mist from the wounds. The dragon screamed. Engine roaring, the plane broke off in a tight turn. Its pilot had seen what had happened to his companion, and he didn't want to chance closing with the dragon, wounded or not.

He would come back to finish the job from farther away. Senaatha was in a flat glide. The bullets hadn't cracked her wing spars or she'd be falling out of the sky, but there were ragged holes in the membranes of her wing. If she strained it too hard, she'd rip it apart by the sheer force of her passage through the air.

The plane turned. Merav and Elazar beat for altitude, but she could see they were on the wrong side. They couldn't get between her and the plane, let alone be ready to dive. Then the pilot would unleash his deadly guns into Senaatha's helpless body, sending her and her human passengers into the Endless Ocean below.

It was up to her.

Already, the plane was lining up.

Azriyqam winged over and dove.

#####

Made in United States
Orlando, FL
04 March 2022

15390139R00237